Taking A Chance

To Andi!
Hope you enjoy a
close look at England.
Celia Martin

Celia Martin

KITSAP PUBLISHING

KITSAP PUBLISHING

Taking A Chance
First edition, published 2019

By Celia Martin

Cover Image Courtesy of
Interior Book Layout: Tim Meikle, Reprospace

ISBN-13: 978-1-942661-02-3

Published by Kitsap Publishing
P.O. Box 572
Poulsbo, WA 98370
www.KitsapPublishing.com

Also by Celia Martin

To Challenge Destiny

"Exquisite passion and breath-taking action! A historical romance feast!"

Curt Locklear - Laramie Award Winner

"Martin proves she has the vision and talent to make bygone times come alive for modern readers."

Anne Hollister, Professional Book Reviews

A Bewitching Dilemma

"A willful heroine cornered by a relentless foe and a dashing sea captain tormented by his past cast their lots against the tides of a history dark with treachery. A compelling read cover to cover."

Michael Donnelly - Author of False Harbor

With Every Breath I take

A love story laced with fun and surprises

---

cmartinbooks.kitsappublishing.com

I would like to thank Linda Reed for her continual encouragement and support. Your friendship and endorsements mean so much.

I would also like to thank Rae, Jo Z., Helene, Deb, and Dorothy for your enthusiastic support and reviews.

Endorsement by C.CA. CAsbrey, author of historically accurate mysteries involving the spying and scientific techniques of the past.

Lovers of historical romance will find this book grabs them from the first line and enfolds them in a firm grip. Set just after the English Civil War, the story follows the fortunes of two beautiful cousins and their respective loves. Throw in a few abductions, highwaymen, and scheming noblemen, and the author takes us on a delightful romp through the sexual mores of the 17th century. Delphine navigates the difficulties faced by women in the 17th century, and having money is no guarantee of happiness. It can even be a liability which makes them a target for fortune hunters, and frustrates the path to true love.

Celia Martin has clearly researched the period deeply. She captures the complex landscape of people dealing with Puritanism which squelches the fun out of life for ordinary people. It all makes a great backdrop for the wonderful heroine to shine as she strives to marry the man she loves.

C. A. Asbrey is the author of a series of 19th century murder mysteries, The Innocents Mysteries Series. She has also written articles on history and forensics for various magazines and periodicals

Endorsement by Trisha J Kelly,
multi-genre, award-winning author.

I found myself absolutely pulled into this, not a book, but another world. A time, a place, which I could vision so clear in my mind. If you could imagine one of the works by the Bronte Sisters, or a renowned period drama on British TV, it would give you an idea of the content of this story.

Taking a Chance by author Celia Martin begins in the setting of Cheshire, England in 1654. The action is forefront as Delphine Lotterby, an extremely wealthy, young single woman, is once again the victim of a proposed abduction.

Set in this time period, with everything so different to modern day, many men will attempt to take her as their wife by force, in order to secure her vast estate. Throughout her life she has loved one man only, Torrance Madigan, though he is not aware of this. Indeed, he in turn, is in love with her beautiful cousin, Venetia.

In a tale of love, twists, and danger, you will find yourself pulled along into the lives of the gentry, the ways of the times, just as if you were there yourself. With such detail in every scene, together with the factual timeline, you can feel every bump in the road as travellers take to coaches from one estate to another.

The highway robbers steal from the Roundheads to assist their King, Charles II. With many dangers to face and relationships to bloom, follow the well-written tale of times gone by. I've no hesitation to recommend this five- star read to new or old readers of historical fiction. I was thoroughly immersed in the storyline

Trisha J. Kelly (author). Living in England, she is a multi-genre author of children and middle grade books, cozy mysteries, and crime thrillers. Winner of Best Children's book 2018 and Best Juvenile Fantasy 2018.

A Collection of Romantic Adventures

Follow the romantic adventures of the D'Arcy, Hayward, and Lotterby families and their captivating friends in seventeenth century England and the American colonies. In Taking A Chance, immensely wealthy heiress, Delphine Lotterby tries to convince Torrance Madigan (Maddy) that he loves her and not her cousin Lady Venetia. Because of her wealth, Delphine must also stay ever vigilant to elude abduction and being forced into an unwanted marriage. And be sure to watch for Precarious Game of Hide and Seek as Lady Rowena Crossly is aided in rescuing her daughter from and unscrupulous Cromwellian by a gang of highwaymen led by Nathaniel D'Arcy.

Excerpt from

Precarious Game of Hide and Seek

At the end of the book.

Visit my web site at:
cmartinbooks.kitsappublishing.com

Chapter 1

Cheshire, England 1654

Delphine Lotterby woke to muffled voices and the heavy tread of footsteps on the stairs. "Which door?" a grating voice demanded. She could not make out the frightened answer to the demand, but she did not need to know what was said. Her hand found the horse pistol on the small table beside her bed.

"Mistress ..." came her maid's querulous voice, and Delphine hissed, "Keep low, Tatty." At the same instant she heard her door latch jiggled, and the grating voice said, "Door is locked."

A second, deeper voice said, "I will take care of that."

Delphine raised the pistol, and holding it steady with both hands, pointed it at her door as it burst open with a loud crash. The lantern from the corridor showed her a bear of a man standing in her doorway. When he took a step toward her, she fired. Sparks and smoke belched from the pistol's mussel and the report roared in her ears. With a yowl, the man smashed back against the door he had busted in, but despite Delphine's cousin's training, the kick of the gun knocked her backwards. Two men pushed past the grimacing bear but were met by Delphine's maid. Though slight of frame and pushing forty, she sprang up from the trundle bed to attack the two men.

One man knocked the maid aside and headed around the bed as Delphine rolled off its far side. Swinging her pistol, she connected with his forehead. He grunted and grabbed at her arm. The second man hopped over the bed, and Delphine found herself trapped between the two assailants. Tatty renewed her attack, tugging from behind at the first man's straggly hair, but a third man entered, and grasping Tatty, pinioned her arms to her side.

Her heart pounding in her ears, Delphine struggled rigorously though she knew she was no match for her adversaries. The pistol was wrested from her hand and one arm was twisted behind her. The pain caused her to cease her struggles. "Ah, now that is better." The man's voice grated in her ear. "You ready to join your new bridegroom?" His comment brought a coarse chuckle from his colleague, but the bear growled, "Damn she-cat! I am bleeding lack a stuck pig, and my shoulder hurts something fierce. Was we not getting paid in hard coin, I would wring her damn neck."

Delphine looked past the bear to a youth holding the lantern in the corridor. Her fear lessened and was replaced by heart-stopping relief as a bed warming pan descended upon the youth's head. Stunned, he slumped and dropped the lantern. Fortunately the lantern did not break, and the light but flickered then resumed its bright glow. With the youth still under attack, a whirlwind blew into the room, bounded across the bed, and landed on the man with the grating voice with enough force to knock him against the wall. Though he did not lose his hold on Delphine's arm, he swore roundly. The whirlwind, in the form of Delphine's cousin, Venetia, dug her teeth into the man's hand. He yelped and released Delphine. She in turn grappled anew with her first assailant. She had almost freed herself when a loud voice demanded, "What is the meaning of this? What goes on here? Can a man not get a decent night's rest?"

She recognized the voice of the corpulent merchant who had joined them at dinner, then she heard her footman Purdy. "Mistress, Mistress, are you harmed?" Her two footmen bounded into the already crowded room. Their appraisal of the situation instant, they attacked the two men struggling with Delphine and Venetia. Purdy's big fisted hand landed a direct blow to the jaw of the man holding Delphine. The assailant sank to the floor. The man with the grating voice extricated himself from Venetia and backed into the corner of the room. His maneuver failed to save him. Delphine's second footman, Anker, pummeled him in the gut before punching him in the nose and then the jaw. The man holding Tatty released her and attempted to run, but his and the wounded bear's escape was blocked by the merchant and a couple of other guests of the inn.

The innkeeper's voice rose above the din. "The constable is on his way."

In a matter of moments, Delphine's footmen, with the help of the inn's guests, had the malefactors bunched and bound. Venetia's maid, who had wielded the warming pan with such enthusiasm, stood aside to let the merchant drag the befuddled youth to his feet. Delphine felt her robe draped about her shoulders, and with Tatty's urging, she slipped her arms into it. Tatty also threw a large fringed shawl over Venetia's shoulders. Delphine realized she and her cousin had been most indecently clad in naught but their sleeping shifts. And though Delphine's footmen had not ogled them, the inn's male guests had not been so circumspect.

By the time the constable and his assistants arrived and carted off the would be abductors, the innkeeper's wife announced she had made a sack posset to calm everyone after the harrowing episode. "I declare," the innkeeper said. "I thought the one man to be a gentleman or I would ne'er have allowed him to stay in my inn. Apparently when all were asleep, he crept down and opened the door to let in the other culprits." He looked sheepishly at Delphine. "They had a knife to me throat, Mistress Lotterby, or I would have ne'er divulged your room."

Delphine smiled. "I know that, sir. What else could you have done? I am but grateful to all of you who came to my aid." She looked around the large public room where guests and staff, mugs of sack posset in hand, sat hunched over the tables. Sleepy-eyed gazes met hers and accepted her gratitude. She raised her mug, and saluting her saviors, took a sip. The frothy drink soothed her palate. Her racing heart was only now settling back into its normal beat. She hoped she would be able to resume her sleep. Come the morrow, they had a long day ahead of them, but did luck go with them, they would reach Harp's Ridge by mid-afternoon.

"I cannot believe such brazenness," the merchant said.

"What were they after?" asked a young man with but one boot on and his shirt tail half in and half out of his breeches.

Delphine had no intention of telling these strangers, kindly though they appeared, what the abductors were after was her. No reason to give anyone else ideas. Instead she said, "They must have thought I traveled with large amounts of jewelry. They were sadly mistaken."

3

"Mistress Lotterby," Tatty said. "I think 'tis best we go back to bed. Purdy has your door mended, and he said he meant to sleep outside your room the remainder of the night."

Delphine nodded. "Aye. 'Tis best we retire." She rose, and Venetia and her maid Bethel followed suit. Venetia smiled and also offered her thanks to the guests and staff. Delphine hid a grin. Her dark-haired, blue-eyed cousin with her dimples that popped in and out, her straight little nose, her sweet, generous mouth, and her creamy white skin left most men bedazzled. The men all stood and near fell over each other in assuring Lady Venetia Lotterby they were her humble servants. Venetia laughed her soft rustling laugh and promised she would report to her brother, the Earl of Grasmere, on how brave they had all been. And did they ever venture near Harp's Ridge, they could always find shelter for the night.

Again the men behaved like befuddled ducks, quacking and displaying, and Delphine tugged at one of Venetia's braids to start her toward the stairs. Did she keep smiling at the poor fools, they would never get another wink of sleep. Delphine doubted she would ever mesmerize any man, let alone a pack of them, as did her cousin. Not that she thought herself unattractive. She had the Lotterby slim aquiline nose, firm mouth, and jutting chin – features, to her thinking, that looked better on a male than a female, but she had her mother's dark wavy hair and ebony-colored eyes, her high cheekbones, thick dark lashes, and perfectly arched brows. Though no great beauty, she was no eyesore. But what she lacked was Venetia's sweet demeanor, that honest desire to be kind and caring that shone in Venetia's eyes and softened the expressions on her face. No, Delphine thought, unlike Venetia, sweetness was not one of her strong points.

Tatty and Bethel were both clucking as they shepherded their charges up to their rooms. That Delphine and Venetia had gone down to the public room and sat amongst strange men in naught but their shifts and night robes, both maids found appalling, and did not mind saying so. "What your dear sweet mother would have said about such conduct," Bethel mumbled. "'Tis a wonder is she not turning in her grave."

Venetia laughed that laugh men found so tantalizing. "Oh, Bethel, had Mother just been through such a brawl, I doubt not but she would have been exuberant. You cannot think I remember her so poorly that I would think her weak-livered."

"Nay, my lady, 'tis most unlikely your mother would ever have been involved in a brawl in the first place." Bethel said the word *brawl* with undisguised disgust. "First, your mother would not be apt to be traveling about the country without a male escort. Second …"

Delphine interrupted her. "Lay the blame on me, Bethel. Scold not Venetia. Did I marry sensibly as I should have years ago, I would not have men attempting to abduct me and force me into marriage to gain control of my wealth. Was I married, Venetia would not be put at risk."

"'Tis not right, Mistress," Tatty spoke up, her gray eyes alight, her pointed nose flaring. "That you have not found a man to meet your standards cannot mean you should lower your standards and settle for anyone just to have a husband. After all, four and twenty is not so old."

Delphine laughed a self-depreciating laugh. "I do appreciate your loyalty, Tatty. But perhaps I should lower my standards. One of us might have been injured tonight."

Venetia grabbed Delphine's hand. "You must not think such thoughts, dear cousin. I can think of nothing more vile than to be married to a man I could not love." She looked to her maid. "Tell her so, Bethel. Tell her you agree."

Bethel shook her head, and a strand of her graying hair slipped out from under her night cap and curled about her sallow cheek. "Does no good do Tattersall or I scold either one of you. Neither of you will pay us any heed." She looked at Delphine. "And, yes, Lady Venetia is correct. A marriage without love can be miserable. Well I remember my own dear mother and the burden she bore in trying to keep my ever-angry father appeased. I cannot think such a life would be worth living."

They reached the door to Delphine's room, and Purdy stood respectfully back. He would spend the remainder of the night in a chair outside her door. Though he could have had no way of knowing the wily abduction scheme was in the works, she knew he faulted himself. He considered himself her protector and tried to be alert to all possible hazards. That her dying grandfather had entrusted her to his care, he had taken to heart. Noah Purdy and Alfa Tattersall had been in her family's employ for as long as she could remember. Neither had ever married, both were devoted to her, and indeed, she trusted them with her life. This was not the first time an attempt had been made to abduct her and force her into marriage to obtain her fortune. The first had been made in her own home in Liverpool where her grandfather lay dying.

Three men had burst into the house, found her beside her grandfather's bed, and attempted to drag her from her home. The house servants had fought them off, but unlike this evening, the would be abductors had escaped. The episode had frightened her grandfather enough, he had had armed guards added to his house retinue. Delphine continued the policy because she promised her grandfather she would, but she preferred not to travel with them. Unlike Purdy and Anker, the guards were rough, coarse, and she was not completely certain she trusted them. Purdy and Anker were not only tall, strong, and excellent marksmen, but was a highway extremely rutted, they could run beside the coach and keep it from tipping over if it hit a dangerous dip.

Interrupting Delphine's train of thoughts, Venetia gave her a fierce hug and said, "Again, I bid thee good night, dear cousin."

Delphine returned the hearty embrace. "Thank you for coming to my rescue. You were a wonder, as was Bethel."

"Was it not fun?" Venetia said in a whisper not meant for Bethel's ears.

Delphine chuckled. "I cannot say I found it any great lark. The brute who had hold of me had the foulest breath. And, I am thinking both Tatty and I will have bruises come the morrow. But as all has ended well, I am content."

Chapter 2

Torrance Madigan winced as another low moan tore at his guts. For the hundredth, or was it the two hundredth time, he wished Cyril Yardley had not agreed to allow his greatly pregnant sister to accompany her husband on their desperate flight to a hoped for safe haven at Harp's Ridge. Seated behind him on a cushioned pillion, Sidonie Yardley Hayward was going into labor, and he knew not what to do. He knew nothing about birthing a child, and her husband was in no condition to help. Had Caleb Hayward not been so badly injured, his wife would now be at home where she belonged. But fearing for her husband's life, Sidonie had refused to be parted from him. Who better to nurse him on their trek to Harp's Ridge than she, she had protested.

"And in my condition, no militiamen on your trail would think to stop you," she declared. She was right. One group of militiamen had thundered past them with nary a backward glance mere hours after they left the Hayward farm. The next group they encountered was at the inn where in their weary flight they were forced to spend their second night. Hayward's injury would allow him to go no further, and they had no friendly family they could bide with as they had done the previous night. Militiamen, lounging in the inn's public room, had done no more than note their entrance before returning to their ale.

The innkeeper had been all solicitude as he conducted Sidonie and Hayward, disguised as his wife's maid, to a private bed chamber. Hayward had managed to make it up the stairs without stumbling, but Madigan, acting as Sidonie's husband, had been right behind him to catch him had he collapsed. The moment the innkeeper left with the promise to return with a light repast for Sidonie, Hayward sank onto the bed.

He had lost a lot of blood. His normally sun-bronzed skin looked pallid, and his green eyes appeared sunken in his face. The gunshot wound to his chest had missed his heart by more than two inches, but getting the ball out had made the wound bleed profusely. He should not have been moved, should not be spending all day on a horse, but they had little choice. Because of house to house searches, the injured Hayward could not stay with his family.

Hayward survived the night, even seemed improved in the morning. The bleeding had finally stopped, and he had taken some nourishment. The strain on Sidonie's heart-shaped face lessened and her brown eyes looked brighter. But by midafternoon, her pangs had begun.

Maneuvering his horse up beside Madigan's, Henry LaBree, Baron Tuftwick – Tuffy to Madigan – his blue eyes glistening, donned his winning grin, swept off his floppy-brimmed hat, and pushed his light brown hair off his brow. "How do you go?" he asked Sidonie.

"I do well," she lied. Madigan knew she lied. She was in pain, and though she tried to hide it, she could not control the moans. "How does my husband?" she asked.

Hayward, slumped on a pillion behind Tuftwick, spoke up, "I do well, wife. Tuftwick gives me his strong back to lean upon. All the same, I will be pleased do we reach Harp's Ridge by nightfall. My arse grows weary."

Her husband's attempt at levity brought a chuckle to Sidonie and helped her cover another groan. But Madigan was not fooled. Dear God, he prayed, let them make it to shelter before the baby thinks to come.

"Look yonder," Tuftwick said, pointing up ahead. "Chapman awaits us."

Madigan glanced up the road, if the narrow, rutted lane they traveled could be called a road. Jack Chapman, looking for all the world like a peddler taking a rest, sat on a grassy knoll off to one side. Would he have good or bad tidings to deliver? He was their guide, though none would guess he had any connection to them. Though he traveled on foot, he could traverse as many miles if not more than they could on horseback. Stemming from a long line of Chapmen, from whence he owed his surname, he knew Cheshire and surrounding counties better than any man with any number of maps.

Brown-haired, square-jawed, and with lively blue-gray eyes, Chap-

8

man greeted them with a bright smile. "Ho, pilgrims, do you take a respite? There is a pond back of this knoll to water your horses," he swept his arm out behind him. "And plenty of grass for the beasts to nibble do you mean to rest them."

"Have we time to rest?" Madigan asked. "Will we reach Harp's Ridge ere night falls?"

Chapman rose. "Aye, you have made good time." He stepped forward. "Here now, Mistress Hayward, allow me to help you down." He held up his arms to Sidonie. She placed her hands on his shoulders, and he carefully lowered her to the ground. When she found her footing, he escorted her over to the knoll, pulled a light blanket from his pack, and spread it out. With his aid, she was soon settled, and her husband was gently deposited at her side. She immediately checked his bandages.

"He is bleeding again," she said, tension in her voice. "Though 'tis slight." Sweeping back her husband's chestnut hair, she put her hand to his forehead. "His fever seems lessened, but I would cool his brow and change his bandage."

"I will get some water," Chapman said. He dug again in his pack and pulled out a tin cup.

"Do you get some fresh bandages from the saddle bag, Maddy," Tuftwick said, "and I will tend to watering the horses."

Madigan did as bid and looked up in time to see Sidonie turn from her husband and grip her stomach as a pain shot through her. Hayward, his eyes closed did not see his wife's pain, but Madigan saw her bite her lower lip until it dripped with blood. She wiped the blood away with the back of her hand and looked up with a smile as she accepted the proffered bandages.

Madigan wondered if any woman would ever love him with such devotion. He doubted it. He doubted he would ever marry. What woman would want him? He had no home. No income. At present, as a member of a gang of highwaymen, he was a wanted man. And even was he not someday caught and hanged, what future had he to offer any woman? He knew women found him attractive with his dark curly hair, dark brown eyes, and regular features, but a woman needed a man to offer more than good looks.

Chapman returned with the cup of water. He first urged Hayward to take a drink, then he pulled a cloth from his pack and dipped it in the water. While Chapman bathed Hayward's forehead Sidonie changed his bandage. She had to stop in the middle of her ministrations as another cramp wracked her body. His eyes closed, Hayward again missed his wife's suffering, but Chapman did not. He glanced up and Madigan met his gaze. Neither could say anything. Neither could do anything but pray Sidonie would last until they reached their destination.

🌱 🌱 🌱 🌱

"Two riders coming," Tuftwick said.

Madigan and Chapman both rose and peered down the road they had journeyed. Neither spoke as they watched the pair draw closer. "Peers to be a merchant and his servant," Chapman said. "That being the case, I can be on my way. Another mile down the road, the road will fork. Take the fork to the left. Follow that lane. It will twist and turn, but take no branches off it. I will meet you outside the village below Harp's Ridge. Do you fail to see me, think not to enter the village. Wait by the roadside. I will be awaiting D'Arcy. He will give us the all clear. Pass this on to Yardley and Preston."

"We will do as bid," Tuftwick said. "Do we pass any other villages we need be wary of?"

"None to fear. We are in the King's country here. You will pass a couple of hamlets. The tenants should be in the fields, but you should be able to quench your thirst at an ale house." He raised his hand. "God's speed," he said and set off down the lane with the forward lean and even paced gait of an experienced walker.

"I will but stretch my legs a bit do you help me to rise Mister Madigan," Sidonie said, and Madigan hurried to her side. She would need time alone to tend her business and to keep her husband from realizing she was going into labor. "Rest easy, my love," she told her husband before waddling off toward a clump of bushes.

Madigan and Tuftwick stood silent as the riders drew closer. Deverette Preston, dressed in merchant's plain garb, and Cyril Yardley, garbed as his servant, raised hands in salute, but neither called out a hallo. Though the area seemed secluded, the undulating swells could hide a shepherd or a hunter. Both men were the sons of baronets, but they had their roles to play, and so they would abide by them. Not until they swung down from their horses did they greet their friends. "How does Caleb?" Yardley asked, concern for his brother-in-law obvious in his voice.

"His fever is lessened and your sister has changed his bandage," Madigan answered. "He rests now. Once you have watered your horses at the pond yonder," he swept his arm behind him, "you may wish to have a word with him. But I do think now he sleeps."

"And my sister?" Yardley looked about, his brown eyes so like Sidonie's, searched the area.

Madigan nodded his head to one side. "She tends her needs."

"In case we are being watched," Preston said to Yardley, "you being the servant, you had best see to our horses. I cannot think we are being spied upon, but we have come too far to give ourselves away at this point."

"Aye," Tuftwick said, "Dev is right. We must not drop our guard." And as if to put the truth to his words, they heard the jingle of bells, the bleat of a goat, and a youthful herder bounded over a distant knoll driving four goats before him. He and the goats partially disappeared behind another rolling swell then reappeared headed in their direction.

The youth waved the staff he carried.

Tuftwick returned the wave, but said, "We best get Hayward up and on the horse and be on our way. Maddy, you give Dev Chapman's instructions while I get the horses."

Madigan passed on Chapman's directions and turned to find Sidonie bending over her husband and gently shaking him. "Wake my love. We must go."

They needed Preston and Yardley to help them get Sidonie and Hayward back on their pillions. "Glad to oblige, glad to oblige, happy to be of service," Preston said in a reverberating voice that no doubt the young herder could hear. "Always ready to help the ladies," he added.

Madigan admired the show Preston put on. He seemed every bit the convivial merchant. "Again, we thank you and your servant, sir, and God's speed to you," he said.

"And to you," Preston said as the youth and his goats trotted up the lane.

Madigan gave the youth a little wave then flicked his reins, and his horse set off at a leisurely pace behind Tuftwick's. He heard the boy greet Preston and Yardley, but he did not turn around. He pitied Yardley that he had not had time to visit with either his sister or his brother-in-law. But perhaps 'twas for the best that he did not know Sidonie was starting her labor. That would be one more worry for him.

Looking up at the sky, Madigan noted the clouds massing to the west. Though the late spring days had been warm and good for their trek, he knew thunderstorms were more apt to appear when the warm air met the cool air coming off the sea. He could feel the air cooling. Dear God, they had to reach Harp's Ridge before a storm broke over them.

Chapter 3

Phillida Lotterby, Lady Grasmere, her thoughts scurrying in all directions, heaved a sigh. She had no sooner welcomed home her sister-in-law, Lady Venetia Lotterby, and Venetia's cousin, Mistress Delphine Lotterby, returned from their visit to a friend in Warwickshire, than her brother, Nathaniel D'Arcy, arrived. He needed her to shelter his band of motely bandits. In addition, they had an injured man and a pregnant woman near her time with them.

"Nate, I swear, do you bring the militia down on us, I will see you horse whipped." She glared at her dark-haired brother with his laughing blue-green eyes.

"Nay, Phillida, why would you be suspected. No one suspects I am in England. They think I am in Holland, or Germany, or wherever the King may be. The militia would have no reason to come here. Besides, the men in my band are gentlemen. None of your servants should suspect them of being aught but friends who met up on their way to various destinations."

"You are wanted, Nate. I believe my servants loyal to us and to the King, but rewards can be tempting. You are worth twenty pounds. A more than goodly sum."

He tugged at a curl of her hair that had slipped out from under her cap. "You worry too much little sister. Where is Grasmere?"

She slapped his hand away. "Berold is making his rounds with our steward. He is a good husbandman and sees to the needs of his grounds and tenants weekly. He has seen to many improvements since his father's passing. God rest his soul, but his father was a poor husbandman." She looked about then said in a lowered voice. "And a poor husband, too." She raised her chin. "But that aside, how long do you mean to stay?"

"I will stay but the night, dear sister, and I will take a couple of my men with me when I leave. But Hayward and his wife will stay until they can travel. And I will leave a couple of other men here that they may attend Hayward's needs and then see his wife home safely."

Phillida frowned. "Must you leave so soon. Might you not stay a day or two? I have not seen you in so long, and I would hear how Kenrick and Blanche do. As neither my oldest brother nor my husband are allowed to leave their parishes, we cannot visit as we would like to do."

Her brother chuckled. "I thought you wanted me away from here as soon as possible."

She shrugged. "I do want you gone, but not before we have had a decent visit. When do your men arrive?"

"I go now to meet Chapman. We will bring them up by the back path and skirt the village. Better the villagers have no knowledge of the number of your guests."

"Ah, ha, so there is some danger."

"Not really, Phillida, but 'tis now my nature to be ever cautious."

"I will do my best to have rooms readied, but I can make no promises. What with Venetia and Delphine returning, all is a'ready muddled."

He kissed her brow. "Do express my thanks to Grasmere does he return ere I do."

She nodded and watched Nathaniel hurry away. She lived in constant dread her beloved brother would end up being shot, or worse, caught and hanged. He could be safe in Europe with the King as was their younger brother, Ranulf. But no, he would stay here in England and play the bandit, the highwayman, with his foolish followers. Now one of them was badly injured, and she was to shelter him, tend him until he healed – or died.

She shook her head. Naught to do but prepare for the onslaught. She was to have a houseful, at least for one night. Beds would need be made, fires laid – despite the warmth of the day, she feared a storm was on its way. She headed for the kitchen. She needed to consult with the cook. He would not be pleased at the short notice she was giving him. In addition to Venetia and Delphine, he would have seven more mouths to feed for supper and then for breakfast. Not to mention the need for a soothing broth for the invalid.

Delphine laughed and swept the giggling little girl up into her arms. "Yes, Timandra, you are still first in our hearts," she assured her cousin Berold's three-year-old daughter. "However, Eliza is a lovely little girl, and your Aunt Venetia and I are happy we got to see her and our dear friend, Clarinda. But now we are happy to be back home with you."

"Mother says Uncle Nate is to visit," the little girl said, her blue-green eyes, so like her mother's, dancing with excitement.

"Is he? Do you know, are any of his friends also visiting?" She tried to sound only mildly interested, but her heart started thumping at her young cousin's announcement. The image of a mop of curly brown hair framing a finely-wrought face with glorious brown eyes under straight, dark brows quickened her pulse.

"I do think so. Mother said she wonders how she will house all his friends."

Without thinking, Delphine enthusiastically hugged the little girl tight enough to make the child squeak. "Oh, dear one, I am sorry. I was but thinking I must go see if I can be of any service to your mother. More guests, and your Aunt Venetia and I just returned home. Mayhap I should offer to vacate my room and move in with your Aunt Venetia." Setting Timandra down, she said, "I must find your mother."

Delphine found Phillida hurrying from the kitchen, a young maid trailing in her wake. "Timandra has informed me you have more guests coming. I thought I would ask if I can help in anyway. And might you be needing my room?"

Stopping, Phillida swiped a strand of her dark hair off her brow. "Oh, yes, Delphine, I fear I will need your room. At least for tonight. I shall put Nate in your room. He plans to leave on the morrow, so you may have your room back when he leaves."

"Happy to oblige. I shall tell Tatty to move my night rail and toiletry items to Venetia's room. Now, how else may I help?"

"You are a dear, Delphine. If you would take Lucy with you," Phillida indicated the spritely young girl behind her, "and find Anna and make sure the rooms are being aired and the sheets are fresh. That will free me to work with the steward to get the table set. Nate says all the men are gentlemen, but I remember not their ranks." Pulling Delphine aside, she whispered, "Last time his gang came through here, they all hid in the stable, then they were gone before the first light. I swear, one of these days, we will find the militia at our door."

Delphine remembered that night well, but hiding her knowledge, she smiled and said, "I am sure all will be fine." Beckoning to the serving girl, she said, "Come Lucy, let us find Anna." Glancing over her shoulder at Phillida. She added, "I will tell Venetia what transpires. She will want to help, do you need her."

Phillida nodded. "I know she will. Do ask her to speak to the cook about heating enough water to see that all the rooms have warm water. Oh, and have her ask Timandra's nurse to see me. Nate says they have a woman with them who is with child and near her time. We may need send for the midwife."

"I will do so," Delphine said, setting off with Lucy at her heels. Hefting her skirts with both hands that she might scurry up the stairs, she quickly found Anna engaged in Phillida's bedchamber cleaning a silver framed looking glass. Pulling Anna from that chore, she set the two young servants to work airing out the guest chambers before hurrying off to find Venetia and Tatty and relay Phillida's needs to them.

Tatty had finished unpacking the trunks and was setting out Delphine's toiletries, when informed they must vacate the room for the night. To Delphine's relief, Tatty pulled no face. She but shrugged, and said she would attend it immediately. Delphine found Venetia in her chamber seated on a stool with Bethel combing out her hair. A tub had been placed before the hearth. Venetia was planning a bath after their long journey home. Upon learning of the multitude of unexpected guests soon to be arriving, Venetia promised she would see to Phillida's requests before she allowed herself the luxury of a hot bath. Delphine, hoping she, too, would find time to bathe before the guests descended upon them, asked Bethel to find her footmen, Purdy and Anker, and ask them to help Phillida's serving men. Carrying water up to all the rooms was a big job. Add in heating enough water for two baths and carrying that water upstairs – no question, additional help would be needed were she and Venetia to get their baths.

After leaving Venetia, Delphine found Anna and Lucy diligently engrossed in their tasks. Needing to give them little direction, she let her thoughts drift back to the last time Nathaniel D'Arcy and his fellow bandits visited Harp's Ridge. 'Twas near a year past. They had arrived in the dark of night. She would never have known about their brief visit had she not been awakened by her maid's coughs. Tatty had been suffering from a cold for several days, and concerned about her loyal servant, Delphine had insisted the woman keep to her bed with a camphor salve and warm flannel compress on her chest.

After checking on her maid and finding her still sleeping, if fitfully, Delphine had started back to bed when she heard footsteps passing her door. Fearing something might be amiss with Timandra who also suffered from a cold, she donned her robe and opened her door. In the dim light cast by a lantern, she made out Berold's figure headed down the stairs. Worried, she hurried after him, and in a loud whisper called to him.

"Berold, what is amiss?"

Turning, he beckoned to her. "Ah, Delphine, what luck. You can help me."

"Is something wrong? Is Timandra all right?"

His dark brown hair falling over his forehead, Berold frowned, and his bold blue eyes met her troubled gaze. "No, no, Timandra is fine. I need help in the kitchen. I am not wanting to awaken the servants, but I need help putting together some food." He leaned closer to her and whispered, "We have some unexpected guests."

"Unexpected guests?"

"Phillida's brother, Nate, and his highwaymen. They are on the run, but they need rest and food before they journey on. We must hurry, but be as quiet as you can."

Following Berold to the kitchen, Delphine wondered how her cousin thought he could keep his servants from discovering his guests' presence. But then, servants worked hard – likely, once finally abed, they slept so soundly they would not hear their master rustling about in the middle of the night. Still, as she helped her cousin gather bread, cheese, left-over ham hock, dried apples, and ale from the kitchen, she wondered how he would explain the food's absence to the cook come morning. And would not the stable hands wonder at the excess horse droppings and diminished hay? She forbore questioning Berold, she but helped him load the food items into cloth sacks and jugs of ale into a basket, then grabbing up the cook's wrap hanging by the door, she helped carry the victuals out to the stable.

Berold held the lantern high to light their way, even so, several times Delphine's slippered feet came in contact with pointed rocks. She suppressed her groans, but wished her cousin had given her time to put on sturdy shoes like he wore. Upon entering the stable, and finding a half-dozen pair of eyes gazing up at her, she was glad she had donned the cook's ponderous cloak. Had she not, the men lounging on their beds of hay would have viewed her in naught but her night shift and robe. Tatty would have been more than a little disapproving.

The men were most appreciative of the food and drink she and Berold passed around to them. She learned they had not eaten since the previous day and had had nothing other than spring water to drink. Oh, but they had made a bountiful haul. Laughing, they related how they relieved a Roundhead of his ill-gained fortune.

His brown eyes alight, a man she remembered named Cyril Yardley, chuckled. "The greedy Puritan. Having purchased confiscated Royalists' properties, he turned tenants who could not produce titles off their rentals, then sold off several large portions of forest land. He was headed back to Derby with his profit, but despite his armed guard, we waylaid him and left him and his guard bound up by the roadside. His quick return on his investment will soon be padding the King's pocket instead."

"Barring a small sum to go to a couple of the tenants turned off their land," interrupted another man in a soft voice, and Delphine turned to him.

"Chapman is right," Yardley admitted. "Plus, we stow a few coins for our own upkeep.

Chapman, blue-gray eyes dancing, chuckled and nodded.

Delphine remembered Chapman well. D'Arcy and the survivors of his troop, having served as an escort to King Charles II in his flight to escape Cromwell following their defeat at Worcester in 1651, relied on Chapman to lead them down hidden lanes, across fallow fields, and through trackless woods safely back to Cheshire. The King himself endured a grueling adventure before escaping to France, and D'Arcy and six members of his troop, believing they would have prices on their heads for fighting for their King, decided to become bandits. "Like Robin Hood," Delphine heard D'Arcy explain to his sister. "Only, we rob from the Puritans to give to the King."

Phillida was not happy with her brother's decision, but her husband was. Confined to his parish in Cheshire after being paroled from Weymouth prison for fighting for Charles I, he regretted he had been unable to fight for Charles II. Consequently, he was pleased to be able to help D'Arcy in his endeavor to fund King Charles, and at the same time, be an irritation to the Roundheads.

Noting D'Arcy was not present, Delphine asked after him.

"He is talking with Phillida in our room," Berold said. "She wanted some private time with him. She does worry about him."

"Rightfully so," said Torrance Madigan, the man Delphine had hoped to see. Maddy to his friends. His dark curly hair drooping over his forehead, his warm brown eyes earnest, he propped himself up on one elbow. "We have had our share of narrow escapes. The trouble with this last endeavor was it took place too close to Manchester. The hue and cry was raised, and the militia was on our tail err we had gone more than a few miles. We had to cache our plunder. In the meantime, our horses have been ridden hard, and they, like us, are in sore need of rest and fodder." At the end of his statement, he chomped into a wedge of cheese.

Delphine smiled at him, but he had turned his attention to his food. She could not blame him for paying her little heed. She must look a fright with her sleep drugged eyes, her hair, hanging below her night cap, scraggy about her shoulders, and the buff colored cloak, despite her height, dragging about her feet.

"How long do you stay?" she asked Chapman. With D'Arcy absent, he seemed in charge.

Berold answered for him. "They leave before first light. They are but giving their horses time to rest. The militia trailing them must also rest, but they have the option of demanding fresh horses from any stabling."

Delphine's heart dropped to the pit of her stomach, and she looked to Chapman. "You are in no danger of being captured, are you?" She could not bear to think of Maddy in prison, or worse, with a rope around his handsome neck.

Yardley chuckled. "Nay, Mistress Lotterby. We are now back in our home country. No one knows this area better than Chapman. No militiaman will be able to follow us."

"Mainly because there will be no trail for them to follow," chimed in Henry LaBree, Baron Tuftwick. He was Maddy's closest friend. Fact was, she would not know Maddy if not for the fun-loving Tuftwick. The two had been bosom friend's since they met in a boy's school in Manchester. Later, in their teens, they had been fostered at Harp's Ridge and at Knightswood Castle, a keep at Grasmere Lake dating from the time of William II. It had been in the Lotterby family since Henry VII awarded the lands to a Lotterby ancestor who fought on his side in the War of the Roses. Delphine's Uncle Gyes, Berold's father, taught them to ride, fence, hunt, and shoot. All requirements for a well brought up gentleman, her uncle had joked. Tuftwick had been expected to continue his education at Oxford, but in forty-two, the eruption of the Civil War put a halt to those plans. Maddy and Tuftwick, along with her cousin, Berold, and her Uncle Gyes, went off to fight for the King.

The King lost. Uncle Gyes was killed in the crushing defeat of the Royalists at Naseby, and Berold was sent to prison. Maddy and Tuftwick had been pardoned with the payment of stiff fines. Tuftwick paid both fines. Maddy had no money. No family that he knew of. But the bond between him and Tuftwick was as strong as any blood bonds. At least, so it seemed to Delphine. She had never seen the two apart.

She would have liked to stay in the stable and talk more with the men, but Berold herded her back to the house. The men needed their rest, and it would not do for her to be found missing from her room. With one last look at Maddy, he was already settled down in the hay, his head pillowed on an arm, she followed Berold back to the house. She thought she would not go to sleep the rest of the night, but she had. When she awoke later than usual in the morning, she hurriedly dressed, and found a reason to visit the stables before she broke her fast, but the bandits were gone. There was nary even a sign they had ever been there.

She never learned what Berold told the cook or his stable hands. And

20

she never told Phillida that she had helped Berold carry food out to the bandits. They left no trail. They just vanished. She could almost believe she had dreamed the whole thing. But she had not. And now they were returning. But this time they would be staying in the house. Sitting down to meals in the dining hall. She would surely have several times she could expect to see Maddy. Oh, she hoped she would have time for a bath. Time for Tatty to put some curls in her hair. Mayhap this time, she would be able to hold Maddy's attention.

Her mind swirling with things she might talk to him about, she followed Anna and Lucy to another chamber. She checked the freshness of sheets they pulled from a chest at the foot of the bed. She wondered which room Maddy would stay in. If she knew, she could put a sachet packet under a pillow. Though Anna and Lucy shook the sheets out well before making the beds, they had not the freshness of sheets just brought in from the wash.

She looked out the window at the darkening sky. She hoped they would arrive before the storm hit. That a storm was coming, she had no doubt. 'Twas the time of year for rains. At least Harp's Ridge was a cozy abode. In 1630, the same year Delphine was born, her Uncle Gyes's had torn down the old fortified manor house on Harp's Ridge and had used his wife's hefty dowry to build a new house. It had all the newest comforts, including hearths in every bedchamber and in every room on the ground floor. Servants' quarters still made do with small coal braziers.

The ground floor had a large dining hall, a smaller dining chamber for just the family, a withdrawing room off the family dining chamber, and a parlor for entertaining guests. All these rooms, plus a library and a room where Berold and his steward conducted business, opened off a formal hall with a broad, baluster staircase and landing. Paneling and plastered walls hung with framed pictures replaced tapestries and wall paintings. Woven or leather carpets graced the floors, and a gallery ran the length of the back of the house.

The kitchen and pantries and the wine and ale butleries, as well as the cook's quarters were in the undercroft. The other house servants lodged on the second floor, the gardeners and stablemen were housed in a dormitory behind the stables. Family and guests' bedchambers, the countess's private sitting room, and the nursery were on the first floor. Berold's father had wanted to put the nursery on the second floor with the servants, but his wife and his mother both rebelled. The children would be close to hand, or there would be no new house.

Delphine's house in Liverpool, which she had not called home since her grandfather died in 1649, dated from the mid sixteenth century. A half-timbered two-storied house, it was not large, only six bedchambers, the grand hall, a small dining chamber, a withdrawing room, and a library, but her grandfather had endeavored to stay up with the newest fashions, so the house had always been beautifully furnished and decorated. After her grandfather's death, for her protection, Berold insisted she move to Harp's Ridge. It had been her home ever since.

"Mistress?" Her reverie was interrupted by her footman, Purdy. He stood just outside the door, a bucket of water in each hand. "We have the water for the pitchers, would we not be in your way, we will fill them."

"Oh, Purdy, please do attend the pitchers." She stepped aside that she would not be in his way and would not be splashed when the water was poured into the white clay pitcher. "The water has been warmed?"

"Yes, Mistress, 'tis piping hot. Do the visitors not arrive too late, should still be warm for their ablutions. And water is being heated for yours and Lady Venetia's baths. And, I have moved your bathing tub over to Lady Venetia's room."

Smiling warmly, she said, "Dear Purdy, what would I do without you?"

Returning her smile, and before turning to his chore, he answered, "God willing, Mistress, may you never need to know."

Delphine counted herself more than a little lucky to have such a devoted servant. Did she ever marry, Purdy would be her steward. Even now, she paid him the wages due a steward for he did services beyond those of a coach footman. She knew she could count on him for anything and everything. Who else would have thought to have her tub removed to Venetia's room, or insisted water for two baths be heated. He was more often than not, a step ahead of her. And, did things go right, Anna and Lucy would be finished with the bedchambers about the same time the water for her bath was ready.

She would get her bath, and she would have Tatty curl her hair. And, were her prayers answered, this time, Maddy would notice her.

Chapter 4

Madigan breathed a heartfelt sigh of deliverance when he reached the top of the low hill, and on the other side of a slight incline, he saw Harp's Ridge Hall. Despite his floppy brimmed hat and his woolen coat, he was drenched. But his greatest concern was for Sidonie. Her labor pains had intensified to the point she could no longer conceal them from her husband. And when her pains struck at their worse, Madigan had to stop his horse, turn in his saddle, and hold Sidonie about the shoulders to keep her from falling off the pillion.

"Almost there," he told her. "And Jack has struck out ahead to give them warning of our arrival." Nudging his tired horse forward, he added, "Soon you will be in a warm bed and delivered of your son."

Her head resting against his back, he felt her nod, and her heard her hoarse voice joke, "You be that certain 'tis a boy, are you, Mister Madigan?"

He managed a chuckle. "Aye, no lass would be causing you so much grief."

Watching Chapman bent slightly forward, arms and legs swinging in harmony, stride effortlessly up the incline, Madigan could not help but admire his comrade's stamina. He believed the man to be the best asset their band possessed. Equally at home on foot or on horseback, he could ride with the best of them when the need arose. But coming from a long line of chapmen, he had learned to ply his trade at an early age alongside his father. He knew every lonely cottage, small hamlet, river or stream crossing, sheltering cave or forest bower, every mountain pass where one seemed not to exist, every phantom trek across heath and moor.

Never without his pack filled with needles and threads, scissors, shears, knives, and ax heads, ribbons and lace, small pots, and various fabric remnants, he visited farms and villages, showing and selling his

24

wares, and unobtrusively learning about the comings and goings of the wealthy Puritans who were not only taking advantage of Royalists' confiscations and sequestrations, but were infringing on the public's activities. Chapman listened to complaints – ale houses closed, theaters closed, race meets and Maypoles prohibited, fines for not attending Sunday services assessed – and he commiserated with his patrons. Some homes became safe havens for D'Arcy's highwaymen. Some provided information on the movements of the militia. No question, much of their success was due to Chapman.

As another deep groan broke from Sidonie's lips, Madigan saw the door open to Chapman's knock. In a matter of moment's, men and women, cloaks donned, were scurrying toward them. A tall, broad-shouldered man with deep-set eyes reached them first. Scooping Sidonie off the back of the horse as though she weighed no more than child, he cradled her gently against his chest as the pains raked her body.

"Easy, Mistress," he crooned, stalking away with her. "Lady Grasmere has made all ready for you." Women hurrying along beside him held a blanket up between them to block the rain off Sidonie's face. A second man carried a lantern to light the path. Though night had not yet fallen, the rain darkened sky made visibility difficult. A third man urged Madigan to follow him. He would see to the horses when they reached the door. Another rather large man, joined by Chapman, helped Hayward down from the back of Tuftwick's horse. They carried Hayward inside the house, and Madigan and Tuftwick, relieved of their mounts, followed after them.

Inside the brightly lit hall that held so many fond memories for Madigan, all was a bustle. Berold Lotterby, the Earl of Grasmere, his often firm mouth widened in a smile, met them at the door, and welcoming first one and then the other of his long-time friends, he urged them over to the fire blazing in the hearth.

"Your chambers are ready," he said, handing each of them a cup of mulled wine, "but I would know, where is D'Arcy, and the others of your band?"

"We had to travel separately," Madigan said after first savoring the warm wine going down his throat. "D'Arcy had to wait for Preston and Yardley to bring them up over the ridge path to avoid the village."

Grasmere nodded. "Aye, well, drink up, then I will see you to your chamber. My wife is seeing to Mistress Hayward, and my valet and Chapman are seeing to Hayward. Once I have you two settled, I will also check in on him."

Eager to strip off his wet clothes, Madigan set his empty cup on a nearby table and followed after Grasmere. With Tuftwick at his heels, he trod up the broad staircase, but at the landing, he cast a glance back over the well apportioned hall with its two tiered candelabras hanging from strong, wide beams, the large stone hearth, wainscoted walls, high-back, red velvet padded chairs lining the walls, and bright patterned woolen carpets in the center of the floor and over several low cabinets. Grasmere's father had done himself proud. And to Grasmere's credit, despite the heavy fines and taxes imposed by Cromwell's government, he had not sold off any of his prized furnishings. Yes, he had been forced to cut down and sell a large portion of his forests that surrounded his Harp's Ridge estate and sell a couple of minor manors, but so far, he was clinging to all his Harp's Ridge land.

Madigan admired Grasmere, but could not avoid being a little envious, though he hoped he never showed that side of himself to Grasmere. Over the years, Grasmere had been a good friend to him. He had never once belittled him or made fun of his lack of money or family. That all accepted Madigan initially came from a genteel family was a given. Otherwise he would not have been sent to the prestigious boys' school in Manchester. That after his mother's death, his stepfather made off with her wealth was also a given, so Madigan was accepted as a gentleman, if an impoverished one, and accorded all the courtesy extended to any person of the gentry class.

Life could be a lot worse, he thought as he entered his warm, cozy bedchamber.

� 🌲 🌲 🌲

Phillida had had her own birthing stool placed in the chamber she selected for Mistress Hayward, but it was soon evident, the poor woman was much too exhausted to use the stool. Directing Delphine's footman, Purdy, to place Mistress Hayward on the bed, Phillida offered a silent prayer thanking God that Delphine and Venetia had returned this same day. How she would have managed to get Mistress Hayward up the stairs without Purdy, she could not imagine. Delphine's other footman, Anker, had just as easily scooped up Mister Hayward and carted him up the stairs. Indeed, Delphine was a fortunate woman to have such capable, strong, and devoted servants in her employ.

With the help of her maids, Anna and Lucy, Phillida got Mistress Hayward's wet clothes stripped off her and a warm shift onto her. She had Timandra's nurse, Delphine's maid, Tattersall, and her own personal maid to help her with the birthing. And was she not mistaken, the babe could be coming at any moment. How the woman had endured the labor pains during the long ride was beyond Phillida. She believed she would never have been able to survive such an ordeal. Birthing Timandra in her own room with a midwife and her mother-in-law present, and maids hovering about ready to help in any manner, had been difficult enough. And according to the midwife, she had had an easy delivery. It had not seemed easy to her, but she knew she had not suffered the way Mistress Hayward was suffering.

"The babe comes, it comes," the nurse cried.

Holding Mistress Hayward's hand, Phillida said, "Push, push, 'tis almost here." And with her fingers aching from Mistress Hayward's tight grip about them, she saw the babe's head emerge. "One more push," she cried, and to her joy and wonder, the full baby appeared, pulled the rest of the way out by Delphine's maid. The cord was cut and the baby was held up for Mistress Hayward to see.

"'Tis a boy, a fine boy," the nurse said. "Now, I will wash him up, wrap him in his swaddling, and he will be in your arms afore you know it."

While the nurse tended to the needs of the baby, Phillida, her hand no longer painfully gripped, patted Mistress Hayward's hand. "You did fine. I shall send a maid to tell your husband he has a handsome son."

Mistress Hayward tilted her head to look up. Her brown eyes in her heart-shaped face looked huge. "My husband, how does he?"

"I am certain he does well. If not, my husband would have made it known to me. But I will tell the maid to ask after him when she tells him of your son."

"Thank you," Mistress Hayward said and licked her lips.

"Oh, dear, you must be parched. I have been remiss." She looked to the maids. "Anna, go now and inform Mister Hayward that his wife is safely delivered of a son. Also, ask how he does. And Tatty, do you please pour Mistress Hayward a cup of wine mixed with some water."

Mistress Hayward clutched at Phillida's hand. "Thank you, thank you."

Phillida patted her hand. "No thanks are needed. You must rest now."

"Lady Grasmere," her maid, Adah, said. "She still bleeds. We have packed her tightly, but she still bleeds."

Phillida knew enough about birthing to know that was not good. Women were known to die did the bleeding not stop. Swallowing, she said, "Then pack her again."

"Here is the wine, milady," Tattersall said, holding out the cup.

Phillida took the cup, and in holding it to Mistress Hayward's mouth, she noted the poor woman's lips were caked in blood. How often must she have bitten her lower lip to keep from crying out in pain. She turned back to Tattersall. "Do please bring me a warm wash cloth that I may bathe Mistress Hayward's face."

"Yes, milady, right after I fetch more rags for Adah."

Phillida brushed Mistress Hayward's moist brown hair off her forehead. "As soon as I have you cleaned up a bit, we will let you hold your baby, but then you must promise me you will sleep. You need the sleep to regain your strength. When you awaken, we will have some nourishing broth for you. And after you eat, you will be able to feed your son."

Managing a smile, Mistress Hayward nodded. "Again, thank you, and all your servants."

"You are most welcome. I am but glad you made it here to have the baby rather than somewhere along the trail."

The tired woman gave a weak laugh. "I agree."

Tattersall handed Phillida a soft damp cloth and said, "I do think the bleeding has lessened. But she has lost a lot of blood. I would like to change the sheets and pack her once more before we let her sleep."

"Yes, but not until after I wash her face. And we must let her hold her baby."

"He is ready to meet his mother," the nurse said. "A big, strong,

28

healthy boy he is, and what a mass of red hair he has. Must take after his father."

Her face wiped clean, Mistress Hayward smiled and reached up for her baby. The nurse, returning her smile, placed the baby in her arms. At that moment, Anna returned with the news that Mistress Hayward's husband was heartened by the news of his son. "But his first concern was for you, Mistress Hayward," the maid said. "I told him you were fine. Only then did he ask about the babe. And he said to tell you that knowing you and the baby are well made him feel much better. He said now he would be able to eat a hearty meal and get a good night's rest."

"Who is with him, Anna?" Phillida asked.

"His lordship is there, milady, but he is having his own man, Docket, stay with Mister Hayward through the night."

Phillida looked down and smiled. "Ah, so you see, your husband will be well cared for. Now, we will roll you about a bit while we get the sheets changed, then we will let you sleep."

"Yes, I would like to sleep," Mistress Hayward said, her eyes drooping.

Phillida nodded to the nurse to take the baby and put him in the cradle. She then let the maids work their magic. In no time, the sheets were changed, Adah and Tattersall had Mistress Hayward repacked, and warm quilts were pulled up over the exhausted woman. Poor dear, Phillida thought, watching her drop into sleep. God, she prayed, please let the bleeding stop.

"Milady," Adah said, her pinched nose raised, "are you to join your guest for supper, we must get you ready. At present, you are a fright."

Phillida half-smiled at her maid. Wiry and thin-faced, Adah was not a woman of great empathy, but she was loyal, she was skilled with a needle, and she could do wonders with hair.

"Let us go repair the damage," she said, but she looked back at the nurse. "Come for me does she not improve."

Chapter 5

Delphine was pleased with her gown and her hair. She and Venetia had both had time to bathe, and Venetia's maid, Bethel, knowing Tatty was helping Phillida, had been diligent in caring for Delphine's needs as well as Venetia's. Delphine had chosen a dark rose gown with tight-fitting bodice and v-shaped waist. The neck line was low and square cut, but a large lace-trimmed white collar was draped over her shoulders, partially concealing the revealing décolletage. Her hair, pulled straight back off her forehead, was parted down the middle and a multitude of curls cascaded down the sides of her head. A small rose-colored cap sat on the crown of her head.

Venetia had chosen a blue gown that accented the brilliant blue of her eyes. A thin belt encircled her waist, and a blue ribbon was entwined in the curls that fell softly about her face. She looked a vision, Delphine thought.

"Shall we descend to the dining hall?" Delphine asked her lovely cousin.

"Yes," Venetia said. "Now that we know Mistress Hayward is delivered of her baby, we can have a merry celebration."

The maid, Anna, at Phillida's direction, had informed them of the safe delivery and had let them know supper would not be delayed.

Delphine was eager to see Maddy. And hopeful she could catch and hold his attention. She longed to gaze deeply into his beautiful brown eyes, and mayhap read in them an attraction for her equal to hers for him. With Venetia following her, Delphine stepped into the corridor and headed for the stairs, but she stopped when she heard a door open down the corridor. Looking over her shoulder, she saw Maddy and Henry LaBree, Lord Tuftwick, emerge from their room.

Her breath catching in her throat, she grabbed Venetia's hand. "Oh, let us wait and greet Mister Madigan and Lord Tuftwick."

Her smile dimpling her cheeks, Venetia turned. "Welcome to Harp's Ridge. Let me see, how long has it been since you have graced our threshold? A good three years, I do believe."

Both men hurried forward. Dressed as gentlemen of fashion; they wore broad falling collars, Tuftwick's trimmed with lace, over short doublet's, Maddy's a soft gold, Tuftwick's a gold-trimmed violet. The sleeves attached to the doublets were full and slit to reveal their white, flare-cuffed shirts. Full breeches tied with garters below the knees, warm woolen stockings, aptly displaying their well-formed calves, and serviceable shoes spoke of prosperity, but not great wealth. They played a role, even when staying in what they hoped was a safe sanctuary.

Though the two men heartily greeted both Delphine and Venetia, Delphine noted they had eyes only for Venetia. Neither man looked at her. All her efforts to make herself appealing were wasted. She could be wearing her shabbiest gown for all they would have noticed. Bethel's efforts with her hair were for naught. She was used to being more or less invisible whenever Venetia was present, but this time it hurt, though she could not resent her cousin. Venetia was as lovely inside as out, and did she have any idea Delphine was in love with Torrance Madigan, she would have done all in her power to nudge him in Delphine's direction.

Delphine had never told anyone of the love she bore Maddy. The love was one of many years standing. She had loved him since she was ten years old – since he had saved her from a vicious dog attack. He had taken several nasty bites to his legs before the dog's owner had called the dog to heal. What she had done to cause the dog to attack her, she never learned. She but knew had Maddy not darted in between her and the dog, she would have been badly mauled, if not killed. The dog's owner apologized profusely, and Delphine's Uncle Gyes harshly chastised the man for not keeping his dog leashed, but not waiting to hear the man's excuses, Delphine followed after the servant who was taking Maddy inside to Aunt Helsa. Her aunt, with the aid of a couple of maids, saw to Maddy's wounds, but he limped around for a couple of weeks after the attack. He was still limping when Delphine and Venetia were sent to Wollowchet Hall to Aunt Helsa's sister, Charissa, Lady Wollowchet, where they were fostered for the next ten years.

Maddy and Tuftwick, though fostered with Delphine's Uncle Gyes, took their holidays at Wollowchet. Baron Wollowchet was Tuftwick's uncle on his mother's side and was his guardian as both Tuftwick's parents died when he was nine. Maddy and Tuftwick would arrive a few days before Delphine and Venetia were scheduled to return to their homes to spend holidays with their families. Until the year of forty-two when Maddy, Tuftwick, Berold and Uncle Gyes went off to fight for King Charles I, Delphine had been able to see Maddy several times a year. Even if those times were brief, and he paid her little attention, she and Venetia still being considered naught but children, she had cherished the sight of him.

During the three years of the first war, she saw Maddy only once. He and Tuftwick arrived at Wollowchet for a brief respite. War had changed Maddy. Turned him into a man. And, oh, what a handsome man he was, with broad shoulders, well-formed calves, and a wary alertness to his luminous brown eyes. She had watched his every move, listened to his every word. To her he was the perfect warrior. She feared for him, but he was fighting for his King. At her youthful age, she found such loyalty commendable.

Then before she knew it, he was gone. Gone to fight a losing battle at Naseby. The King suffered a devastating defeat, and Delphine's Uncle Gyes was killed in battle. Her cousin, Berold, became the Earl of Grasmere. To all the world, he was no longer Berold, Baron Standage, he was Lord Grasmere.

Berold spent nine months in prison then was paroled on his sworn oath he would never again take up arms against Parliament. Maddy and Tuftwick went home to Tuftwick Hall after they, too, swore not to take up arms against Parliament. Maddy, having no lands, had a minimal fine, but Tuftwick's fine was substantial enough he had need to borrow from his uncle, Lord Wollowchet, who had not taken up arms, though he had surreptitiously given financial aid to the King's forces. For the next few years, Tuftwick, with Maddy's support, worked diligently to repay his uncle and pay the fine to buy back his sequestered estate, consequently Delphine saw little of Maddy except when he and Tuftwick made brief visits to Wollowchet.

In forty-eight, when a number of Royalists again took up arms on behalf of the King, Maddy and Tuftwick, after consulting with Berold, remained faithful to their oaths. But in fifty-one, the two, unable to resist Charles II's call to arms, joined D'Arcy's cavalry unit and rode off to war. Having avoided capture, yet wishing to aid their King, with Nathaniel D'Arcy as their leader, they turned to highway robbery. They never considered their robberies of the Roundheads crimes. Nor could Delphine think of them as criminals. They were acting in support of their King, the rightful ruler of England. Now, here they were at Harp's Ridge, on the run, but appearing as naught but two gentlemen seeking shelter for the night.

Upon descending to the great hall, Delphine saw Berold, Jack Chapman, and Nathaniel D'Arcy, Phillida's brother, who would be occupying her room for the night. The men were chatting and enjoying the glowing fire in the large hearth, but D'Arcy swept off his hat and greeted Delphine with elaborate courtesy.

"Mistress Lotterby, I cannot begin to thank you enough for surrendering your room to me. And, I find, I must also thank you for the aid your footman, Purdy, provided me. He had a warm fire in the grate, warm water in the pitcher. And as Grasmere's serving men were helping Preston and Yardley, these clothes I am wearing, Purdy laid out for me. A marvel he is."

Accepting D'Arcy's gratitude, Delphine smiled. "Purdy is a wonder. I cannot think I could get on well without him. I am glad he was of service to you."

"He was indeed." He looked past her to Venetia and again bowed. "Lady Venetia, may I say you have grown even more lovely than when I last saw you."

Venetia laughed the rustling laugh men so adored and said, "Now, Mister D'Arcy, such blandishments will turn my head. Mister Madigan and Lord Tuftwick have been offering equally flattering sentiments." She looked at her brother. "Berold, you must tell these men they are to have pity on me. They will put my head in a swirl."

Berold chuckled. "Seems Maddy and Tuftwick have at last noticed you are no longer a schoolroom miss. I am thinking when last they saw you, they had naught but flight on their minds. Is that not right?" He looked at his two friends. "Fresh from the battle at Worcester with the Roundheads beating the bushes for any Royalists. You had little thought for flirtations."

D'Arcy slapped Berold on the back. "You are indeed correct, Grasmere. 'Twas the first time we came fleeing here in the dead of night, looking for shelter and sustenance, but 'twas not the last. And ne'er have you failed us."

"Would that I could do more, but do I break my parole, I could lose not only by land, but my head. And now, with a daughter to think of, I dare not chance anything more adventuresome than offering you my home. I am allowed a trek to and from Knightswood Castle once a year to tend the estate. Otherwise, I must not step foot outside my parish."

"Do you go to Knightswood soon?" D'Arcy asked.

"Aye. In a couple of weeks the rains will lessen and the roads will be fit for travel."

"Good, that will give the Haywards time to heal. Time for Mistress Hayward, and the new son I have been told she bore, to grow strong that they may be returned to their home."

Delphine had not seen the Haywards when they arrived. She had been soaking in her tub, but she knew the birthing had not come easy. Even at the distance from one end of the corridor to the other, she had heard the woman's cries. Bearing children was a difficult and often frightening experience for women, yet mankind would soon be extinguished did women not accept their fate. Someday, she would marry. Hopefully Maddy. And she, too, would bear children. She had been but six when her mother died in childbirth. A third miscarriage. Her father and her grandfather had been devastated. Her father never thought to remarry. He but continued to work diligently for her grandfather until the ague carried him away in forty-five, the same year Uncle Gyes died at Naseby.

"Ah, here comes my wife," Berold said, directing Delphine's thoughts away from her departed parents. "You look charming, my dear," Berold added, holding out his hand to Phillida as she neared the hearth.

Though impeccably dressed from head to toe, Delphine thought Phillida looked tired. And rightfully so. She had supervised the preparations for the numerous guests they were housing and entertaining, and had also helped deliver a baby. Yet, when she took her husband's

34

hand and gazed into his eyes, a beauty possessed her and the weariness that had shown in her face evaporated to be replaced by a loving smile.

Delphine would love to see such devotion in Maddy's eyes when he looked at her. Instead, she watched him gaze longingly at Venetia. Tuftwick had the same besotted look in his eyes. No doubt, both men would vie for a place at Venetia's side throughout the evening. Venetia, though used to such attention, and normally immune to men's flirtatious behavior, seemed to be enjoying Maddy's and Tuftwick's adulation. Not that Delphine could blame her. Both men were handsome, well-formed, and well-spoken. Superior in all ways to the parish locals. Not since the Spring of fifty-one when Venetia's Aunt Charissa had taken them to London had they encountered men of equal wit and charm.

Their dear friend, Clarinda Seldon, had met her husband Vincent Tilbury on their London visit. Delphine believed had she not already been in love with Maddy, she might also have made a match. She and Venetia met several men they liked, but neither met a man they wished to wed. Still, experiencing London had been thrilling, and they were pleased Clarinda, being naught but the daughter of Lord Wollochet's steward, had made such an estimable match. She had married a member of the gentry with a substantial estate in Warwickshire.

Having just returned from a visit to Merrywic House, the Tilbury estate, Delphine could not help but be a little envious of her friend. Clarinda, happy in her marriage, her home, her station in life, and with her beautiful baby daughter, had everything Delphine hoped someday to have. But until she could find a way to win Maddy's love, Delphine feared she would continue to be pursued by men eager to gain control of her vast fortune. At least, if someday she did marry Maddy, she could be certain 'twas not her fortune that brought him to her bed. Had he been interested in her wealth, he would now be pursuing her instead of Venetia.

Lost in her own thoughts, she paid little heed to the conversations buzzing around her. Not until Berold told D'Arcy he would like to have Maddy and Tuftwick ride with them to Knightswood. Then her heart skipped a beat. Maddy to travel with them to Knightswood! "These are uncertain times," Berold continued, and with a grin and a slight tilt to his head, added, "Can never tell when some highwaymen will attack."

D'Arcy chuckled. "'Tis true. I have heard there has been a rash of attacks over the past three years. Some right here in Cheshire."

Berold sobered. "'Tis more the miscreants hoping to abduct Delphine that I worry most about. She is under my protection. Just last night in an inn not a day's ride from here, an attempt was made to abduct her. It is now the fifth such attempt. I have no fear for her safety here, but when we travel, we are vulnerable. Two more men who know how to use their weapons would make me feel more secure. Especially as I travel with my wife and daughter."

Turning his gaze on Delphine, D'Arcy nodded and said, "I believe I could spare Maddy and Tuftwick, but I fear such abduction attempts will not cease until Mistress Lotterby is wed."

Berold frowned. "So I have been telling her for a number of years now. Near from the time her grandfather died, and I brought her here to live."

Blushing, Delphine raised her chin and glared at her cousin. "You need not speak of me as though I have no hearing or am not present, Berold. As I have told you many times over, when I am ready to wed, I will wed. Do you grow tired of providing me protection, I can return to my home in Liverpool."

"Humph! We have had this quarrel before."

"And you will not have it again at this time," Phillida said, laying a hand on her husband's arm. "Look, Mister Preston and Mister Yardley join us. 'Tis time we go into supper. I know everyone must be starved."

Delphine had hoped to go into supper on Maddy's arm, but D'Arcy offered his arm, and she had no choice but to accept and follow after Venetia and Tuftwick. The other men, having no ladies to escort, trailed along behind. At the table, Delphine found herself seated between D'Arcy and Preston, and directly across from Venetia, Maddy, and Tuftwick. Well, if she could not be seated beside Maddy, at least she could feast her eyes on him. And that was exactly what she did, though vaguely listening to the conversations on either side of her.

D'Arcy was telling Phillida about their eldest brother Kenrick and his children. Preston was telling Yardley about the tongue lashing he received from his father the last time he secretly visited his home. From what Delphine could gather of Preston's conversation, his father was not pleased with his son's current occupation, if being a highwayman could be considered an occupation. Delphine could not blame Preston's father for being perturbed.

Yardley chuckled. "My father is no more pleased with me, nor is Hayward's father pleased with him, but I asked my father would he rather I had surrendered to the Roundheads. I could have ended up in prison or have possibly be placed in servitude and sent to the islands. At least neither your father, nor mine, nor Hayward's was involved in the fighting, so they have had no land confiscated. Nor have the Roundheads been able to prove our fathers gave any aid to King Charles I. And the Roundheads have no idea we are the highwaymen who have been terrifying Puritans in counties all over England."

"Aye," Preston said, "my father knows I could not have surrendered. He but wishes I had fled the country. He thinks I would be safer trailing around after the King in Europe. What he thinks I would do to earn my bread over there, I have no idea, nor did I press him. 'Twould but have furthered the argument."

"Watch your tongues," Chapman hissed from across the table, "the servants have ears." He had been involved in a conversation with Berold, but he must have heard Preston and Yardley. Delphine knew caution, even around Berold's loyal servants, was a necessity. The servants knew D'Arcy was wanted. They knew he had fought for Charles I and II, but they were not apt to risk losing employment for a twenty pound reward, though for most, it was more than they would make in five years' time. Nor would they want to cause their beloved lady any grief. However, did they know Harp's Ridge was housing notorious highwaymen, they might think the reward for turning them in well worth the loss of employment. Fact was, the reward could be enough so they might never need work again.

Preston flushed a bright red. "You are right, Jack. Forgive me." He glanced over his shoulder. Fortunately, none of the servants were in the dining chamber, but he knew he and Yardley had put all at the table at risk.

Yardley, too, looked contrite. "I fear I relaxed my guard too much here in such comfortable surroundings, sitting with ladies at the table, eating and drinking food better than I have tasted in many a day." He looked at Berold. "Begging your pardon, Grasmere. It will not happen again."

Berold nodded. "No harm done. Enjoy your meal. After we are finished eating and the ladies retire, we will adjourn to my study where we may talk more freely."

Changing the subject, Berold asked Yardley if he had seen his new born nephew, and as Yardley commenced praising young William, named for his brother who had died at Worcester, Preston turned to Delphine. "I want to thank you, Mistress Lotterby, for directing your footmen ready the water pitcher for Cyril and me this evening. Purdy and Anker, I believe are their names. We made certain to give them substantial tips."

She smiled at the handsome youth with his generous mouth and well-formed lips, his light hazel eyes, and thick brown hair pushed back from a broad forehead. She guessed he could be little older than she, yet he had been to war, had helped his King escape capture, and had lived a life on the run for the past three years. She could not fault him for letting his guard down. Being constantly vigilant had to be exhausting in itself.

"That was kind of you," she said. "I am sure they appreciated it, but they are of such value to me, I see they are both well remunerated. They have been at my side for many a year."

"They never went off to war then?" he questioned.

"Nay. That was not their calling. Both swore oaths to my grandfather they would see to my care. And they have never broken their oaths. Ever they are at my side."

"You are fortunate to have such loyal servants."

"Indeed, I know it well and give daily thanks for such blessings. But you, Mister Preston, have you a large family?" She asked the question more to keep him talking rather than any real interest. Her real interest was centered on the man across the table who was doing his best to hold Venetia's attention. Oh, Maddy, she thought, might I not have even a crumb?

"Both my parents are alive and well," Preston was saying, and Delphine smiled and nodded. "I have three younger sisters. One is recently

38

betrothed to a neighbor. They have ever been sweet on each other, so 'tis no wonder. My other two sisters are yet in the school room." His hazel eyes saddened. "I had a younger brother. We were close. He died when I was but sixteen, he but fourteen. The ague that came 'round that year and struck so many. Took my grandmother, as well."

"Was that the year of forty-five?"

He nodded. "Aye."

She gave him a half smile. "Yes, that year it took my father. Not enough we had a war taking lives, destroying property, we had to have the ague as well."

"I was not old enough to fight in the first war, and father convinced me not join King Charles I and his supporters in their second attempt. He was certain they had no chance, and he was right. Too many former Royalists were unwilling to break their oaths, so the King had poor backing. And those who did break their oaths, lost their lives, or much of their fortunes." He looked about to ascertain no servants were hovering near him, then leaning closer to Delphine, he whispered. "When D'Arcy came asking for volunteers to fight for Charles II, I could not say no." He leaned back, and shrugging, said, "And so here I am today, traipsing about the country in the guise of a semi-prosperous merchant."

Servants were popping in and out of the dining chamber bringing various dishes, and refilling wine goblets. If any of them looked at their lord's guests suspiciously, she had not seen it. And she had been alert to them. Over the years, after five abduction attempts, she had learned to watch for surreptitious eye movements, for jittery or shaking hands, for hidden glances, the kind of glances she had been directing at Maddy all evening. Purdy and Anker were alert to such things as well. They would inform her did they suspect any of the servants were suspicious of the numerous guests who had descended on the hall at one time.

Of course, many of the servants knew Maddy and Tuftwick. After all, both men had been fostered at Harp's Ridge, but none of the servants knew the two had fought in D'Arcy's cavalry unit. They were D'Arcy's only recruits from outside Cheshire. She guessed even Tuftwick's own servants at Tuftwick Hall had no notion their lord was involved in Charles II's debacle. Since Tuftwick was nine, a steward appointed by his uncle had managed the Tuftwick estate. Over the years, Tuftwick spent little time in his home, a small barony in the foothills of the Pennines in Lancashire. His absence would be of little note. And situated as the estate was in an isolated area, 'twas unlikely a concerted effort would ever be made to discover Tuftwick's comings and goings. Fact was, had he and Maddy not been captured at Naseby, no one would have known they had fought for Charles I. They would never have been fined. And due to their youth, and Tuftwick's negligible importance in the peerage, once their fines were paid, they had not been confined to their parish as were Berold and his brother-in-law, Kenrick D'Arcy, the Earl of Tyneford.

Chapman and Hayward, not being of the nobility or the gentry, escaped notice by the Roundheads searching for the King's followers. They could return to their homes and families, unmolested and were never suspected of having fought for the King. Yet, like Maddy and Tuftwick, the two men chose to ride with D'Arcy. Yardley and Preston, not having broken any oaths, probably could have escaped with naught but fines, but they, too, had thrown in their lot with D'Arcy, who could have chosen to be with his younger brother somewhere on the continent in the company of Charles II. What made these seven men willing to risk certain hanging if caught in the commission of highway robbery was something Delphine found honorable yet perhaps foolhardy in the risk they were taking.

Berold understood them, wished he could join in their dangerous escapades. She decided it must be a man thing. Surely women had better sense. Yet did Maddy but crook his little finger at her, she would follow. Share in his hardships, just to be at his side. So, indeed, she supposed she could not claim to have better sense than did the man she loved.

With the meal ended, she reluctantly rose with Phillida and Venetia, and with one last look at Maddy, she exited the dining chamber and followed Venetia to Phillida's sitting room. Phillida, worn out as she was from her busy day, had to check on her two patients before she could at last retire for the evening.

Chapter 6

Phillida took a peek at the sleeping baby. He had put his mother through a lot, but he was a strong, healthy looking boy. Tattersall assured her Sidonie's bleeding had stopped, and the poor woman, after eating a bowl of beef broth with shredded beef, was sleeping peacefully. She had nursed her new son before giving in to her exhaustion. "The babe will be waking again in an hour or so, ready for another feeding," Tattersall added, "but Mistress Hayward will have no trouble feeding him."

"I thank you for sitting with her, Tattersall, but who is seeing to Delphine's needs?"

"As Mistress Delphine is sleeping in Lady Venetia's room, Bethel will see to her. I told Nurse she should put Lady Timandra to bed, and that I would stay here for the night. Anna is coming back to make up the trundle bed for me. I will be on hand to help Mistress Hayward with her baby. Now, if you know how her husband fares, that I may assure her he is well, she will sleep better. Questions about her husband are constantly on her lips."

Phillida looked down at the sleeping woman. She could understand her concern. She would feel the same was Berold the one lying injured in another room. "Tell her he is resting peacefully. Lord Grasmere's own man is with him. We will keep Mister Hayward to his bed yet another day to insure his wound will not again start bleeding, but is all well the following day, we will let him visit her."

Looking questioningly at Tattersall, Phillida said, "You look tired yourself, Tatty. Should I not have Anna spell you? Have you eaten?"

"I have eaten, and once the trundle is made up, and young William has his next feeding, I will go to sleep myself."

"I cannot think how I would go on without you. I am ever so grateful you returned today. I fear Adah would not be near so good at caring for

Mistress Hayward as you are."

Tattersall chuckled. "Adah has her merits. When others might have panicked that we had no midwife and the babe was coming so quickly, she remained calm. She may have ice in her veins, but at times that can be a good thing."

Phillida had to agree with Tattersall's assessment of Adah. Her maid might shed few tears for another person's misery, but then, neither would she be blinded by her emotions. "Well, I shall leave you, but do you need me, you must not hesitate to send for me. I will tell Anna to be near to hand should you want for anything."

"Thank you, milady," Tattersall answered.

With another glance at the baby, then at Mistress Hayward, Phillida exited. Oh, how she was ready for her bed, but she had yet a couple of letters to write. Nate meant to visit their older brother, Kenrick, at Wealdburh, the family's principal residence, and he promised to take letters to her brother and his wife for her. At times Phillida missed her home by the sea on the Wirral Peninsula. Wealdburh had been the D'Arcy principal seat since the first D'Arcy had come over as a knight with the Conqueror. The keep was old and had few of the modern conveniences she enjoyed at Harp's Ridge, but it was the home of her childhood, and she loved it. She hated that Berold's confinement to his parish or the Knightswood Castle estate near Lake Grasmere prevented her from visiting her home and brother on a yearly basis.

Treading softly down the corridor to her chamber, she prayed Venetia and Delphine were equally tired after their long journey, and that they would not want to stay up talking about the evening's events.

❀ ❀ ❀ ❀

Venetia eyed her cousin from under her lowered lashes. Since settling onto cushions in Phillida's sitting room, Delphine had done little more than give monosyllable answers to Venetia's questions or statements. Did Delphine not think Lord Tuftwick and Mister Madigan the two most handsome men of their acquaintance? Yes. Were they not the most amusing and courteous of any men they had met since their visit to London? Yes. Was it not exciting to think they might accompany them to Knightswood Castle? Yes. Was it not wondrous to see both men again after so long a time? Yes. Did she think they had changed greatly since last they saw them? No. Did she enjoy her conversation with Mister Preston? Yes. Did she have any conversation with Phillida's brother? Not really.

"You are rather quiet, Delphine. I do hope you are not overly upset by Berold again taking on about you finding a husband. You should just ignore him."

Delphine at last turned and looked at her. She shook her head. "No, I cannot say I was even thinking about our little spat this evening until you just now brought it up. But mayhap, he is right. Mayhap I should marry."

"Oh, Delphine, not unless you fall in love. You cannot marry just to be marrying someone. You would be so unhappy, and if you are unhappy, I will be unhappy."

Delphine laughed. "Dear sweet one, if you could but see the concern on your face. It warms my heart to know you love me so much."

"I do indeed love you. Now you must promise me you will not be marrying just to please my brother or anyone else. Promise!" Leaning forward, Venetia's eyes bored into Delphine's.

Again laughing, Delphine raised her hand. "I do so swear I will not marry anyone not of my own choosing."

Frowning, Venetia leaned back into her cushions. She was not certain Delphine's promise was the promise she wanted from her. She wanted her beloved cousin to promise she would not marry unless she loved the man, but she decided not to push the issue at this time. She could understand how frustrated Delphine must feel after yet another attempt to abduct her and to force her into marriage in order to gain control of her wealth. What a shame it was a woman's property became her husband's once she married. At times she thought a woman's lot in life to be most unfair. But then, did one find the right man – a man to love who would protect his wife as Berold loved and protected Phillida – then marriage would be naught but joy.

With Delphine again immersed in silence, Venetia let her thoughts drift back over the evening's banter with Tuftwick and Madigan. She liked both men, but she believed she was a bit more attracted to Tuftwick. She admitted, some of the added attraction might be centered around his position and wealth. Tuftwick was titled, and though his barony was not extensive or of great wealth, he was also the heir to Wollowchet Hall. His uncle, Lord Wollowchet, having no children, had already made out his will in Tuftwick's favor. She knew about the will because Lord Wollowchet's wife, her Aunt Charissa, had told her Tuftwick was to inherit the estate, though not the title which would go to some distant cousin.

Madigan was dear and sweet, and mayhap even more handsome than Tuftwick, but he was virtually penniless. The most he could hope for was to be steward to one of Tuftwick's manors. Clarinda's father had prospered as Lord Wollowchet's steward, but her dear friend's dowry had been provided by her father's older brother, who, as was the norm, had inherited the entire Seldon estate. Clarinda's father had been forced to make his own way in the world. Such was often the fate of younger sons. But even if well paid, an estate steward was but barely considered a member of the gentry.

As Tuftwick's bosom friend, Madigan had ever been treated as an equal, but because he was without means of his own support, Venetia knew Berold would never let her marry him. So she had best not fall in love with him. She might enjoy his banter and his flattery, but she must guard her heart.

She looked up when the door opened and her sister-in-law entered the sitting room. Jumping to her feet, she exclaimed, "Oh, poor Phillida, you look so very tired."

"Indeed, what a day you have had," Delphine said, also rising. "We but waited to bid you a goodnight, and we will be off to our bed."

"Yes," Venetia said, giving Phillida a kiss on the cheek. "Adah awaits you in your bedchamber. Now, do you get some rest."

Phillida smiled weakly and nodded. "Thank you. I am very weary. As must you also be after your exhausting journey." She looked at Delphine. "Your dear Tattersall is staying the night with Mistress Hayward. She assured me Bethel would see to your needs."

"And so she shall," Venetia said, taking Delphine's hand. "Let us to bed."

"Indeed. To bed. Again, goodnight, Phillida," Delphine said, following after Venetia.

Candles burning in sconces on the corridor walls gave them all the light they needed to find their way to their room without bumping into benches or cabinets covered in decorative carpets or topped with family busts situated against the walls. Venetia loved her home and was happy to be back in it. Happy to be safe, and warm, and pampered. And she was more than a little ready for a good night's sleep.

❧ ❧ ❧ ❧

Madigan tossed on the trundle bed he had insisted he take in the room he shared with Tuftwick. He wondered that his friend had so quickly fallen to sleep, but he could hear the even breathing he knew so well after the many years they had spent together. Madigan often wondered what would have befallen him had he and Tuftwick not met at the boy's school in Manchester. They had both been nine years old. He had been sent away from his mother and his home in Ireland by his step-father. Tuftwick had just lost both his parents. Both he and Tuftwick had been lonely and afraid and had turned to each other for comfort. A bond had formed, and when Madigan's step-father stopped paying for his schooling, and Madigan at the age of thirteen was kicked out onto the streets, Tuftwick left with him.

The two boys, with little in the way of funds and carrying what belongings they could, walked from Manchester to Wollowchet. Because it was mid-morning before they set out, they were forced to spend the night curled up together next to a fallen tree. But the weather had been balmy, and being youthful, they had suffered no dire consequences. By noon the next day, footsore and hungry, they arrived at Wollowchet.

Having received a message from the school that Tuftwick had left with Madigan, Lord Wollowchet had not been surprised to see them, and when Tuftwick insisted he would not return to the school without Madigan, his uncle chuckled and promised to make other arrangements. In the meantime, the boys enjoyed being at leisure at Wollowchet and being pampered by Lady Wollowchet. Madigan, being young, had not realized how much charity he was receiving from Lord Wollowchet. He had but accepted it and been grateful.

He had known when his step-father, Millard Lawford, stopped paying for his schooling that his mother had died. On his behalf, Lord Wollowchet had written to the mayor of Ballyfermot, a small village a few miles from Dublin, and had learned that indeed Madigan's mother had died, and soon after her burial, his step-father had left Ballyfermot taking his young daughter, Madigan's half-sister that he had never even seen. The mayor had no idea where Lawford had gone. Nor was there any indication that any of Madigan's mother's inheritance had been left for her son.

Madigan had not been home since sent away. He had spent his holidays with Tuftwick at Wollowchet. Letters came from his mother, begging him to write to her. And how often he had written her, but she never seemed to get his letters. He could only assume his step-father was not giving her his letters. But he prized her letters, had saved every one of them. They were now the only possessions he had that he could truly call his own. His horse and saddle, gun and sword, even his clothing he owed to Tuftwick. At times, it bothered him that he had no way to repay his friend, no way to repay him but to stay by his side and make sure no harm came to him.

Tossing from right side to left, he let his mind drift over the evening's events. That he had fallen in love, he had no doubt. Venetia Lotterby was the most beautiful woman he had ever seen. The sweetest he had ever known. To think the number of times he had seen her at Wollowchet and had paid her no heed, now here she was, casting spells over him, and putting thoughts into his head he should not be having about a proper lady. Even now, just thinking about her and a sweat rose on his forehead, his heart started pounding, and his arousal could well prove embarrassing. He and Tuftwick had vied for her attention the whole evening. What a joy it had been to be the one to make her laugh. And oh, how he loved to hear her throaty laugh.

He knew he was foolish to be dreaming about the daughter of an Earl. He would never have a chance to marry such a woman, and yet, he could not give up on the possibility of some miracle happening. If he could but win her heart, might there not be some hope for them? Mayhap he could find his step-father and claim the inheritance stolen from him. Mayhap the King would return to the throne and reward

46

those who had helped fund him in his exile. Anything could happen. He could not give up hope, not yet, not when he had just discovered Venetia. He would let his dreams drift for the time being and would revel in the fact he would be escorting her to Grasmere. He would have days in her presence. Days that he could hold in his memory for the rest of his life, for he could never imagine loving another woman.

Chapter 7

Phillida was pleased with the progress Sidonie Hayward had made. Naught but a week had passed since she had given birth, and though she should have spent another week in bed, she was up and about and eager to help in the care of her husband. Caleb Hayward was mending more slowly than his wife. The gunshot wound, the loss of blood, the travel when he should have been in a bed had played havoc with his stamina, but Phillida believed she could assure Sidonie her husband was out of danger.

Phillida liked that she and Sidonie were on a first name basis. And she was pleased she and Berold had been able to stand in as Godparents for Sidonie's brother and sister at little William's christening. She found Sidonie an amazing woman. Though near to giving birth, when she should have been confined to her lying in room, she had insisted on journeying with the fleeing highwaymen that she could see to the care of her husband. All the men agreed they could not have succeeded in their flight had Sidonie not been with them. She gave them the cover they needed. Caleb Hayward owed his life to his wife. Phillida wondered if she would have had the same courage had she and Berold been in the same situation. She loved her husband so dearly, yet the thought of traveling on horseback over sometimes rugged country for long hours with a baby due at any time, and no other woman about to help should the baby start to come – well, Phillida hated to admit it, but she was not certain she could have done it.

Berold had decided he would take the Haywards with him to Knightswood Castle. "Better they stay away from the Hayward farm for the time being. Mistress Hayward having her new babe, and Hayward with his wound slow to heal, neither one is fit to flee again should the reason for their absence not be believed by the local authorities. Besides, the beauty of Grasmere will do them both good. Between our coach and

Delphine's, we will have no trouble safely transporting them."

"Will not their families worry about them?" Phillida asked.

"Nay, your brother, Nate, is sending Chapman with a message to the Hayward and Yardley families that Hayward and his wife survived the trek, and that the babe is healthy and strong. I will send an additional message letting the families know Mistress Hayward and the babe will not be returning until the autumn. No doubt by then, is he asked to do so, Hayward will be well enough to rejoin your brother and his men. In the meantime, a summer with us, time for husband and wife to recover their strength, will be good for the both of them."

Phillida kissed her husband on the cheek. "You are a thoughtful man, Berold. And I love you for it."

Grabbing her around the waist, and pulling her closer, he said, "I can be even more thoughtful, my wife, and I will prove that to you in our bed tonight."

Chuckling, she placed a palm on his face. "I will have that to look forward to all day."

And so she did. For the past week, busy with caring for the Haywards and entertaining Tuftwick and Madigan, she and Berold had fallen into bed too tired to think of love making. Unlike many married couples, Berold's parents being a prime example, she and Berold shared a bed all the night. She had her sitting room off the bedchamber, and he had his closet where he kept some of his prized possessions, but neither his man, Docket, nor her maid, Adah, slept in the closet or the sitting room. She and Berold liked their privacy and saw no reason to have any servants that close to hand.

The thought of having Sidonie and her sweet little baby spending the summer with them at Grasmere brought a smile to Phillida. Her sister-in-law, Venetia, was a dear, and Delphine was always amusing, but the two were so close, and they spent so much time together, that Phillida often felt left out. Not that they ever meant to make her feel that way. All the same, she would enjoy Sidonie's company.

That Berold enjoyed having Tuftwick and Madigan about was more than evident. The three had spent much time together as youths, then in forty-two had gone off to war together. Tuftwick and Madigan had helped console Berold when he lost his father at Naseby. And while

Berold was in Weymouth Prison and his estates sequestrated, Tuftwick, with Lord Wollowchet's help, had at Berold's instruction, bought the lands back for the assessed fines. It had cost Berold much of his forests, and they were the poorer for it, but at least they still had both principal manors. A smaller manor near Chester, he had not been able to save. Adjoining some crown land, its value and fine assessment had been too great. It was, at least temporarily, lost to the Lotterby family, as were a couple of small manors in Shropshire.

Delphine had offered to buy back the land near Chester for Berold. Certainly her fortune would never miss the sum needed to buy it, but Berold had refused her offer. The asking price was too high. He knew the manor's worth. Eventually, the present owners would be happy to sell it at a lower price. Especially since they had run off many of the tenants, cut down most of the forests, and now had little left to give them an income off the estate.

Tuftwick and Madigan were lucky, they had not spent even a day in prison. That was fortunate for Berold for they had saved him his lands. They had been true friends to him. Now, it would seem, both Tuftwick and Madigan had fallen in love with Venetia. Phillida liked Madigan, but she pitied him. Even did Venetia choose Madigan over Tuftwick, Berold, as her guardian, would never let her marry Madigan. He had no money, no lands, no future income other than what Tuftwick provided him. Poor man, his inheritance had been stolen by his step-father. And though he was a gentleman, he was a penniless gentleman. His best bet would be to find an older, rich widow who wanted a youthful companion in her bed.

Phillida decided she would write some of her friends on Madigan's behalf. One of them might know of a widow needing a husband. And Madigan, a kind and caring man, would make some woman a very good husband.

❧ ❧ ❧ ❧

His heart plummeting into his stomach, Madigan stared at his friend. "Are you certain, Tuffy? You have known her but a week." Tuftwick had just told him he meant to ask for Venetia's hand in marriage. He knew his friend had been enjoying his flirt with Venetia, but he had been so wrapped up in his own feelings for Venetia, he had paid no attention to Tuftwick's.

"Nay, Maddy, I have known her half my life. Do you not remember her when we first came here to begin our training with Berold's father. Or our holidays at Wollowchet when Lady Venetia and Mistress Lotterby were there?"

"Aye, I remember them, but I cannot remember you paying them any heed."

"Nor would I pay them heed. They were but young lassies then, but now ... I can think of no vision more lovely than Venetia. I think I fell in love with her the moment my eyes first rested on her when, standing there in the corridor, she turned to welcome us to Harp's Ridge."

Swallowing hard Madigan asked, "Has the lady indicated she returns your love?"

Brushing his light brown hair off his forehead, Tuftwick frowned. "I cannot say. She is ever cheerful in my presence, and she has not pulled away or objected when I held her hand a bit too long. She has seemed to listen with interest when I described to her my manor. She asked questions and begged me tell her more about it. Was she but being polite, I could not say."

His world crashing down around him, Madigan tried to hide his pain. "Do you speak to the lady first, or to her brother."

His blue eyes brimming with hope, Tuftwick asked, "What would you advise, Maddy?"

Madigan shook his head. "I have no idea. I have never asked for a lady's hand. Mayhap you should ask the lady would she object should you ask her brother for her hand." Though the ache in his heart was near overwhelming him, Madigan could do naught but aid his friend. He owed Tuftwick too much. Most likely his very life. Surely he would have died on the streets when the school kicked him out had Tuftwick not joined him and taken him to Wollowchet. Now he must support Tuftwick and help him win his love though it tore out his own heart.

Tuftwick's grin brightened his face. "Maddy, you are superb. That is what I will do. I will speak first with Lady Venetia, the angel. But you must help me get a moment alone with her. She is ever with Mistress

Lotterby. You must draw Mistress Lotterby from Lady Venetia's side that I may speak with her."

His eyes lowered, Madigan slowly nodded. "Aye, I will find a way to draw Mistress Lotterby away."

Tuftwick clamped a hand on Madigan's shoulder. "You are the best comrade any man could ever ask for. I bless the day we met."

Madigan looked up and met his friend's steady gaze. "Aye, Tuffy. I bless the day we met. I owe you more than I will ever be able to repay you."

"Ah, now let us not start that again. You have more than repaid me. At Naseby, had you not blocked that blow to my head, I would be dead. That we both know. So enough. Now let us make plans on how you may distract Mistress Lotterby."

Giving Tuftwick a shallow smile, Madigan nodded. Now, even did Venetia by some wild chance say she loved him and not Tuftwick, Madigan knew he could never claim that love. He could never bring such heartache to his friend. His own heart breaking, Madigan assured his friend they would find a way to give him time alone with Venetia.

※ ※ ※ ※

Venetia sat lost in her thoughts as Bethel gently combed out her hair. Bethel would dress her hair becomingly before Venetia donned a new gown of deep blue, as deep a blue as her eyes. She wanted to look her best. She had a feeling Lord Tuftwick might be set on declaring his love for her. She knew he loved her. She could tell, and Delphine agreed with her.

"But do you love him?" Delphine had asked.

That had set Venetia to thinking. Did she love Henry LaBree, Lord Tuftwick? She had known him most of her life. She had been but five when he and Madigan first came to Harp's Ridge to train, under her father's direction, to be chevaliers. She had scarcely ever seen them. Only when her nurse took her outside, and she chanced to see them practicing at their sword play in the courtyard behind the house. Yet they seemed to ever be a part of her memories, whether at Harp's Ridge, or Knightswood Castle, or Wollowchet Hall where she and Delphine were fostered. Then the war had come. They and her father and her brother had ridden off to war. Her father had not come home.

With her father dead and her brother in prison for nine months, she had lived at Wollowchet Hall or with Delphine in her home in Liverpool. Several times she saw Tuftwick and Madigan at Wollowchet. She knew Lord Wollowchet helped Tuftwick pay his fine and also helped him make the necessary arrangements to sell off portions of Harp's Ridge forest lands to pay her brother's fines and buy back the sequestered Harp's Ridge and Knightswood Castle manors. But she had been but a child, still confined to the schoolroom. Though neither man noticed her, she had noticed them and found both men handsome and dashing. She still found both of them handsome and bright and witty. But did she love Tuftwick?

When in London with her Aunt Charissa and Delphine and Clarinda, she had let a man, really he was little more than a youth but very handsome and the son of a Duke, she had let him kiss her. She could not say she found the kiss very appealing. Rather slobbery. The youth had pledged his undying love and had asked her to marry him, but he stirred no flurry in her heart as Tuftwick did just by taking her hand in his. Could that mean she loved Tuftwick. She felt a slight tingle when Madigan took her hand. She liked it, and she enjoyed the love for her she saw in his eyes. At least, she thought it was love. Delphine told her it was more like adoration which she swore was not the same thing as love.

"Love is everlasting," Delphine said. "Adoration can come and go like the brightness of spring flowers. So lovely, but in time they fade and wilt away."

Well, she would be foolish to let herself fall in love with Madigan. She could never marry him. But did she fall in love with Tuftwick, her brother would be very happy. No question, she would have to kiss Tuftwick. She could in no way be certain she loved him did she not kiss him first. She wondered if she should also kiss Madigan. Just to have a comparison. Did she get the same thrill from kissing both men, then mayhap neither one was the right man for her. She did so want to be certain she truly loved the man she married. And she needed to know the man she loved would love her as faithfully.

She had no wish to be treated like her father had treated her mother. Everyone knew he had had several paramours. She was not supposed to know, but she had overheard servants talking. She learned she had two illegitimate half-brothers by different mothers. She also knew her father's will had provided for them, though he had not named them as his sons. Berold had honored his father's bequest despite the financial hardship the war had placed on him. He had sent both boys off to school. Venetia believed she might also have a half-sister. Shortly after her brother was released from prison, a woman with a young girl in tow called on her brother. They met privately in the room where Berold and their father before him conducted business. When they emerged the woman was smiling and thanking Berold. When Venetia questioned Berold about the meeting, he had been evasive, but she had little doubt the little girl was her sister. She looked entirely too much like a Lotterby not to be a Lotterby.

Venetia often wondered how much her mother had known of her husband's various trysts. She feared her mother knew about all of them. If her mother had ever chastised her husband, or even been cross with him, Venetia had never heard it. Oh, but she had heard her grandmother, her father's mother, lay into him often enough. Dear Grandmother Marietta. Venetia had always been told she was the image of her Grandmother Marietta. People said that in her youth, no one was more beautiful than Marietta Lotterby. Certainly the portrait of her that hung in the most prominent place in the gallery showed her to be a beautiful woman.

Grandmother Marietta was also a fun woman. She enjoyed life and laughed a lot. That she out lived her husband and both her sons and daughters-in-law, Marietta found sad. But she loved her grandchildren and her great grandchild, Timandra, and all were ever welcome in her home. At eighty-two, she chose to live in a small house in Frodsham. She said she liked seeing the people passing by on the main road through the village. She liked wondering where they might be going and on what business. "And Phillida has no need to have me underfoot," she adamantly stated, though Phillida declared she would love nothing more than to have Grandmother Marietta living at Harp's Ridge.

Venetia wished her grandmother was there now. She would like her advice. Mayhap on the morrow, she and Delphine might ride into Frod-sham that she might seek her grandmother's counsel. Yes, she would talk to Delphine at dinner. She knew her dear cousin would accompany her. Delphine loved their grandmother as much as she did. And could be, Delphine might want to talk with Grandmother Marietta as well. Something was bothering Delphine. She was not her usual self. Her mind seemed ever off when Venetia tried to talk to her. Surely their grandmother could help the both of them.

Chapter 8

Madigan was taken completely by surprise when he exited his room and bumped smack into Venetia. She laughed her enthralling laugh when he grabbed her to keep her from tumbling backwards.

"Goodness Mister Madigan, you are indeed in a hurry. But then had I not been hurrying up the back stairs, we would not have collided." She blushed. "I fear I was visiting the kitchen seeking a morsel to munch before dinner. I slept late and failed to break my fast this morning." Still in his arms and looking sideways at him, she asked, "And what is your hurry?"

He knew he should release her, but she felt so heavenly there in his arms, and it could well be the only time he would ever get to hold her. "I have no excuse," he answered. "I stopped in my room to retrieve my fork, so I would have it come dinner."

Pulling away from him, she looked up, her blue eyes dancing with merriment. "And what think you of the use of forks?"

He shrugged. "For the most part, I suppose I like them. The fingers get less greasy."

Again she laughed. "I agree." She looked at his mouth. "The mouth also gets less greasy. And smaller bites are easier to chew. Do you not agree?"

He was having trouble breathing. Though no longer in his arms, she was standing so close to him. Her face turned up to his. She licked her lips. It was more than he could stand. He drew her back into his arms, and gently, ever so gently tasted her sweet lips. A soft sweet kiss. Oh, God help him, what was he doing? She would be marrying his dearest friend. Yet he could not stop himself. He started to tell her of his love for her, but she put her hands to his chest and pushed away from him.

"That was very sweet, Mister Madigan. I rather liked it. Yet my heart is not pounding uncontrollably." She took his hand and held it to her breast. "See. No flurry. I rather think there should be a flurry." She released his hand and stepped back. "I must ready for dinner." And she left him there staring after her, dumbfounded, his lungs collapsing, his breath in spurts, his heart hammering in his head.

Oh God, oh God, he thought.

He was still standing there when Mistress Lotterby touched his shoulder. "So do you love Venetia so very much?"

Without thinking he said, "She is a Venus."

Mistress Lotterby twisted her mouth thoughtfully. "Yes, I do believe you are correct. But sweeter than any reports I have read about Venus. Do you plan to ask Venetia to marry you?"

Reality returning, he shook his head. "I am penniless, Mistress Lotterby. I can have no hopes of winning her hand. Besides, I am not the only one who loves her." He could not think why he was confiding so in the woman beside him. She was eyeing him curiously.

"Yes. Lord Tuftwick is also in love with her. And so you choose not to fight for her?"

"I owe Tuffy more than I can ever repay him. Even did I suddenly come into a fortune, I would not try to win Lady Venetia's love." He was feeling a bit angry. Why was she asking him these things, and why was he admitting them to her?

"Then you are a fool. Did I love a man, I would do all in my power to win his love. Whatever it might take."

He had turned from her, looking for a way to escape, but he snapped back around at her words. "That is a callous thing to say."

"Mayhap, but did I have the chance to win the love of the man I loved, I would never let that chance slip through my fingers." She smiled, and like Venetia, she said, "I must ready for dinner," and her head high, she walked lightly down the corridor.

He watched her until she disappeared into her chamber. Since arriving at Harp's Ridge, he had paid little attention to Mistress Lotterby. All his thoughts, all his actions had been centered on Venetia. He had not even had a conversation with Mistress Lotterby, and yet, he had just confessed to her his love for Venetia as well as Tuftwick's. Not that she had seemed at all surprised. He supposed they had both been more than a little obvious in their attentions to Venetia. Had he not fallen so instantly in love with Venetia, he might have looked more than once at Mistress Lotterby.

Though not beautiful like Venetia, he admitted she was a handsome woman. She had the Lotterby firm mouth, jutting chin, and slim, slightly aquiline nose, but her coloring was dark. With her ebony eyes, thick dark wavy hair, thick dark lashes under perfectly arched brows, and high cheek bones, she looked regal. And she carried herself like a duchess or even a queen. Tall and well endowed, she moved with an easy grace, almost like she glided along the corridor.

He shrugged. Why had his thoughts turned to her when he could be reliving the kiss he shared with Venetia. How sweet and soft were her lips. She had given him a memory he would cherish for the rest of his life. It would tantalize his waking hours and stimulate his dreams. 'Twas an indescribable gift.

✿ ✿ ✿ ✿

Delphine stood with her back to her chamber door. She was relieved Tatty was not in the room. She needed time to collect her wits. Coming up the back stairs a little behind Venetia, she had been astounded to find her cousin locked in Madigan's arms. At first mad rage possessed her. What was Venetia doing? She could never marry Maddy, why tempt him? Torture him? She had to know he was hopelessly in love with her. But when Venetia pulled away from Maddy and told him he caused no flurry in her heart, Delphine felt a relief like none she had ever known. Venetia had been but testing herself like she did in London when she kissed the Duke's son.

Her dear cousin was a romantic. She sought the kind of love Berold and Phillida had. Delphine believed Venetia could well find that love with Tuftwick. A baron, destined to inherit an even greater estate than his own barony, Tuftwick would be able to give her the kind of life she was used to leading. Maddy on the other hand, could give her naught but love, and love could soon turn sour when the comforts one was used to could not be provided.

She, on the other hand, had no need to marry a rich man or a peer. She was twenty-four, past time she should marry, and she could marry anyone she chose. And she chose Maddy. He might not love her, but despite his little lapse there with Venetia, she believed he would be true to her. She had loved him for so long, and that love had done naught but grow over the years. She had little doubt Venetia would accept Tuftwick's proposal. That would mean Maddy would have to keep his distance from her. And since Tuftwick and Maddy would be accompanying them to Knightswood Castle, it would give her plenty of time to court him.

She smiled. Yes, the man should do the courting, but in this case, Maddy would never have the gumption to court her. So it was left up to her. She supposed she would also have to do the proposing. Berold would object. Maddy was nobody. He had no family, no money, but Berold had no say over whom she married, and she intended to marry Maddy.

After dinner, she and Venetia were to ride into Frodsham to visit their grandmother. Tuftwick and Maddy, as well as Purdy and Anker, would accompany them. Delphine could go nowhere on her own. She hoped once she was married, that would change. She would also need to have a couple of children as quickly as possible. Unless she had heirs, Maddy could be at risk. Those who would attempt to abduct her could well make attempts on Maddy's life. That did worry her, but then, was Maddy off with Nate D'Arcy, would be killers would never be able to find him. For three years now, D'Arcy had kept his men safe and alive. Despite Hayward's wound, Delphine trusted D'Arcy to continue to do so.

The thought of children set a flush rising up Delphine's neck. She basically knew what to expect in the marriage bed. The looks she caught passing between Phillida and Berold told her it should be a pleasant experience. She had no doubt Maddy would be gentle with her. Of course, did he love her, she believed the experience would be even more profound. But love could come. He could grow to love her. If not, she had enough love for the both of them.

Pushing away from the door, she went to stand at the window. Looking out on the courtyard at Harp's Ridge had always been something she enjoyed. The gardener kept the grounds immaculate. Flowers bloomed in the spring and summer and brilliant orange and yellow leaves brightened the outer regions come fall. Only winter could sometimes appear drab. How often had she stood at this window and watched Maddy and Tuftwick train. They had never been aware of her, but she had ever been aware of Maddy.

Now, with him accompanying them to Knightswood Castle, she would have at least ten days in his company. She would insure she rode beside him. She would engage him in conversation. He could well be glum because he had lost in love. She would have to do her best to cheer him. Did he think of her as amusing, cheerful, he could be more willing to share his life with her.

Traveling to Lake Grasmere was never a swift process. With so many wagons and coaches, so many articles to take, and with the roads so poor, they were lucky did they manage ten miles a day. Normally they stayed with Berold's friends along the way. A stopover could often extend into a couple of days of feasting and merriment. So no matter how she looked at it, time was on her side. Time, if not to win Maddy's love, time to win his respect and friendship.

❀ ❀ ❀ ❀

Phillida laughed softly as the baby's tiny hand curled around her finger. She so wanted another child herself. She and Berold were active in bed, yet a second child was not forth coming. "He looks much like his father, does he not?" Phillida said, looking up to catch Sidonie's eyes on her.

Nodding, Sidonie agreed her son was the image of his father. "Now I but hope he will grow up not only as handsome as his father, but as gentle and caring. 'Twas Caleb's handsome countenance that first set my heart to whirling, but 'twas his concern for the well-being of others that won my love. The Haywards, being our neighbors, and my brothers ever being involved in play or school or mischief with Caleb and his brother, Adler, I was in constant contact with Caleb. I cannot tell you when I realized I had fallen in love with him, but I think I could not have been more than fifteen. My father always liked the Haywards, yet he would have preferred I marry someone more in my class. The Haywards are yeomen, though freeholders. Well off they are, but yeomen all the same, and father is a baronet." She giggled. "Of course that is nothing compared to being a peer. Still, father …" Shrugging, her voice tapered off.

"I understand what you are saying," Phillida answered. "My father was most particular about whom I should marry. Fortunately, Berold and I fell in love the moment we met. My brother Kenrick, having met Berold when fighting for King Charles I, liked Berold and brought him for a visit to Wealdburh, our principal family home on the Wirral. I met Berold in forty-four. I was seventeen, he had just turned twenty-one. Our fathers agreed to our betrothal, but due to the war and Berold's and my oldest brother Kenrick's imprisonment after their capture at Naseby, then their paroles, and of course the need of both estates to pay off the sequestration fees, we could not be married until forty-nine. Since Berold was confined to his parish and Kenrick to his, Kenrick could not attend the wedding. The wedding had to take place here at Harp's Ridge. At that time, my mother was not well enough to travel. She was yet grieving over the death of my father. He died the year before." She smiled. "But my brothers, Nate and Ranulf, came, and Kenrick's wife. She stood as my witness.

"Berold's mother did all she could to make me feel welcome and to make my wedding a beautiful memory. I bless her and miss her terribly. She was truly one of the kindest women I have ever had the privilege of knowing. She died but two years ago. The ague carried her off. I do still miss her. At least my mother's health has improved enough to allow the occasional visit. When she visits, she does spoil Timandra."

The baby started fussing, and Sidonie reached for him. "I am thinking he must be hungry." Once she had the babe at her breast, she said, "Caleb and I were married in January of fifty-one. It was a cold winter day, but the house was filled with friends and neighbors, and father's tenants had a bonfire glowing outside and trestle tables laden with food. Since father was giving them a holiday and providing them with ale and roast of beef and various other treats, they seemed not to mind the cold. I can remember looking out my window and seeing the children running hither and yon, laughing and shouting with joy."

She looked down at her nursing babe then back up. "Oh, it was a glorious day. I was just turned twenty and Caleb was twenty-two. It had taken me a good year to convince my father I would marry Caleb or no one. It helped that both my brothers, Cyril and William, were on my side. The fact that I was choosing to marry the younger brother, and his inheritance was limited, made Father even more leery. But when Mister Hayward agreed to give Caleb a piece of bottom land that adjoined the piece of land father was giving as my dowry, Father finally consented. Of course, now that Caleb's older brother, Adler, has fled England, and swears he has no plans to return, all the Hayward land will go to Caleb. My father could not help but be pleased with that, though the Haywards were devastated when Adler left his family for the new world.

"As it has turned out, Adler need not have fled. Neither he nor my Caleb were ever suspected of fighting for the King in fifty-one. My brothers were known to have fought for Charles II, and your brothers were, and Mister Preston was, but Caleb has been able to come and go freely. He rides off with your brother when he comes to collect him. The rest of the time, he is at home to help his father with the farm. My poor brother, Cyril, must ever stay on the run. His wife's house and my parents' house are periodically watched. Do my parents or sister or Cyril's wife and little daughter wish to see him, they must come to the Hayward home. There he can be safely hidden, the Haywards having but one servant and my maid living on the premises except at harvest time. But Cyril dare not show himself if any of the Hayward day laborers are about."

Tilting her head and gnawing her lower lip, Sidonie added thoughtfully, "I am not certain what may be the consequences for us now. Because the recent robbery that got my husband shot was so close to home, Mister D'Arcy feared the militia would be searching all the houses. That is why we had to flee. Caleb's parents were to destroy anything with blood on it from bedding to Caleb's clothing. The militia knew one of the highwaymen had been shot. It was just a matter of time before their search reached our home."

Phillida placed her hands over her heart. "How truly terrifying for you. To have your husband brought to you, wounded, and then to discover you cannot keep him safely in his bed. I am in fear for Nate all the time. Every time he comes here, I fear it will be the last time I will ever see him."

"I would be well pleased, as would Caleb's parents, did Caleb give up this crazy pursuit. We all know at any time the whole group could be killed or captured, but after Caleb received a personal note of thanks from King Charles, he has felt obliged to continue serving him."

Frowning, Phillida said, "I know it cannot be easy for the King, maintaining a court while having no income and feeling responsible for the people who fled into exile with him. At the same time, how long can this continue to go on? I see no end in sight."

Sidonie switched the baby to her other breast before responding. "I know. Cromwell grows ever stronger. The militia seem to be everywhere. My father complains of the large increase in taxes he has to pay. For now, I cannot see things getting better." She smiled. "Except for this wonderful respite you are giving me and my husband by taking us with you to Lake Grasmere. I have never traveled far from home. I look forward to seeing more of the country."

"I always enjoy my time at Knightswood Castle," Phillida said with a nod. "It is little better than a keep, and nowhere near as comfortable as Harp's Ridge, but the area is so lovely in the summer. 'Tis the perfect place for quiet walks and for the two of you to make complete recoveries." She shrugged. "However, the journey is never pleasant. The roads are poor, time in the coach can grow tedious, but we stopover with friends each night so we have clean bedding at night and tasty meals. And often some good entertainment."

"I feel certain I shall enjoy the entire adventure. I am so pleased at how well Caleb has recovered. Soon he will be well enough to make the journey. And now that he is able to be up and around, he is enjoying talking with Lord Grasmere about the soil improvements Lord Grasmere has seen since he started rotating clover with wheat in his fields." A wide grin crinkled the corners of her dark eyes. "I love watching how excited he gets whenever he learns new ways of bettering his land. He does so love his land."

Taking the sleeping babe from her breast and handing him to Phillida to burp him while she readjusted her clothing, Sidonie said, "Speaking on a different thought, am I mistaken, or might Lady Venetia and Lord Tuftwick be having a flirt?"

Phillida patted the baby's back, and smiled. "Berold and I both hope it may be more than a flirt. Lord Tuftwick is a genial soul, at the same time, very stable and sensible. And he is one of Berold's dearest friends. We would welcome a betrothal between them."

Sidonie nodded. "Yes, I can see that would be a good thing. Well, as Lord Tuftwick and Mister Madigan will be accompanying us to Lake Grasmere, there should be time for the romance to blossom."

"I hope you may be right, dear Sidonie," she said as a little burp resounded. Baby William was ready for his nap. Rising, Phillida gently placed the baby in the crib. Having stood in as godmother for Sidonie's sister at William's christening, she felt a special tie to the babe. But she hoped the crib would soon be filled with another babe of her own.

Chapter 9

"Oh, Grandmother, you are such a dear soul," Venetia said, placing her arms carefully around her fragile grandmother. Though her blue eyes were clouded, and her once gracile frame shrunken, Dowager Lady Grasmere's bright wit and sweet smile bound her two granddaughters to her with deep affection.

Delphine held back a chuckle. Venetia had just received her grandmother's approval of her plan to ride, if not all, at least part of the way to Grasmere on horseback. "Do you give your approval, Berold cannot deny me, I am decided. He will not question your judgement."

From the moment Delphine told Venetia of her determination, was the weather cooperative, to ride horseback rather than in her coach, Venetia had determined she would do the same. Unlike Delphine, though, Venetia had to contend with her brother, who was also her guardian. Venetia thought she would be wise to first get her grandmother's approval before she broached the matter with Berold.

As Delphine and Venetia were both accomplished riders, Delphine thought their plan would be accepted without too much argument on her cousin's part, but having their adored grandmother's approval would be an added precaution. Not that Delphine needed Berold's permission, but she had no wish to become involved in an argument with him. She wanted nothing to mar her courtship of Torrance Madigan.

"Do you miss journeying to Grasmere, Grandmother?" Delphine asked.

Extricating herself from Venetia's hug, and giving Venetia a loving pat, their grandmother said, "Nay, my bones are far too weary for such a trip." She looked around her spacious sitting room with its yellow curtains and yellow and white striped chairs and daybed. "I sit here in my sunny room and look out at the village and the green hillsides. I watch the white fluffy clouds float by in the blue sky and the white fluffy sheep dotting the grassy meadows and grazing contentedly, and I think back over my many years here on this earth. Sometimes I wonder when the heavenly father will call me." She held up her lace-gloved hands. "No, I need not your protests. I am old, but I still find much pleasure in my life. My dear maid, Lila, reads to me in her sweet soothing voice, she puts me to bed when I grow weary, rubs my neck and shoulders do they ache, and my cook does all in his power to tempt me with my favorite foods.

"And I have my lovely granddaughters who come to visit me. Now, tell me, at my age, could I ask for a better life?"

"I am certainly glad Lila takes such good care of you," Delphine said. "We feared when your dear Beth passed on, you would be so lonely, but how fortunate Beth's widowed niece was there to step into Beth's shoes."

Her grandmother smiled. "I love Lila, and she will be well rewarded for her service and care for me, but my dear Beth will always have a special place in my heart. She served me for over fifty years. She was not just my maid, she was my friend and companion. Times there were when I fear I could not have managed without her at my side.

"But enough of such talk. Much as I enjoyed seeing Lord Tuftwick and Mister Madigan again, I cannot believe you two came here with them, only to send them on a useless errand to fetch me a cinnamon tart from the bakers, did you not have more to discuss than your desire to ride your horses to Grasmere as opposed to traveling in your coach. Am I not right?"

"You are right, Grandmother," Venetia said, grabbing her grandmother's hands and leaning in close to her. "I believe Lord Tuftwick may be thinking of asking for my hand."

"Does that please you, my dear child?"

Venetia slowly shook her head. "I cannot say for certain. I like him very much. He is always merry, and I enjoy being in his company, but do I love him? I wish I knew."

"Do you think Berold will approve of his suit?"

"I am certain he will. Lord Tuftwick is one of his dearest friends. And though his barony is of no great income, he will someday inherit Wollowchet Hall."

Their grandmother glanced aside before returning her gaze to Venetia. "In my day, the question of love was never of any consideration. Marriages were contracts. Did love blossom between the married couple, all the better, but it was of no real import.

"I had no say in my marriage to your grandfather." She smiled a sad smile. "My father had no great wealth. Yes, he was the younger son of an Earl, so his blood line was considered good, but he had no title, and his income was limited to the land left him by his mother. But I was considered a beauty and was put on display to be more or less sold to the highest bidder."

"Oh, no, Grandmother!" Venetia exclaimed, but Delphine was not shocked by her grandmother's statement. Her maternal grandfather had once hinted he doubted her paternal grandmother had chosen to wed Lord Grasmere.

"You my, dear granddaughter," he had said, placing a hand on Delphine's head, "you shall choose the man you wish to wed, like your mother was allowed to choose to marry your father. Like your mother's mother chose to marry me. And oh, what a marriage we had." His eyes got dreamy. "Nothing can ever be better than a marriage based on love."

That her grandfather had loved his wife very much, and she him, Delphine never doubted. That he allowed her mother to choose to marry Thayne Lotterby, a younger son with no landed income, having only his good looks and his wit to make his way in the world, Delphine realized was a rare phenomenon. Few women, not even the daughters of her cousin's tenants, had much of a say in whom they married. Like her grandmother proclaimed, marriages were contracts, and peers and tenants, merchants and yeomen, all were involved in matrimonial bargaining.

"None of you grandchildren ever knew your grandfather," Lady Grasmere continued. "He died long before any of you were born. As he was not a part of your lives, you had few questions concerning him. I doubt you have even paid much heed to his portrait in the gallery. Not that it is a good likeness. But so shall I tell you more of him now.

"Gerald Lotterby, the third Earl of Grasmere, was thirty years my senior. A recent widower with no children, he had hopes a young wife would give him the heirs he so desperately wanted. Once he met me, he told me he determined he would have no other. I was but sixteen. My dowry was naught but my horse and saddle and a lovely leather chest that held my clothing and toiletries. Gerald, your grandfather, settled on me two-hundred fifty pounds a year upon his death plus this house here in Frodsham. And on my father, he agreed to a settlement of one thousand pounds to be paid to my father on my first son's first birthday.

"To your grandfather's great disappointment, my first two children were girls. Both died before reaching their first birthdays." Again the sad smile touched her lips. "I think it might have been the cold in the old dwelling. Their little bodies were always so chilled." She looked at Venetia. "I was very pleased when your father tore down that heap of stones and built the home you now live in. Indeed, I thank the good Lord you were raised in a healthier home.

"Anyway, when I was twenty-one, Gyes was born. And what a healthy babe he was. He seemed to thrive on the cold. And I was older and stronger, and had grown more used to the cold that descended over Harp's Ridge in the winters." She looked at Delphine. "Five years later, along came your father. He, too, thrived, and my husband could not have been more happy with me. I had given him the healthy sons he so desired.

"Ten years later, I was a widow with two sons to guide. I believe I did a better job with Thayne than with Gyes."

"Why would you say that, Grandmother?" Venetia asked, but Delphine guessed her cousin knew the answer. Everyone knew Gyes had not been faithful to his wife. Whereas, Delphine's father had not only been faithful to Delphine's mother but to her mother's memory. Delphine could not imagine her father ever consorting with other women. His evenings he spent at home with her and her grandfather. And he was forever telling her stories about her mother so that Delphine had grown to believe she had experienced the various events he described though she knew she had been too young to remember them.

When she turned ten, her father and grandfather, both believing she needed a woman's influence in her life, sent her to Harp's Ridge. That same year, she, along with Venetia, was fostered at Wollowchet. Her father's letters to her had been constant. Those letters had been filled with little reminders of her mother. Her father wanted her to know how much her mother loved her and how much he loved her mother. Thanks to her father, she believed she knew her mother near as well as Venetia knew her mother.

Pursing her mouth, her grandmother tilted her head before replying to Venetia's question. "I say that because your father, like his father, married not for love, but for profit. Sadly, my dear, neither your dear mother, whom I loved greatly, nor your sweet aunt, were allowed to choose their husbands. Their father, as you know, was a wealthy woolen merchant. He wanted his daughters to marry peers of the realm. He and his father had fought their way up the ladder until their wealth rivaled a King's ransom. Your grandfather wanted his grandchildren to be peers. His daughters' dowries were substantial, their inheritances even greater. Your mother ended up with an Earl. Your aunt with a Baron of ancient linage."

"Yes," Venetia said, a frown puckering her lovely forehead. "I know Mother and Father failed to share the kind of love in their marriage that I want to know in mine. Not that Mother ever complained about Father. She never said a harsh word to him or about him. At least not in my hearing. But she could not always hide her discontent. Times I thought her melancholy."

"Times she was melancholy, but she loved you and Berold. She was proud of both of you, and so pleased Berold married for love." She chuckled. "It did amuse her that her father was ever on a rant because her sister bore no children. Still, she was sad for her sister. Charissa would have made a beautiful mother. Certainly she was the perfect foster mother for you girls.

"Do you, Venetia, decide to marry Lord Tuftwick, you may know you will be pleasing your mother's father in his grave, for through you, his great-grandchildren will inherit the fortune he bestowed on Lord Wollowchet. They may not have the ancient title he craved, but at least his wealth will stay in his family. And do you have a son, he will be a Baron, even if not one of ancient heritage.

"But back to your concern. I never knew the love that romantic stories are written about, though I read my share of romantic tales. And I have had the good fortunate to observe the love between Berold and

Phillida." She put her hand to her heart. "You can see the love in Berold's eyes when he looks at Phillida. I see that same look in Tuftwick's eyes when he looks at you."

"Do you, Grandmother?" Venetia cried. "And what of Mister Madigan? Do you see that look in his eyes?"

"I am sorry, dear. I failed to observe him. Though I have always liked Mister Madigan, I cannot think you and he would suit."

"Because he has no money, no land, and Berold would not approve of him?"

Shaking her head, their grandmother laughed sweetly. "Nay, he would not suit because he is too serious. Lord Tuftwick is ever bright and cheery. Mister Madigan may never know that lightness. His family, his fortune were stolen from him. 'Tis hard to know peace when your heart is ever in tumult. That would not be good for you, Venetia. You are a merry soul. You are capable of great love, but you need someone to share your joy of living with you. Not someone you would forever be having to cheer."

"I must say," Delphine said, "I cannot but think Grandmother speaks the truth. Lord Tuftwick has ever the genial laugh, ever the sparkle in his eyes. I do believe you would lead a merry life together."

Venetia looked from her grandmother to Delphine and slowly nodded. "I do enjoy his company. I would like very much did he set my heart to fluttering, but do I not love him now, mayhap I will grow to love him. Certainly, I have met no other man who pleases me more." She again took her grandmother's hands. "Thank you, Grandmother. Still, does he ever get around to kissing me, and do I like it, I do think, does he propose, so shall I accept him."

She looked at Delphine. "Would you mind terribly, dear cousin, did I abandon you?"

Delphine tossed back her head and laughed. "Dear Venetia, you could never abandon me. We will ever be the dearest of friends. Besides, I know whenever Lord Tuftwick rides off with Mister D'Arcy, you will want me at your side. And who but me would you want to be holding your hand when you give birth to your first child. Nay, dear one, have no thoughts that we will ever be long parted."

Venetia beamed. "So right you are. We shall never be long parted.

That I promise."

"I do believe I hear the two men in question returning," their grandmother said. "Tell me quickly. Do they indeed, both still ride with that too handsome rapscallion, Nathaniel D'Arcy?"

Delphine and Venetia both nodded. "They do."

Their grandmother shook her head as her serving man announced Tuftwick and Maddy. "Pity," she said, though her smile was in place when the two men, a basket of tarts in hand, entered her sitting room.

Chapter 10

The weather being more balmy than had been the usual of late, Venetia consented to a walk in the garden with Lord Tuftwick. Nervous and jittery, she knew Lord Tuftwick was going to propose. She had been very bold the day before in her grandmother's house, proclaiming that she would accept his proposal, but now she was not feeling so certain. Was she ready to commit to marriage? She liked Tuftwick better than any other men she knew, but was that enough? What if she agreed to marry him, then on the journey to Knightswood, she fell in love with someone else? She had traveled the same trek many times over, and she had never met any men who interested her. But did that mean she could not meet one on this trip, or the next one. Oh, what foolishness! Why must she keep thinking the man who would fulfill all her dreams was always just up the road, just around the next bend.

She had immersed herself in the same old dreams when she and Delphine visited their dear friend, Clarinda, in Warwickshire. Surely she would find the man who would sweep her off her feet, leave her panting for breath. But no. Though they had been royally entertained by Clarinda and her husband, none of the men invited to various gatherings had caught her fancy. Nor Delphine's. How sad for the both of them, she thought.

Her attention was brought back to the man walking by her side when he said, "'Twas a treat to see your grandmother again yesterday. When Maddy and I were young and first came here to begin our training with your father, she made us feel so welcome. I never knew either of my grandmothers, and with my mother dying when I was but nine, I think I had been longing for a woman's gentleness, for a sweet smile, an encouraging word."

Looking up into Tuftwick's smiling blue eyes, Venetia felt the first little quickening in her heart. "Yes, Grandmother is a dear," she said.

Tuftwick was a handsome man, a warm-hearted and gentle man. Must love be an exhilarating tumble down a hill? Might it not instead be a slow, sweet ascent, moving ever upwards toward a pinnacle of mutual delights? She had kissed Madigan. It had been sweet. What might Tuftwick's kiss be like? Would it be as sweet, mayhap sweeter? She had no intention of answering yes or no to his proposal until she kissed him.

She noted he was directing their steps toward a stand of trees that would shield them from prying eyes. Not that her brother would mind did she kiss Tuftwick. She had no doubt Berold was hoping she and Tuftwick would become betrothed. She had seen him watching them at dinner and supper near every day. True, he directed more of his attention to Caleb Hayward now Hayward was able to be up and around, but she had seen Berold's sideways glance rest on her often enough.

"You seem pensive today, Lady Venetia. Do you think about the journey we will soon be taking?" Tuftwick asked.

Shaking her head, she lied, "I was thinking of Mister Hayward and of his sweet wife and new baby. The Haywards seem so much in love."

"Indeed they are," Tuftwick answered. "Mistress Hayward is a very brave woman to have undertaken such a journey when her babe was so near due. Yet, had she not accompanied us, I fear we could well have been caught. But the militia never looked twice at men traveling with a pregnant woman."

By the time he finished speaking, they were amongst the trees, and he stopped.

She looked up at him. "It must be wonderful to be so very much in love. Berold and Phillida love each other in the same manner. It is lovely to see."

He took her hands in his. "I could wish we might share such a love, Lady Venetia."

She widened her eyes. "Indeed?"

He stepped closer to her, and she backed up until she was brushing against a tree. He now stood so close to her, she could feel his breath on her face as he raised her hands to his lips and kissed her fingertips. His gaze locked with hers, he said, "I can promise you a never ending, undying love, Lady Venetia. Your loveliness caught my eye when Maddy and I stumbled upon you in the corridor our first night back here at

Harp's Ridge. But 'tis much more than your lovely face that binds my heart to you."

"And what might that be, Lord Tuftwick?" She found her breath quickening, and she was unable to look away from his intense gaze. Nor could she pull her hands free. He held them close against his chest.

"'Tis your gentleness with all who are around you, be they servants or family or guests. You have ever a bright smile to bestow on everyone, no matter how menial. Your laughter brightens all who hear you, yet you are ready with a helping hand are you needed. I have watched you with Mistress Hayward and with her new babe. And with Lady Timandra. I have no doubt you will be a wonderful and caring mother.

"I know I am not worthy of you, Lady Venetia, but I would like very much would you give me the chance to try to win your love."

He was not asking for hand, not asking could he speak to Berold. He was not trying to rush her into making a decision. How well that pleased her.

"We will have days together as we travel to Knightswood," he said, bending so close their noses were almost touching. "I beg you, do say you will allow me to court you."

"Yes, Lord Tuftwick, you may pay me court. I am honored you choose to do so."

He drew in his breath then released it slowly. "Thank you, dear lady."

He was so close to her, she had been so sure he was going to kiss her, just as Madigan had done, but still holding her hands, he drew back, and turning her hands over, he ran a fingertip down first one palm, then the other, causing tingles to race up her spine. She was not certain what all his courtship would entail, but she was now eagerly looking forward to it. And to kissing him. She licked her lips, moistening them, but he made no attempt kiss her. He instead tucked her hand back in the crook of his arm, and they resumed their walk.

"Shall I tell you more about me, Lady Venetia, and about Tuftwick Hall? 'Tis not a grand estate, 'tis old, but I have plans for it."

"What sort of plans, Lord Tuftwick? Do tell me."

He looked pleased she showed an interest in his plans. Why would she not? Did she decide she would marry him, she should know something of the home she would be moving to. She knew his home was not

74

far from Wollowchet, but she also knew it was more isolated.

"It is an old house," he told her, "but my father and his father before him, each made some improvements." He chuckled. "The hall now has a fine marble hearth and mantel. The hall was once two-stories high with massive arched rafters, but Father built a floor over the hall, and the room he created above it serves as a grand parlor. The house is in the shape of an H with many windows and chimneys. 'Tis timber-framed with brick and plaster fill, and it has rounded turrets that are three-stories high. The house was built during Queen Elizabeth's reign before separate living space was provided for servants. Servants slept in the hall or in their master's room or just outside his door. There are few servants now, as I am seldom at the hall. What servants do live at the house have rooms in the undercroft or rooms off the kitchen which is in a separate building.

"The bedchambers for guests are in the turrets. They will need redoing. Naught has been done to them since my parents died." He looked downcast for a moment, but before Venetia could express her sympathy, he brightened and said, "There is a portico at the rear of the house that stretches from turret to turret. I have plans to enclose it, make it a gallery, a place to stroll when the weather is inclement. Then I mean to build a corridor above it to make easier access to the parlor and the bedchambers."

He stopped and looked down at her. "I cannot promise to do all the changes immediately. Such things take time and money, and I have yet to fully pay back my uncle, though he will not press me for it. He says the sum will someday be mine, but my aunt and uncle, God willing, may live many years to come. I cannot take advantage of them, any more than Berold was willing to take advantage of your cousin." He shrugged. "Oh, I know of her offers to pay his fines that he would not have to sell off his woods or his lands, but he would have naught but a loan."

Venetia knew her brother's pride, his refusal to do no more than borrow the necessary funds from Delphine until he could sell off the forested land he loved and repay her, was a part of who he was. He had been adamant, he would not take advantage of his cousin, especially not when her father was dead and her grandfather was on his deathbed, and anyone might think he was abusing their relationship. Not that Venetia believed anyone would be able to take advantage of Delphine. She was strong and wise, and she had capable men vigilantly looking after her interests. Firms that had worked for grandfather and great-grandfather for generations. But in knowing her brother's feelings, she could better understand Tuftwick's.

"Because I spent so little time at my home," Tuftwick continued, "my staff is small, but do you agree to marry me, you may increase the staff to whatever you think needed to provide you with the care you are used to."

"And does that mean you would give up your exploits with Phillida's brother, Nate?"

He stopped and turned to face her. "Did you wish it. Yes."

"But you would not wish to desert the others, would you?"

He shook his head. "Nay, we are all dependent upon each other. We succeed because we have worked together for so many years now. We each know our role. Caleb being shot was a fluke that should not have happened and will not happen again. We knew our target was risky, but the haul was so immense, we thought it worth the risk. D'Arcy will re-examine our plans. He will determine where we were at fault, and our next venture will have no casualties."

Tilting her head and narrowing her eyes, Venetia asked, "Where is this immense haul?"

He chuckled. "Oh, my pretty one, it is safe and secure and awaits but the right time to be removed and sent to the King. But I can tell you nothing of it or where it is hidden."

"I would guess as Phillida's brother has allowed you to escort us to Knightswood, Nate has no current nefarious plans."

He coughed. "None that involve me or Maddy or Caleb, that is for certain."

"Ah, and did you know of any plans, you would not be telling me, now would you?"

He smiled and ignoring her question, said, "Shall I tell you about my parents? At least what I can remember about them and about my childhood before I was sent off to school."

She laughed. "Very well, I can tell our discussion of your adventures

76

is over. So do tell me about your youth."

※　※　※　※

Madigan sighed. He had done as he promised Tuftwick he would, he distracted Mistress Lotterby so Tuftwick could have time alone with Lady Venetia. Watching his dearest friend walk away with the woman they both loved on his arm had caused a pain in his gut like he had never known. No, not even when he learned his mother had died, and he was being kicked out of his school. Set adrift with nowhere to turn. But Tuftwick had been there for him. Now he would return the favor though his heart felt it would never be whole again.

He had involved Mistress Lotterby in a game of chess, but he had been unable to concentrate. She quickly defeated him then suggested he might like to see her new gelding. Not knowing what else to do, he agreed to accompany her. "I have always had mares," she said. "Their mouths are generally more tender, and they are easier to manage. But when I saw Fire Dancer, I could not resist him."

As soon as he saw the horse, Madigan understood why Mistress Lotterby was taken with the animal. A chestnut with a jagged white blaze down the center of his noble nose, he flicked his ears and pranced up to greet them when they drew near his stall.

"Hello, my handsome boy," Mistress Lotterby said, reaching out to scratch his nose. "Let me introduce to you a friend of mine. This is Mister Madigan. He will be accompanying us to Knightswood Castle." She turned to Madigan. "Is he not as fine as I said?"

Madigan nuzzled the horse's soft nose with his fingertips. "Oh, you are indeed right, Mistress Lotterby. Have you ridden him, yet?"

"Nay, he was but brought here last night, but I have been watching him grow since he was a young colt. When I sought a new horse, as my mare, Aldora, is aging, I went to see an Irishman, by the name of O'Gibbon, who does naught but breed and train horses on a small acreage outside Frodsham. Fire Dancer was barely a week old, but I knew I had to have him. Even then, I could see the intelligence in his eyes, his perkiness, his friendliness. He came right up to me. Had no fear." She laughed. "I paid royally for him, too. But I have watched O'Gibbon train him to saddle. He had no need to gentle him, for he was never wild." She gave the horse a pat and scratched an ear. "I did hate to geld him, poor dear, but though I am an accomplished rider, I feared a stallion might at times prove troublesome."

Madigan nodded. "We all ride geldings. Cannot afford to have a stallion catch the scent of a mare and lose his senses and ..." He started to say more but caught himself. He was speaking to a lady not a man. He had felt so comfortable there in the stables with Mistress Lotterby, he had almost forgotten himself.

She laughed. A pleasant laugh. Not a sensuous laugh like Venetia's, but a laugh filled with merriment, and the smile that graced her lips reached her ebony eyes and set them to twinkling. To his wonder, he joined in her laughter, and whatever embarrassment he had felt quickly fled.

"I will be riding him to Knightswood Castle," she said, "but I hope to take him out for a canter before supper. Would you care to accompany me?"

He nodded enthusiastically. "Aye, I could do with an outing myself."

"Splendid. I will need but a short time to change into my riding costume. Do you tell the stablemen to ready our mounts. I should return in short order."

"Agreed," he answered, pleased to have something to take his mind off his lost love.

Chapter 11

Delphine thrilled to the wind in her face as leaning slightly forward, she gave Fire Dancer his head, and they dashed across the meadow, scattering sheep and tossing up tuffs of turf in their rear. Glancing to her side, she saw Maddy draw up beside her. He had a fine horse. Dark brown with black mane and tail, sturdy legs, and a massive chest, the animal had the look of a runner. No doubt he carried Maddy swiftly away from any pursuers.

When she finally drew up as they approached a wooded area, she could not keep from laughing with exhilaration. Maddy drew up beside her. "I think you chose well, Mistress Lotterby. Few horses are a match for Lucan, here," he said, patting his horse's neck.

"Yes, I do believe Fire Dancer will be all I hoped he would be." Patting her horse, she noted Purdy and Anker who had followed at a discreet distance were circling around them and putting themselves between her and the woods. Shaking her head, she frowned.

"What brings the sudden gloom to your face Mistress Lotterby?" Maddy asked. "Surely you find no fault with your mount."

Forcing a smile, she said, "Nay, look you at my two ever cautious footmen. Note how they have maneuvered themselves between me and the forest. They must be ever on the alert. I fear I am a great trouble to my servants and my family."

Maddy looked to the footmen then back at her. "A great trouble? How is that?"

"As Berold told you, there are men who would abduct me to force me into marriage. My footmen must keep me safe. And indeed they do, but I grow weary of having my freedom curtailed. I can never take a walk on my own, never enter a forest on a hot day to relax in its shade. We never know when someone may be lurking, waiting for an unguarded moment to snatch me away." Skewering her mouth to one side, she said,

"My fortune has its trials as well as its benefits."

He looked again at her footmen. "They are devoted to you."

"They are indeed." She flicked her reins, and urged Fire Dancer into a gentle walk. "Let us start back. I am too near the woods. I wish not to make my footmen nervous."

Maddy turned his mount and fell in beside her, his horse matching his stride to her horse's. "Well, I thank you for the race, Mistress Lotterby. Any time you wish to ride, I will be happy to accompany you. Help keep you safe. 'Tis a shame the law does so little to protect you."

"Yes," she agreed then narrowed her eyes. Now was her chance. She had to take it. What had she to lose. "Mister Madigan," she said, catching his eyes. "What would you think of marrying me?"

She watched him closely. At first he seemed not to comprehend what she had asked him. He shook his head like he was trying to clear his thoughts. Finally he thrust his head forward and stared at her.

"Did you fail to hear me, sir? I asked you if you would marry me." There, she had done it. An outright proposal.

Again he shook his head. "In truth, I cannot believe I have heard you correctly." He gave a half-hearted, nervous chuckle. "Could you have said you want to marry me?"

"That is precisely what I said, Mister Madigan. If I am to ever know any peace, ever be secure in my own home, I must marry. Since this most recent abduction attempt, I have been considering the need to marry." That was partially true. It was only true if she could convince Maddy to marry her. "And why should I not marry you. I like you. And I think you like me." She gave him no chance to answer her. "I trust you. I have known you a goodly portion of my life. I do believe we would suit each other quite admirably."

Yet again he shook his head, making his unruly hair fly about his face. He let out a heavy sigh and scratched his neck. His eyes looked at her, looked away, looked back at her. "Nay, 'twould never suit. I am penniless. You … you … are a woman of great wealth and prestige. You should be marrying a lord … an earl, a marquess, mayhap even a duke. Nay. Besides, Berold would never consent."

She smiled at his confusion. "I have no need for Berold to consent. He is not my guardian. I am free to choose whomever I wish to marry, and I am choosing to marry you, Mister Madigan, would you but consent." She held up a hand as again he started to protest. "I have been to London. I have met Dukes and Earls. I cared not a whit for any of them. And I have no wish to be married for my fortune."

"But all would think that is why I married you," Maddy blurted out.

She shrugged and raised an eyebrow. "Am I that hideous you think no one could think you might find me appealing?"

"Oh, nay," he said, pulling up his horse, and she pulled up hers.

"Nay, that is not what I meant, Mistress Lotterby. Why, indeed, you are most attractive. But as you know ... as you saw ... I love Lady Venetia."

"Yes, so you have said, yet you also said you will not try to win her hand. My guess is she will agree to marry Lord Tuftwick - if he courts her properly. Where does that leave you, Maddy, if I may be so bold to call you such. Can you love Venetia and live in the same home with her when she is married to your dearest friend?"

Bowing his head, he nudged his horses flanks to again set his horse in motion. She followed suit. "I had not thought that far ahead, but no, I could not continue to live with Tuffy at Tuftwick Hall."

"I would think not." She reached over and touched his hand to get him to look at her. When he looked up, she said, "We leave for Knightswood Castle in a few days. We will have any number of days during the trip to become better acquainted. You need not decide at this moment whether you will marry me or not. Take your time. Think about what I have said. I must marry," she stated adamantly, her gaze holding his. "I am sick to death of these abduction attempts. In my twenty-four years, I have met no one I wanted to spend the rest of my life with. No one until you, Maddy. And I have met a good many men. As I said, I like you. I think we can be good friends. Do you wish to continue to ride with Mister D'Arcy, I would not interfere."

They were nearing the edge of the field. "At least promise me you will consider my proposal. Will you not at least promise me that?" She was feeling frightened. What if she could not convince Maddy to marry her. What if he loved Venetia too dearly. Or he was too concerned about what people would think, what Berold would think.

Then he nodded. "I will think on your proposal," he at last agreed, and she let out a silent sigh. Now she but had to court him as Tuftwick would court Venetia, and mayhap by the time they reached Knightswood, both she and Venetia would be planning their weddings.

※ ※ ※ ※

Madigan stared after Delphine as she strode toward the house. He told her he preferred to stay and see to Lucan himself, which he did, but he really needed time to think. In walking Lucan around the courtyard behind the stablemen walking the other three horses, he let his thoughts race in all directions. Why would Delphine want to marry him? What would Berold think? Worse, what would Venetia think? She had to know he loved her. Everyone would believe he was marrying Delphine for her money. What else could they think? He had no future. Tuftwick was as dear to him as anyone alive, but as he admitted to Delphine, he could not continue in Tuftwick's company did Tuftwick marry Venetia. What would he then do? His education was limited. Because of the war, neither he nor Tuftwick had continued their education. He was not competent enough to even serve as an estate's steward. He could ride, shoot, and fight with a sword, but he knew nothing of managing a property, nothing of the law.

His thoughts went racing back to his first question. Why did Delphine want to marry him? Her wealth was immense. Her father was the son of an Earl. And, when he thought about her looks, he realized she was an attractive woman. Not a goddess like Venetia, but not a woman a sensible man would shun. He could understand her frustration with the number of attempts at abduction she had endured, but surely she could find someone more suitable to take to husband than him. So why him? What could he possibly offer her?

She said she believed they would be well suited. She said she liked him, trusted him. He slowly nodded his head. Trust would be important. She would want a man who would not run through her fortune. He could guarantee her that. She had agents and lawyers and business men who presently looked after her interests. He would have no wish to interfere with them. He had no estate that needed her money to put it back to rights. He was not a gambler. He owed no financial debts to anyone. With her wealth, she could marry a peer of the realm. But many of the peers were in debt, were old or unappealing, or were already married. And like Delphine said, she wanted to marry, needed to marry to be safe from continued attempts to abduct her and force her into a marriage she could not abide.

So why not him? At least it was worth considering. Like she said, they could be friends. He enjoyed talking with her. She was bright and had a good sense of humor. And when he thought about it, he would have no trouble bedding her. Fact was, the thought rather appealed to him. He had known few women. There had been little time for women in his life, and few women had been available. Somehow, paying a woman for her favors had never appealed to him. Tuftwick felt much the same, saying a woman who takes coin for the bedding could be giving you more than you might want in exchange. The pox was something Lord Wollowchet had warned them about numerous times over. Both had been cautious. He had been tempted on several occasions, but had normally relied on his hand to squelch his desire.

But to be married. To have a woman to share his bed. A woman who stirred his desire. A woman who would give him children. To have a family of his own was not something he ever let himself contemplate. It had always been too painful. Now. Now he wanted to think about it. To be a father. To have little sons and daughters to love, to protect, to hold in his arms. Yes, the more he thought about the idea of marrying Delphine, the better he liked it.

Then, just before leading Lucan into the stable, he saw Venetia. She walked beside Tuftwick, her head tilted back, her laughter floating out over the evening air. Something had amused her. Even at a distance, he could see the sparkle in her heavenly blue eyes. She saw him and waved. Tuftwick waved, too, before he directed Venetia toward the door.

Absently returning their waves, Madigan turned his horse over to one of the stablemen. How could he think of marrying Delphine when his heart ached for Venetia? What kind of a husband would he be, lying abed with Delphine, but dreaming of Venetia? Nay, 'twould not be fair to either woman. Though why it would not be fair to Venetia, he was not certain. Mayhap he simply could not want her thinking of him bedding her cousin. He wanted her thoughts of him to be pure. Why? What foolishness!

Shrugging, he headed back to the house. He had to ready himself for supper, and at the moment, he smelled of horses and leather. Facing Delphine and Venetia would not be easy. Both women had his thoughts scurrying in all directions. Somehow he would have to sit at the table, make conversation, and act like he bore no love for Venetia and that Delphine had not asked him to marry her. At least Caleb Hayward would be at the table. Hopefully he would be able to engage him in a conversation that would allow him to avoid conversation with Venetia or Delphine.

Chapter 12

The first two days on the road had been glorious. Bright sunshine and chirping birds greeted them both mornings, but clouds sitting on the horizon this, their third day out, threatened to turn their day's journey into a nightmare. Phillida frowned as she peered out the coach window. Delphine and Venetia were still mounted and riding beside Madigan and Tuftwick, but with the dark clouds rapidly advancing, she knew Berold, much to his sister's and his cousin's objections, would soon have them switching to a coach.

At Delphine's insistence, Phillida and Sidonie, along with Timandra, baby William, and Timandra's nurse were riding in Delphine's coach. It was incredibly luxurious with all the most modern mechanisms to make for a smooth ride as the coach made its way along the rutted road. The maids, Tattersall, Bethel, and Adah, as well as the Harp's Ridge cook, whom Phillida would not go to Knightswood without, were riding in her coach, but did Venetia and Delphine have to move inside, Adah and the cook would have to remove to the servants' coach with the younger maids, Lucy and Anna.

Besides the three coaches, two wagons loaded with various household items, clothing, food supplies, and books and games followed the coaches and inevitably slowed their progress, but despite the loveliness of Grasmere Lake, the castle could be dark and dreary did Phillida not take her favorite items to enliven the hall and the cold bedchambers. Bringing up the rear of their procession were extra horses for riding and for the coaches and wagons should any of the horses go lame on the journey.

Caleb Hayward had insisted upon riding, promising his wife that did his wound start to bleed, he would remove to the coach. With the storm moving in, Sidonie was already insisting her husband join them in the coach. At first he balked but at last relented. He looked wane, and seemed more than willing, after giving his son a kiss, to settle into the corner of the coach and close his eyes.

Phillida could not help but envy Sidonie her baby. He was such a sturdy and bright-eyed little fellow. He had a healthy appetite, and as long as he was kept fed and dry, he seemed to have little to fuss about. Even when the wind came up and rattled the coach window shutters, he slept peacefully in his little basket.

When the first splatters of rain arrived, the procession stopped again that Delphine and Venetia could dismount and settle into their coach. Phillida knew Adah would hate being relegated to the less comfortable servants' coach. No doubt she would be full of complaints in the evening when she readied Phillida for bed.

"I do believe the men will be royally soaked despite their hats and cloaks ere we reach our night's destination," Sidonie said, interrupting Phillida's thoughts.

Peering at Sidonie in the dim light seeping through the shutters, Phillida nodded. "Aye, they will all be ready for some warm ale, 'tis certain. I feel the most sorry for the coachmen and the footmen. Does the ground get too soggy, the wheels get stuck in the mud, and getting the coach or wagon unstuck is most difficult. The poor footmen must push and try to lift the coach or wagon enough to set it rolling again. Is our coach stuck, we might well have to get out. Berold always has a canvas set up for us to stand under, but there is still no way to keep from getting wet in this kind of rain."

"Let us pray we will reach our destination before the roads get too soggy," Sidonie said. "I cannot wish William to be exposed to this downpour." She chuckled softly. "Besides, I had enough rain to last me on the night we arrived at Harp's Ridge."

Half-smiling, Phillida said, "Indeed you did. I am yet wondering how you managed such a feat. I know I could never have done it."

"Oh, yes you could have. I see the love between you and Lord Grasmere. Was your husband in danger, you would do whatever you had to do to save him."

"I hope I would. But I pray I will never be put to the test as you were. But on a brighter note, do we reach Sir Hammet's Beaulieu Hall without incidence, I am thinking Berold may choose to stay over an extra

86

day or two does this rain continue. You will like Beaulieu. It is quite lovely and the Phelpses are very gracious and hospitable."

"If they are anything like our hosts the past two nights, I know we will find all most amiable. The Barclays and the Haskells could not have been more accommodating to Caleb and me. Especially kind as we were complete strangers to them."

"I would expect nothing less from them. Both families have long been friends of the Lotterbys. I understand Berold's father and his father before him always stayed with them when traveling to Grasmere. Fact is, most of the homes we stay in on our trek have long been stopovers for the Lotterbys."

"Lord Grasmere must know a great many people."

Phillida pursed her lips. "I believe Berold's father was good at cultivating friendships. Of course, being an Earl and serving in the House of Lords for so many years, he met many people. Did favors for many I would guess. Now with the House of Lords no longer sitting, Berold has not the same influence his father had, but thankfully, the homes are still open to us. Most members of the gentry here in the west are still Royalists at heart. Or so it seems."

"Milady," the nurse said, "Lady Timandra is stirring from her nap. I am thinking she will be in need of a respite, but how shall we manage it in this rain?"

"I could use a respite myself," Phillida said. "We should have managed something before the rain started." She turned to Sidonie. "I am guessing you are also in need."

"Aye," Sidonie said, "I would be pleased to relieve myself. I would also be pleased to be off my buttocks for a bit as well, comfortable as these cushions are."

Squiggling into an upright position, Timandra rubbed her eyes and said, "Mother, I need the chamber pot."

"Yes, dear, let me see can I get someone's attention. Mayhap we are nearing a village." Pulling the shutters back enough to see out, Phillida could not see any riders near to hand. She had no choice but to stick her arm out the window and wave it in the hope of attracting someone's attention. Her arm and shoulder were drenched by the time her husband rode up, and bending forward on his horse, peered in at her.

"What is amiss, my love? You must be drenched now."

"I am soaked, but we must have a respite, Berold. We are all in need. Are we by chance near a village?"

He shook his head. "Nay." Straightening in his saddle, he looked ahead then bent back over. "I see a cottage up ahead. It will at least offer shelter while you tend your needs. I will ride ahead and arrange what comfort I can for you."

"Thank you, dear," Phillida answered and hastily reclosed the shutter. She reached over to pat her daughter's knee. "You need but hold it a bit longer, Timandra. Can you do that?"

"Yes, Mother," Timandra answered, "but I hope we hurry."

❊ ❊ ❊ ❊

The wattle and daub cottage was but two rooms, rustic and poorly furnished, but the husbandman and his wife hurried out to greet the coaches when they pulled up in front of their home. Bowing and offering to help in any manner they could, the couple paid no heed to the rain as they ushered their unexpected guests into their humble home. Three wide-eyed children in ragged clothes backed up against the wall as Phillida hurried in behind the nurse carrying Timandra and Sidonie with William tucked under her cloak.

The footmen held tarpaulins up to shield the women from the rain as they dashed from the coaches into the cottage. Another tarpaulin had been spread across the ground in front of the cottage to help protect the women's shoes from the mud.

A low fire burning on a flagstone in the center of the main room offered the only heat. Smoke drifted about the room, some rising to a hole in the roof that allowed drops of rain in as the smoke escaped. The husbandman, setting aside a pot of simmering porridge and adding more wood to the fire, said, "Come and warm yourselves while me daughter pours ye some ale." He beckoned to the oldest child, a skinny girl with stringy yellow hair. She hurried to a rough-hewn cupboard, took a couple of wooden noggins from a shelf, pulled a plug from a worn barrel, and tilting it, started filling the noggins.

Taking the wife aside, Phillida said, "'Tis the necessary we are most in want of. Especially for my daughter."

The woman stared blankly at her and questioned, "The necessary, milady?"

"We must need relieve ourselves. Have you no pot?" Phillida squatted a bit and lifted her skirt in an attempt to demonstrate what she needed.

The woman brightened. "Oh, you be needing the pot. Come. I have one in me bed chamber."

"We are all in need," Phillida said, indicating Delphine and Venetia, Sidonie and Timandra, and all the female servants.

"Oh, my," the woman said. "Well, does it fill up, I will empty it. Come."

The bed chamber was a small windowless room. A fagot from the fire in hand, Goody Kemp, so Phillida learned was the woman's name, hurried to light the wick of a rushlight attached to the wall. The room held naught but a bed, a stool, several pegs on the wall, and a small table. Goody Kemp pulled a cracked earthenware pot with a handle out from under the table. She set the pot on the sturdy four-legged stool, then stepped back. "Help yerselves."

The chamber being small, the servants waited their turn in the main room. "Men are lucky," Phillida said as she settled Timandra on the pot. "They can relieve themselves anywhere. I have been in some homes where when the women leave the dining area, the men use the hearth to relieve themselves. I know this because Berold laughed at me once when I complained about the smell in a particular house." She looked over at Venetia and chuckled. "No, I will not be naming which home, so you need not query me."

When all the women had relieved themselves and were scurrying back into the coaches, Phillida saw Delphine press a coin purse into Goody Kemp's hand. Phillida knew her husband had paid the husband-man handsomely for the man had thanked him repeatedly.

"Buy the children some new shoes and coats come winter," she heard Delphine say.

Clutching the purse, the woman, her pale eyes wide, said, "God be blessing ye, milady."

Delphine harrumphed. "I am Mistress Lotterby. I am not titled." She patted the woman's hand. "Make sure that goes for the children. Do I pass here again and find them poorly shod, I will not again be so generous."

"Oh, yes, Mistress. Indeed. They will have new shoes."

"Good. And I thank you and your husband for the ale. It helped warm my innards."

Phillida had noted that both Delphine and Venetia had taken sips of the ale from the noggins. Fearing the cups would not be clean, she had not been so brave herself. Her husband, though, accepted the drink and praised it before passing the cup on to Caleb Hayward. That the family made do with but the three cups spoke sadly of their poverty. Well, they were considerably richer this day all because the women had needed a respite, and the Kemp's had graciously, if humbly, cared for their needs.

"I hope we may not have need to stop again before we reach our night's destination," Timandra's nurse said. "Even shielding Lady Timandra as best I could, her hair is damp. I worry she might take a chill."

"I, too, hope we will soon reach Beaulieu," Phillida said. "I doubt a little dampness will hurt Timandra, but here, use my shawl to dry her hair." Taking her shawl from her shoulders, she handed it to the nurse. The coach interior being even darker as the sun dipped lower in the sky, Phillida could not see her daughter. She could but be grateful her child had always been a healthy child, and that her brief exposure to the rain would not bring on the ague. She hoped it would not make any of the men, riding through the downpour, ill. With a silent prayer that the rain would soon stop, she settled back into her corner of the coach and closed her eyes. What a dreary day.

Chapter 13

Trying not to be obvious in his perusal, Madigan glanced sideways at Malcolm Phelps, Sir Hammet's son. A handsome youth with hazel eyes, light brown hair, and sporting a trim mustache but no beard, he had an open countenance and an engaging smile. Madigan guessed him no more than twenty, but from the moment Delphine entered the house and until she and the other women were escorted up to their rooms by Lady Phelps, the youth had been at Delphine's side. He had fussed over her, complimented her, and praised her. Then bowing over Delphine's hand, Phelps said, "I have requested Mother seat me beside you at the table. We have much to catch up on since your last visit."

Smiling brightly at the youth, Delphine answered, "Indeed we have, Mister Phelps. I expect you to tell me how you fared at Oxford since last we met."

"Delighted," he said. "My studies went well. I shall be honored to tell you more."

"Splendid," Delphine answered, and reclaiming her hand, she turned and followed Lady Phelps up the narrow winding stairs leading to the first floor bedchambers.

Phelps stared after her until she disappeared then joined his father before the hearth. Sir Hammet had mugs of steaming ale for all the men, and he assured Berold, that Berold's men servants would be fed and bedded comfortably once the horses were cared for and the portmanteaus distributed to the appropriate rooms. Madigan and Tuftwick would as usual share a room, and both Berold and Hayward would get to share rooms with their wives. Berold, ever expedient, had dispatched messages to all the hosts they would be staying with that they would need additional accommodations for the four extra people traveling with him. So far, at each home, all had been in readiness.

Madigan knew Berold was relieved they had arrived at Beaulieu without encountering any major difficulties. One wagon had been stuck, but by adding two extra horses to the team, and with the footmen pushing from behind, the wagon had been extricated without having to unload any of the cargo.

"You cannot tell me you will be wishing to travel on the morrow, Grasmere," Sir Hammet said. "Does this rain continue through the night, the roads will be naught but a soddy mire. I recommend you spend an extra day here. Give your women a day of rest, and I can tell you, my wife will enjoy their company. Now days, we seldom go far from home. Certainly no reason to go to London or even Manchester. Can never forgive the people of Manchester for supporting the Round-heads over the King."

Another re-fighting of the war was not something Madigan wanted to take part in. Sir Hammet, like many members of the gentry in the west, had endured confiscation of his property, but like many others, he managed to pay his fine and keep his home, but his wealth was dimin-ished he proclaimed, and Berold offered him sympathy. Young Phelps added his witticisms about the cotton linen merchants of Manchester, and how they had prospered. "Many now look to set themselves up as landowners, having bought Royalists' lands." He mocked them as Ja-nus-faced fribble thinking to join the ranks of their betters.

Madigan guessed the Phelpses had not been members of the gentry for too many generations, but he said nothing. Instead he let his mind drift over the last three days. To his surprise, he had found himself enjoying riding beside Delphine. She made for a good companion, chatting about horses, books she had read, her favorite foods, and her descriptions of London were intriguing.

"I cannot care much for the city," she declared. "It is crowded, dirty, and noisy, but the variety of shops and homes and people, from the merchants to the downtrodden, are most interesting. I enjoyed several boat outings on the Thames, but I could never imagine living in such a place."

Never once did she bring up the subject of marriage. By their second day out, he had relaxed completely in her presence and had been more than a little disappointed when came the afternoon, the weather drove her into the coach. Her lively companionship helped keep his mind off Venetia. He occasionally heard Venetia's laughter, but as she and Tuftwick rode behind him and Delphine, he was not forced to watch his friend court the woman he loved.

Another thing he liked about Delphine was her generous nature. She was ever ready with a handsome tip for servants, and he had seen her give a coin purse to Goody Kemp. He had not heard what she said to the woman, but he had seen the gratitude on the woman's face. In their conversations, he discovered Delphine was not particularly religious, yet she seemed ready to follow Christ's teachings concerning the act of giving.

He could not help but wonder whether young Phelps was attempting to court Delphine. Her wealth would be a boost to the Phelps family. As it would to anyone's, but that was what Delphine declared she was sick to death of – being courted for her wealth. If she suspected the youth of such intentions, she had shown no annoyance, but being a guest in the Phelpses' home, she would be unlikely to express any contempt.

"What do you say to that, Maddy?" Tuftwick broke in on Madigan's thoughts.

"I beg pardon, Tuffy, I was wool-gathering. What did you say?"

Tuftwick spread his arms wide and looked about the hall. Madigan's gaze followed his friend's. The stone walls, aglow from sconces on the walls and candles in heavy chandeliers hanging from rafters, were hung with bright tapestries. Beaulieu was an old house, dating from the fourteen hundreds, but it had only been in the Phelpses' family for three generations, or so Berold had told him and Tuftwick before they arrived.

"Sir Hammet thinks we should have a sword dueling tournament here in the hall tomorrow," Tuftwick said, "does Berold consent to stay an extra day until the roads can dry. What would you say to a tournament?"

Madigan frowned. "'Twould be a small tournament, there not being many of us to compete. Hayward, even was he well enough, is not a swordsman."

"Sir Hammet says Lord Rigdale, who is but a short ride from here, has two youths fostered with him that he has been training. Plus Lord Rigdale himself is a noted swordsman. Could be good fun. Keep us in practice."

Madigan looked to Berold. "If you say we are to delay a day, I will join in whatever entertainment Sir Hammet wishes."

"Splendid," Sir Hammet said, his hazel eyes under bushy brows, alight. "What say you Grasmere, do I send word to Lord Rigdale?"

Berold beckoned to a servant hovering nearby. "Does it yet rain?"

"I will see, my lord," the man said and hurried off.

"By the by, Mister Hayward," young Phelps said. "How came you by your wound?"

Frowning, Hayward shook his head, and repeated the story told to the Lotterby servants and their other hosts. "'Twas a tavern brawl. My wife and I had just walked in the door when the fight broke out and a stray shot hit me instead of the intended victim."

"Good heavens!" Sir Hammet said.

"Good heavens is right," chimed in Tuftwick. "Maddy and I had recommended the inn. But not thinking the inn the best place for Hayward to recover, when he was well enough, we decided 'twould be best did we take him on to Berold's. However, the worry for her husband brought on Mistress Hayward's baby. She barely made it to Harp's Ridge for the delivery."

"Should never have allowed her to travel with me in the first place," Hayward said, "but she had never traveled far from home, and she pleaded so, that I relented."

"What was the purpose of your journey?" Malcom Phelps asked.

"'Twas our doing," broke in Tuftwick, "mine and Maddy's. Hayward's family gave us solace after the defeat at Naseby. We were too weary to continue home, and they cared for us until we were mended. Anyway, we were on a visit, and knowing Berold was having good luck with rotating his crops with clover, we thought Hayward would find it of interest. So, Hayward having seen his ploughing done, we suggested he take a holiday and come see Berold's fields."

"And am I glad I did," Hayward said. "It was near worth the wound to see the benefits of the clover. The bees seem to like the clover, too. Means more honey. Mayhap enough to sell."

How clever of Tuftwick, Maddy thought. The perfect answer to the Hayward's presence. None of the Lotterby servants or the other hosts

94

they stayed with had questioned the Haywards' presence. They had but accepted that the Haywards were having a holiday and going to Lake Grasmere after Hayward's injury and the birth of their child. But Tuftwick had taken a half-truth – for 'twas true the Haywards had given them solace, but 'twas after Charles II's defeat at Worcester, not after Charles's father's defeat at Naseby. He and Tuftwick never admitted they had fought for Charles II. One never knew who might turn them in were they in need of some coin.

"Now Hayward's holiday has been extended," Berold said. "I insisted he and his wife spend the summer with us while he recuperates. Seems only right."

"Excuse me, my lord," said the servant who had been sent to check on the rain. "It is still raining, though 'tis not as heavy as it was when you arrived."

"Thank you," Berold said. Turning back to Sir Hammet, he slowly nodded his head. "I do believe we would be well served did we stay the extra day with you. And we appreciate your hospitality. I know it means more work for your wife."

Sir Hammet's face spread in a wide grin. "Nonsense. As I said, my wife will be thrilled to have the extended company. She has been bored this long winter. Our nearest neighbor is Rigdale, and his wife died over four years ago, so Mildred must make do with naught but her servants does she wish for female companionship, what with our daughters being fostered at her cousin's for the past two years. Though they will be home this summer."

"So we shall have the tournament," young Phelps said, beaming. "I will tell you all, I won every tournament I entered at Oxford."

Tuftwick laughed. "Well, I will tell you all that I have not used my sword for anything but decoration for a couple of years, so I will ask you to have mercy on me."

"I must send word to Rigdale," Sir Hammet said. "I should have word back from him ere we have finished our supper. I would say by now, the ladies are settling comfortably into their chambers. I think 'twould be safe for you men to venture up." He beckoned to the servant. "Adkins, see Lord Grasmere and Mister Hayward to their chambers, then escort Lord Tuftwick and Mister Madigan to theirs."

"Yes, Sir Hammet." The servant nodded to Berold and then the others. "This way, please."

Madigan was not particularly looking forward to spending an extra day with the Phelpses, especially if Malcom Phelps was to be spending his time trying to impress Delphine. Why that would bother him, he was not sure, but he had to admit, it did. Following after Tuftwick, he glanced back once more at Phelps. He was a bright cheerful lad. Nothing not to like about him, but Madigan did dislike him. Yes, that youth would bear watching.

❦ ❦ ❦ ❦

Delphine smiled at her reflection in the mirror as Tatty combed out her hair. "What a tangled mess," her beloved servant said. "'Twas the wind whipped it up afore you took to the coach. Then the rain hitting it when we had to nip into that shoddy cottage. How I am to get all these tangles out in time to dress you for supper is what I am wondering."

"We will manage, dear Tatty, I am certain. Here let me have the comb while you lay out my clothing. Nothing too revealing tonight. I am in no mood to encourage young Phelps." Or was she, she wondered, absently taking the comb from Tatty. Mayhap she should encourage the youth. She had seen Madigan, a slight frown on his face, watching her and Phelps. For once, Maddy's eyes had been on her, not Venetia. Could he possibly be jealous?

"On second thought, Tatty, lay out my red gown with the red and gold pleated petticoat. Why should I not enjoy a flirt?"

Narrowing her eyes, Tatty looked at her for a long moment. "'Tis chill tonight, Mistress Delphine. That décolletage is cut low and off the shoulders. You could be cold."

"You are right. I best have my gold shawl. It may be flimsy, but it should be enough."

Tatty frowned but resumed delving through Delphine's trunk. "Yes, Mistress, and I suppose you will be wanting your red slippers."

"Yes, thank you, Tatty," Delphine said, and turning back to her reflection, she began tugging at the knots in her hair. She found Phelps a handsome, amusing youth. The previous year on the Lotterbys' return trip from Lake Grasmere, Phelps had been preparing to return to Oxford. She had known him for years for the Lotterbys always stayed with the Phelpses, but the previous year, Malcolm, or more likely his father, had decided he was old enough to flirt with her.

She had little doubt his father had told him to try to win her hand. Single men of all ages, from youths in their teens to doddering old peers, sought her fortune. What made any of them think they would be the one she would consent to wed always intrigued her. She never encouraged any of them, but this night, she might give Malcolm some false hope. 'Twas not a kind thing to do, she knew, but she had to see if mayhap she could catch a spark of jealousy in Maddy's eyes. She might even use a little color on her cheeks.

She smiled again. This could be an entertaining evening.

Chapter 14

Venetia was pleased they were to spend an extra day at Beaulieu. Though they had been on the road but three days, she was ready for a change in the routine. She liked riding beside Tuftwick. He was ever amusing, ever attentive, but she had yet to find a chance to kiss him. She thought she might be falling in love with him, but how could she be certain did he not kiss her. To her way of thinking, he was being entirely too circumspect. Was he concerned Berold might think him too forward?

Madigan had not been afraid to kiss her. She had liked the kiss. Indeed, kisses were most pleasant. But a kiss needed to be more than pleasant. It needed to start her heart pounding, her head spinning. At least, that is what she wanted a kiss to do. Surely that is what Juliette felt when she kissed Romeo. With a sigh, Venetia wondered if mayhap she was expecting too much, being overly romantic, but she saw the way Berold and Phillida looked at each other. And the way the Haywards' looked at each other, so she knew such love as she wanted existed. It was not mere fantasy.

Squiggling around in the bed, she was glad she and Delphine were not having to share a room. She liked sharing secrets with her cousin, but this night as she tossed and turned, she knew she would be keeping Delphine from sleeping. Delphine would insist upon knowing what troubled her. She would end up telling Delphine all about her frustrations with Tuftwick and her scheme to get him alone that she might tempt him to kiss her. Delphine would not find fault with her, might even be willing to help her, but she knew Delphine set no store in letting a kiss determine true love or not.

Tapping Venetia's breast, Delphine had once said, "Your heart should tell you if your love is true. A kiss should not be needed. When you are in the presence of the one you love, you should feel all aquiver inside and out. Then yes, I would guess when you kiss him, you could well soar into the air, float on the clouds." She shook her head. "That I would not know, but I would think the love should come before the kiss."

Venetia thought Delphine must be mistaken. And what would Delphine know of love anyway. Numerous men had paid her court, but she had never given any of them any encouragement. At least not until this evening. She would swear, Delphine had actually been flirting with Malcolm Phelps. The youth was certainly handsome enough, and well-spoken, but surely Delphine could not be attracted to a youth not yet finished with his years at the University.

Rubbing her chin and pursing her lips, Venetia ran the evening back through her mind. Supper was served in the hall. A trestle table had been set up to accommodate all the guests. She had been seated between Tuftwick and Sidonie Hayward. Delphine, across the table, had been seated between Phelps and Madigan, and though Delphine had seemed to be enjoying Madigan's company when riding beside him, she seemed almost to ignore him at the table and directed the majority of her attention on Phelps. Certainly Phelps carried on a constant flirt with her. He was full of brags about the coming tournament on the morrow. Delphine praised him and promised she would cheer him on. Such behavior was not normal for Delphine.

Her thoughts shifted to Madigan. She had thought him in love with her, but he had paid her little heed since he kissed her. Oh, she had seen him gaze longingly at her a time or two, but not since they had started on their journey. Riding beside Delphine, he had been more jocular than she could remember him being in the norm. He had been ever present to hand Delphine down from her horse. And this evening, did she not know better, she could swear he was jealous of Phelps. But surely that could not be. Unless he was beginning to form a tender for Delphine. Oh, but that would never do. Or would it? Madigan was landless, penniless, but he was a member of the gentry. He was quite handsome. Berold would never approve of him as a suitable match for Delphine, but then Berold could not tell Delphine whom she could or could not marry.

Venetia smiled. Would it not be wonderful if Madigan were to fall in love with Delphine and Delphine with him! Then, if she and Tuftwick were to marry, Delphine, with her fortune, could buy a home near to Tuftwick Hall, and she would not have to be separated from her dear cousin. Oh, it would be so perfect! In her excitement, she squeaked.

"Be you in need of something, milady?" Bethel asked from the near-by trundle bed.

"I am sorry, Bethel. Did I waken you? All is fine. I am but pleased we will not be setting out on our trip tomorrow. I am glad of the respite, and my pleasure bubbled over."

"Yes, I too, am glad of the respite. But you must get your sleep."

"I will. Good-night, again."

"Good-night, milady."

Venetia knew she needed to go to sleep, but how when she was so excited at the prospect of a romance between Madigan and Delphine. She wondered if she could do anything to encourage either of them. She would have to think on it. In the meantime, she had her own romance to forward. Somehow she had to get Tuftwick to kiss her. Even did she have to ask him to do so.

※　※　※　※

Madigan rose early. He had slept poorly and was eager to get out of bed. Tuftwick still slept heavily, so he was careful to move quietly in the dimly lit room. It was not yet dawn, but the predawn glow seeping in through a crack between the window curtains cast enough light for him to find his clothes and quietly don them. After tugging on his boots, he tiptoed to the door and slipped out. The corridor, lit by sconces, was empty, but he could hear faint noises coming from the hall downstairs. Servants would be up, readying the hall for the day's activities.

Sir Hammet's neighbor, Lord Rigdale had sent back word that he and the two youths he was fostering would be delighted to come to a tournament. He also had a guest, a Sir Milton Flynn, who expressed an interest in joining in the sport. After the tournament they would have dinner, and after that, dancing, could Sir Hammet entice a couple of his more musically talented tenants to leave their fields to play for them.

Madigan could not remember when he had last used his sword. It was naught but ornamentation for the most part. Once or twice he had needed to draw it when they were robbing Cromwellians, but that was rare, and he had not used it. D'Arcy always wanted them to avoid violence if possible. In the three years since they began their clandestine path as highwaymen, they had, to Madigan's knowledge, killed no one, though they had been forced to wound four men. Most of the servants, from outriders to coachmen, seemed none too willing to forfeit their lives to save their master's purse.

As he made his way down to the more brightly lit hall, Madigan contemplated his situation. He had no home to call his own. He had no skills beyond those of a cavalry man, or highwayman. Did D'Arcy tire of leading his band of highwaymen and decide to join his brother and the king in Europe, Madigan wondered what would then be his options. He supposed he too could go to Europe and join one of the armies there. Europe always had a war going on. But he really had no desire to go to war. He had no real taste for killing. Or for being killed.

"Good morning, sir," one of the servants said, stopping in his chore of sprinkling fresh flowers amongst the reeds on the hall's stone floor. "Do you wish to break your fast, a buffet will soon be set up in the dining chamber." He pointed to a door leading off the hall.

"Thank you," Madigan answered. "Has the rain stopped, I plan to check on my horse."

"Aye, the rain has stopped and the sun has come out. Looks to be a glorious day, sir."

"Splendid." Madigan flipped the man a ha'penny and wished it could be more, but his own purse was none too plump. The lack of coin could easily be remedied did he accept Delphine's offer of marriage. Exiting the hall, he stopped to watch the sun begin its rise over a distant hill. It did look like it would be a glorious day. Not a cloud in the sky for as far as he could see. The sun would help dry the roads. He wished they were setting out immediately. He really had no desire to be part of the tournament. How he would hate to be defeated by the boastful Phelps. He really had no good reason to dislike the youth, and yet he could not like him.

Delphine seemed to like Phelps. She had spent the previous evening laughing at his quips and admiring his floundering attempts at poetry. Why had she given him so much attention? She said she needed to marry someone. But surely she would not consider Phelps. Striking off toward the stables, he clamped his hand on his sword hilt. No! Delphine could not marry Phelps. She was too superior to the likes of that whelp.

Upon entering the stables, Madigan saw Noah Purdy examining Delphine's horse's legs. When the footman straightened, he noted Madigan watching him. "Good morning to you, Mister Madigan. Looks to be a fine day for your tournament games. Mayhap the tournament can even be held out of doors."

Madigan nodded then asked, "What do you look for on Mistress Lotterby's horse?"

Purdy shrugged, his deep set eyes looking directly into Madigan's eyes. "Anything and everything," he said. "I must ever be alert. I check all the horses and the coaches and wagons. When we travel, 'tis better does nothing go amiss."

"You have been with Mistress Lotterby many years, I understand."

"Aye, her grandfather charged me with her care. Before that, I took care of her father." Purdy chuckled. "Mister Lotterby was ever intent on forwarding the Torrington enterprises, especially after his wife died. 'Tis not for me to say, but I believe staying busy helped ease his pain. He felt the loss of his wife deeply. He traveled from the salt mines, to the Liverpool warehouses, to the Torrington ships. He called on various merchants and farms across Cheshire. I accompanied him and made sure he arrived at his appropriate destination. He was not a good one for directions. His mind would be on accounts and transactions, and he would pay little heed to where he was going."

Cocking his head to one side, Madigan questioned, "Then, 'twas not until after his death you were charged with watching after Mistress Lotterby in the same manner as you watched after her father?"

"Aye. And I would give my life for her should it be necessary."

"Such loyalty is admirable."

"'Tis owed her. My father was secretary to Mister Torrington, Mistress Lotterby's grandfather. Ezra Torrington took note of my brother and me. He made certain we both attended a good school, and when my brother Benjamin showed promise with the books, he paid for him to attend Oxford and then sent him on to Gray's Inn. Benjamin is now an attorney with the firm of Filmarr, Eadwyn, Norwell, and Thorndyke

102

which represents the Torrington businesses. Benjamin is directly responsible for overseeing Mistress Lotterby's estates and assets."

Frowning, Purdy admitted, "I had no love of schooling. I had no wish to sit in an office. But Benjamin is now a gentleman, married a baronet's daughter, has two children and another on the way. He has a fine house and sits down to dinner at a table with a white linen tablecloth. I am proud of his accomplishments, but I envy him not. As I said, I would ne'er be good at poking at figures and writing out legal documents. I like being outdoors."

"I cannot blame you there," Madigan said, thinking that accept for his birth into the ranks of the gentry, he was little different than Purdy. "I cannot think I would be much good in an office either. My schooling, too, is limited. I learned to ride and shoot and fence, then got to put them to use fighting for Charles I, but I have had little use for them since. Though I was once good with the sword, I doubt I will fare well in the tournament."

"Might be well you should get back into practice, sir. You, too, are now charged with protecting Mistress Lotterby. I fear more attempts at abduction. Even here, we must be watchful."

Drawing his brows together, Madigan shook his head in surprise. "Here! On the road, yes, but here?"

"At a dance hosted by the Thorndykes in Liverpool, Mistress Lotterby was dancing with a Sir Elias Bannon. 'Twas summer, the doors to the garden were open. Sir Elias, after the dance ended, led Mistress Lotterby toward an open door. Two men rushed in the door and swooped up Mistress Lotterby. Sir Elias blocked attempts by various men in the room to rush to Mistress Lotterby's rescue, and the abductors raced toward a coach waiting outside the gate. They, of course, never made the gate. Anker and I had been alert to them from the moment the coach drove up and the two men furtively advanced onto the Thorndyke grounds."

"Gramercy!" Madigan knew of the most recent attempt to abduct Delphine, but that an attempt had been made while she attended a dance at a respected attorney's home shocked him. "What of the two men and this Sir Elias, what happened to them."

"Sir Elias denied any part in the abduction attempt, and as his bungling antics could not be proven to be malicious interference, no charges were brought against him. The two men we caught were charged with trespassing, a more serious offence than abduction in the eyes of the court. I believe transportation was their lot. Sadly, they never divulged the name of the person who hired them. The coachman was never caught. He drove away when he saw the fate of his two henchmen. We had no proof he nor the others were hired by Sir Elias. Consequently, Bannon is still welcome in most homes in Liverpool."

Madigan pushed his hat up from his brow. "After hearing this tale, I believe you are right. I will tell Lord Tuftwick, we must be more alert to all around us. And mayhap this tournament will be a good practice for the both of us."

Chapter 15

Her gaze riveted on the match before her, her pulse pounding in her brain, Delphine watched the final two contestants in the fencing tournament, Maddy and Phelps. The day was so beautiful, Sir Hammet had decided to hold the tournament in his courtyard. Benches and chairs were brought outside. Servants hovering near-by, ready to attend Sir Hammet's guests, were also intent on the contests. The two youths Lord Rigdale was fostering were the first ones eliminated, but that had surprised no one. The slightly rotund Lord Rigdale and his guest, Sir Milton Flynn, were next to be eliminated. Tuftwick defeated Berold, but then lost to Maddy.

Now Maddy and Phelps were locked in a fierce battle. Delphine hoped Maddy would win. She had praised Phelps when he defeated his previous competitors, but had said nothing to Maddy. Was Maddy wondering why she was ignoring him? Was he wondering why she was having a flirt with Phelps? She noted Maddy eyeing her whenever she talked to Phelps. Or to Sir Milton Flynn.

There was something about Flynn she could not like. He held her hand a tad too long when introduced to her. His eyes traveled up and down her in an impudent manner she found offensive. He was not an unattractive man, neither was he attractive. She guessed him to be in his mid to late thirties. He had broad shoulders and had not yet developed a paunch around his belly, but his gray eyes were hard and cold, his mouth small, and his thin lips pursed in a pompous way when he spoke. To Delphine, his blond mustache and pointed goatee gave him a fiendish look. Indeed, she could not like him, yet throughout the morning, she felt his gaze upon her. She was glad she was seated between Venetia and Phillida, and he could not wedge his way into a seat beside her. When they went into dinner after the tournament, she planned to tell Lady Phelps she wished not to be seated anywhere near Sir Milton.

A lunge, a thrust, a parry. A gasp caught in Delphine's throat. Maddy had barely blocked a superbly executed attack. But both men were tiring. By rights, they should be tired. They had both fought several duels before being pitted against each other. Phelps was younger, quicker, but he was not as tall as Maddy, and had not the same reach. Maddy's broad shoulders and sturdy legs also gave him an advantage over the trimmer Phelps. But it was the look on Maddy's face that told Delphine the man she loved so desperately was determined to win the match.

Then Maddy dropped back, seemed to stumble. Phelps pressed him, his blade hitting punishing blows against Maddy's. Maddy looked to be weakening under the onslaught. With each step Maddy took backward, Phelps grew bolder and advanced more and more aggressively. A triumphant smile lighting his face, Phelps raised his sword on high to come down with the winning blow. At the same time, Maddy straightened and brought his sword up with a powerful swing. The ringing clash of metal on metal sang through the air, and Phelps's sword, knocked from his hand, flew through the air to land with a clatter on the cobble stone courtyard. In the next instant, Maddy's sword point was at Phelps's throat.

For a moment silence held reign, then Tuftwick burst out with a cheer. More cheers followed as Maddy lowered his sword, and gave Phelps a slight bow. Phelps, his face red, lips thinned, and eyes watery, returned the bow before walking over to pick up his sword.

"A remarkable display of swordsmanship," Sir Hammet said, coming over to pound Maddy on the shoulder.

"Indeed," Berold said, joining them. "In that last flurry, you could see the difference in age and experience over youthful exuberance." He looked at Phelps. "This will be a good learning experience for you. Never be over confident. Maddy looked tired, but he was tiring you out. By the time you thought you could land the final blow, you had not the strength left to match the blow he brought up against you. I remember well, 'twas a lesson my father drilled into us, did he not Maddy? Never under estimate your opponent." Clamping a hand on Phelps's shoulder, he added, "Nevertheless, well played, the both of you."

Delphine saw Phelps glance in her direction, and she gave him a bright smile, but inside, she was near bursting with pride for Maddy.

106

He used not only skill, but wit to defeat his younger opponent. She could not help but feel a little sorry for Phelps. He had wanted to impress her. Perhaps she had been unfair to seem to be encouraging him. Now, did she try to discourage him, he would think 'twas because he lost the match. That would not do. She would have to continue their flirt until she departed the next day. Oh, but she did so hope she would have a chance to dance with Maddy this evening. She longed for the touch of his hand on hers, longed to see his smile that lit up his dark eyes.

Sir Hammet called for everyone's attention. "My wife says 'tis time we all refreshed ourselves and changed for dinner." He turned to his guests. "Lord Rigdale, let me show you and your youths and Sir Milton where you may wash and change." He waved his arm. "I think the rest of you can find your way back to your rooms."

Pleased with the morning's event, Delphine linked arms with Venetia, and they headed back into the hall, but in glancing back at Maddy, her gaze instead fell on Flynn. His hard eyes glittering, he smiled at her in a way that sent a chill racing up her spine. Forcing herself to return his smile before turning back around, she hoped she could find some way not to have to dance with him that evening. She decided, at first chance, she would discuss her feelings with Venetia. She might need her cousin's help in avoiding the man.

※　※　※　※

Stripped down to his bare skin, Madigan sloshed warm water over himself before taking the rough soap bar and applying it to his under arms then his torso. Gads, but he reeked. He would not be fit company for the ladies unless he could wash away his stench. That last match against Phelps had not only been fatiguing, it had made him sweat profusely.

"Here, now," Tuftwick said. "You are not the only one in need of that soap." Like Madigan, he was stripped down to bare skin and had just finished sloshing himself with water from the white glazed crockery bowl on the table by the door. Hoping not to soil the floor, both men stood on towels, but some water landed on the flooring. "Do I not smell sweet enough, Lady Venetia may not let me near her. And can I not get near her, I cannot court her."

Madigan passed the soap to his friend, but he could not face him. Any discussion of Venetia hurt too much, and he could not let Tuftwick see the pain in his eyes. He knew he could never have Venetia himself, so he hoped his friend could win her love. At the same time, seeing them together was a constant source of anguish.

"What think you of young Phelps?" Tuftwick asked, placing the soap back on its dish.

Using a cloth to wash away the soap, Madigan said, "He fought well."

"No, I mean what do you think of the way he has been flirting with Mistress Lotterby? And for that matter, she with him?"

Madigan was not certain what he thought, but he had known he could not let Phelps win the tournament. He had wanted to show Delphine that Phelps was but a youthful braggart. "I think, mayhap, Sir Hammet would like to see his son marry such a wealthy heiress, but I cannot think Mistress Lotterby has any real interest in the youth."

"I think you must be right. Lady Venetia has naught but praise for her cousin. She says Mistress Lotterby is ever kind to everyone. Must be she is but being kind to Phelps. But what think you of Sir Milton? Before the tournament, he, too, seemed most attentive to Mistress Lotterby."

"Did he? I paid little heed to the man," Madigan answered, but he had. He had seen Flynn take Delphine's hand and hold it, to his way of thinking, much too long, but he had seen nothing in the man that would make Delphine show him any special attention. The man was cold. His smile never reached his eyes. No, Delphine would not be drawn to Flynn as she seemed to be drawn to the merry Phelps.

After he and Tuftwick dried off and wiped up the floor, Madigan donned his only other set of clothes. When they went marauding with D'Arcy, they took but one change of clothes – the change that served as their disguise, jaunty members of the gentry. Having such a limited wardrobe meant he and Tuftwick had needed to borrow shirts and hose from Berold in order to accompany Berold's party to Grasmere. Hayward had needed to borrow an entire wardrobe, he having arrived at Harp's Ridge dressed as a woman. Fortunately, explaining Hayward's apparel to the Lotterby servants had not proven to be a problem, as only

Delphine's footman, Anker, Berold's valet, and Chapman had seen to getting Hayward into the house, up to his room, and out of the gown. The gown he had worn had then disappeared. When at last Hayward was able to be up and around, had anyone noted the clothing he wore looked like clothing they had seen Lord Grasmere wear, no one said anything.

Being naught but a yeoman, Hayward at first complained of the constraints of a gentleman's clothing, but he adjusted and was playing his role as a member of the gentry well. Sidonie, born into the ranks of the gentry, a daughter of a baronet, guided her husband when necessary. Now that her husband had recovered enough to travel, and her baby was strong and healthy, Sidonie showed every sign of fully enjoying her adventure. She and Lady Grasmere seemed to have developed a comradery, and the dark eyes Madigan had seen racked in agony from her labor pangs now glowed with joy and excitement. After what she had been through, she deserved to be pampered and spoiled. Hayward was a lucky man to have such a wife.

"This would seem to be the best we can do," Tuftwick said, adjusting the collar at his neck. "Shall we venture downstairs?"

Madigan nodded. "Aye. I am ready. I do hope dinner will be on the table. I am starved."

"Well you should be after that swordsmanship display. You did yourself proud, dear friend. Lady Venetia was much impressed."

"Was she?" Madigan could not keep the tremor of excitement Tuftwick's words gave him from his voice. To his relief, Tuftwick seemed not to notice.

"She was," Tuftwick answered, "as was Mistress Lotterby. I know she is having a flirt with young Phelps, but she applauded with sheer joy when you won."

Madigan could not think why, but the fact that Delphine had applauded him, pleased him. Finally, he said, "'Twas kind of her."

"I am quite certain I heard her say, 'Boldly done, Maddy, boldly done. Called you Maddy, she did."

"Aye, I did so give her leave as we are riding together every day."

"Mmmm, I wish I could get Lady Venetia to be less formal with me," Tuftwick said, then slapped Madigan on the back. "Here we stand jawing, and you are starved. Let us go to table."

※ ※ ※ ※

Wiping her mouth with her napkin, Venetia glanced across the table at her cousin. Delphine might seem to be enjoying her flirt with Phelps, but Venetia had seen her gaze fly down the table to land on Madigan more than once during the extended meal. The Phelpses were feasting their guests royally, and Sir Hammet had arranged to have music and dancing after the dinner ended. Venetia knew her job was to do her best to keep Sir Milton away from Delphine. That Delphine found the man cold and unpleasant was not surprising. Venetia could not think him pleasant either.

Delphine had enlisted Lady Phelps's aid in seating Sir Milton at the far end of the table from her. No doubt Lady Phelps had been pleased to do so. Less competition for her son. And certainly Phelps was taking advantage of his place beside Delphine. Ignoring his mother, seated to his left, he concentrated all his attention on attempting to amuse and impress Delphine. That meant Tuftwick, seated on Lady Phelps' right, was forced to devote much of his attention to Lady Phelps and not Venetia, but Venetia cared not. She was enjoying a flirt of her own with one of Lord Rigdale's fostered youths. Mayhap did Tuftwick get a tad jealous, she might be able to get that kiss she wanted from him.

Gads, but she was longing to kiss Tuftwick. She was beginning to believe she truly was falling in love with him. When he grinned at her in a playful fashion, her heart did a little flip. He looked so alluring. And he would lean in so close to her when giving her compliments, she would be certain he meant to kiss her. But no. He but tempted her. Teased her. Would serve him right did she refuse his kiss when at last he did attempt to kiss her. But she knew she would not refuse his kiss. No, she meant to entice him into kissing her.

Seeing Sir Hammet rise, she turned her attention to him as did others at the table. He announced the meal at an end, and once the table had been cleared and removed, they would have dancing. "My musicians be not highly skilled, but they can pick a merry tune or a ballad on the viol and lute that make fair to dancing."

Venetia followed the other women back up to their rooms where they would refresh themselves before the next festivities started. "Do you remember to keep Sir Milton from me," Delphine said, grabbing Venetia's arm.

"I will do my best, cousin. And I will ask Lord Tuftwick to help. I, too, find Sir Milton unappealing. His eyes are too bold. I cannot like the way he looks at me. Almost as though he was seeing me in my chemise."

"Yes," Delphine answered. "That is how I feel. I fear he may be another after my fortune, though why he would imagine I would be interested in him, I cannot think."

Venetia laughed. "I do believe some men have an elevated view of themselves. Sir Milton falls into that category." Lifting the latch on the door, she looked back at Delphine. "Does he pester you more than you could wish, you can always plead the headache and return to your room."

"I have thought of that, but then I would but sit here and sulk and miss all the fun and the music." Giving Venetia a kiss on the cheek, she said, "Do your best for me, dear one," and headed on to her own room.

Venetia entered her room to find Bethel waiting to help her ready herself for the dance. She looked forward to dancing with Tuftwick. But she hoped to get him out into the garden and somehow manage that kiss.

☙ ☙ ☙ ☙

Phillida was enjoying the day. She had laughed at Berold's attempts at swordsmanship, as he laughed at himself. He was much out of practice. But she had been surprised at how competent Tuftwick, and particularly, Madigan still were. She supposed the difference was in ever having to be alert. It kept the body agile.

What grabbed her attention, though, was seeing the enthusiasm Delphine displayed when Madigan defeated Phelps. She had thought Delphine enjoying her flirt with the handsome young Phelps. She had even started to wonder if she should encourage the flirtation. Mayhap it could lead to an eventual betrothal. Delphine needed to marry. Phelps might be young, but he was bright and witty, and though but the son of a baronet, he would one day inherit Beaulieu Hall. It was an impressive estate despite the fines Sir Hammet had been forced to pay to buy the estate back after its sequestration. With Delphine's wealth, the house could be made more comfortable. But was Delphine's flirtation with Phelps nothing more than a cover for her real feelings? Could Delphine be interested in, nay, could she be in love with Madigan?

If so, it would never do. Berold would never condone the match. Madigan was of good stock. He was handsome and had good bearing, but he was penniless. Yes, she had hoped to find him a wealthy widow to wed. Had written to a couple of her dear friends, expounding his virtues, but what might do for an unknown widow would not be suitable for Delphine.

Determined to keep an eye on her husband's headstrong cousin, Phillida watched Delphine at the dinner table. Though Delphine continued her flirt with Phelps, her eyes often glanced down the table to where Madigan sat. And when the dancing started, though Delphine danced with all the men, she definitely sparkled when in Madigan's company.

Phillida could not determine what Madigan's feelings toward Delphine might be. She thought him in love with Venetia, but knew him wise enough to know he could never marry her. But might he consider marrying Delphine? He seemed to be treating her more as a friend, or even a sister, but such feelings could change. Delphine was an attractive woman. Not as beautiful as Venetia, but then who was. And for a penniless gentleman, Delphine's wealth would make her even more attractive. The situation would bear watching.

Chapter 16

Delphine was glad Lord Rigdale and his entourage, which included Sir Milton, planned to leave shortly after the dancing, Lord Rigdale choosing not to stay for supper, but wanting to return to his home before the sun disappeared. "'Twas a fine display of swordsmanship this day," Lord Rigdale professed. "A good experience for my foster youths." He turned to Lady Phelps and took her hand. "As always, Lady Phelps, you set a fine table."

"Thank you, Lord Rigdale," Lady Phelps answered with a slight bow of her head. "We are ever honored when you attend us."

Out of politeness, Delphine remained present as the guests prepared to depart, but she hung back, hoping she would not have to endure another lingering interlude with Sir Milton fondling her hand. To her disgruntlement, her luck abandoned her. Sir Milton sought her out. Her skin crawled when he took her hand and raised it to his lips, but before his lips could caress her fingertips, Maddy slapped a hand on Sir Milton's shoulder, forcing him to release his grip.

A wide grin spreading across his face, Maddy proclaimed, "'Twas a pleasure watching your swordsmanship, Sir Milton. At one point, I was certain you would defeat Tuftwick."

What else he might say to Sir Milton, she had no interest in knowing. She but wanted to escape. Hurrying up the stairs, she stood in the dimly lit corridor awaiting the departure sounds to disappear. A smile played at her lips. Maddy had saved her. He must have been watching her, or he would not have seen Sir Milton approach her. But she questioned whether he had rescued her because he realized she found Sir Milton disgusting and wanted to help her – or was he mayhap jealous? Did he think Sir Milton might be a rival for her hand. Either way, it meant he had some kind of feelings for her.

With Venetia and Tuftwick's help, she had managed to avoid all but one dance with Sir Milton. Each time Sir Milton attempted to approach her, Venetia stepped in front of him with some kind of question. She would only release him when the music started, and Delphine was dancing with one of the other men. As the men greatly outnumbered the women – five women to ten men – she had never lacked for a partner eager to take a whirl with her. The two beardless youths, and Phelps had been ever at the ready to lead her onto the floor. Lady Phelps, Phillida, and Sidonie, as Mistress Hayward insisted Delphine and Venetia address her, had never lacked for partners either, but after several rousing dances, Lady Phelps excused herself, saying she would join her husband and Lord Rigdale on a cushioned bench – both older men retiring after only a couple of dances.

The musicians' tune repertory being limited, all the dances were country dances but for a couple of ballads. Delphine preferred the country dances as they limited the contact she had with her partners – though she would have enjoyed a more stately, processional dance with Maddy. During her dance with Sir Milton, as they wove in and out of formation, conversation was limited, and she managed to turn his compliments aside or redirect them to Lady Phelps or Phillida. She had no wish for him to think she fancied him or his flattery.

She owed Venetia and Tuftwick a favor for their help in keeping Sir Milton from her. Hearing the servants bustling in the hall, she hurried back down the stairs. Catching Venetia's hand, she gave her a kiss on the cheek. "You were wonderful. I cannot thank you enough for keeping that jackanapes from me."

Venetia squeezed her hand, and said, "I was glad I had Lord Tuftwick at my side. I would not have wanted to confront him on my own. Did he know what I was about, I cannot say, but the last time I stepped in his path, he near bared his teeth at me."

"Well, I owe you. I thought mayhap, as the sun has not yet set, you and I and Lord Tuftwick, and perhaps Mister Madigan might take a stroll in the gardens."

Venetia grinned and slanted her eyes. "Oh, I do think that a fine idea. Let us suggest it."

They found Tuftwick and Madigan with Berold and Hayward. The four men were discussing their plans for the next day. Berold was hoping for an early start. "We will be up and ready," Venetia promised, "do you release Lord Tuftwick and Mister Madigan to us now. We are wishing to see Sir Hammet's gardens. I understand Lady Phelps is most proud of them."

"Yes, my wife is rightly proud of them," Sir Hammet said, joining the men. "I am having tables set up that we may indulge in a game of cards or draughts while we await supper, would you be interested in a game, Grasmere? My wife is retiring to her solar with Lady Grasmere and Mistress Hayward. They feel in need of a rest after all the excitement." He looked at Venetia and Delphine. "But you two still look bright and hearty. I cannot but think you would indeed enjoy a stroll in the gardens. I will tell Malcolm to join you. He can show you about. And then Madigan, here, can make up a foursome for a card game." Turning, he called to his son.

Delphine's heart dropped. She glanced at Maddy. She thought he, too, looked disappointed, but the look vanished, and he assured Sir Hammet he would enjoy a game of cards. Phelps, looking pleased, sidled up to Delphine. "A stroll in the gardens is just what we need after such a busy, but entertaining day."

Agreeing, she took his proffered arm, and they led the way out a back entrance and down a set of steps to a graveled path making its way through topiary shrubbery toward a fountain with an urn tipped partially on its side. Benches were situated along the path, and Delphine abruptly sat down on one. "Oh," she said. "I have a pebble in my shoe."

Taking great pains to remove the non-existent stone, she said, "These dance slippers are not made for walking on this gravel." She looked up at Venetia. "I would advise you to set off upon the grass, dear, do you think to continue your stroll. I fear, I must sit here a bit. My foot does pain me."

"My poor dear," Venetia said, the concern on her face looking real. "Might we help you back inside?"

Delphine shook her head. "No, I but wish to sit here. I have no doubt my foot will soon feel better. If not, Mister Phelps will help me hobble back inside." Glancing off toward the fountain, she added. "Or, I can call to Purdy, and he can carry me in." As usual Purdy and Anker had exited before her, most likely had searched the gardens, and now stood watch on the off chance someone might again attempt to abduct her. Gads, but she longed to get married. She was so tired of constantly having to be on the alert. If Maddy would but consent to wed her, she would insist the ceremony be held immediately, and hopefully she would soon be with child. That thought brought a flush to her cheeks, but she covered it by looking back down at her foot and urging Venetia, "Go have your stroll, but do be careful not to scuff up any pebbles."

"Do you insist, my dear. I am in need of a stroll before supper. Thankfully after our feast today, Lady Phelps has promised a simple supper for this evening."

Phelps laughed. "Enjoy your walk and do work up your appetite. Mother may say the supper will be simple, but she will not want to be thought miserly, so I would count on the meal being substantial."

Venetia's dimples dented her cheeks and her soft rustling laugh floated out over the still air. "Very well." She took Tuftwick's arm. "Come, let us have our walk. Does Lady Phelps put another spread before us, we must do it justice that we may not offend her."

Tuftwick also chuckled. "As you wish Lady Venetia. But do mind your step."

Leaving the path to cut across the cropped grass, the pair headed for the path, and Delphine looked up at Phelps. "Do sit, Mister Phelps. I am straining my neck looking up at you."

Appearing happy to be invited to sit beside her, Phelps seated himself. "I am sorry I am not able to show you the garden. Or the summer house." Leaning forward, he pointed toward a peaked roof pavilion at the farthest corner of the gardens. "During the summers, before the war, we would oft use it as a banqueting house. At least, Mother and Father did. I fear I was at that time considered too young to join the adults." He shrugged. "Now I am an adult, many of our friends, like Father, are confined to their parishes. We have to make do with local parish gentry and Lord Rigdale." His eyes capturing hers, he said, "'Tis always a treat for us that each year Lord Grasmere deigns to stay with us as he travels to and from his parish confinements."

"Ah, Mister Phelps, 'tis we who are grateful your family extends us such a resplendent welcome each year. How pleasant that you could be home from university during our visit." She was pleased he had been home. She had hopes his flirtation with her had made Maddy jealous.

"Trinity term begins soon, so I must be returning to Oxford, but when it ends, I will again return home. I expect to be here when you are on your way back to Harp's Ridge as the Michaelmas Term will not begin until late October. This will be my last year at the University."

"Will you miss the University life when you have completed your studies?"

Shaking his head, he stated adamantly, "Nay. With the Puritans running things, I cannot say it has been particularly pleasant. Not at all as Father described it when he went there." Phelps made a face. "Good rousing fun, Father had, but the Puritans have banned all forms of sport. I will have my education, but sadly, I will not get my Grand Tour of Europe. Father says we cannot afford it. 'Tis a bad state we Royalists are in."

Delphine nodded sympathetically. "'Tis a bad state. We can but be thankful the Puritans allowed those who fought for the King to pay a fine and receive their land back. They could have confiscated all the estates as they did the King's and the Church's estates."

"I suppose you are right." For a moment he looked glum, but then he brightened. "Does your foot feel better, we could go for that stroll now."

"It still pains me a bit," she lied. "I wonder, might you give me your arm. I should like to go back inside. I am feeling more tired than I thought, and I am also thirsty."

Springing to his feet, Phelps offered her his arm. "'Tis no wonder you are tired. You danced near every dance am I not mistaken."

"You are not mistaken," she said, rising. "But I could not have enjoyed myself more. Your father's musicians played well."

Pursing his lips, he waggled his head back and forth. "Their skills are sadly lacking, I am thinking. They are much better to suited to their own class, but then, they are better than nothing. When I was young, Father had real musicians on staff."

Taking Phelps' arm and walking with a slight limp, she said, "So many things you have had to miss out on, Mister Phelps. However, we must not give up hope that someday we will see the return of our monarch."

"I pray you may be right, but I fear I hold out little hope." He paused. "Are you able to manage to walk back up the steps?"

"Oh, yes, with your strong arm to lean upon, I shall manage quite well." Phelps's spirits had drooped, and she meant to give him an ego boost.

Her words worked, for he beamed down at her. "I shall not fail you, Mistress Lotterby."

Once inside, she saw the men were playing at cards, but a draughts table had been set up, and she suggested she and Phelps should have a game. He readily accepted, and soon they were seated at the table with mugs of ale near to hand. They had to explain why their walk had been cut short to Berold and Sir Hammet. Both men harrumphed and returned to their game. Delphine thought Maddy had looked sympathetic, but she could have imagined his look of concern. Still, at least she was in the same room with Maddy instead of wandering around outside with Phelps.

She did hope Venetia would at last get the kiss she craved. Certainly, she and Tuftwick would have time to themselves with no one around. Even Purdy and Anker had come back inside. Wherever she went, they went.

Oh, Maddy, she wanted to scream. Marry me, marry me!

❀ ❀ ❀ ❀

Venetia felt like stamping her foot and demanding Tuftwick explain why he would not kiss her. They were alone in the summer house, far from any prying eyes, yet he made no advances. Delphine had done a superb job of giving her a chance to be alone with Tuftwick, but he was not taking advantage of the situation. Oh, he had been ever so solicitous, making sure she was careful where she stepped, holding her arm firmly, but gently, when he helped her over a low hedge. He told her more about his plans for his home. Told her he would not forever continue as a highwayman. And he was a good listener. He made appropriate comments to the things she told him about the various sights she had seen in London and about her visit with her dear friend, Clarinda.

They talked about the Phelpses' garden, and when she admired the fountain, he told her he could not think why he could not have a fountain put in the garden at Tuftwick Hall. "Not that the grounds have much of a garden. But that can be changed," he promised, looking so deep into her eyes, she had been so certain he meant to kiss her. But no. No kiss.

"Where are your thoughts, my dear Lady Venetia," he asked, bringing her out of her reverie.

She had been gazing sightlessly out at the garden, but she turned back around and looked up at him. "I was wondering …" But she stopped herself. She wanted to ask him why he would not kiss her, but she could not bring herself to ask him to kiss her. He had to want to kiss her.

"Yes," he said, "you were wondering?"

"I was wondering if you and Mister Madigan might be staying at Knightswood for a while, or if you would be off on another raid somewhere."

He moved closer to her. "Would you like us to stay, Lady Venetia?"

Not looking at him, she shrugged. "You are pleasant company."

Putting his hands on her shoulders, he gently turned her to face him. "If it would help me to win your heart, indeed, I would stay." He cocked his head to one side. "I wonder might I ask a favor of you."

She widened her eyes. Was he going to ask permission to kiss her? "Of course, you may ask a favor, Lord Tuftwick."

"Would you be offended, did I ask you to call me by my given name, Henry. I have been called Tuftwick since my father died, and I became Baron. I would like very much to hear my given name on your sweet lips."

His request was not what she hoped for, yet she could understand it. A given name was so much more intimate than a title. "Yes, I would be honored to call you Henry. But likewise, you must call me Venetia. We have, after all, known each other for a good many years. I believe such formalities as titles can be put aside between friends."

The light in his eyes danced. "You have made me a happy man – Venetia." He hesitated before addressing her by just her given name. "But I hope I will soon be more than a friend to you. Can you tell me, think you I have a chance of winning your love."

Raising her chin, she slanted her eyes to one side. "I would say you have a chance – Henry." You would have a better chance did you kiss me, she thought, but he simply stood their grinning his absurdly handsome grin. She did love his brightness. She had no doubt he had his low moods, but she had yet to see him doleful.

He caught her hands and brought them to his chest. "Could you but feel the patter of my heart that your words have provoked. And to hear my name said so sweetly, you have raised my spirits more than I can tell you. But come, 'tis time we return. I would not have your brother thinking I have taken liberties with you."

He turned before he could see the frown she bestowed on him. She should tell him Berold would be pleased did he take liberties. She knew her brother was hoping she would marry Henry. Falling into step beside her too circumspect beau, she sighed and wondered what it would take to make him kiss her. But until he kissed her, she would not consent to marry him, or even admit she was falling in love with him.

Chapter 17

The sky was blue, the ground was dry, and Madigan was happy to be back in the saddle. He had not enjoyed the sojourn at Beaulieu. Yes, the Phelpses had been all that graciousness could demand. Yes, the food had been delicious, the bed comfortable, but he had been irritated the entire stay. He told himself 'twas the pain in his heart causing his irritation. Seeing Venetia and Tuftwick together, walking, talking, laughing, cozying up when they talked in whispers at the table or before the hearth after supper.

He had danced one dance with Venetia, but that had caused him more torment than joy. He found next to nothing to talk to her about. Not that the rousing dances lent much time for conversation. Yet when he danced with Delphine, he had been full of tidbits he wanted to impart to her in the brief moments when they stood next to each other before they went flying off following the lead of another couple. He had managed only two dances with Delphine. Phelps and Rigdale's foster youths had monopolized her time as Tuftwick had monopolized Venetia's.

What surprised him was the anger that built up in him when Delphine danced with Flynn. There was something about the man he could not like. Flynn was a good swordsman. Naught but a slip of his foot prevented him from defeating Tuftwick in their match. Tuftwick had been able to take advantage of Flynn's off balance moment and had swiped Flynn's sword from his hand. Madigan had talked little with Flynn, but he overheard Flynn telling Berold he had been a member of Prince Rupert's cavalry. That might explain some of his arrogance. Rupert and his men were known for their egotistical natures.

But that could not explain his dislike of Sir Milton Flynn. His dislike seemed to stem from Flynn's bold effrontery when introduced to Delphine. Reading the look on Delphine's face, he knew she found the man brazen. Flynn held her hand too long, stared at her under lowered lids in an offensive, measuring manner. The one time Delphine danced with Flynn, he noted she did her best to have as little physical contact with Flynn as possible. When the dance ended, in escaping Flynn's outstretched hand, she had near run over to Phillida. No, Delphine should not have to be subjected to such a man as Flynn.

Madigan admitted he had missed Delphine's company, her bright, entertaining conversation. At Beaulieu, she had been seated next to Phelps at every meal. She seemed to enjoy the youth's company. And why should she not. Phelps was handsome, witty, and of a good family with a promising inheritance. Yet, he was not man enough for Delphine. Madigan doubted a woman of Delphine's intellect could be happy with a youthful braggart who thought to impress her with his sword play and tales of his life at the University.

Hearing a chuckle, Madigan looked over at Delphine. She was smiling at him. "I have been watching you, Maddy. You have gone from a smile to a glare to a frown. Whatever might you be contemplating?"

He offered her a smile in return. "Thoughts do fly on this bright sunny day. I am pleased we are again on the move, but I thought, too, of what your man Purdy has told me. We must ever be on the alert. Too often your safety has been put at risk."

Cocking her head, and glancing at him out of the corners of her eyes, she said, "That is what I have told you, Maddy. I trust you are yet giving my proposition consideration."

He flushed. "The question has been in my thoughts, Delphine." She had insisted, as she called him by his nick name, he must address her by her given name. At least when they were on their own.

"Splendid," she said. "Now to change the subject. I must tell you an amusing story I have just remembered. Concerns the governess attempting to teach Venetia, Clarinda, and me Greek. You remember, I told you of Clarinda?"

"Yes, the daughter of the Wollowchet's steward. I remember Mister Seldon, and I vaguely remember his daughter."

"Of course." She nodded. "Well, I fear our governess was such a poor student of the Greek language herself, that she had a miserable time trying to teach us the alphabet. Eventually, Lady Wollowchet told her to forget Greek, just concentrate on Latin and French. Were Venetia,

122

Clarinda, and I ever grateful about that."

"I can well imagine," Madigan said. "Greek was never a subject I cared for. Fact is, I doubt I even remember much of it any more. Though I can still read Latin and French."

"Funny how Greek is considered important to education. At least to a boy's education. I believe 'tis seldom taught to girls. But anyway, one day we were seated in the garden. 'Twas a wondrously hot day. Mistress Morse, on a bench, was fanning herself while Venetia, Clarinda, and I were seated on the ground, struggling with our sentences. All of a sudden a rat ran right across our feet." She giggled. "Oh, did we scream. Our hornbooks went flying. We tumbled over backwards as the house cat went chasing after the rat. Mistress Morse screeched, the gardener came running, all was chaos. But what made the whole thing so funny was the cat caught that rat. And he was so proud of himself, he thought he had to show off his accomplishment. We had finally calmed down, the gardener had assured himself we were in no danger, and we picked up our books and were resuming our seats when the cat came trotting up with that rat in his mouth."

"You screamed again?" Madigan asked, imaging the young girls settled on the grass, their skirts billowing around them.

Delphine laughed. "Before we knew what was happening, the cat jumped up on the bench and deposited the rat in Mistress Morse's lap. But the rat was not dead! Jumping up, Mistress Morse screeched again, we screamed and fell backward again to avoid the rat which was attempting to escape. So off went the rat and the cat. I know not whether the cat caught the rat a second time, but if he did, he must have decided he would not again present him to us.

"With all the screaming, one of the maids from the house ran out to see what was wrong, the gardener came running back. We girls started laughing uncontrollably, but poor Mistress Morse was in a state. The maid told Lady Wollowchet what happened, and the dear lady came out to comfort Mistress Morse. Wrapping an arm around Mistress Morse, Lady Wollowchet urged her back into the house. She should rest in her room, and we were to have the rest of the day off. Glaring over her shoulder at us, Lady Wollowchet bid us calm ourselves and go take a walk about the grounds. And that we did, greatly enjoying our unexpected holiday."

Grinning and shaking his head, Madigan said, "And did your Mistress Morse recover?"

Delphine chuckled. "Not until the next morning. She had a light supper in her room, and Lady Wollowchet gave her some laudanum so she could sleep. Even so, she was rather pale the next day. Lady Wollowchet made us promise we would be on our best behavior." She looked over at Madigan. "Oh, now you must not laugh. We were good. Poor woman. We were but glad the cat had not dropped that rat in our laps."

"I cannot say I would care to have a rat dropped in my lap either," Madigan said, still grinning. "Not even a dead one." Riding beside Delphine did keep him entertained, making the monotony of the slow moving caravan less tiring. He was used to D'Arcy's fast moving jaunts. They could travel back and forth across the breadth of the island in but a few days did they learn of a particularly lucrative objective.

"Tell me, Maddy," Delphine said, "are you ever scared when you do those robberies?"

He frowned. D'Arcy preferred they not talk about their deeds, yet he trusted Delphine, and he knew D'Arcy had told Berold about some of their adventures. "I cannot help but feel a tenseness when we wait in hiding for our target to arrive. Fear? More wariness, I think. Though I guess I felt some fear at our first robbery.

"To make certain we would not be recognized, though we do wear our kerchiefs over our faces, Nate decided our first robbery should be in Derbyshire. We went to Derby, a large enough town to have any number of inns. We split up with plans to meet on the outskirts of town in the early morning. Our job was to sit in the inn's public room, stay in the shadows, and listen. Most wealthy travelers are Puritans. Many Royalists are confined to their parishes or are struggling to pay their fines and have no money for traveling. We watched the travelers arrive. 'Twas easy to spot those with money. They are given the best rooms and are never forced to share a bed with other travelers. We gleaned what we could of the wealthy travelers. Where they were headed, what road they would be taking, and in the morning when we met after a restless night's sleep on my part, we compared what we learned."

"Is that normal? Staying at the inns?"

"Now, that I should not have told you."

"I would let them cut out my tongue before I would breathe a word of what you tell me, Maddy. I find what you do admirable if mayhap foolhardy."

His chuckle more a scoff, he acknowledged, "Foolhardy, indeed. We have always been so careful. That Caleb should have been shot is unforgiveable. We had but one moment of carelessness, and it near cost Caleb his life."

"What happened?"

He shook his head. "That I cannot tell you, nor can I tell you why I will not tell you." But the memory stung him. They had struck a Cheshire tax collector on his way to London, just after he crossed into Shropshire. His coach was well guarded, but as usual, they had planned their attack well. D'Arcy left no detail to chance. There being a bright full moon, the tax collector had determined he would travel at night. 'Fewer vehicles on the highway,' Preston and Yardley heard the collector tell his guard. His coachman had agreed with him. The guard of six well-armed, experienced soldiers gave D'Arcy minimal pause. But they had encountered larger forces and prevailed. Surprise in the right place at the right time was their foremost tool.

"You were telling me of your first robbery, Maddy." Delphine brought his focus back to the present. "My but your mind is wandering today."

"Yes. Must be the sunshine. Sets one to dreaming."

"Hmmm. By the expression on your face, I would say your dreams were not pleasant."

"Thoughts can often go off in unexpected directions," he said, a brief smile touching his lips. "But let me resume my tale. After conferencing, we selected our first quarry, a woolen merchant traveling from his home in Manchester to London. According to Caleb and Cyril, who stayed at the inn where the merchant lodged, he was a braggart. Had too much to drink, and despite his wife's pleas for him to follow her to bed, he was too much enjoying himself. He had gathered quite the audience. Seems he made his recent fortune buying up sheep off Royalists' confiscated properties. He was on his way to London to select new furnishings for the Royalist manor he had but recently purchased. He was our perfect target."

"He does sound like an unpleasant fellow."

"Our biggest worry was others might attempt to waylay him before we got to him."

"You mean other highwaymen were listening to him."

"Undoubtedly. But others are not as organized as we are. And they are out only for themselves. They are not out to aid our King. But a man who brags or displays his wealth in an inn is asking to be robbed. Wonder he had not been robbed before we chanced upon him.

"To his credit, he had two armed outriders as well as two footmen running beside his coach. D'Arcy guessed the men would be wary, maybe have their arms out when they entered a wooded area south of Derby." He glanced at Delphine. "Wooded areas easily conceal would be robbers."

"Yes, Purdy is ever on the alert when we pass through any forested area," Delphine said.

Madigan nodded, his mind going back to his first robbery. In describing it to Delphine, he was there again. A vivid imagery danced before him. A cloudy day with light drizzle, the sun well hidden in the darkened sky. D'Arcy chose a barren area rather than a wooded area that the outriders would be less on guard. 'Twas a section of the road next to a hill high enough to conceal their horses from the view of anyone approaching from either direction on the highway. On the opposite side of the road was a low stone fence, but it was high enough to hide the men crouching behind it. A lone tree, bare of leaves, was on the fence side of the road, bushes climbing up the hill on the other side. One end of a rope was wrapped around the trunk of the tree, the other end was attached to a scruffy but sturdy bush across the road. The hemp rope lying on the slightly muddy road was near invisible.

"All right, Dev," D'Arcy told Preston. "When I give you the signal, you give a good yank on that rope. With any luck, it will send the lead outrider tumbling. That will cause the coachman to pull up."

At Preston's nod, D'Arcy turned to Madigan. "Maddy, you will need to be quick. Make your pitch count. We need the rear outrider's horse to throw him or at least keep him off balance until you can level your gun on him."

Like Preston, Madigan nodded. His job was to throw a sharp stone at

126

the rear outrider's horse's flank, causing the horse to buck. He dare not miss. If he did, he might have to shoot the outrider, and D'Arcy wanted no one injured, especially not the innocent men guarding their chosen target. In the confusion, the rest of the gang, with the exception of Chapman who was minding the horses, would leap over the wall, their pistols raised, and would order the footmen and coachman to drop their weapons. Their target would then be ordered out of the coach.

"We will relieve him of his purse, mayhap some of his wife's jewelry, but none she might claim to be family heirlooms. A wife is subject to her husband. She cannot help he is a fool."

'Twas the waiting Madigan hated the most. His heart hammered in his chest each time he heard hoof beats splatting along the muddied road. A couple of riders passed them, a farmer headed into Derby with his produce rumbled along on his wagon, an old coach pulled by tired looking horses ambled past. Though his woolen coat kept him warm and protected him from the light rain, crouching behind the fence in the muddied field, Madigan soon had moisture creeping up through his stockings and breeches. He was beginning to think he was not cut out to be a highwayman. Then came the coach.

Though mud-splashed, it was a quality coach. Six matching grays pulled it, their legs mushing gingerly along the mired road. His muscles tense, Madigan gripped his stone, and glanced down the fence to D'Arcy. His leader had removed his hat and just the barest portion of his head poked over the fence so he could watch the coach advance. Head bowed against the drizzle, the front outrider rode past, the coach followed, but not too closely. D'Arcy gave his signal. Up went the rope. It caught the outrider's horse between the legs, tripping the animal and setting it to stumbling. Near falling, the horse righted itself, but the outrider had jumped free so he would not be caught under the horse if it fell on its side in the muddy road.

As the coachman pulled up on his reins, Madigan rose and aimed his rock at the back outrider's horse. The rock hit the horse's flank, startling the already nervous animal. The horse started bucking. The outrider, unable to reach for his gun, was at Madigan's mercy by the time he had his mount under control. D'Arcy, Yardley, Tuftwick, and Hayward had the coachman and the footmen disarmed, and Preston had the front outrider covered. Madigan was relieved to see the first horse, though still staggering, was apparently not seriously harmed.

"Out of the coach, sir," D'Arcy demanded of the merchant. Nodding to a footman, he added, "Help your master and mistress from the coach."

The footman hurried to do as instructed. He lowered the step and opened the coach door, then reached up a hand to give assistance to the coach occupants. "Out," D'Arcy again demanded. "We offer you no harm."

A stocky middle-aged man with a craggy face descended. His dark eyes scowling, the merchant huffed, "What is the meaning of this!"

D'Arcy chuckled. "'Tis a robbery. We mean to relieve you of your purse. Now I need your wife to descend also."

"She carries no purse," the merchant protested.

"No, but I need to search the inside of the coach, so she must exit, though I regret the destruction of her shoes in this mire." Looking at the footman, D'Arcy said, "Help your mistress out." Again the footman reached out his hand, and a plump woman in traveling attire emerged.

While D'Arcy searched the inside of the coach, where he found the merchant's purse hidden under a cushion, Yardley climbed on top of the coach and inspected the couple's luggage. With a whoop, he tossed down a jewelry box to D'Arcy.

"Oh, not my jewelry," the wife cried, tears welling in her round eyes.

"We will not take all. Fact is, do you have some treasured items," he held the box out to her, "do pick them out, and those we will leave with you."

The woman looked at D'Arcy in surprise before hastily opening the ornamented case and drawing out several items. D'Arcy nodded. "Fine choices. Sorry, but I must relieve you of the remainder. However, I will not take your lovely case." After emptying the box into his coat pocket, he handed the jewelry box back to the wife, and she clutched it to her bosom.

Madigan felt sorry for the woman. She was probably scared, cold – he could see her shivering – and distressed by the loss of her beloved jewelry. From atop the coach, Yardley had pulled several clothing items from the trunks. He handed them down to Hayward. The articles

128

he took were plainer clothes; shifts and shirts, a couple of petticoats and non-descript breeches, items that could be given to the poor, but never identified as too fine for a poor man or woman to be owning or wearing.

"All right," D'Arcy said, "back in the coach." He nodded to the footman to help the merchant and his wife back in. "Now, you two outriders, let us have you join them."

The outriders looked confused, but with guns trained on them, they did as directed. With the outriders tucked inside the coach, D'Arcy ordered the footmen to fall in at the rear of the coach. Lastly, the two horses were tied to the back of the coach. D'Arcy examined the legs of the horse that had been tripped. "Forelock appears a bit swollen," he told the footman, "but does the pace not go too fast, he should heal.

"Now, watch what I am doing with your guns that you may return to claim them. You may have need of them later during your journey. They will be muddy, but you can clean them." To Madigan's surprise, D'Arcy tossed all the weaponry out into the field as far as he could fling them. Afterwards, he walked up to the coachman. "I recommend you drive on up the road until you find an area where you can safely turn this coach around. You would be best to return for the guns. Most likely the outriders paid for the ones they carry themselves. No reason they should be out their guns or horses. I also recommend, for your master's sake, that you return to Derby where he is known, that he may be able to arrange credit for the remainder of his trip." Smiling, he slapped a rear horse on its rump. "Good journey to you," he said, and when the coachman shook his reins the coach lurched forward.

"And that was that," Madigan told Delphine. "The whole episode took but a matter of moments. We scurried over the hill, retrieved our horses, and set off across the country side."

"But what happened to the money and the other items you took?" Delphine asked.

"D'Arcy has a couple of safe places he keeps them until he can pass them on to his younger brother, Ranulf, who gives them to the King." He shook his head. "Oh, you must not look at me in that suspicious way. D'Arcy is not keeping the treasure for himself."

"I know that. I have known Phillida's brother long enough to know he is devoted to King Charles. But what if something happened to him. How would anyone know where to find the things you stole?"

"My guess is Chapman also knows where the items are stashed."

"So after you robbed the merchant, what then?"

"Chapman led us down various country roads skirting around Derby until we returned to the highway leading north from Derby to Sheffield, where we would look for our next quarry. We had to split up at that time. Too large a group traveling together makes people suspicious and starts tongues wagging. So Tuffy and I pair up. Yardley and Hayward and Preston travel together, and D'Arcy and Chapman ride together unless Chapman assumes his peddler disguise and goes on foot."

"Do you not keep any of the prizes for yourselves? Do you not need to pay your way?"

"Indeed, we keep some, but Tuffy has an income, which also keeps me in coin, and Nate's older brother makes certain he never lacks for funds. Chapman has a store in Cheshire that his sister oversees, and that keeps him well enough. Yardley, Hayward, and Preston get some funds from their families, but our needs are really rather simple. Feed for the horses, food and drink for us and a bed at night, and we are well maintained."

He raised one hand. "Look at Tuffy and me now. We have no need for coin except to tip the servants at the homes where we stay. We eat well, have good beds." Smiling, he glanced sideways at her. "And we want not for good company."

She returned his smile. "I thank you for that compliment. I, too, am enjoying your company. You have made this trip much more entertaining than is its norm."

Madigan nodded. He liked her smile. It was full of good cheer. And with his heart breaking, he needed to be cheered. While talking to Delphine, he could almost forget about Venetia. Forget that she rode right behind him, chatting merrily with his dearest friend.

Chapter 18

Delphine was pleased with the whole day. She and Maddy had been most compatible during the long ride. She had been able to make him laugh, and she enjoyed his tale about his first highway robbery. She liked knowing his feelings. She liked that he had worried about the horse, had felt sorry for the merchant's wife, cold and scared, and that he had not wanted to have to shoot anyone. He was a kind and considerate person. She just knew he would make a good husband. If he would but commit to being her husband.

Her only disappointment came when they arrived at their night's destination, Woodburn Hall, and found Sir Milton Flynn was also a guest at their night's abode. Greeted at the door to the stark, sparsely furnished hall by the house steward, Berold's entourage followed the stiff-back young man to the brightly lit, fashionably furnished parlor where Flynn joined the Creswell family in greeting them. Delphine's hackles rose as Flynn's eyes raked her up and down, and he again held her hand longer than he should. "Mistress Lotterby, what luck to find you are staying here. I hope we may sit for a chat later this evening."

To her relief, before she had to answer Flynn, Venetia rescued her. "Why, Sir Milton," Venetia said, stepping in front of him and forcing him to release Delphine, "what an extraordinary happening that we should find you in our midst. Last night, I thought you told me you were bound for your home."

Flynn's face at first showed aggravation, but he abruptly changed his demeanor. A smile replaced his frown, and bowing graciously, he said, "Indeed, Lady Venetia, I am headed for home, but my servant's horse came up lame, and I begged shelter for the night."

Mustache twitching, Ambrose Creswell, their jovial host, his rotund belly fashionably covered in a bright yellow jerkin ornamented with enough gold buttons to evince his wealth, slapped Flynn on the back.

"Begged shelter. What poppycock. You know well you are ever welcome here, Sir Milton. Do not my wife and daughter brighten when you visit?"

Slipping past the posturing Creswell, Delphine greeted Mistress Creswell and her daughter, Anna. Both women were dressed for a formal supper. The slender Mistress Creswell, wearing a spring floral patterned gown, draped at the neck with a broad laced collar that matched the cuffs on the sleeves of her tight-fitting bodice, embraced Delphine and gave her a kiss on the cheek. "How grand to see you again, my dear. And do I understand you have not yet found yourself a husband?"

"Oh, Mother!" Dressed in a green silk gown with a short-waisted bodice and very low décolletage, the pretty, blond Anna chastised her mother before also giving Delphine a kiss on the cheek. "You must not mind Mother. She cannot think any woman is whole until she is wed." Glancing in Sir Milton's direction, she added, "She is thrilled to have Sir Milton staying with us. She thinks him quite eligible." Delphine could understand why the two women would be happy to see Sir Milton. Anna was of marriageable age and could well think Flynn a promising suitor.

"He is eligible," Mistress Creswell said, unperturbed by her daughter's chastisement. "His principal seat, though I have heard 'tis encumbered, is extensive. And he is a baronet. So neither I nor Anna's father could object did Sir Milton make an offer for Anna's hand." Believing her family worthy of marrying into a baronetcy at the minimum, she looked toward the hearth, and Delphine's gaze followed hers to rest on a shield hanging in a place of honor above the mantel and displaying the Creswell Coat of Arms – two birds in flight over what appeared to be a chalice. Mister Creswell's, great grandfather had been knighted by Queen Elizabeth, and they could not be more proud of their heritage, though the same ancestor made his fortune as a butter and eggs broker. According to Berold, the current Mister Creswell dabbled in trade, but most of his income came from his estate.

"'Twould be pleasing did Anna marry a man we have known for any number of years. Knew his father. And his principal residence is not a day's ride from here. With Anna so close, I would not feel so forlorn when she must leave me. I have no other daughter you know, just the

132

three boys, and they are all away at school more time than not." Mistress Creswell dabbed at the corner of one eye with a silk kerchief.

"I suppose that would be comforting," Delphine said, silently pleased the Creswell boys had not yet returned from their school in Manchester. They were bright lads, but boisterous, and she had experienced their jubilance often enough she could not say she missed seeing them.

Mistress Creswell cocked her head and narrowed her eyes. "Would you also be finding Sir Milton an eligible match, Mistress Lotterby?"

"Mother!" Shaking her head, Anna again chastised her mother, but Delphine laughed.

"Oh, my no, Mistress Creswell," Delphine heartily assured her hostess. "I barely know the man, and I fear I may be looking for someone of a more studious nature."

Looking pleased, Mistress Creswell beamed at her before turning to greet Phillida and Sidonie. The conversation turned to their rooms for the night. The maids, Lucy with baby William, and the nurse with Timandra had already been shown to their mistresses' rooms. Soon the women would be escorted up to their chambers, and after a rousing drink or two, the men would follow. Delphine was glad to be encircled by the group of women. It kept Sir Milton at bay. She could not help but wonder if Anna was as taken with Flynn as was her mother. She feared the man might have a cruel streak in him, and she would not like to see Anna wed to such a man.

"I will look forward to seeing your new baby, Mistress Hayward," Anna said. "But is he not young to be making such a long journey?"

Again, the Hayward's story had to be retold. Again, oohs and ahs were forth coming, then it was time to go up to their rooms to change for supper. After spending the day on a horse, Delphine had no doubt she likely smelled like a horse. She was looking forward to washing and toweling off. With the added guests, Delphine was not surprised she and Venetia would be sharing a room and a bed. Bethel and Tatty would have to share the truckle bed. Poor dears. She knew they must be tired, bouncing around in the coach all day. She and Venetia must try not to keep them up too late.

As they ascended the stairs behind Mistress Creswell, Phillida, and Sidonie, Delphine caught Venetia's hand. "Thank you for rescuing me," she whispered.

"'My pleasure," Venetia answered, her voice lowered. "I cannot find Sir Milton very pleasant. I must say, I was more than a little disappointed to find him here."

"You were!" Delphine hissed. "I near turned and ran back out the door."

Venetia's sensuous, throaty laugh floated up the stairs. "Let us hope Mistress Creswell thinks not to seat him beside you at table tonight," she stated, her tone hushed.

"I cannot think she will. I believe Anna will have the pleasure of being seated next to him. Mistress Creswell thinks he would make a fine husband for Anna."

"Oh, I hope not. Anna is too sweet for such a man."

"I agree." Their conversation ended as Mistress Creswell showed first Phillida and then Sidonie to their rooms before leading Delphine and Venetia to the end of the corridor. A bright smile on her face, Mistress Creswell stopped in front of the door to their bedchamber. "I do hope this room will be satisfactory. We need more rooms. I keep telling Ambrose we should add another wing to the house, but then ..."

"No, no, Mistress Creswell, you must not fret. We will be perfectly comfortable, I am certain," Delphine said, grasping Mistress Creswell's hand and giving it a pat.

"Indeed we shall," Venetia said. "Delphine and I are used to occasionally sharing a room. Now, think no more about it. We will be fine."

Mistress Creswell smiled back at them. "Well, then, I will leave you to your ablutions. And I must see to mine. I have been on the run all day." With a little wave, she hurried off, and Delphine, followed by Venetia, entered their room.

It was a pretty room with green curtains on the glazed windows, green canopy and curtains on the four-poster bed, two washstands against the half wains-coated wall, a gold framed mirror above one stand, a rack of linen towels above the other. Copper pitchers filled with warm water and lovely hammered copper basins were atop both stands. Little bowls of rose-scented soft soap were on the shelves under them. Bethel and Tatty had laid out gowns, petticoats, and stockings on the bed, and had set out combs and personal mouth fresheners on

134

a stand beside the bed that also held a three-tiered lighted candelabra. The trunks and portmanteaus were tucked away in a corner so no one would stumble over them, and two chairs with tufted green cushions were placed before a dimly glowing fire in the hearth.

"Are you wishing to rest a bit before we ready you for supper?" Tatty asked.

Delphine shook her head. "Nay, I think we had best get washed. And Tatty, I must put on a clean shift. I can feel this one sticking to me."

"As you wish. Let me but help you out of your riding costume."

Allowing Tatty to help her disrobe, Delphine let her mind wander. How would she keep away from Sir Milton and how would she manage to be seated next to Maddy? Both important questions, but how to manage either she had no real idea.

❦ ❦ ❦ ❦

Madigan liked Woodburn Hall. Though 'twas smaller, it reminded him of Wollowchet. He had spent many a happy summer at Wollowchet with Tuftwick. During those days of unbridled leisure and liberality, he had been able to forget the loss of his mother, his home, his birthright. Lady Wollowchet had coddled both him and Tuftwick, and Lord Wollowchet had given them free rein to wander the estate, to fish, to swim, to hunt, to just enjoy being young, healthy, and alive.

Like Wollowchet, Woodburn Hall dated from the mid fourteen hundreds. It was still surrounded by a thick protective wall with a guardhouse and gate. The wall had turrets at all four corners, though neither the Creswell nor the Wollowchet house had turrets. Madigan smiled, remembering the mock battles he and Tuftwick had fought in the wall turrets at Wollowchet. Also, like Wollowchet, Woodburn had seen little change to the outside of the building, but both houses had seen considerable change on the inside, Wollowchet more than Woodburn.

The Creswell's had made few changes to their hall. Tapestries were hung on the cold stone walls, and a large wall hearth had replaced the raised center hearth, but, unlike Wollowchet, a ceiling had not been added to create a chamber above the hall. The heavy, high arching beams, hung with giant candelabras, held up the imposing, smoke-darkened, wood-framed ceiling reaching three stories high. Madigan was amused to see the servants setting up a trestle table on the dais. The house had no separate dining room and the parlor was not large enough to provide seating for all the Creswells' guests, so apparently Mister Creswell intended to play the role of lord of the household. He, his wife, and the more important guests, that would be Lord and Lady Grasmere, would share his table. The other guests would sit at the trestle table below the dais. Madigan was pleased with the set up. It would give him a better chance to sit next to Delphine and to protect her from Sir Milton.

Upon their arrival that evening, he had been trailing into the parlor behind the Haywards when he saw Sir Milton was again in their midst. To his disgust, Sir Milton again had Delphine in his clutches. Before he could make his way around the Haywards to come to Delphine's aid, Venetia intervened, and Delphine escaped to be greeted by their hostess. Inwardly, he applauded Venetia. Not only was she sweet and beautiful, she was courageous. But she would never be his, and he needed to stop thinking about her. He needed to give more thought to Delphine's proposal. The more time he spent with her, the more he began to believe they might be well suited to one another.

Neither of them expected love in the marriage. Delphine but needed a husband to put a stop to all the abduction attempts. A friendship was developing between them, and he saw no reason they would not be quite compatible. Other than his friendship and protection, he had little he could offer Delphine. But she had no need of additional wealth, and had she wanted a title, she could have married long ago. She knew of his love for Venetia, and it seemed not to concern her. Had she ever expected romantic love in a marriage, she must have long since given up such notions, did she ever have them to begin with.

Hastily completing his ablutions, he left Tuftwick deciding whether to wear his shoes or his boots, and hurried down stairs. He meant to be on hand when Delphine arrived in the parlor. He was determined to protect her from Sir Milton. Finding the parlor empty, he wandered into the hall and spent some time admiring the tapestries, but hearing voices, he returned to the parlor. There he found Creswell, Grasmere, and Tuftwick lounging before the hearth. Tuftwick was admiring the Creswell coat of arms.

Chin raised, Creswell stated, "My great grandfather made his fortune in trade, supplying butter and eggs to Liverpool and Manchester. He was knighted by Queen Elizabeth because he used some of that fortune to build a ship to help protect England from the Spanish Armada. He used another portion of that fortune to buy this estate from Lord Bryson who needed the funds to play the courtier in London. My tenants grow rye and oats to feed the cattle they raise. They turn milk from those cows into cheese and butter which I, like my father and grandfather, sell to merchants in Manchester and Liverpool."

He looked directly at each of his guests and inhaled deeply, puffing out his chest. "'Tis naught I have ever been ashamed to admit to."

"Nor should you be," Grasmere said. "I sell my cattle for their meat and hides, my sheep for their mutton and wool. Any excess grain, I sell as well. 'Tis no shame in profiting from the surplus of your land. Shows good management. 'Tis why I must travel to Grasmere each year. 'Tis not to enjoy the scenery. 'Tis to make sure my steward is caring for Knightswood properly."

"Aye," Tuftwick said. "I am fortunate to have a good steward, and to have an uncle to keep an eye on my steward while I go visiting friends instead of minding my land."

"You are fortunate indeed," Sir Milton said, having joined them as Tuftwick proclaimed his poor stewardship of his land. "I have three estates. One to the south of here, a day's ride from Lord Rigdale's, another less than a day's ride north of here. My third estate is in Derbyshire." He looked at Lord Grasmere. "Like you, I must travel from estate to estate, not for the change of scenery, but to make certain it is being managed properly."

Madigan believed Sir Milton had a reason for telling Grasmere about his estates. But what was the reason? Was he trying to impress him with his wealth? He could not tell whether Grasmere was impressed, and the conversation turned to taxes and complaints about the Puritans until Hayward and the ladies arrived. They then went into the hall for supper. Mister Creswell led the way with Lady Grasmere on his arm, they were followed by Lord Grasmere and Mistress Creswell, Tuftwick and Venetia went next. According to status, Sir Milton should have had Delphine on his arm, but Mistress Creswell had paired him with her daughter, Anna. The Haywards went next, Sidonie being the daughter of a baronet, and to Madigan's delight, he and Delphine brought up the rear.

At the table, he found he was seated between Delphine and Anna, and the Haywards were across from them. Sir Milton was at the exact opposite end of the table from Delphine. She would not have to speak to him or even look at him. It boded well to be an enjoyable meal.

Chapter 19

Once supper ended, and everyone adjourned to the parlor, Delphine stayed close by Maddy. She was thrilled that he seemed eager to keep her at his side. Tables for cards or backgammon had been set up, and she arranged a game of cards for her and Maddy against Mister Creswell and Phillida. Sidonie, saying she needed to see to her baby, bid all a good night, and with a kiss for her husband swept up the stairs. No doubt her babe was in need of a feeding.

Anna asked Sir Milton to join her in a game of backgammon, but to Mistress Creswell's obvious chagrin, he told Anna he was a poor study at the game, preferring cards, so Anna, not looking at all perturbed, sat down to a game of backgammon with Mister Hayward. After a few moments of fluttering around, Mistress Creswell joined Venetia and Tuftwick for a tete-a-tete. Delphine had to smile. She could tell by the expression on Venetia's face, that her cousin was not desirous of Mistress Creswell's company. Venetia had yet to get Tuftwick to kiss her, and she was getting more and more frustrated – and irritated. It amused Delphine. She believed Venetia was falling more and more in love with Tuftwick, but would not recognize her love because she was so set on the importance of a kiss.

What was not amusing was the amount of time Sir Milton was spending talking with Berold. A couple of times she saw Berold look in her direction. If the conversation involved her, it could not be good. She was not surprised when the evening broke up after desserts and wine were served, to be caught by Sir Milton when she started to ascend the stairs to her bedchamber. Berold had called Maddy to his side. Mistress Creswell again had Venetia's ear. Hayward had already gone up as had Phillida. She had no one she could turn to for aid when Sir Milton caught her elbow, halting her and turning her to face him.

"Mistress Lotterby," he said, "I have spoken with your cousin, Lord

Grasmere, and he has given me his permission to speak with you. Though he did tell me he had no need to give his permission. Still, I thought it appropriate to speak to him of my wish to pay you court."

Delphine was expecting his speech, but before she could answer him, he smiled what she considered a repugnant grimace and said, "And so I ask you, Mistress Lotterby, may I pay you court? Lord Grasmere has offered me lodging at Knightswood Castle do you give your consent."

Though she felt no honor at Sir Milton's request, she gave him her standard courtesy answer. "Sir Milton, you are most kind to make me an offer, and I am indeed honored, but I cannot wish you to pay me court. I know we would not suit."

Anger jumped to his eyes, but his voice remained calm. "How can you know we would not suit, Mistress Lotterby. You barely know me. Did I pay you court, you might find I can be most charming."

"I have no doubt you can be charming when you choose, Sir Milton, but this is not one of those moments. I wish you to release me." She looked down at his hand still gripping her elbow, but he did not release her.

His eyes narrowing and his lips firming, he said, "I know there have been attempts made to abduct you and force you into a marriage not of your choosing. You are in need of a husband. For your own protection, you should consider my request."

Her own eyes narrowed, she stated, "You still hold my arm, Sir Milton. I ask you again to release me."

This time he did release her, and she looked him straight in his eyes. "As I said, I am honored you would wish to pay me court, but 'tis most obvious to me we would not suit. Now I wish you a good-night, Sir Milton." With that, she turned from him and walked regally up the stairs. The man was much too bold, and she prayed she had put an end to his pursuit of her.

❈ ❈ ❈ ❈

Hoping she would not awaken Tatty and Bethel, Venetia slipped quietly into the bedchamber she shared with Delphine. She was delighted to find Delphine sitting up in bed waiting for her. Both maids, settled on the truckle bed, were snoring lightly. After hastily disrobing with Delphine's help and slipping into her night shift, Venetia, her legs crossed under her, settled down for a quiet chat with Delphine.

"Tell me what Sir Milton said," she demanded in a low whisper. "I was that perturbed with Tuftwick that he failed to go to your aid when I was detained by Mistress Creswell. She is a dear lady, but she must ask was I planning to wed Tuftwick. I was telling her I could not know, and I was shooting arrows at Tuftwick, but he but stood smiling at me while Berold held Mister Madigan at his side. So was Sir Milton as brazen as he seemed?"

Delphine chuckled. "He was brazen. Said he wished to court me, but I abused him of that idea. So do let us put the scene from our minds. I take it you had no time to get Tuftwick alone."

Shaking her head, Venetia frowned. "I had thought we might go back to the hall. It has such history, and Tuftwick and I both thought it much like Wollowchet. But when Mistress Creswell joined us, she would have to talk on about her plans for the house if Mister Creswell would but give his consent to them. We had no chance to escape her. Next thing I knew, she was insisting we join her to see the trellises she added to the back of the house. She is training roses to grow up them."

"I am sure it will be lovely," Delphine said, amusement in her voice.

"I suppose it will be," Venetia agreed, shaking her head, "but I pitied the two serving men having to hold their lanterns above their heads that Mistress Creswell might show us how high the trellises went up the walls and how high the roses would climb." She cocked her head to one side. "Still when the rose bushes are mature and the roses are in bloom, they will make a lovely scent that could well waft in the open windows when the weather warms. 'Tis a most thoughtful idea. I will be giving it some consideration do I decide to marry Tuftwick."

"Ah, so you are thinking more about marrying him?" Delphine asked.

Before answering, Venetia gnawed her lower lip. "I do like him. But how can I know if I love him? I have yet to feel his arms around me. Yet to taste his lips. He is handsome, yes. He is ever cheery, yes. Ever considerate. I enjoy talking with him, and he does so often make me laugh, which is good, but are those things enough?"

"Answer me this, dear heart," Delphine said. "How would you feel did you know you would never see Tuftwick again?"

Venetia straightened. "Never see Henry again?" For a moment she stared off into space then looked back at Delphine. "I would be very unhappy did I never see Henry again. Especially if something evil befell him. But does that mean I love him? I would feel the same did I think I would never see you again, my dear cousin. And I am still often saddened that I will never see my mother or father again. But, yes, I would not like it did Henry decide not to pursue his court of me. I admit, I would be most devastated. Yet, I cannot tell you that I love him."

"Well, by the end of summer, does he stay with us at Knightswood Castle, you should know your feelings for him," Delphine said.

Venetia nodded, "Yes, but I would rather know sooner. I cannot think why he will not kiss me, but I am determined I will not ask him to kiss me."

Delphine chuckled. "No, that you should not have to do. But kiss you he will, of that I have no doubt. And I believe you will enjoy it very much."

"I do hope you are right, dear cousin." She looked at the guttering candle. "I suppose we should put out that candle and go to sleep. Berold said something about making an early start as tomorrow will be a long day ere we arrive at the Leeds."

Delphine leaned over and kissed Venetia on the cheek. "Good night, dear. Blow out the candle and let us hope for a restful night."

Venetia blew out the candle and snuggled down under the woolen blankets. The bed was soft, the pillows plush, she was tired, and she soon drifted into sleep.

☙ ☙ ☙ ☙

Pleased he was not sharing a bed with Tuftwick, and instead had his own bed, albeit little wider than a cot, Madigan stretched out in the middle on the overly soft mattress. From his years of sleeping on cots or the hard ground, he was not finding the squashy beds the treat he had at first enjoyed at Harp's Ridge. He supposed, did he decide to marry Delphine, he would have to adjust to a downy bed, but his back was wishing for firmer support.

Marriage to Delphine. He was beginning to like the idea more and more. She had a way of amusing him and keeping his mind off his hopeless love for Venetia. He envied the Haywards and Berold and his lady their love. He would never know that kind of love for the woman of his dreams would someday marry his dearest friend.

Turning his thoughts away from what he could not have, he relived the gaiety of the evening. They had been seated across from the Haywards and had enjoyed conversing with them. When Mister Creswell called an end to supper and suggested they all adjourn to the parlor, Sidonie had excused herself to go see to her baby, but she had thanked him and Delphine for being such enjoyable table partners.

Delphine thanked the Haywards in turn, then looked up at him and asked if he would enjoy a game of whist with her and Creswell and Lady Grasmere. He would, indeed, he would. Just knowing he was keeping Flynn away from Delphine gave him an uplifting feeling. Something about the man, he could not like.

The card game and banter had been uplifting. Creswell was a jovial host, and Lady Grasmere was, as ever, charming, though he could not help but think he caught her several times eyeing him circumspectly. He decided he must be mistaken, though, as she never blushed or in any way tried to look away when his gaze met hers. By the time the game ended, and Mister Creswell suggested 'twas time to serve the dessert, he was in a pleasant mood. He was especially pleased to hear Delphine tell Anna Creswell about Malcolm Phelps.

"I do think you would like him, Anna," Delphine said. "He is bright and personable and will finish at University this year. Do you wish, I will speak to your mother about him. And does she approve, I will write to his mother. I cannot help but think you two would suit."

Wrinkling her nose distastefully in Flynn's direction, Anna looked back at Delphine and readily approved the idea. That Delphine thought Anna and Phelps would suit proved that Delphine had not been interested in the youth herself. She had just been courteous to the young Phelps, him being the son of their hosts. She had never considered him as a possible husband. He was not sure why that perked up his spirits, but it did.

Tossing around on the over soft mattress, he ground his teeth. How could Berold have even considered letting Flynn address Delphine? When Berold called him to his side, he had no choice but to leave Delphine on her own. Before she could escape up the stairs, Flynn caught her. He had the nerve to grab her arm. Only Berold's hand on his arm had kept him from rushing to Delphine's defense. He saw various expressions flash across Delphine's face. Annoyance turned to aggravation. Her look finally became haughty, and Flynn released her. She then proceeded up the stairs, her head high, her step regal.

When Flynn turned around, Madigan saw the anger on his face, but as Creswell advanced on him, his frown turned into a cheery smile. He thanked his host and said he was off to his bed. He also said he would be departing early in the morning. That pleased Madigan. They would all be well served did they not have to bid Flynn a God speed.

With that pleasant thought, he smiled, shut his eyes, and drifted into sleep.

Chapter 20

Leaning back against the coach's soft cushions, Phillida cuddled baby William to her heart and patted his bottom. The babe was finally sleeping peacefully after suffering through another coughing spell. Poor little dear had a cold. His mother blamed their stay at the Leeds'. And indeed, though as always, the Leeds did their best to accommodate their guests, unlike the Creswell's renovated hall, the Leeds' rustic old home was drafty and smoky. The bedchambers were small, and rather than hearths, they had but braziers with coal fires offering a pitiable warmth. Fortunately the Hallman House, where they stayed the next night, though also an older house, was not so rustic or drafty. The motherly Mistress Hallman warmed a mixture of honey and sweet wine for the baby. The drink had eased his cough and helped him sleep. Mistress Hallman put some of the mixture in a bottle capped with a sponge so the babe could be given more of the soothing mixture did his cough continue during their journey, as it had.

In her worry for her baby, Sidonie had gotten little sleep the past two nights, and Timandra's nurse, after struggling to get Timandra away from the two younger Hallman children and to bed the previous night, was near as weary as Sidonie. Between staying up late and being overwrought at parting, Timandra had exhausted herself and her nurse. Thus, while the nurse, Timandra, and Sidonie napped, the care of William had fallen to Phillida, and she loved it. She so wanted another child. A playmate for Timandra. Smiling at Timandra, her head pillowed on the dozing nurse's lap, Phillida felt a biding sorrow that her daughter so seldom had any children to play with. The child had delighted in her time with the Hallman children and had cried great tears when forced to say good-bye to them and climb back into the coach.

Well, the naps would be good for all her companions. The bumping and jiggling of the coach seemed not to bother them. They dozed peacefully. The day was bright, sunny, and warm, and the gauze shades on the window let in the soft light but kept the dust from blowing in on them. They all had full stomachs, having enjoyed a simple, but satisfying dinner at an inn the Grasmeres had patronized on their yearly sojourns to Knightswood Castle for many an eon. No longer bothered by any distractions, Phillida let her thoughts drift back three nights past to their stay at the Creswell's.

That night, playing cards with Delphine and Madigan, she had been able to casually observe both of them. She had little doubt they had fallen in love. She had originally believed Madigan, like Tuftwick, had fallen in love with Venetia, but 'twas plain to see, even did he not yet recognize it, Madigan was in love with Delphine. Berold would not be pleased. He wanted Delphine to marry, but he wanted her to marry a Duke or an Earl. And Delphine could, did she so choose. She was the grand-daughter of an Earl, and she was as wealthy as Croesus. Yet she had fallen in love with a man who had not a penny to his name. Everything he possessed, from his horse, to his clothes, to his sword, he owed to Tuftwick's generosity. 'Twas sad he had been done out of his birthright by his step-father. She could pity him, but she could not think him a proper match for Delphine. All the same, did Delphine decide she wanted to marry Madigan, nothing anyone could say or do would dissuade her.

However, Madigan was an honorable man. He would know he was not a suitable match for Delphine. Could be, did Berold speak to him, Berold could convince him such a match would not be acceptable. Still, if Delphine had her heart set on marrying Madigan – did she truly love him, would it be fair to separate the two lovers? Delphine was stubborn enough that she might decide never to marry was she not able to marry the man she loved. And Berold would forever be needing to protect her from would be abductors. She sighed. What a dilemma.

Staring out the window, she was surprised when the coach drew to a stop. Was something blocking the road? The highway was narrow, mayhap a coach or wagon coming from the other direction needed to pass. Raising the shade so she could see out better, she spotted a number of horsemen advancing. Surely they were not highwaymen. For a moment, fear gripped her heart, then she recognized the lead rider. It was Sir Milton Flynn. Relief flooded her, and she readied herself to give him a wave when he road past her. She did not particularly like the man, and she knew Delphine found him abhorrent, all the same, he was a strong Royalist and a friend of several of their friends. 'Twould not do to be discourteous.

Seeing Sir Milton stop to talk to her husband while the men accompanying him streamed past them, she idly patted the baby. She hoped the delay would be brief. She was eager to get to their evening's destination. They would be staying with the Blomsters in Lancaster. Mayhap they would stay an extra day with them. Do some shopping. Buy some fabric. She could use a couple of new gowns, and Timandra was fast outgrowing her gowns. From Lancaster, it was but three and a half days to Grasmere. It would be pleasant to have a rest before continuing on.

Beside her, Sidonie stirred. "Do we have a halt here?"

"We have but again met up with Sir Milton Flynn. He is headed south with some other men, but he has stopped to talk with Berold."

She heard the two men laugh, and Berold's voice carried to the coach as he said, "Well, have a safe journey."

She looked at Sidonie and smiled. "Go back to sleep. Your babe is fine. He sleeps. We will soon start again."

Sidonie nodded, settled back in her corner, and closed her eyes. Phillida looked back out the window, prepared to give Flynn a polite wave. She saw him nod to Delphine and Madigan. She knew he was disappointed Delphine had rebuffed his attempt to court her, but she could not say she blamed Delphine in the least.

Stopping beside Venetia, Flynn cocked his head to one side and said in a loud voice, "Now is the time men." With those words, he drew his pistol and pointed it at Venetia's heart.

Phillida gasped, and in looking about, she saw all the men with Flynn had their weapons drawn, and they had them aimed at Berold's men and at Tuftwick, Madigan, Hayward, and Berold. Had Flynn gone mad. Surely he could not mean to rob them.

※ ※ ※ ※

Wary of the smirk on Flynn's face when he passed her, Delphine swung around in her saddle to watch him depart. The instant he drew his pistol and pointed it at Venetia, she understood the reason for his smirk. He meant to abduct her by using Venetia as his pawn.

"What is the meaning of this!" demanded Tuftwick, and at the alarm in Tuftwick's voice, Maddy turned around.

"Pay heed!" Flynn said, his voice raised. "I wish not to hurt Lady Venetia or any of the rest of you, but my men have been told to shoot to kill do any of you not obey my orders. You must now, all of you, drop your weapons. That means your coachmen, footmen, and outriders." He looked directly at Tuftwick. "And you, Lord Tuftwick, very carefully drop your pistol and your sword. You, too, Madigan."

"Flynn! Have you gone mad!" Berold spat out, joining the group around Venetia.

Delphine could not see Berold. Her eyes were on Venetia and Flynn, but she could imagine his face turning red, his eyes narrowing to slits of anger.

"Do all of you not immediately drop your weapons," Flynn stated, ignoring Berold, "my men will start shooting. This could end very badly."

"Berold! Tell your men to do as he says," Delphine said. "He is after me. Do you cooperate, no one will be hurt."

A smile momentarily played on Flynn's lips, but his eyes remained on the men around her, and his pistol stayed pointed at Venetia's heart. "Mistress Lotterby is correct. Do you obey, no one will be harmed."

"Do as he says," Berold growled, his voice hoarse with anger. "Drop your weapons. All of you."

"You will not get away with this, Flynn," Maddy said, dropping first his pistol then his sword. Delphine felt her heart quicken. Was his concern for her? Or for Venetia? Surely it was for Venetia. After all, despite Flynn's admission he meant to abduct her, his pistol was pointed at Venetia's heart.

Venetia sat very still, her hand holding her mare steady. No fear showed in her eyes, just contempt. Delphine could but hope Venetia would not do something rash like trying to grab Flynn's gun. Even did he not mean to shoot, the gun could go off accidentally. That could start

148

Flynn's men to shooting.

The three coachmen, as well as the two men driving the wagons, dropped their guns. Purdy and Anker dropped their pistols, but a glance at them told Delphine they were shrewdly watching Flynn and his men. They would do nothing to put Venetia's life in danger, but their job was to protect their mistress. They would do whatever was necessary to insure she came to no harm, and that Flynn's scheme was frustrated.

"Now, all of you – off your horses," Flynn ordered.

"Do as he says," Berold snarled, swinging down from his mount.

Delphine started to dismount, but Flynn said, "Not you, Mistress Lotterby." She knew he had not meant her to dismount, she had but meant to aggravate him.

"Lord Grasmere," Flynn said, "I am sorry to discommode you like this, but I fear I must take your riding horses with me. However, I am not stealing them. There is a village not five miles up the road. You can see the church steeple on the hillside from here. I have made arrangements to leave your horses with the blacksmith there."

"You are a fool, Flynn. Why do you do this?" Berold demanded.

"Because I am in need of a wife. Come this evening, I will be a happy bridegroom."

"You cannot marry my sister. I am her guardian. I will never give my consent."

"I mean not to marry Lady Venetia. 'Tis Mistress Lotterby I mean to marry. And you have already given me your consent to court her."

"You cannot force her to marry you!" Maddy said, his voice low with anger.

"No, I mean not to force her. I think she will willingly marry me. But now we must go." He waved his pistol in the air. "Treadwell, the rest of you, make sure you get the horses that are tied to the back of the wagons. I want no riding horses left." He glanced in Berold's direction. "Notice, Grasmere, I make no move to take your coach horses. I mean no harm to your lady or her women. But Lady Venetia, I fear I will be taking with me."

"You cannot take her!" Tuftwick ground out between gritted teeth.

Flynn chuckled. "Worry not about your lady love, Tuftwick. Grasmere told me his party will be staying with the Blomsters in Lancaster.

Do all of you cooperate, Lady Venetia will join you there tomorrow. But today, she is coming with me."

"We have the horses, Sir Milton," a shaggy haired man with a grisly beard said.

"Splendid," Flynn said. "You keep me covered, Treadwell." He raised his voice. "The rest of you men, let us head for Lancaster. I am soon to be married."

"You will never get away with this, Flynn," Berold said, reaching out to grab the reins of Venetia's horse.

Flynn cocked the hammer on his pistol. "Release her horse, Grasmere. Your sister will come to no harm." He looked at Venetia. "Shall we ride, my lady?"

Venetia smiled at her brother. "Fear not for me, Berold." Glancing down at Tuftwick, she said, "No doubt, I will see you soon." She then set her heel to her horse's flank, and it started moving forward alongside Flynn's horse.

"You will be coming with us, Mistress Lotterby?" Flynn asked, his voice syrupy.

"You know well I will, Sir Milton," she answered and turning her horse, she glanced at Purdy, met his eyes, and gave him a near imperceptible nod. She then looked at Maddy. He looked angry, bewildered, and ashamed. Ashamed he had not been able to protect her. And he was looking at her. His gaze was not following Venetia. He would come for her. That she knew.

Putting her heel to her horse, she caught up with Flynn and Venetia, and at Flynn's word, they set off at a gallop, his man, Treadwell, bringing up the rear.

Chapter 21

Like Tuftwick, Berold, and Hayward, the first thing Madigan did was grab his pistol and his sword up off the ground. Berold and Tuftwick were both shouting, Lady Grasmere was calling to her husband. The coachmen, postilions, and outriders were clamoring to know what they should do. Chaos ruled, but Delphine's footman Purdy raised his voice above the rest and said, "Lord Grasmere, Anker and I will be setting off for the village immediately. I would suggest Mister Madigan and Lord Tuftwick follow on the front postilion horses as soon as possible. Anker and I will need the use of yours and Mister Hayward's horses once we reach the blacksmith's are we to reach Mistress Lotterby before Flynn can force her to marry him. We want not to have to kill him."

Madigan jerked his head up at Purdy's last statement. The man's loyalty to Delphine knew no bounds. Did he have to kill to protect his mistress he would. Madigan felt that way himself. He realized, he would have no trouble putting a bullet through Flynn's heart.

"How do you know where to find them?" Berold asked, after demanding everyone, including his wife, be quiet. He also bid Lady Grasmere stay in the coach.

"Someone in the village will know where he is going. Anker and I will learn his whereabouts. 'Tis hard to keep secrets from curious eyes and ears."

"I heard Flynn say to his men to head to Lancaster. 'Tis a large enough town to hide in," Tuftwick said.

"His words were meant to throw us off. He could not ride into Lancaster with a pistol pointed at Lady Venetia's heart. No. He has some secluded place he is taking them. But we are wasting time." He looked at Madigan, then Tuftwick. "We will meet you at the blacksmith's." Before Madigan could answer, Purdy and Anker set off at a lope. Footmen had to be conditioned to run long distances carrying messages or a lantern in front of a coach traveling at night or beside it to keep it from tipping over on poorly maintained roads. And though no longer in the prime of life, Purdy and Anker would reach the village way before he and Tuftwick, of that Madigan had no doubt. He but hoped Purdy would be able to discover where Flynn was taking Delphine and Venetia. He knew one thing for certain. Did Flynn force Delphine into marriage, he would not live long enough to enjoy the marriage.

☙ ☙ ☙ ☙

Bouncing along on the coach horse, Madigan found the postilion's meager saddle to be bruising to the rump, but he was pleased upon arriving at the blacksmith's shop to find all of the horses Flynn had taken awaiting them. The blacksmith, a youthful man with a shock of gold hair and a dangling mustache, told him and Tuftwick that Purdy and Anker had said they would return shortly. The smith also imparted the same information he said he had given the footmen.

"Yes, sir, I saw the two ladies. I would not have guessed them under duress, but Sir Milton kept them at a distance. His men left the horses here. Told me Lord Grasmere would pay the fee for keeping them for him. Then I saw Sir Milton hand over a fistful of coins to three of the men with him. Those men tipped their hats to him and set off on their own. T'other three stayed with Sir Milton and the ladies. They headed on up through the village. I could not say did they turn off at any point. I went back to me work."

"Have you seen Sir Milton often?" Madigan asked.

"Not until as of late. Stopped here once to have his horse reshod. He went acrost to the inn to wait until I was done. Another time I saw him coming out of the inn aside one of the men with him today. Fellow is what I would call unsavory looking. Guess I noticed him because I thought it strange a man like Sir Milton would be in company with such a character."

"Does the man live in this village?" Tuftwick asked.

"Nay, but he comes through here often enough. Did I have to be guessing the reason, I would say he is a bandit that preys on lone travelers. He stops here to refresh himself before or after he commits his crime. I could not say. But from time to time, after one of his stop-overs, a traveler will come stumbling into the village, devoid of most of his clothes, his purse, and his horse. Poor fellow has no idea who 'twas that robbed him."

"Was this unsavory man you described one of the men Sir Milton paid off."

"Aye, he was. The three men who continued on with Sir Milton looked to be less disreputable. I would think mayhap they are men in Sir Milton's permanent employ."

"Might the man's name be Treadwell?"

The smith shook his head. "That I could not say."

"No matter. You have been a big help to us," Tuftwick said, pulling out his purse and handing a coin to the smith. "We will take our horses and two for Purdy and Anker. Lord Grasmere should be arriving to collect the rest of the horses shortly."

The smith cocked his head. "Well, now, sir, you be looking the part of gentlemen, but how am I to be knowing you are not just taking the horses, and they are not truly yours."

Tuftwick snorted and nodded his head. "You have no way of know-ing. Here." He dumped half his purse out on a bench. "You keep these coins until Lord Grasmere arrives. Does that satisfy you?"

Scooping up the coins and dropping them into his apron pocket, the smith said, "Aye, I will help you ready the horses. I see your other com-panions returning."

Looking over his shoulder, Madigan saw Purdy and Anker trotting back to the smith's. "What news?" he said, hoping Purdy had discov-ered Flynn's destination.

The grim smile on Purdy's face told him the footman had indeed learned Flynn's destination. "Flynn has a cousin lives not ten miles from here. Lives near the town of Glasson. Barmaid has been seeing one of Flynn's men." Purdy patted his coat pocket. "Asked me would I give him a message for her. Seems she has to work tomorrow evening and cannot see him until after she gets off. She gave me a note for her beau and good directions on how to find Crutcher's estate. So let us mount up and ride."

"I am with you," Tuftwick said, and in a matter of moments, the horses were saddled, and they were headed off through the village.

※ ※ ※ ※

Delphine pitied Vernon Crutcher. Wringing his fleshy white hands, he looked both confused and concerned. "Dear Mistress Lotterby, Lady Venetia, I am sorry I have no woman here for you." He looked accusingly at his cousin. "When Milton told me he was bringing his future bride here, I but assumed you would have your own maid with you."

Flynn had ushered them into his cousin's house where Crutcher, patting his paunch then smoothing his mustache and goatee, had greeted them warmly. He directed them into his small, but tastefully furnished parlor where a fire blazed gaily in the large stone hearth, but Venetia's angry countenance plus their bedraggled appearance told him something was amiss.

"Let that not trouble you, Mister Crutcher," Delphine said, smiling at their unhappy host. "Lady Venetia and I can see to each other, do you but show us to our room."

"Not quite yet, Mistress Lotterby. I would have your consent to wed me before you refresh yourself."

"She will not wed you, Flynn. Never will she wed you!" Venetia snapped, her eyes narrowed to slits as she glared at her abductor.

Flynn stepped closer to Venetia and clasped a lock of her hair, holding it firm enough Venetia could not pull away from him. His eyes meeting Delphine's, he said, "'Twould be a shame did Lady Venetia lose some of her lovely curls."

"Pay him no heed, Delphine," Venetia said, slapping Flynn's hand and tugging free. "He could cut off all my fingers and toes, and I would still not have you marry him."

Delphine smiled at her cousin. "Nay, Venetia, I would not have him harm you in anyway. Not even the tiniest little hair. Besides, as we know, I must marry someone."

"No you will not marry him." Venetia glared at Flynn. "Do you force her to marry you, her lawyers will have the marriage annulled."

His eyes still on Delphine, he answered Venetia. "Ah, but she must agree she is marrying me of her own free will. Here before my cousin and his staff and my retainers." He glanced at Crutcher who had turned a pale gray. He apparently had not been made privy to Flynn's nefarious plans. "Then, after our wedding celebration supper, we will be off to Glasson as man and wife. There we will take a boat to Ireland and from there a ship to France where we will stay until our first child is born."

Venetia fumed, but Delphine said, "You have it all planned, do you Sir Milton?"

Raising his eyebrows he gave her a slight nod. "I have no doubt your lawyers might try to annul the marriage, but once you have a child, you would not want the child to be deemed a bastard. So when you have given birth to the future baronet, we will return to England. With your wealth, I will reclaim my lost lands." He chuckled. "and buy more land around my principal residence. You will see. Do you please me, you will find me a most accommodating and thoughtful husband."

"The banns! The banns!" Venetia exclaimed. "The Puritan Parliament requires banns be read for the marriage to be legal!"

Flynn chuckled. "But they have been read, Lady Venetia. Tell her, Vernon."

Crutcher, looking even more uncomfortable, stated, "Milton has been in residency with me here for the past month. He met with the Registrar, and banns have been posted in the market for the past three weeks. But believe me. I had no notion you might not wish to marry Milton, Mistress Lotterby."

His eyes again on Delphine, the smirk she so despised contorting his lips, Flynn waved his cousin to silence and said, "When I explained to the Registrar that you had no permanent residence due to your constant travels, he was quite content that the banns posted in Glasson would be sufficient for him to extend us a license. Soon the Justice of the Peace will be arriving to perform the ceremony. So now that we understand each other, do you wish to refresh yourselves, I think Vernon's steward may show you to your room."

"No, I will not stand for this!" Venetia stamped her foot, but Delphine took her hand. "Come dear, I am greatly in deed of the necessary.

Let us not tarry."

Crutcher directed his steward to show them upstairs to a room he had readied for them. "Are you in need of anything, Mistress Lotterby, Lady Venetia, just tell Simpson."

"I have need of a sword to slit your cousin's throat," Venetia snarled, but with Flynn's chuckles following them from the hall, she allowed Delphine to pull her up the stairs.

The stone house was old but well appointed. Delphine was pleased with the room they were given and its heavy wooden door. Opening the door wide for them, the stately, middle-aged steward stepped aside and said in a cultured voice, "You will find mulled wine on the table. Fresh warm water in the pitcher and clean towels there on the bed." He first indicated a delicate table with two crystal goblets brimming with a ruby colored wine, then a sturdy washstand with hammered copper washbowl and pitcher atop it, and finally a stack of cream-colored towels on the four poster bed bedecked with pink flower printed drapes and canopy. The cold stone walls had not been wainscoted, but were instead white-washed and warmed by three decorative tapestries depicting bright spring landscapes.

A log fire blazed in the hearth, and the chimney had a good draw for little smoke escaped into the room. The wax candles in two candelabras on the mantel gave a soft glow to the room. Clearing his throat, the steward said, "You will find the ah ... the ah ... necessary in the closet." He nodded toward a door at the back of the room on the side wall near the hearth.

"Thank you," Delphine said. "Now, I wonder, might you please bring us some bread and cheese. We are both quite famished. I know Mister Crutcher has a fine supper planned, but I could well starve before 'tis time to eat."

"As you wish, Mistress Lotterby," Simpson said. "And will there be anything else?"

"Not at the moment."

"Very good," he answered, and with a nod, left, closing the door behind him.

"How can you be thinking of food at a time like this?" Venetia demanded. "We must think of some plan of escape. You cannot marry

Flynn."

Smiling, Delphine took Venetia's hands in hers. "I have no intention of marrying the fiend, dear cousin. You cannot think I would, but we must buy time. Listen," she said, cocking her head slightly. "Even with the window closed, you can hear the roar of the sea. And I smelled the salt air as we approached the house. I would say we are very near the ocean and in the dark, we know not what dangers we might encounter did we somehow manage to sneak from the house. We could be on a cliff. No, we must make ourselves as comfortable as possible in this room. And it will serve us no purpose to sit here with our stomachs growling."

Her lower lip pouting, Venetia asked, "You mean to just wait for the Justice of the Peace to arrive? Then what? Humph! You think the Justice of the Peace will help us. No doubt Flynn has paid him off."

"Yes, you are right, the Justice of the Peace will not help us. He will be in Flynn's employ. But we are not waiting for him. We are waiting for Purdy to arrive."

"Purdy!"

"Of course. You cannot think he is not on his way. He would never forgive himself did he allow any harm to come to me."

Pulling her hands free, Venetia glanced aside, then looked back at Delphine. "And just how is Purdy to know where we are?"

"Come now, Venetia, were you a tavern maid, and did Purdy want to know where he might find Sir Milton, would you be refusing to tell him."

Delphine smiled as she watched the expressions dancing across Venetia's face. She knew her cousin was picturing Purdy, and imagining a grinning young woman eagerly flirting with the tall, muscular footman with his dark, deep set eyes and provocative smile.

Tilting her head to one side and eyeing Delphine through slanted eyes, Venetia said, "Suppose the maid has no knowledge of where Sir Milton lives. After all, he has been staying here with his cousin for but a month."

"She will know. A man like Flynn will not go unnoticed. And should she not know, she will know who would know. Now, go relieve yourself. As soon the steward returns with our food, we must securely bolt that door."

Venetia's gaze darted to the door. A sturdy iron bolt adorned it. For the first time since they had arrived at Crutcher's ancient abode, she smiled. "If Purdy is coming to our aid, I would guess Tuftwick will be with him."

Delphine returned Venetia's smile. "Aye, no doubt he and Mister Madigan will come to our rescue. Now, I hear footsteps. Go see to your needs."

As Venetia turned to the closet, Delphine answered their door. Simpson had returned with some seed cakes and jam as well as the bread and two kinds of cheese. Placing his tray on a drop-leaf table, he asked, "Will there be aught else, Mistress Lotterby?"

"No, thank you, Simpson."

He nodded, started to leave, but looked back over his shoulder. "'Twould take a powerful ax to break through this door, mistress." He raised his eyebrows. "Could an ax be found."

Opening her eyes wide, before bursting out in a grin, Delphine said, "Thank you, Simpson. I trust one will not be found."

He nodded. "Safe evening to you, Mistress Lotterby," and closed the door behind him.

Delphine wrapped her arms about her shoulders. Oh, do please hurry Purdy. And do please have Maddy with you.

Chapter 22

After caring to their needs and refreshing themselves, Delphine and Venetia enjoyed their repast before lying down on the bed to get what rest they could. After their strenuous ride, Flynn not giving them even the slightest respite until they arrived at Crutcher's, they needed to replenish their energy, yet they were both so tense waiting for the knock on the door that was sure to come, neither could fully relax. Delphine tried to lessen their tension by talking about nonsensical things, like how chilly she had been at the Leeds's, or how she hoped baby William would soon be over his cold. She even suggested they might play a wishing game like they had played in their youth, but finally, Venetia patted her hand and said, "Enough, Delphine. I am as nervous as you are, but you need not try to pretend for my sake."

Delphine chuckled. "I believe I am chattering on more for my own sake than for yours. My nerves are frayed. How I wish Purdy could arrive before the Justice of the Peace."

"Even does he arrive first, what then? There will be a fight, will there not?"

"I fear there will be. But at least Flynn has but three retainers with him. And certainly none of Mister Crutcher's staff will offer any aid to Flynn. I must admit I am a bit frightened one of our rescuers might be injured." Turning her head on her pillow to look at Venetia, she added, "'Tis one time we can be grateful Tuftwick and Maddy are well experienced in clandestine activities. No doubt, they will plan their attack carefully."

She had barely finished speaking when they heard a rap at the door. "Mistress Lotterby, Sir Milton has sent me to tell you the Justice of the Peace has arrived. He requests your presence downstairs."

Delphine recognized Simpson's voice, and she smiled. "Do please tell him I am not yet ready, Mister Simpson."

"Yes, Mistress Lotterby."

Delphine's eyes met Venetia's. "It begins," she said, sitting up on the bed and swinging her legs off the edge.

❀ ❀ ❀ ❀

Standing side by side in the center of the room, Delphine and Venetia had not long to wait before they heard heavy footsteps in the corridor, then a loud hammering on the door.

"Mistress Lotterby, I will have you downstairs now."

Delphine had no trouble recognizing Flynn's voice. "No, Sir Milton. I think not. I am resting. Both Lady Venetia and I are tired. We will not be coming down at this time."

His voice tense with anger, Flynn said, "You will come down this instant or regret the consequences. I will not play games with you."

"Nor I with you," Delphine answered, her pulse beating in her ears. Would he find an ax? Would he be able to beat down the door? She felt for her knife in its scabbard at her waist. She hoped she would not have to use it to defend herself, but she would fight before she would surrender to Flynn.

"Simpson. Go get me an ax," Flynn commanded.

"Yes, Sir Milton," Simpson answered.

"You are going to regret this, Mistress Lotterby. Both you and Lady Venetia will be made to regret trying my patience."

"You are the one who will regret your actions," spoke up Venetia. "Do you harm either of us, my brother or Lord Tuftwick will see you punished."

"Sir Milton, what goes here?" A voice Delphine failed to recognize questioned Flynn.

"Mister Spice, I told you to wait in the parlor," Flynn growled.

"Yes, but the hour grows late," the man whined. "Your man brought me here with the understanding I would perform the ceremony, we would have a genial supper, and you and your bride would return with me to Glasson, your retainers lighting our way. The moon is half hidden by clouds and rain threatens. I wish to be done with this and return to my home and bed."

"My future bride has turned shy. For the moment, she is refusing to come out of her room. But I will deal with the situation. Fear not, even do we have to forgo the supper, you will be returned safely to your home. And I and my bride have a boat sailing with the tide that we must catch does it rain or not."

"Must be the Justice of the Peace," Delphine whispered to Venetia.

Venetia nodded and smiled. "Aye, and he is not sounding happy."

Delphine heard herself being addressed by the man she assumed was the Justice of the Peace. "Come now, Mistress Lotterby. Your shyness does you credit, but the evening grows late and my wife awaits me. She will start to worry. And your groom grows anxious. As he has said, you have a boat to catch."

"No, Mister Spice," Delphine said. "I believe that is your name. No, I will not come out for I have no intention of marrying Sir Milton. Are you ready for your bed, I suggest you start for your home on your own."

"You will go nowhere," Flynn snarled. "I am paying you and paying you well to perform this ceremony." He paused. "I have a thought, could you not perform it through the door?"

"Through the door? Not see the lady? Good heavens, no. Besides, she must sign the license, and she must say her vows to you."

"I care naught about her vows, and she can sign the license when I get this door busted down. Where is Simpson with that ax? Vernon! Vernon! Where is your steward!"

"Here … here he comes, Milton," Vernon's wavering voice could barely be heard.

"Where is the ax?" Flynn's voice boomed through the door.

"I am sorry, Sir Milton," Simpson said in a sonorous tone, "but it is not in the woodshed. Seems it must have been left in the woods. Mister Crutcher ordered a number of logs cut to prepare for Mistress Lotterby's visit, and the gardener, logging not being his usual chore, says he carried the logs to the house and forgot to go back for the ax. We have a woodman from the village who normally takes care of our wood supply. And the gardener loaned his hatchet to a neighbor boy after he trimmed up the logs."

"No!" screamed Flynn. "No, no, no! Vernon! This is your fault! Why must you have iron bolts on these doors?"

His voice shaking, Crutcher said, "I have tried to keep the house as near to its original state as possible. It was a block house. Meant to protect the coast. Its sturdiness is its charm. This room was the solar and a stronghold for the knight's family did invaders make it into the house."

"Damn you!" Along with that curse Delphine heard a whack against the door, and an, Ouch!" She feared Flynn had just slung his cousin into the door.

"You are choking me!" gurgled Crutcher's voice, but another voice brought Delphine's chin up. "I think you had best release him and draw your sword, Flynn."

"Maddy!" Delphine whispered.

"'Tis Mister Madigan!" Venetia affirmed, her eyes glowing. "They have come for us." She hugged Delphine. "You were right, Delphine, you were right."

Freeing herself from her cousin's embrace that she might concentrate on what was happening outside the door, Delphine heard Maddy repeat, "Arm yourself, Flynn."

"Madigan! You will be made to regret your interference!"

In a matter of moments, the sound of steel against steel resonated through the door.

"Let us see what is happening," Venetia said, and together she and Delphine tugged the heavy bolt back and cracked open the sturdy door. The corridor was dimly lit by wall sconces, but Delphine could see the two shadowy figures engaged in a life and death struggle. In an attempt to stay out of the way, but still view the combat, Crutcher, Simpson, and Spice stood with their backs pressed against the stone wall. Crutcher, his mouth open, clutched his throat, but his gaze was glued on the combatants.

Returning her attention to the fight, Delphine's breath drained from her lungs when Flynn lunged at Maddy, but Maddy parried the thrust and sliced a corner of Flynn's coat. The two swordsmen were evenly matched in skill. And in anger. But Flynn's anger was hot and desperate. Maddy's was cold and intense.

"Look, there's Henry," Venetia said, with a tug to Delphine's sleeve.

Delphine gave but a hasty glance to the top of the stairs where Tuftwick stood watching his friend fight, his hand on his sword hilt. Delphine knew did any harm come to Maddy, Tuftwick would take his revenge on Flynn.

Thrust, parry, thrust, parry, the sound of sword on sword reverberated off the walls. Boots scuffing over the rough stone floor and harsh pants as the two combatants tired were the only other sounds. No one else seemed even to be breathing.

Then Maddy caught Flynn's sword handle, gave a twist to his wrist, and Flynn's sword went flying before clattering down on the floor. Maddy's sword was then at Flynn's neck.

"No, you must not kill him," Delphine cried, darting from the room.

Not looking at her, Maddy asked, "And why should I not?"

"Because it will involve having to have the coroner come here. We will have to give testament. It could greatly delay our departure." And though she despised Flynn and knew he would not hesitate to kill Maddy were the situation reversed, she could not want Flynn's death at Maddy's hand, or on his conscience.

"She speaks the truth," Tuftwick said, joining them. "We shall bind him as we have done his henchmen. Here." He dangled a rope in his hand. "I shall tie his hands, then we will take him down and deposit him in the hall with the others."

His breath still harsh, Maddy nodded. "Bind him tight." His eyes narrowed, he added, "I almost wish he would attempt to escape."

"Mister Madigan, Lord Tuftwick, all is well?"

Delphine turned to see Purdy looming at the head of the stairs. His eyes were on her, a slight smile touched his lips. "You were not harmed, Mistress?"

"No, Purdy, I am not harmed, nor is Lady Venetia. And we thank you," she swept her arm to include Maddy and Tuftwick, "all of you for coming so hastily to our rescue."

"'Twas Purdy knew how to find you," Tuftwick said. "The man is amazing."

"That he is," Maddy added. "Now let us get Flynn downstairs."

Delphine held up her hand. "Oh, but let me first introduce Mister Crutcher and his so wonderful steward, Mister Simpson. Mister Crutcher knew nothing of Flynn's plans. He was not part of the abduction scheme, or the forced marriage plan, as I fear Mister Spice was."

She indicated Spice, who now cringed against the wall.

"I ... I ... should be go ... going," Spice stuttered.

"You will go nowhere except downstairs," Tuftwick said. "We will determine what is to be done with you. Purdy, do you, please, keep watch on Spice." He looked at Crutcher. "And Mister Crutcher, do you and your steward lead the way downstairs. We will bring Flynn."

Flynn had been silent since he lost the fight, but his eyes burned with hatred. Delphine glanced at him then looked away. She hoped she had not made a mistake in asking Maddy to spare Flynn's life.

❈ ❈ ❈ ❈

Venetia had been standing silent in the doorway until Tuftwick turned and looked at her. She felt neglected. If Tuftwick loved her, should he not have immediately come to her side to see that she was unharmed? She raised her chin, and met his eyes with a defiant gaze. Then in two steps he was standing there before her.

"Has Flynn in anyway harmed you?" he asked.

"No." Her nose flared. "But if not for Delphine's shrewdness, he might have."

His mouth thinned, teeth gritted, he snarled, "Had Flynn harmed a hair on your head, he would now be dead." And before she knew what was happening, he scooped her into his arms, tilted her head back, and with lips firm, yet gentle, he claimed hers with a passion she had but hoped he possessed.

When he released her, she stood breathless in his arms, looking up at him in wonder. "You cannot believe the pain I have been in since Flynn abducted you" he said. "The fear for your safety that has racked my guts. To see you now, safe and well, brings me more relief than I can ever tell you, my dear lady."

Her heart beating a little tattoo in her chest, she smiled up at him. "And I cannot tell you how greatly relieved we are to be freed from Flynn's clutches."

"We will hear more of your ordeal later," Madigan said. "Let us get this vermin downstairs and dealt with."

"Aye." Holding out his arm, Tuftwick said, "Come, Lady Venetia, allow me to escort you."

She took his arm as Madigan gave Flynn a shove. With Delphine following Madigan, they headed downstairs. Bringing up the rear, and clutching Tuftwick's arm to steady herself from the emotions Tuftwick's kiss had sent rushing through her, Venetia gasped when she saw Madigan at the next to last step, stick out a foot and trip Flynn.

Flynn went flying, landing hard on his knees. Unable to catch himself with his hands bound behind him, his face, too, crashed into the stone flooring. A harsh cry erupted from his lips, then a moan as Madigan gripped him by the neck of his shirt and jerked him to his feet. His knees bloodied, blood dripping from his nose and chin, Flynn glared at Madigan, but Madigan's face showed no emotion.

Just what Flynn deserved, Venetia thought, after all he had done to her and Delphine. She had no pity for him as Madigan yanked him around and pushed him toward a corner of the hall where three other men, Flynn's retainers, sat trussed and gagged. Delphine's two footmen stood guard over the bound men, and Mister Spice stood shaking nervously next to Purdy.

Limping badly, Flynn joined his men. Anker pulled out a long cord of rope, and after pushing Flynn to the floor trussed him neck to feet. Then tearing a strip off an already demolished shirt lying on the floor, he gagged Flynn.

"What are we to do with Mister Spice, here?" Purdy asked, pushing the quivering man forward. His wig askew, froth dribbling from his mouth onto his pointed beard, Spice swallowed hard, his Adam's apple bobbing up and down in his throat.

Glancing at Flynn, Spice began stuttering, "I … I had no … no idea Flynn was abducting these women. He paid m…m…me to come here tonight to … to perform the … the ceremony. He never told me the … the lady had no wish to marry him."

"My guess is, Mister Spice would not have protested had he known I was being forced to marry Flynn because of Flynn's threats to my cousin," Delphine said. "But he did refuse to perform the ceremony through the door to our chamber, as Flynn requested he do. He said he must see me in person, and hear me take the vows. So mayhap, he is not to be treated too harshly."

"She is right, she is right," Spice cried.

Madigan looked at Crutcher. "What do you know of Spice? Should we let him go?"

Crutcher, near as nervous as Spice, said, "I know him little. He is of the Calvinist faith and fought with Cromwell, but I have not heard evil of him."

Madigan sighed and looked questioningly at Tuftwick, who looked at Venetia. "What say you, Lady Venetia?"

Venetia gazed up at him. His eyes were brimming with love for her, and her heart did a little flip. She swallowed and said, "I leave that decision to Delphine."

Delphine said, "Then I say, send him home to his wife."

"Thank you, thank you and bless you, Mistress Lotterby." Vigorously nodding his head, he looked from her to Madigan to Purdy whose impassioned gaze set him to quivering again.

"Very well. Is your horse in the stable?" Madigan asked.

"It is, it is."

Venetia could not help but feel a little pity for the frightened, round-face man as he tried to right his wig on his head and straighten his coat. "My … my cloak and hat, Mister Crutcher? And … and mayhap a lantern to light my way?"

Crutcher nodded to Spice. "Simpson, will you retrieve Mister Spice's hat and cloak and see do we have a lantern to light his way."

"Yes, sir, Mister Crutcher," Simpson said, but before Spice was allowed to claim his articles, Madigan grabbed him by his coat lapels.

"I had best never see you again, Spice," Madigan ground out in slow syllables.

"No, sir, no, sir," Spice said, fumbling with his cloak before donning it and his hat, and with the lantern Simpson gave him in hand, he scurried out the door.

"Have you more lanterns?" Madigan asked. "I fear we will have need of several."

"Oh, but sir, you cannot think to leave tonight," Crutcher said. "'Tis raining. You cannot think to take the ladies out in the rain. And they have had little to eat. I have a supper prepared. Though it grows cold. But surely you must stay the night and set out fresh in the morning."

166

Madigan looked to Tuftwick. "What do you think, Tuffy?"

Tuftwick looked down at Venetia. "I think we would be fools to set out in the rain and the dark when Mister Crutcher is offering us his hospitality. What think you, Lady Venetia?"

She loved the way he cared about what she thought, what she wanted. She looked to Delphine. "I think we should stay the night. Delphine and I already know how comfortable the bed in our chamber is."

Delphine chuckled. "After today's ride, I have no wish to set out again. However, I would like to know if my Fire Dancer has been properly cared for."

"I will see to him," Purdy said.

"Thank you, Purdy. Besides being my avenging angel, you see to my every need."

"I try, Mistress."

"I will go with you," Simpson said. "I must see extra wood is brought in and extra water drawn and heated that the gentlemen may see to their ablutions before supper is served."

Delphine caught Simpson's hand. "I thank you, Simpson. For all you did for us."

He nodded. "'Twas but right, Mistress Lotterby."

Madigan turned to Anker. "Would you and Purdy be comfortable bedding down here tonight that you might take turns guarding these jackanapes?"

Glancing down at the men at his feet, Anker scoffed, "I but wish they would give me cause to whack them again. 'Twill be near a pleasure to stand guard over them. Could I make them any more miserable, I would. What they did to Mistress Lotterby and Lady Venetia is not to be forgotten or forgiven."

Venetia widened her eyes. Anker was always so quiet. Fact was, she seldom ever heard him speak. Now to make such a speech. Delphine had certainly earned and held her footmen's loyalty. She doubted even King Charles could claim any more devotion from his royalists subjects. Thank God for that loyalty. Otherwise, Delphine might now be married to Flynn.

Chapter 23

Seated around Crutcher's dining table, Crutcher's guests enjoyed a late and slightly cold supper, but Madigan noted no one seemed to mind. They were all ravenous, and only after initial hunger was appeased, did they begin to tell their tales. Delphine and Venetia first described their ordeal; their fast, hard ride with nary a respite, Flynn's threats, their fears that they would not be rescued before Flynn found some way to beat down the door to their chamber. They praised Simpson for all his help, but in particular for insuring no ax could be found. Tuftwick swore he would see the man well rewarded.

Madigan felt shamed that he could not make such an offer. Having nothing he could call his own was beginning to prick his pride. As Tuftwick explained how they discovered where Flynn was taking his captives and lauded Purdy's initiative and resourcefulness, Madigan looked sourly down at his plate. Delphine's hand on his made him glance up. Her smile radiant, she asked, "Do tell how you managed to take Flynn's men without any disturbance. We heard nothing from our room."

"That was Maddy's doing all right," Tuftwick said, "but let us not get ahead on our tale. We should have been here sooner for we, too, rode hard, and our horses had been rested, but we had to keep stopping at various cottages to ask were we on the right trace. When we learned from a cottager that Crutcher's Hall was just around the next bend, on a low cliff, not but a short ride up the lane, we had to draw up and formulate our attack. We had learned from the smith that Flynn had paid off three of his men, but he still had three with him when he left the village. We could but assume they were yet with him. Dark was falling fast, but we needed to reconnoiter."

Delphine touched Madigan's hand again. "Did you do the reconnoitering, Maddy?"

He turned to her. Her eyes, looking into his, were so trustful. She had been in his protection, and he had let her be abducted, had been unable to do anything to stop the abduction, yet she seemed not to hold him at fault. That she was now safe he knew was primarily due to her footman's astuteness. Purdy had discovered her captor's destination, but once they reached the hall, Purdy let him and Tuftwick plan the attack. Trying to think what D'Arcy would do, Madigan had decided Purdy and Anker should stay with the horses while he and Tuftwick scouted the grounds. D'Arcy would want to know what and who they had to contend with. Madigan hoped they would be but four against four.

"The unknown was Crutcher and his staff," he said. "Were they also Flynn's cohorts? Once we had the hall in view, Tuffy and I dismounted and worked our way around to the back of the hall." He recounted the sun, lingering in the sky, casting shadows that gave them cover as they raced from tree to bush to outbuildings. "Spying the stables, we were set to dash across an open area to reach it when a man rode up, and a stableman came out to take his horse."

"We have since learned that man was Spice," Tuftwick threw in.

"Aye," Maddy agreed. "Spice made his way to the stairs leading up to the hall, and we saw Flynn greet him. We then knew we had found you." He looked at Delphine, and her smile encouraged him to continue.

"The stableman led Spice's horse into the stable, and Tuffy and I determined I should have a talk with the stableman. Learn what I could about the location of Flynn's men while Tuffy returned for Purdy and Anker. I was prepared to use whatever methods I needed to use to get the information from the stableman, but I found the man more than willing to be of help. He had no love for Flynn or his henchmen."

For a moment, Madigan let his thoughts sift back over the stableman's comments. "Two o' 'em be above, sleepin' in me bed. Been that way for near a month now," he grumbled. "Me stuck on a cot down here wi' the horses. T'other one be in the hall wi' Sir Milton. More his personal servant, he is. Them other two," he raised his eyes upward, "they jest be a couple o' mullipuffs. Eat, sleep, and ride out when Sir Milton goes anywhere. That be all they do. Poor Mister Crutcher. He is not wantin' 'em here, but he is that afraid o' his cousin."

Seeing Delphine looking at him questioningly, he smiled and resumed his tale. "I learned two of Flynn's henchmen were in the stable loft, and once Tuffy arrived with Anker and Purdy, it was easy to sneak up and overpower them. The next question was how to get into the hall unseen. That question was easily answered when Simpson came out to hide the ax and hatchet and to warn the gardener to hide anything else that might be of use to Flynn. We found Simpson more than ready to help. He, too, had had his fill of Flynn. We learned Flynn's third man was in the kitchen, annoying Crutcher's cook and tormenting the scullery lad who is not all right in his head. Simpson agreed to distract Flynn's man. A blow to the man's head, and he was out until he woke up in the hall, trussed up like a chicken ready for the spit."

"Soon as we entered the kitchen, we heard Flynn bellowing," Tuftwick said, "but Simpson assured us he could in no way beat down the door to your chamber." He looked at Venetia. "That is all that kept me from dashing up the stairs to you. I helped Anker and Purdy and the stablemen get the three men into the hall while Maddy, being the better swordsman, went up to put a stop to the bellowing."

"And none too soon," Crutcher said, rubbing his throat. "I feared he meant to kill me."

"I am but grateful the door to our chamber was so sturdy and the lock so strong," Delphine said, smiling warmly at Crutcher.

She has a generous heart, Madigan thought. But these abductions and attempted abductions must be stopped. And he knew how he could stop them.

"Like I told Milton," Crutcher was saying, "I bought this hall because its history intrigued me. I left much of the hall unaltered, including the chamber you were in, Mistress Lotterby. I am a quiet man. I like to read, to walk in my garden on sunny days. The estate is enough distance from Glasson to give me my privacy, but not so far we cannot go into town for any needs we may have."

He glanced at Simpson who was pouring more wine for everyone. "I cannot say how I would manage without Simpson. He is my personal servant, he serves my meals, and as my steward, he sees to the smooth functioning of the hall. Sadly, we have no women to tend your needs." He looked first to Delphine and then to Venetia. "But once a week the woodcutter's wife comes to do our laundry, and their daughter does any cleaning we may need doing."

"Well you have a lovely home, Mister Crutcher," Delphine said, and their host looked pleased by the compliment.

"When this was a knight's hall, guarding the shore, this room was the chapel," he said. "Like the hall and the kitchen, it was two stories high. Its ceiling was the beams of the roof as you see in the hall. Did the knight and his lady not wish to join their servants for the morning service which was held every morning, they could view it from the solar above. I added this ceiling to insert the second floor." He looked up at the delicate swirls in the white plaster ceiling. "I wanted my bed chamber above this room, so when I look up at night, I could see the chapel beams." He smiled. "Somehow it is soothing to me."

"What of your ground floor?" Tuftwick asked. "I noted the main entrance is here on the first floor. I would guess that would have been for defense purposes."

"Yes. In fact the stairs leading up to the hall entrance were originally of wood and could be drawn up inside was the hall attacked. The knight who built this hall would have used half the ground floor to store supplies, and half to hold any prized animals during an attack. Now, I too use half for supplies, the other half I partitioned into rooms for some of my staff. There is a small room off the solar where Simpson normally sleeps, but he will see it made up for you and Mister Madigan tonight."

"Here, now, after all he has done for us and our ladies, I cannot feel right putting him from his room," Tuftwick said, and Madigan agreed with him.

"Begging your pardons, sirs," Simpson said, "but whenever Mister Crutcher has overnight guests, 'tis the norm that I move in with the cook. I would not feel comfortable did I not see his guests suitably accommodated."

"You are too good, Simpson," Delphine said. "Indeed, you are."

"You are kind, Mistress," Simpson said with a deferential nod of his head.

"She is right," Venetia said, her lovely eyes glowing, and making Madigan marvel at her beauty and sweetness. He could not help but notice the besotted look on Tuftwick's face. His friend was so very much in love.

"You – and Mister Crutcher, too," Venetia continued, "and the stableman, and all the staff have been most heroic. But I have a worry. On the morrow, after we leave, Mister Crutcher, you will have to free your cousin and his men? Will Flynn not be very angry with you and with Simpson? Might he try to harm either of you?"

"I admit that has worried me, too," Madigan said. "Even did we take them into Glasson to the constable, my guess is they would soon be freed, and could be even more angry."

Frowning, Crutcher nodded his head. "Yes, yes, that does pose a problem, but Milton owes me a substantial sum for a loan I gave him to pay one of his fines. I have no need of the funds at this time. Fact is, I doubted Milton would ever pay me back. Do I forgive him the loan, I believe he will not be overtly abusive."

"I hope you may be correct," Delphine said, "but do allow me to reimburse you. I have no wish to aid Flynn in any manner, but I would not like to see you suffer for helping to protect me. And doubt me not, I can easily afford it. 'Tis why Flynn wanted to force me into marriage."

Crutcher shook his head. "No, no, Mistress Lotterby, I could not take your money."

"Nonsense," Venetia said. "She will never miss it. My sister-in-law is always claiming Delphine is as rich as Croesus. Just be certain Flynn never learns she is paying you and thereby paying his fine for him."

Crutcher still looked unsure, but when Delphine again insisted, he demurred and agreed to accept a sum. Madigan wondered just how wealthy Delphine was. He knew men were after her fortune, but he was beginning to think that fortune must be immense.

"Normally I would invite my guests to remove to the parlor at supper's end," Crutcher said, "but as the hour is already late, and it has been a trying day for everyone, mayhap you would prefer to retire to your chambers."

"Aye, as we must rise early, I think that might be best," Tuftwick said. "We will want to arrive in Lancaster as soon as possible to relieve Lord Grasmere's worry for his sister and his cousin."

"I will make certain all is well with Purdy and Anker," Madigan said.

"I saw the stableman had set up a cot for them. They intend to alternate standing guard over Flynn and his men. Not that I think they could escape their bounds, but 'tis best not to take chances."

"Your men have been given their suppers, sir," Simpson said, "and I have left them blankets, extra candles, and some ale. I trust you will find them comfortable. Now I will see to your room while the scullery lad clears the table. All will soon be ready for you."

"Thank you, Simpson," Madigan said, rising as Crutcher rose to indicate an end to the meal. Delphine and Venetia bid their host goodnight, and with a candle to light their way headed up the stairs behind Simpson.

Madigan and Tuftwick stopped in the hall to insure all was well.

"The stableman retrieved our horses, and the gardener helped him brush them down," Purdy said. "And as I told Mistress Lotterby, her horse and Lady Venetia's horse had both been well cared for. Mister Crutcher has himself a fine stableman who knows his horseflesh, and he knows how to properly care for the needs of his horses."

Madigan looked at Flynn and his men. They could not look much more uncomfortable. Good. After what they had done, they deserved nothing better.

"Gave them each a swig of ale," Purdy said, "but their stomachs will have to rumble tonight. I figure they will be less likely to want to chase after us on the morrow do they first need to assuage their hunger and tend their business. That is have they not soiled their breeches by the time they are released."

Tuftwick chuckled, but Madigan asked, "Think you they would be likely to follow us?"

Purdy cocked his head thoughtfully. "For Flynn to be so brazen in his abduction of Mistress Lotterby, I am guessing he is in desperate straits. In none of the other abduction attempts has the person behind the attempts revealed himself. There have been paid henchmen, but the identity of whomever had paid them has never been determined. So, will Flynn make another attempt?" He shrugged.

"I see," Madigan said. He was becoming even more determined Delphine would not again experience such terror. He wished he had run his sword through Flynn when he had the chance. The man was malevolent. Though he was gaged, his eyes spoke his hate and anger.

"Let us find our room," Tuftwick said. "I want to be fresh and alert in the morning. We have a long ride, and two dear ladies to protect."

"Aye, tomorrow will be a long day." He looked back at Purdy. "Do you need us for any reason, just give a loud holler."

"That we will Mister Madigan, and good night to you, and to you, Lord Tuftwick."

In arriving at their allotted room, they found Simpson, his arms loaded with used sheets, headed out. "Your bed is made," Simpson said, "however, you will find what was once the privy, is now a closet for the solar, and is strictly for the use of the occupants of the solar. You will find a chamber pot under the bed do you find yourself in need."

"Did I not know how highly Crutcher values you," Tuftwick said, "I would be attempting to lure you away from him. You have served our ladies well, and we are in your debt."

Ever dignified, Simpson said, "I could tell you I was from a family that lost its wealth, but the truth is, I am of humble origins. My father was a peasant farmer. My brother still is." He shook his head. "I had no wish to end my days shackled to a plow. Though I had little formal training, I watched and learned. Luck was with me, and I was given work in Mister Crutcher's father's home. Mister Crutcher saw potential in me, saw to my education, and employed me first as his personal servant, then when he bought this hall, I also became his steward. I will ever be grateful to him, and I serve him to the best of my ability."

"Indeed, you serve him well," Tuftwick said.

"Mister Crutcher is a good man. I could tell how upset he was once he learned Mistress Lotterby had no wish to marry Sir Milton. 'Twas then my duty to help protect the ladies."

"And so you have," Tuftwick said, and pulling his purse from his pocket, he handed Simpson several coins. "Please take these with our gratitude."

Holding the coins in his open palm, Simpson said, "'Tis not necessary, Lord Tuftwick."

Tuftwick folded Simpson's fingers around the coins. "Yes, it is. If not for your benefit, then for ours. We would feel we were remiss did we not reward you in some manner, and our thanks alone seems inadequate."

Simpson bowed his head ever so slightly. "Then I accept your generosity, and I thank you. And I bid you a peaceful night's sleep."

Madigan watched Simpson head back down the stairs. A good man. As loyal to Crutcher as Purdy and Anker were to Delphine. But Delphine needed more than the loyalty of her servants. His mind resolved, he said, "I wish to ascertain Mistress Lotterby has fastened her lock. I cannot think anything will go amiss, all the same, best to take all precautions. I shall return momentarily."

"Wise, very wise," Tuftwick said as Madigan headed down the corridor to tap on Delphine's door.

As he had hoped, Delphine answered his knock. Frowning, he shook his head. "Your door should be bolted."

With but a single candle lighting the room, she stood in the shadows. "Have no fear," she said. "Venetia and I are readied for bed. I was coming to throw the bolt into place when I heard your knock."

"You should also ascertain who is knocking before opening the door," he said, putting off what he wanted to say.

She stepped closer and for the first time, he realized she had shed her riding costume and was in naught but her shift with her coat draped over her shoulders. "I promise, Maddy, I will bolt the door and will not again open it until I know 'tis safe," she said smiling up at him.

He could recall no time in his life he had ever been so nervous, but there was nothing for it but to blurt it out. "Delphine, if you are still of a mind that you wish to marry me, I have decided to accept the proposal you made." Before she could answer, he held up a hand. "But I understand, have you reconsidered."

Her smile broadened until it seemed to encompass her whole face. "Oh, Maddy, you have made me very happy. And would it not distress you, I would wish to be wed as soon as we may have banns read when we reach Grasmere. I will feel so safe having you as my husband."

"I am of the same mind. I believe we need be married as soon as possible. These abduction attempts must stop. And the only way I can see them stopping is for you to marry. I but pray you will not come to wish you had married someone of a higher station."

She caught his hand. "I know I will be completely content. You will

175

see, we are well matched." Raising his hand to her lips, she kissed his fingertips. "Good night, my savior."

For a moment after she released his hand and closed the door, and he heard the heavy bar thrown into place, he could do nothing but stare at the door. What had he done? He had committed himself to marriage to Delphine Lotterby. Shaking his head, he turned back toward his room. What had he done?

Chapter 24

Hugging herself, Delphine leaned back against the door. The wish she had feared would never become reality had at last come true. She was to marry Torrance Madigan, the only man she ever had or ever would love. Happy tingles raced up and down her spine, and she shivered.

"Whatever are you doing, Delphine, just standing there shivering. Are you cold, come to bed." Venetia had already climbed into the bed and had the blankets pulled up to her chin.

Her heart pounding joyously in her chest, Delphine said, "Yes, yes, I am coming," and she hurried to the bed, dropped her coat on the chair with the rest of her clothing, and crawled in beside her cousin. Snuggling under the covers, she caught Venetia's hand. "What a wonderful night this is," she said.

"Wonderful night! Have you gone mad? You were near forced into marriage with that odious Flynn. How can you call this wonderful?"

Squeezing Venetia's fingers until she yelped and jerked her hand away, Delphine chuckled and said, "Oh, but dear one, we have been rescued. Is that not wonderful?" Before Venetia could answer, she added, "And you have finally been kissed by Lord Tuftwick. Was it is as marvelous as you had hoped?"

Venetia sat up in bed and caught her knees to her chin. "Oh, Delphine, 'twas even more marvelous than I had imagined. I have no doubt now that I have fallen in love with Henry. Does he but ask me to marry him, I will say yes."

"You tell me Lord Tuftwick has not already asked you to marry him?"

"He has said nothing more since the day he asked if he could court me. But now that he has kissed me, I feel he will ask Berold for my hand."

"I have no doubt he will. The man loves you deeply. 'Tis easy to see."

177

Lying back down, Venetia said, "Yes, I believe he does."

After rising enough to blow out the candle, Delphine plopped back down on the bed. Though the room was dark but for occasional glimpses of the moon when it peeked from behind the rain clouds and the glow of the banked fire in the hearth, Delphine could feel Venetia turn to her. "I cannot begin to describe to you how I felt when Henry wrapped me in his arms and kissed me. 'Twas so unexpected yet so exhilarating. My heart pounded in my temples. My legs went weak. I wanted the kiss to never end. And I cannot wait until he may kiss me again."

"'Twas better then than any other kiss you have experienced?" Delphine could not ask Venetia if the kiss was better than when Maddy had kissed her. Venetia was not aware Delphine had witnessed that kiss.

"Oh, yes, far better. 'Twas sweet. Gentle, yet demanding. Oh, 'tis hard to describe. Not that I have had all that many kisses to compare to Henry's, but 'twas not just the kiss. 'Twas the way he looked at me, the way he held me, the way he knew he needed to kiss me to prove his concern for my well-being." She bounced the bed as she changed her position. "Dear Delphine, I feel ashamed to tell you, but I was feeling neglected. All attention was directed to you and your safety. Yet I, too, had been through an ordeal."

"Indeed you had, dear, and you need feel no shame at wanting your courage to be acknowledged."

"Oh, but I do feel ashamed. But the wonderful thing is, Henry recognized my need. His kiss told me he knew what I had endured, and he was ever so relieved I was unharmed. I needed that acknowledgement."

"And you deserve it, for you were immensely brave. You showed no fear in standing up to Flynn on my behalf, and I treasure your love for me. But I am glad you have decided Lord Tuftwick is the lover you have been hoping to find. I think he will suit you well."

"Yes, I believe he will, but you must promise you will come to stay with us often. Otherwise, I will miss you terribly."

"I do so promise. Now let us go to sleep. The morrow will be upon us all too soon."

Delphine felt Venetia turn to her side, and she hoped her cousin would soon be asleep. She wanted time to think about Maddy. To recall his words and the look on his face. She had chosen not to tell Venetia about hers and Maddy's decision to marry. She wanted to keep it wrapped safely in her heart for at least this night. Just her own joyous secret. On the morrow, she would ask Maddy when he would like to make the announcement. She could not doubt that both Venetia and Tuftwick would be delighted for them.

At first, Berold would not be pleased, but he would come around quickly enough. He liked Maddy, and he wanted her married so he no longer had to be concerned with her safety. Well, she planned to see they were married as soon as possible. She cared nothing for a big wedding, she but wanted to be wed to the man she loved. And she would win his love. She knew she would. She already had his respect, his friendship. Surely love would follow.

She had not expected to easily go to sleep. She had thought her joy and excitement might well keep her awake long into the night, but being emotionally drained by a long and frightening day, and an exhilarating evening, her tired body cried out for rest, and her mind gave in to her body's pleas, and she slept.

※　※　※　※

Venetia heard Delphine's even breathing and knew her cousin had fallen asleep. She wanted to go to sleep herself, but her mind kept tripping over the events of the day. The abduction, the fast-paced, forced ride that had her worried about her mare, Flynn's threats and the plans he had made to force Delphine into marrying him. What might they have done had the door to their room not been so sturdy, and had Simpson not been so ready to help them, to keep the ax away from Flynn? What if Delphine's footman, Purdy, had not discovered where Flynn had taken them? And what would she and Delphine have done if they had not been rescued?

She knew Delphine would never have let Flynn harm her. So Delphine would have ended up being married to Flynn. He would have carted Delphine off to France. She had no doubt Delphine would have fought Flynn. But Flynn was powerful. He would have won. The thought nearly made her gag. That her dear Delphine could have been cruelly taken by a man she hated was too horrid to contemplate. Somehow, she had to get Delphine safely married. If only Delphine would not be so picky. No. That was not fair. She was as picky herself. She could not expect Delphine to be less so. Still, her fear for her beloved cousin was overriding her joy in Henry's kiss. She wished she could be kissing him at this very moment. His kiss would turn her mind away from this horrid day and her myriad of fears for Delphine.

Oh, sleep, sleep, please take me, she prayed. And let me dream of Henry. Dream of our wedding, and our wedding night. Henry's kiss had stirred feelings in her she had never before felt. Yearnings that confused her, but she believed only Henry could satisfy. She touched the nether region between her legs. Yes, the sensations stirring throughout her body were new and appealing. With her thoughts at last turned away from the day's trauma, she felt her tenseness evaporate, and soon she drifted into sleep.

❀ ❀ ❀ ❀

Phillida stared blankly at the dark ceiling. She wished Berold would come to bed. She hated being in a strange bed without him. She knew he was terribly worried about his sister. She could not blame him, but somehow, she just knew no harm would come to Venetia or Delphine. Tuftwick and Madigan would find them in time, before Flynn could harm Venetia or force Delphine to marry him. The message Tuftwick had left at the smith's said they were certain of where Flynn was taking his captives. They said they would rescue Venetia and Delphine and rejoin them at the Blomsters' in Lancaster.

Caleb Hayward had repeatedly assured Berold he should not worry. "Tuftwick and Maddy have had three years of training with D'Arcy. They will know what to do to bring your sister and cousin safely back to you. Trust me. I know them well."

"As indeed he should," Sidonie added. "Did they not get Caleb and me safely to Harp's Ridge despite mine and Caleb's impairments?"

Berold nodded his head, but Phillida believed he had been only half listening to the Haywards' assurances. He had hated being stuck in the coach, but his and Hayward's horses had been taken by Purdy and

Anker. By the time they arrived at the Blomsters', he was in a foul mood which had not dissipated as the evening progressed. The aging Blomsters were lovely hosts. They had served them a sumptuous supper with plenty of wine, but Berold had remained cross and uncommunicative, his forehead in a continual frown.

Phillida had been grateful for Sidonie's presence. Sidonie had kept up a flow of congenial chatter that helped relieve the tension and hopefully assured the Blomsters that their gracious hospitality was appreciated. As Sidonie needed to feed her baby, and Phillida was exhausted, Mistress Blomster, the smile on her wrinkled countenance showing the strain of the evening, had taken them up to their rooms, saying she, too, would retire and leave the men to their grousing.

Normally their stopover at the Blomsters' was the high point of the trek to Grasmere, but the shopping Phillida had been looking forward to would not come to pass. She could not go out and enjoy the city and its shops and sights until Venetia and Delphine had been returned to their bosoms. She knew Berold was concerned for his sister and his cousin, but she knew his anger had increased as the long day progressed into night. He blamed Delphine for the abduction.

"Had she married years ago as she rightfully should have," he proclaimed, his hands flat on the table, his fingers drumming, "Venetia would not now be in the hands of that black-hearted villain. Delphine has had many a chance to marry. In fact, could have married your older son." He looked at Mister Blomster who was trying to look supportive.

The dear man pulled at his beard and coughed. "Well, Wilbur might not have been a good match for Mistress Lotterby. She being a dear lady, but mayhap a bit headstrong. Indeed, Wilbur is very pleased with his wife. She has recently given him a fine son."

"Calling Delphine headstrong is an understatement," Berold snapped, ignoring the fact Blomster seemed glad his son had not married Delphine. "Could have married a Duke or an Earl, but no, she could not love them. She could have grown to love them."

"Now, dear," Phillida interjected. "Delphine grew up seeing the love her father bore her mother. Then, when fostered at the Wollowchets', she saw their love for one another." She held up her hand as he started to protest. "And she has seen the love you and I share. So how can you blame her for wanting to marry someone she could love?"

"I blame her because she has put my sister's life in danger. That is how I can blame her. Call it unreasonable if you will, I care not. My intent is to keep her away from Venetia from now on. Until Delphine is married, Venetia can no longer be in her company. That is my intent!"

His face red, his eyes fuming, Phillida had known better than to say anything else. That was when Sidonie said, "Oh, my, I am tired, and no doubt William is ready for his feeding."

"Yes, I am also tired," Phillida said, and Mistress Blomster had eagerly escorted them to their rooms. Now, lying in bed wishing she had her husband beside her, she wondered how Venetia and Delphine would take Berold's pronouncement that he meant to separate them. Well, maybe that would not be necessary. Mayhap Lord Tuftwick would separate them. She was certain Tuftwick and Venetia had fallen in love. It was but a matter of time before Tuftwick asked Berold for Venetia's hand. Once Venetia was married, Delphine would not be so insensitive as to think she could continue to spend all her time with her cousin.

Phillida sighed. She knew Berold was chastising himself for giving Flynn his blessing to court Delphine. He believed he had encouraged Flynn. Made Flynn think he would approve his forcing Delphine into marriage, just to have her married. Berold might be furious with Delphine at the moment, but he would never want her to be stuck in an unhappy marriage despite his claims that she could grow to love whomever she might marry.

In thinking of Flynn's behavior, Phillida decided on the morrow, she must write to Mistress Creswell. 'Twould never do for Creswell's daughter, Anna, to marry such a fiend. She would hope, too, that Mistress Creswell would tell Lord Rigdale of Flynn's abduction of Venetia and Delphine. The man should not be allowed in good homes. That is if he was still alive.

She had seen the look on Madigan's face. She had no doubt, had Flynn forced Delphine into marriage, Flynn was a dead man. Tuftwick's eyes had been cold and worried, yes, but not murderous. But he had known the woman he loved was not the one to be forced into an unwanted marriage. Envisioning Madigan and Tuftwick setting off to retrieve their ladies, she had no fear they would not accomplish their

182

goal. Hayward was right. Flynn was no match for them. They had three years of experience in clandestine pursuits. They would not fail.

Deciding she must give up on her hope Berold would soon be joining her, she shut her eyes. She let her thoughts drift to sweet little William. Oh, how she wished for another baby. A brother or sister for Timandra. She was glad William seemed to be getting over his cough, though the poor little dear still had a stuffy nose that made his feeding difficult for him. At least he was a sturdy little fellow. He should soon be well again. And having him and Sidonie with her on this journey was making it the most pleasant of any of her previous trips to Grasmere.

Half-smiling, she let visions of Knightswood and her plans for the summer take command of her thoughts. Eventually, Berold would come to bed.

Chapter 25

Having broken their fast, everyone rose from the table, eager to start their day. Delphine again thanked Crutcher for his gracious hospitality. She complimented him on the comfortable bed, the cleanliness of the linens, and the filling meals he provided them. "Oh, and I do hope Flynn will not harm you for your aid to us."

Crutcher looked worried, but firmed his lips. "I think he will not. I believe he must know himself to be in enough trouble already. Besides, before I release him, I will have my staff here with me. He will bluster as he is oft to do, but after a night in his cramped condition, I think he will not wish to attempt to throttle me as he did last night."

"Does he harm you," Tuftwick said, dropping a hand on Crutcher's shoulder, "he will find himself again answering to us. I will remind him of that."

Entering the dining chamber from the hall, Simpson said, "The stableman has informed me your horses are ready, and your men await you."

"Thank you," Maddy said. "We should go." He had barely looked at Delphine all morning, and she had begun to wonder if she had dreamed his proposal, or worse, was he regretting it, but when he turned to her, he gave her a little wink. He winked at her. They were sharing a secret, and he was enjoying it. Happy day!

When they entered the hall, Tuftwick issued his warning to Flynn, but Flynn was making so many noises and grunts, and indicating his gag should be removed that Tuftwick warily pulled it down. "You have something you want to say?"

Flynn, his eyes glaring, spit a couple of times then, his gaze on Delphine, he said, "You are promised to me. Before witnesses including my cousin, you promised to marry me."

Delphine raised her brows. "Nay, Sir Milton, never did I make such a promise. I said I must marry someone, but I never said it would be you. It will never be you." She put her hand on the hilt of her knife in its scabbard at her girdle. "Marry you, no. Drive my knife into you, yes."

"You will not get away with this. The banns have been read."

"I gave no consent to the banns. They are worthless."

"You ..." Flynn tried to say more but Tuftwick stuck the gag back in his mouth. Still Flynn made angry noises, until Maddy looked down at him and said, "Enough of this! Mistress Lotterby is marrying me. And do you ever come near her again, you are a dead man."

Delphine heard Venetia's gasp and Tuftwick's, "What!"

"What did you just say!" Venetia demanded, looking first at Maddy, then to Delphine.

Delphine laughed at the expression on her cousin's and Tuftwick's faces, but Maddy said, "You heard correctly. Delphine and I have long been promised. Even had Flynn forced her into marriage, it would not be legal as she did plight her troth with me."

Venetia grabbed Delphine. "How could you not have told me this!"

Delphine glanced at Maddy. It had been near six weeks since she had asked him to marry her. He had not given her his answer until just the previous evening, but did he consider them betrothed since her proposal, then so did she. "We thought to wait until we reached Grasmere. All were so busy what with Mistress Hayward's baby, and the plans for our trek to Knightswood. Then, too, Maddy had some concern about Berold."

"Oh, poo on Berold!" Venetia said, giving Delphine another hug. "I am just so very happy for you. I must say, ever in each other's company as you have been, I had a feeling the two of you had fallen in love. Did you not think so, Henry?"

"Sorry, my dear, but I have had eyes only for you. I spent little time watching Maddy or Mistress Lotterby. But I will say, I could not be happier for the both of you," he added, with a glance at Delphine before pulling Maddy into an embrace and pounding his back.

Extricating himself from Tuftwick's embrace, Maddy said, "I think we must be going. Berold will be worried."

"Yes, yes," Delphine said, "we must be going." She turned to Crutcher. "Thank you again. You have been a most gracious host."

"Congratulations to you, Mistress Lotterby." He looked at Maddy. "And congratulations to you Mister Madigan," he said, escorting them to his door.

Delphine knew she would have to immediately tell Purdy and Anker of her betrothal. They were her dear and loyal servants. She owed them much, and she would not have them learn of her betrothal except from her own lips. She determined before they even set out, she would tell them. And as she expected, though they were, as always, differential, she could tell they were pleased. That pleased her. It meant they liked Maddy and that was important to her. She hoped Tatty would be as approving.

Her heart fluttering with joy, she let Maddy boost her up onto her saddle, and in a matter of moments, they were on their way to Lancaster.

☙ ☙ ☙ ☙

Venetia could scarcely control her excitement. Delphine was to marry Madigan. How Delphine kept news of her betrothal from her all these weeks, she could not imagine. She would never be able to keep silent were she and Henry betrothed. And she had little doubt but they would very soon be betrothed. Funny how she had thought Madigan was in love with her. After all, he had kissed her. She thunked her hand to her forehead. Of course, that was it. He had kissed her and realized he was not in love with her. She was so right about how important a kiss could be. She was so glad Henry had finally kissed her. She had thought herself in love with him, but had not been positive. Not until he kissed her. Now she knew he was everything she had hoped for, brave, caring, and passionate.

She wondered how Berold would take Madigan and Delphine's announcement. He might at first be annoyed that Delphine had not married a duke, but he would come round. He liked Madigan. And he wanted Delphine married. She chuckled, soon he would be quite happy about the match, of that she had no doubt.

She looked forward to when she could be alone with Delphine. She had so many questions for her cousin. Their trek to Lancaster should take less than two hours according to Crutcher. He had given directions to Henry and Madigan, and once they reached Lancaster, Purdy would know how to direct them to the Blomsters. Certainly they had been there often enough over the years. She looked forward to being reunited with her family. She knew they would be terribly worried about her and Delphine. With any luck, they should arrive in time to wash up, change their clothing, and rest before dinner.

And at some point, before or after dinner, Henry would speak to Berold. Berold would gladly give his permission for them to be wed, and by supper, she could well be betrothed to Henry. And come night, as they snuggled under the covers, she and Delphine could start planning their weddings.

🌿 🌿 🌿 🌿

When Berold finally released his sister from a scrunching embrace and was assured she was unharmed, he stepped around her to clasp Delphine in a quick hug then stood back, his arms holding her by the shoulders. "You are not married to that blackguard?"

Shaking her head, Delphine laughed. "Nay, nay. We have much to tell you of our eventful evening and of our daring rescue," she glanced at Maddy and Tuftwick, "but we are in need of rest and refreshment first."

"Of course you are," the motherly Mistress Blomster said. "I have your room all ready for you. Ah, and here come your maids ready to greet you." As she spoke, Tatty and Bethel came rushing into the hall.

Bethel joyfully but circumspectly greeted Venetia, but Tatty, great tears running down her withered cheeks, flung her arms around Delphine, and weeping onto her shoulder cried, "Oh, my dear one, I have not known a moment's peace since that fiend abducted you. Tell me true, did he abuse you? Did he force you to marry him?"

Delphine laughed and patted her devoted servant's back. "Nay, Tatty, I was not abused, nor did Flynn force me to marry him. 'Tis a long story. I will tell you more when we are in our chamber, and you may help me out of these worn and dusty garments."

Drying her tears on the back of her hand, Tatty said, "Yes, yes, you must be exhausted after such an ordeal. You and Lady Venetia both."

She looked to Mistress Blomster. "We must have plenty of hot water that they may wash, and some ale to wash the dust from their throats."

Delphine chuckled. Her maid would not normally so boldly address the lady of the house, but all Tatty could see was her duty to Delphine, and was she being untoward, she would not care as long as Delphine's needs were being met.

Fortunately, Mistress Blomster took no umbrage, saying, "I have already ordered that water be heated and taken up to their room as soon as possible. And I will see Cook delays dinner until Lady Venetia and Mistress Lotterby are rested. Now, are they ready, you may escort them to their room."

Phillida, too, embraced Venetia and Delphine before they could depart for their room. "I am so relieved you are returned safe to us. Mister Hayward did assure us Lord Tuftwick and Mister Madigan were most capable and would have no trouble defeating Flynn. I trusted him, but Berold has been beside himself with worry. But now all is well, and come dinner, we will hear your tale. So, go wash and rest."

Delphine could not remember when she had ever so longed for a hot soaking bath in a tub. Such a bath though would have to wait, most likely until they reached Knightswood Castle. For the present, she feared she and Venetia would have to make do with a kitty bath, washing themselves from buckets of water poured into basins. She was pleasantly surprised to find a foot tub in their room, and she learned Tatty and Bethel had both insisted one be readied for their return. She smiled to see the mound of towels being warmed by the fire in the hearth, and dinner clothes spread out upon the tops of their trunks.

"Mistress Hayward did assure us you would be returning before dinner," Bethel said. "When I asked her how she could be so certain, she said she had known Lord Tuftwick and Mister Madigan for too many years not to know they would succeed in their mission."

"Aye," Tatty agreed. "She was quite adamant, so we insisted all be readied for you."

Delphine knew why the Haywards could be so certain Maddy and Tuftwick would succeed in rescuing them. After all, Hayward had ridden with them for three years. He would know well how competent they were. And his wife would know because she trusted her husband's life to their competence every time he rode away with them.

"You must tell Tatty your news," Venetia said. "Oh, and I cannot wait to see Berold's face when you and Mister Madigan tell him."

"What news?" Tatty asked, concern on her face.

Delphine laughed. "Good news, Tatty, look not so frightened. I am to be married. I am to marry Mister Madigan."

Tatty's gray eye's widened, and her pointed nose quivered. "You are to marry? To marry Mister Madigan?" Her eyes narrowed. "You want to marry him? You are not being forced into this because of something that horrid Sir Milton did?"

"Oh, no. I want very much to marry Mister Madigan. I promise you."

"They have been betrothed since before we left Harp's Ridge," Venetia said. "They just chose not to tell anyone, not even me, until they reached Knightswood." She glanced with a pout at Delphine. "But because of yet another abduction, Mister Madigan determined, for Delphine's safety, 'twould be best did all know of the betrothal. They will tell Berold at dinner. So you see, you two have been told even before my brother knows."

Tatty was eyeing Delphine during Venetia's speech, her eyes searching, questioning. She must have been content with what she saw for she smiled broadly and gave Delphine a hug. "At long last, you have found a man who pleases you."

"I have, Tatty, now do be a dear and help me out of this riding costume. And do please see it is well brushed before I must don it again when we continue our trip."

Tatty and Bethel both jumped into action, and by the time the hot water arrived, Delphine and Venetia were down to their shifts and ready to take their turns in the foot tub.

※　※　※　※

Madigan could not help but be happy for his friend. After the women left the parlor, Tuftwick had asked Berold for Venetia's hand did she consent, and Berold had happily given him his blessing. Madigan thought his heart should be breaking. The woman he loved was to marry another, yet his heart was not being wrenched from his chest. Yes, his brain kept saying, you should be bereft. You should be drowning in grief, but he found he could accept his loss with no emotion. He told himself he would feel the pain when he settled in his bed to sleep. Or mayhap on the morrow when the knowledge sank into his soul. But for the moment, his thoughts kept turning to Delphine. How she had looked when he accepted her proposal. She had glowed. She needed him. Needed him to keep her safe. And though he might not bear her the love he bore Venetia, he would strive to be a good and faithful husband to her.

"Your thoughts are far away," Tuftwick said, flicking a speck of lint from the arm of his dinner coat. After Berold had given Tuftwick his blessing, he and Madigan had gone up to their chamber to wash up and change for dinner. His gaze returning to Madigan, Tuftwick said, "I asked if you are ready to go down to dinner?"

"Aye," Madigan said. "I cannot help but think on what Berold will say when Delphine and I tell him of our betrothal."

Remembering what Delphine had said on the ride to Lancaster, he tried to be confident. "Berold is not my guardian, Maddy," she stated. "You need not ask him for my hand. Truth be, 'twould be best do we announce our betrothal to all at the dinner table. That way Berold may not think he has the right to decide whom I may choose to marry."

Venetia had agreed with Delphine. All the same Madigan could not help being apprehensive. He liked Berold, respected him, and would not want Berold to think he was being discourteous or insolent in not first applying to him for Delphine's hand.

"Trust me," Tuftwick said, again bringing Madigan's thoughts back to the present. "Berold will be delighted. You may not be a member of the peerage, but you will be a husband for Mistress Lotterby, and that is what Berold wants more than anything else. He feels a responsibility to protect her even if he is not her guardian. To have her safely married is his greatest wish. Besides, he likes you. Have the three of us not been friends for many years?" He slapped Madigan on the back. "Come now, let us go down and refill these mugs with some of Mistress Blomster's homebrewed ale."

Hoping his friend would be right, and Berold would be pleased, Madigan picked his empty mug up off the table beside the bed and followed Tuftwick out the door.

190

Chapter 26

"Oh, you sly ones," Phillida said. She had at first been taken aback by Delphine's and Madigan's betrothal announcement. She had suspected a tender was forming between them, but she had not suspected they had been betrothed since before they left Harp's Ridge.

Berold had been taken completely by surprise, but then her husband had never been one to observe the interplay between potential lovers. Oh, he had known Tuftwick wanted to marry Venetia because Tuftwick had asked permission to court her, but he had paid no heed to the love blossoming between Delphine and Madigan. Sidonie had seen it and remarked on it. And now she was wishing them her hearty congratulations, as was her dumbfounded husband. Hayward, no more aware of the developing romance than Berold, had risen from his seat to pound Madigan on his back and assure him he would find marriage the best thing to ever happen to him. Then, a beaming smile creasing his face, he looked at his wife. His love for her shone in his eyes.

The Blomsters, too, were full of congratulations, and Mister Blomster ordered his steward to open one of his best bottles of wine that he had been saving for just such a special occasion.

Frowning, Berold at last spoke. "I am not Delphine's guardian, as no doubt she has told you, Maddy. She has reminded me of it often enough over the years. But Maddy, as much as I like you, I must say, I could have liked a match more suitable to her status." He held up a hand as Delphine started to protest. "However, Delphine has chosen you, and I have no doubt you will be a good husband to her. I know you well enough to know that about you. I can but give you both my blessing and hope you plan to marry soon."

Delphine laughed. "No sooner have we reached Grasmere, and we will have the banns read. Neither of us has a wish for a large wedding. I could wish Grandmother could attend, but I know she will understand the need for our hasty wedding. As Maddy has said, these abductions must stop." She looked at Madigan. "Had we announced our betrothal sooner, mayhap Sir Milton would never have abducted me."

Phillida wondered about their betrothal. 'Twas hard to imagine Madigan proposing to Delphine when Phillida had been so certain both he and Tuftwick were in love with Venetia. Could be Madigan, realizing he could never hope to marry Venetia, had decided, like so many other fortune hunters, to try his luck with Delphine. But that was unfair. She could not believe Madigan to be like the many fortune hunters who pursued Delphine over the years. Yet, he would go from being a penniless dependent to a very wealthy man in a matter of weeks.

However, she believed Madigan, if not already in love with Delphine, was fast falling in love with her. And she had not the slightest doubt Delphine was in love with Madigan. Not that she could blame Delphine. Madigan was an exceptionally handsome man with his dark unruly hair and deep brown eyes. He was genteel and polite, and he could be most charming, and most importantly, he was capable of defending and protecting Delphine. Could be Delphine had made a much more suitable choice than she and Berold suspected.

※　※　※　※

Dinner lasted long into the afternoon. Madigan was beginning to think it would never end, but Delphine and Venetia had had their tale to tell, and he and Tuftwick had theirs to tell, both of them giving much credit to Purdy and Anker. Crutcher and Simpson had also been commended, and Mister Blomster said, as he was friends with the shire sheriff, he would ask him to check in on Crutcher to see all was well with him. Blomster understood Delphine and Venetia would not want to have Flynn arrested, for a trial would delay their journey to Knightswood, or cause them to have to return to Lancaster. Plus a trial would cause a scandal, and Lord Grasmere wanted no scandal attached to his sister's name.

When finally the dinner ended with Sidonie saying she must see to her baby, and Mistress Blomster saying she must consult the steward and the cook about meal provisions for supper and the following day, what with her guests staying over an extra day. "Nay, nay," she exclaimed when Lady Grasmere apologized for the extra work and inconvenience. "I made sure you would be staying as you have yet to have your visit to our shops. I know well you wish to make some purchases, as does Mistress Hayward. And Lady Venetia and Mistress Lotterby have always enjoyed shopping here in Lancaster ere they go to Grasmere where so little is offered."

"Ah, dear Ethel, you are ever so good and kind," Lady Grasmere said. "Year upon year you grant us the most hospitable reception."

"Nonsense," spoke up Mister Blomster. "She loves having you stay with us. She brags to all her friends that she is most happy to entertain Lord and Lady Grasmere. Did you ever decide not to stay with us on your way to Grasmere, she would be devastated." He looked at Berold. "And I would miss your company, Grasmere. We are far from London and far from the powers that now rule our realm. You always have the latest news of the escapades taking place. The little on dits that are not common knowledge. 'Tis good to know what to expect."

"I am fortunate to have friends still residing in London," Berold said. "They are good to keep me apprised of what transpires."

Madigan knew much of what Berold learned, he learned from D'Arcy. D'Arcy had contacts everywhere, and a master of disguise, he was in and out of London on a regular basis. Berold's parole from Weymouth tying him to his two estates, he would not be near the fount of information did not D'Arcy keep him abreast of the latest tidings.

"You men can discuss your Parliamentary Acts all you wish," Lady Grasmere said, rising with Mistress Blomster. "I have letters I need to write. I should have written them this morning, but I was too tense, awaiting Venetia's and Delphine's return to us. I will attend them now."

"Myself," Delphine said, her eyes seeking Madigan's. "I would enjoy a stroll in the Blomsters' garden. 'Tis always lovely."

"After last night's rain, it may be a little muddy," Mistress Blomster cautioned, "so be careful where you step. I will send a servant out to dry off the benches do you choose to sit. I must say, this spring I find the roses exceptionally lovely."

"Thank you," Delphine said. "Maddy, do you join me, we have much to discuss."

"Aye," he agreed. "At this point, do you leave the house, I am not apt to let you out of my sight unless Purdy and Anker are with you."

"Wise thinking," Berold said. "The sooner you two are married, the sooner I can breathe more freely."

Venetia's soft rustling laugh floated across the table. "And here Mister Madigan was fearful you would not be pleased about the marriage. I told him he need have no fear. You have been trying to get Delphine to marry someone, anyone, for the past four years."

Berold frowned at his sister, but did not dispute her claim, and Venetia said, "Lord Tuftwick, I would also enjoy a stroll in the garden. Might you accompany me?"

Tuftwick was instantly on his feet. "I would be delighted to accompany you, Lady Venetia, delighted."

She smiled that smile that brought out her dimples, and Madigan thought her the most beautiful woman he had ever seen. She glowed with a heavenly sweetness, and he knew she would soon accept Tuftwick's offer of marriage. She would be lost to him forever. His fate rested with the ebony-eyed, strong-willed woman sitting beside him. Turning to her, he said, "Let us take that stroll. But you might find you need your wrap."

Delphine's gown with its horizontal, low cut décolletage exposed a daring amount of her creamy bust, and he had not been unaware of it. In fact, it had been a bit of a distraction during the meal. Not an unpleasant distraction by any means. No, definitely not unpleasant, but it had made keeping up with some of the conversation buzzing around him more difficult.

Delphine gave him a smile. "A wise idea, Maddy. I shall go up and get a wrap and meet you by the garden door."

He agreed and when she rose, he rose. Venetia, believing she, too, should get a wrap traipsed after Delphine, and with a look from Tuftwick, Madigan followed his friend from the dining chamber leaving Berold and Hayward to discuss the political climate with Blomster.

※ ※ ※ ※

Delphine was pleased when Venetia said she wished to see more of the garden rather than sit on a bench amongst the roses. Her hand on Tuftwick's arm, they continued down a grassy path toward some boxed hedges surrounding a small round pond.

"This bench seems dry, Maddy. I believe we may sit for a spell."

"Do you so wish, Delphine." He pulled out a kerchief. "But here, let me make certain 'tis dry." He wiped the kerchief over the bench, and after returning it to his pocket, he bid her sit.

"'Tis lovely," Delphine said. "The day after a rain is always so glorious. Puddles sparkle with rainbows and drops of water on leaves and flowers look like little drops of crystal."

"You are very poetic today, Delphine."

She breathed deeply of the fresh air. "I cannot help but be poetic, Maddy. I am soon to be a bride." She gave him as smile. "And I can put yesterday's fearful episode behind me. I am safe here with you."

"I hope you found no fault with my claim we were betrothed since you first made your proposal to me?"

"Indeed, I thought it brilliant. No need anyone should ever know differently. Certainly you came to my rescue like a man coming to save his betrothed."

Maddy shook his head. "I never trusted Flynn. Never liked him. When I saw him lay his hand on you at the Creswell's, I could have slain him then."

She looked at him in surprise. "That is very gallant of you. I had no notion you were aware Flynn had accosted me."

"I was very much aware," he admitted. "Berold asked Tuffy and me to be part of his escort that we might see to your safety. I could tell you had no liking for Flynn, and I did my best to stay at your side. Unfortunately, Berold was not as distrustful of Flynn. He purposely gave Flynn the chance to speak with you. My instinct told me Flynn was rotten. I should have had my gun drawn and should have warned Tuffy as well to be alert to Flynn's knavery. D'Arcy would be ashamed of both of us. Are we not alert to all around us, we are dead. I could not help but blame myself that Flynn managed to abduct you right there in our presence."

She patted his hand. "There was naught you could do. Berold accepted Flynn as a gentleman. If he allowed him to proceed through our midst, you had little choice but to follow his lead."

"You are most fortunate to have a man like Purdy working for you. He knew exactly what to do when the rest of us were caterwauling and wringing our hands."

"Well, that would be Purdy. He has been protecting me for many a year. No doubt, he, too, was suspicious of Flynn, but like you, he could do little did Berold allow Flynn to pass through our midst. I plan to make Purdy our house steward when we have a home." She cocked her head. "If you concur."

"Could not think who would be better. I like the man immensely. I like Anker as well."

"Yes, Anker will be second in command. When Purdy has his days off, or wishes to take several weeks off to visit his brother, Anker can fill in for him."

"Splendid idea. But you mention setting up our home. I understand you have a home in Liverpool. Is that where you wish to live?"

"Nay. We would stay there from time to time, but I have no wish to live in Liverpool. Would it not distress you, I would like to purchase a small estate near Lord Tuftwick, that Venetia and I might visit often. That is, of course, assuming Lord Tuftwick offers for her hand and she accepts. Which I do think likely." She narrowed her eyes and watched him closely, trying to judge his feelings. "Of course, does being close to Lord Tuftwick and Venetia once they are married cause you grief, we could instead purchase an estate near Berold."

Maddy shook his head. "I would like an estate near Tuffy. He is dearer to me than any brother could be. Has done more for me. I would like to remain close to him. As to my feelings for Venetia, I have made my peace with them. I will strive to put them behind me." He frowned. "Did you not already know of my love for Venetia, we would not now be having this discussion. I sit here beside you, inhaling the fragrant smell of the roses, knowing we are soon to be wed. I wish you to forget that I once loved Venetia. As I plan to do."

Taking his hands in hers, Delphine said, "Then mayhap we should start our fabrication with a kiss. You have yet to kiss me, Maddy."

He looked like he meant to complain about her use of the word fabrication, but stopped himself. What could he say. Until he realized he was not in love with Venetia, they would be but masquerading. Still, she had waited years upon years to feel Maddy's lips on hers, and she could not wait another moment. Her gaze locked with his, she tilted up her chin. Would he kiss her?

Leaning forward, his lips lightly brushed hers. Not that she had ever been kissed before to know what a kiss should be, but the light brushing of her lips was not what she would call a kiss. Certainly it was not how he had kissed Venetia. Before she could protest, he leaned forward again and slipped an arm around her back, drawing her closer to him. His lips soft, but firm, he planted tentative kisses on her lips before his kiss lengthened and became more demanding. At that point she closed her eyes and let herself float in the long awaited dream. And how wondrous it was. She had needed no kiss to know she loved Maddy, but all the same, she had longed to feel his lips on hers. To her, the moment was sacred. But what would it mean to Maddy.

¥ ¥ ¥ ¥

That Tuftwick had asked Venetia to marry him, and that she had accepted, surprised no one. At the supper table, Mister Blomster ordered another of his best bottles of wine be served to toast the newly betrothed couple. "We have set no time for the wedding," Venetia said, then looking at Tuftwick, she added, "But Henry thinks the sooner the better."

"I cannot blame him there," Hayward said. "We know not what fate awaits us."

Madigan knew Hayward was referring to when D'Arcy might next need their services, and he imagined Tuftwick was eager to have time with his bride err he again rode off with D'Arcy. He wondered if Tuftwick would continue to ride with D'Arcy once he was married. He would not blame Tuftwick if he chose not to continue the dangerous exploits that helped keep their King solvent, or at least with a roof over his head and clothes on his back.

Madigan appreciated that Delphine had told him she would not interfere with his covert jaunts, but he had no intention of setting out with D'Arcy until he and Delphine were safely married – and bedded. He found himself looking more and more eagerly to their wedding night. When he kissed Delphine in the rose garden, he was so quickly aroused, he had needed to hastily end the kiss for fear of embarrassing himself. He was glad his coat was buttoned and came down long, covering his groin. Delphine had looked at him questioningly when he abruptly pulled away from her. He had mumbled something about being circumspect, and she had laughed.

"I believe Venetia complained of Lord Tuftwick being too circumspect. I might say the same. I liked the kiss, Maddy. I have never kissed anyone before. I am not certain I did it right."

That she had never before been kissed surprised Madigan. She was twenty-four. He would have suspected someone would have kissed her. But he rather liked that she had absolutely no experience. Having little experience himself, he would not feel such a dunce when they did consummate their marriage. He had had few opportunities in his youth to be with a woman. Lord Wollowchet had strictly forbidden any dalliances with the maids at the house. Then a week before he and Tuftwick left to join King Charles I, Lord Wollowchet took them into the village to the home of a man dying of the French Pox. The wretched man not only looked grotesque, he was in agony, and his mind was addled.

"Do you not wish to end up like him," Lord Wollowchet said, "you had best think twice or even thrice about relations with the women who follow the armies about."

The sight had made a lasting impression on both him and Tuftwick. There was many the time a dunk in a cold stream or the methodic use of his hand had relieved his youthful needs. A couple of times he had given in to his urges, but even now, he thanked the Lord he had not been infected with the pox.

Reining in his thoughts, he had said, "Have no fear, Delphine, your kiss was lovely." He looked at her with her dark eyes glowing and her lips a little parted as if waiting for another kiss, and he had to fight to restrain himself. Indeed, she looked very comely and desirable. She was not Venetia, but Delphine was a prize, a lovely jewel of a prize, and he could not but think himself very fortunate.

"And so Maddy, do you accompany the ladies when they go shopping tomorrow?" Berold asked from his end of the table, putting a halt to

198

Madigan's desirous thoughts and redirecting them to his duty to protect Delphine.

"I will indeed be accompanying them. And I will expect Delphine's footmen will also be with us." He looked at Tuftwick. "And you, Tuffy, do you join us."

"If Lady Venetia is going shopping, then, yes, I will be going."

"Splendid," Berold said. "I will not have to worry about their safety. Tonight I will make up for the sleep I failed to get last night."

"Amen to that," his wife said. "Amen to that."

Chapter 27

With the women having enjoyed a day of shopping in Lancaster, everyone was in good spirits the next day when they resumed their journey. To Madigan's vast relief, the remainder of their trip was accomplished without incident. The weather cooperated, none of the horses for the coaches or the wagons threw a shoe, no wheels broke off or needed repair – and no one attempted to abduct Delphine. Madigan had remained on the alert, as had Tuftwick. They would not again be betrayed by perceived innocence. Everything and everyone merited scrutiny.

They were to arrive at Knightswood Castle by mid-afternoon. Berold sent one of his out-riders to inform the couple caring for the keep that their arrival was imminent. They had stopped at a tavern for their dinner, but Berold had rushed them through it. He was eager to see that all was well with his manor. With the Puritans in charge, he had to worry constantly that his lands might in some way be compromised – woodland cut, sheep other than his own grazed in his pastures, his boundaries encroached upon. The rights of Royalists were often overlooked, and men pushing for leveling believed they had the right to take what land they wanted.

Madigan had not been to Knightswood in many years. He and Tuftwick had spent a portion of a couple of summers at Knightswood while they were still in training with Berold's father. An old keep, it had had few of the modern conveniences found at Harp's Ridge, but the area was so incredibly beautiful, he could understand how Lady Grasmere looked forward to her sojourn there, and why she believed Sidonie and her husband would benefit from a restive visit. Not that Hayward any longer seemed to be suffering any debility. Still, it was a new experience for Sidonie, and she seemed to be thoroughly enjoying herself. After what she had been through, Madigan believed she was owed some pampered amusement. Fortunately, too, William had recovered from his cold and gave all signs of being a healthy, hearty, and happy baby.

Delphine told him Lady Grasmere had insisted Berold make some major improvements to the square, dark stone, two-story keep. A decorative screen now cut the great hall in half. The front portion of the hall was still used for greeting guests and for Berold to meet with his tenants or to hold court to settle disputes. The back half, with its new chimney, was now a dining chamber. Lady Grasmere also had the chapel remade into two bedchambers. One was a dormitory for their female servants and guests' servants, the other was for the couple who maintained the keep and were its only inhabitants nine months of the year. She retained the solar for her and Berold. It served as their bedchamber and private parlor. The rest of the first floor she turned into four small bedchambers to house Timandra and her nurse, Delphine and Venetia, and any guests, which they had more often than not.

Within the surrounding courtyard, she had insisted the separate kitchen be rebuilt in stone. She also wanted the stables further from the keep. The male servants who came with them from Harp's Ridge should be housed in a dormitory closer to the keep. All the other various out buildings from pig sty to hen coop to dovecot to laundry shed were located beyond the gardens next to the back wall. The keep had a bowling green on one side and a small formal garden on the other side where the ladies could sit beneath beech trees and talk or read or sew. And to please his wife, Berold built a small pavilion just outside the wall where Lady Grasmere could enjoy a view of the lake and the hills and the village of Grasmere.

When they passed through Grasmere on the way to Knightswood, villagers turned out to greet them. Delphine and Venetia threw coins to the children and to souls who looked as though they were in dire need of assistance. Grasmere was not part of the Knightswood Castle manor, but its residents had long been on good terms with the Lotterbys.

Madigan was looking forward to seeing all the changes at Knightswood, but he was not prepared for the immense swath of denuded land beyond the keep that had once been woodland and was now but stumps and grassland filled with grazing sheep. He guessed the lack of woodland created a hardship for the Lotterby tenants who would depend on the wood for fires and the acorns for feed for their pigs.

"Sad, is it not," Delphine said, riding up beside him. "Between the fine and the remodeling of the keep, the woodland had to be sacrificed. Trees were cut from here and from Harp's Ridge, but 'tis not as noticeable at Harp's Ridge. The woodland cut from Harp's Ridge is not within view of the house as it is here. Still, Berold can now graze more sheep, and wool is profitable."

"What of his tenants? How do they fare?"

"'Tis not unlike Harp's Ridge. Most still farm, but some work the fulling mill, others raise cows and make cheese, some are growing hemp, and others are grazing more sheep. These tenants have tenure that allows them more freedom than in many sections of England. Many have prospered and are yeoman farmers or close to it. The fells still supply many of their needs, not just for fuel, but for thatching, and peat is available if the wood is hard come by. I think 'tis the beauty that is missed as much as the woods and the acorns."

"I am glad to hear things are better than they appear."

"Indeed they are. But now, I wonder, are you of a mind to go into Grasmere on the morrow and see the Registrar that we may post our banns."

"Very willing. I near suggested we stop today as we passed through, but I feared delaying Lady Grasmere's arrival. And Berold's. He seems anxious to see all is well with Knightswood." Having made up his mind that he would marry Delphine, Madigan was eager to have it accomplished.

Delphine laughed. "Much as he wants me married, Berold would not have wanted to stop for any reason today. Tomorrow will suit us fine." She pointed to the courtyard gate. "Look, Berold's outrider and Mister Burch are opening the gate. I have no doubt Mistress Burch will have all in readiness for our arrival. She is ever efficient. I cannot think how Berold will manage when someday she and Mister Burch are too old to continue in their present capacity."

"I remember the Burches. They have been with the Lotterbys for many a year."

"Indeed they have." She pointed again to the gate. "Oh, but look. Is that not Mister D'Arcy waving a greeting."

Madigan looked hard at the man waving his arm to Berold. Indeed it was Nate D'Arcy. Now what was he doing here? If he thought he was going to take him away before he had a chance to marry Delphine, he would have to think again.

❧ ❧ ❧ ❧

Phillida could not be more pleased to have finally arrived at Knightswood. The journey had been long, if not arduous, owing to the comfort of Delphine's coach and to Sidonie Hayward's company. All the same, what with Delphine's and Venetia's abduction, the baby's cold, and Berold's grumpiness, she was ready not to spend any more days bouncing along in the coach.

She was overjoyed to find her brother had arrived at Knightswood before them. He had Chapman, Preston, and Yardley with him, and Tomas and Claudia Burch had seen to their comfort and their sleeping arrangements.

"I have thought to put Lady Timandra and her nurse in the dormitory room with your maids," Claudia said, "and the chamber that normally serves them, I have made up for your guests, the Haywards and their baby. Tomas put an extra cot in each guest chamber, and your brother is sharing a room with Mister Preston and Mister Yardley. I have the second guest room arranged for Mister Chapman, Mister Madigan, and Lord Tuftwick. Naturally, Lady Venetia and Mistress Lotterby have their normal bedchamber."

"How perfect you are, Mistress Burch."

The woman acknowledged the compliment with a smile but added, "I have arranged for a couple of the young tenant girls to come help with the daily chores. I know you have your maids who make the beds and see to the hearth fires, but they are not apt to be doing the scullery labors. I notified the laundress that we will be needing her each week, and the gardener, in anticipation of your arrival, has had several lads working with him to have your garden pruned. And the vegetable garden is coming along grandly. Hopefully your cook will find all to his satisfaction."

Phillida shook her head. "Again, I can say naught but how wonderfully efficient you are. Now, my brother says they have been here for two days. I hope their unexpected arrival was not a terrible inconvenience for you."

Claudia's husband, Tomas, spoke up, "Mister D'Arcy is never an inconvenience. Cares for his own horse and clothing, eats whatever he is served and exclaims over it, is ever congenial, and Claudia says she enjoys just looking at him. And that young Mister Preston she finds quite attractive, as well."

Claudia thumped her husband on the shoulder. "Go on with you. Here you stand jawing when you should be helping unload those wagons and coaches."

He laughed. "You are right, you are right. I must make haste, or they may put the wrong trunks in the wrong rooms." Still chuckling, he hurried away.

Claudia turned to Sidonie. "Mistress Hayward, do you wish, I will show you to your room. Water is being heated, and we should soon have it up to you. And I had the cradle brought up from the cellar. 'Tis cleaned and awaiting your baby."

"Thank you, Mistress Burch," Sidonie said before turning to Phillida with a questioning look.

Phillida patted her hand. "Yes, dear, you go ahead with Mistress Burch. I must need direct things down here before I go up. Get some rest, and we will call you in time to ready yourself for supper. I will send Anna to help you."

"I do think I could use a rest," Sidonie said, "but it is so lovely here, I am eager to see more. On the morrow, I hope you may show me around."

"I will, never fear. Now get some rest."

Venetia and Delphine had already ascended the steep and winding staircase to their chamber. Neither looked tired, but then they were both newly betrothed and in love. That was enough to buoy anyone's spirits. That Berold had readily accepted a marriage between Delphine and Madigan told Phillida much about how desperate Berold was to have his cousin married. The last abduction that had put his sister's life in danger had been more than he could tolerate.

She wondered what Nate would say when he learned both Madigan and Tuftwick were betrothed. And would either one decide they no longer wanted to put their lives in danger so they could continue to support their King in exile in Europe. How long should they continue to take these risks? Loyalty to the King was admirable, but was it worth a possible rope around the neck? She thought not, and she knew Sidonie, too, was in constant fear that her husband would be killed or captured.

Nate often said, "Look around you, Phillida. The people are tiring of this Puritan rule. One day we will have our King restored to us."

She hoped he was right, but she feared 'twas little more than wishful thinking. Well, she had no time to worry about the future. She needed to deal with the present. The wagons and coaches were being unloaded, and she needed to direct the placement and destination of the various items. Soon the furnishings she brought from Harp's Ridge would brighten up the darkness of the old keep. Cook would unload his favored pots and pans and he would set about preparing their supper from the various options Phillida was certain Claudia Burch would have secured for him. And then, everyone would go off to bed. And she would cuddle in Berold's arms, and all would be right in her world.

Chapter 28

That D'Arcy was happy for both him and Tuftwick at first surprised Madigan. He had thought D'Arcy might fear he was losing two of his men, but D'Arcy had been more than ready to accept their decision to quit his gang of highwaymen, was that their choice. Madigan had said he would continue, at least for a while. Tuftwick was less certain. He had not yet fully discussed the matter with Venetia. He intended to let her make the decision.

D'Arcy and Chapman had stopped over at Knightswood on their way to the tiny fishing village of Ellenfoot where D'Arcy was to meet his brother and hand over their plunder to Ranulf to take back to King Charles. Preston and Yardley had come along with them to Knightswood to see how the Haywards fared. On their way to Grasmere, the four men had chanced upon a Puritan tax collector and had relieved him of his pouch.

"'Twas almost too easy," Preston told Madigan and Tuftwick while they were rambling up the denuded hillside to get a better view of the lake. "We stopped for dinner in a tavern and overheard a yeoman complaining about the collector and the increase in his taxes. He mentioned the collector rode a fine chestnut horse, and he thought mayhap the animal had been purchased with some of the taxes he collected.

"Now, no sooner had we set off again but what did we see in the road ahead of us but a man in a dark coat and sugar-loaf hat and riding a fine chestnut. Well, we took to the fields and skirted the rider, and before he could reach the next village, we waylaid him. He was the tax collector all right. He sputtered and fumed and issued all kinds of dire warnings, so D'Arcy decided we would take his coat and hat and breeches, and we shooed his horse off into the field."

"Gave us enough time to get well ahead of him," Yardley said, taking over the tale. "By the time he could make his way into the village on foot and find a magistrate, we were long gone. I know what you are thinking, D'Arcy prefers not to pull any robberies in Cheshire or Lancashire, but this was just too easy to pass up. We were well masked, so 'tis not likely did that tax collector ever encounter us again he would recognize us. Even the horses we ride are all nondescript. Never want a recognizable horse like that chestnut."

"Where do you go next?" Tuftwick asked.

Yardley shrugged. "Does Grasmere not object to our company for a few more day, we will stay here until D'Arcy returns. What he has planned for us, we know not."

"For certain we will return for your wedding, Maddy," Preston said. "You are a lucky man. Not only a wealthy heiress, but a beauty in the bargain."

Madigan had not thought of Delphine as a beauty. Attractive, yes, but compared to Venetia, a true beauty, no, so he was surprised by Preston's statement. What was Preston seeing that he had missed? Mayhap he should look more closely at the woman he would soon marry.

"After your wedding," Yardley said, "we will escort Caleb, Sidonie, and baby William home. Both sets of grandparents are eager to see their first grandson."

"What are your wedding plans, Tuftwick?" Preston asked.

"Again, I must defer to Lady Venetia. I feel I am beyond fortunate that she consented to wed me. She is an angel, and I leave all in her hands."

"Well, you are both lucky," Preston said. "Never did we think when Berold asked to have you two accompany him to Grasmere to help protect Mistress Lotterby that the both of you would wind up betrothed."

"Nor did we, but I admit to having been hopeful," Tuftwick said. "I fell in love with Lady Venetia the moment I saw her. I cannot believe all the years she was fostered at my aunt and uncle's and I never paid her any mind." He shook his head. "Now, I cannot get enough of just looking at her."

"I know how you feel," Yardley said. "For years, Tamar lived on the next estate over. I paid her little heed until one day she came round to visit – 'twas a spring day and she had flowers in her hair and a basket of flowers on her arm." Eyes dreamy, he shook his head. "My god, but she looked like a woodland fairy, so fresh with bright eyes and rosy cheeks. You will not believe this, but I leaped down the front steps, took her hand, and right there, asked her to marry me.

"She of course laughed, but I told her I was serious, and she said did I feel the same way on the morrow, to come round her house and ask her father for permission to court her. Bright and early the next morning, I was at her door. Her father seemed surprised to see me. When Tamar told him of my proposal, he had thought I was drunk. And I was. I was drunk with my love for her." Sighing, he frowned. "Lord how I miss being with her. Was I not a wanted man, I would give up this highway robbery and spend my days with my wife and daughter. Sometimes I wish I had served my time like Grasmere did, then I could be out by now and with my wife."

"Had you served your time," Preston said, "she might not be your wife. She might have grown tired of waiting for you to get out of prison and instead married someone else."

"Never!" Yardley said, looking indignant. "Her love for me is as true as mine for her."

Chuckling, Preston slapped him on the back. "Do we not all know it. Any woman willing to marry a man on the run with a price on his head, and have but one night with him before he must flee again, that is a woman in love."

Over and over, Madigan saw his friends in love and marrying the women they loved. How fortunate they were. He knew they thought him fortunate to be marrying Delphine. And he was fortunate. As he could not marry Venetia, Delphine would make him a good wife. But how he envied his friends the love they shared with their mates. From Berold and his lady, to Hayward and Sidonie, to Yardley and Tamar, and to Tuftwick and Venetia, they would ever have something he would never have.

🌿 🌿 🌿 🌿

Delphine shuddered at the thought of Maddy going off with D'Arcy and committing more highway robberies, but she had promised him she would not interfere. She but hoped after their wedding, she would have enough time with him to find herself with child. She hoped to have a number of children. That could well be the only way to keep Maddy safe. Men like Flynn would not think twice about making her a widow. Sometimes she wished she was not nearly so wealthy. But then, that was not fair to her grandfather who had diligently striven to build his fortune. He built it not so much for himself, but for her mother and her. And, she had to admit, having the best of everything was agreeable. Being able to donate to worthwhile charities as well as needy individuals made her feel good. Knowing she could buy an estate near Tuftwick Hall was of utmost importance.

Having told Purdy she wanted him to be her steward once she had a home of her own, she had asked him to research the area near Tuftwick Hall. Purdy objected to leaving her. Until she was wed, and even afterward, he believed his job was to insure her safety, but assuring him Maddy would guard her closely, she insisted he go.

"Do you find an estate you believe suitable, whether 'tis but land we must build a new home on, or whether 'tis an old house that needs remodeling, ask your brother to look it over. I would not think of buying an estate did Benjamin not give his approval. I know 'twill be a trek for him, and will take him from his family, but I must know I am not being cheated."

"I will do my best, Mistress Lotterby. As will Benjamin. I know he will not mind coming to east Lancashire. He will be that happy that you are to wed and settle into your own home."

Tuftwick had given Purdy a letter to his steward, telling his steward to assist Purdy in any way he could and to extend him every courtesy. "Do you and Maddy have an estate near Tuftwick Hall," Tuftwick said, joining Delphine to watch Purdy ride out the courtyard gate. "I could not think of anything that would make Venetia and me happier. To have our two dearest companions near to hand – what else could we ask for."

Standing at his side, Venetia said, "The return of the King so you will no longer be riding off with D'Arcy." She looked at Delphine. "Yes, Delphine, I surrendered and will allow Henry to continue to ride with D'Arcy. I support the King and would not have him starve, but I cannot say I like it. And when they ride off, you and I must be together. Truth is, you must plan to stay at Tuftwick Hall until your new home is ready for occupancy."

Delphine smiled at her cousin, and taking Maddy's arm, she said, "That sounds like the best way to console each other, but now that our men have returned from their exploration of the hillside, let us take a stroll in the garden. 'Tis cooler there, and the sun is unusually warm today."

"No," Venetia said. "You and Mister Madigan go ahead. Henry and I have things we must discuss, as do you two."

"Very well," Delphine said. "'Tis hard to think we have less than three weeks to plan our wedding. It will be simple, all the same, we must have some kind of celebration."

She looked up at Maddy and thought he was eyeing her differently than she had seen him look at her before. What could he be thinking. She prayed he had not changed his mind. Well, if he had, she would refuse to release him from his vow. Like it or not, he was committed to marry her, and she would not let him out of the bargain.

"Shall we take that stroll in the garden, Delphine?" Maddy asked.

She nodded and they set off to the garden side of the keep as Venetia and Henry headed for the gate. Would Venetia give in to Henry's wishes that they post their banns and be married as soon as possible, or would she hold out and insist they be married at Harp's Ridge that their grandmother might attend the wedding of at least one of her granddaughters.

"Delphine," Maddy said as they fell into step together, "I have little doubt you and Lady Grasmere will work out all the details of our wedding celebration. 'Tis our wedding night that I have been studying on."

She had been thinking of their wedding night as well, but his mention of it made her blush. She prayed she would not disappoint him. If she could but satisfy him in bed, mayhap he would grow to love her.

"The trouble is," Maddy continued. "I cannot think how we will have our own chamber here at Knightswood. Not with all the other guests. When we posted our banns, I saw a small inn in Grasmere. I am wondering if I should arrange a room for us there."

Shaking her head and smiling, Delphine said, "Nay, Maddy, 'tis all arranged. You and I are to have the solar for a week. Phillida will bunk with Venetia, and Berold will take your bed."

Maddy stopped short, and turned Delphine to face him. "You cannot mean it? Berold and Lady Grasmere are to give up their chamber to us?"

"Indeed I do mean it. 'Twas Phillida's idea. And Berold approves of it. He wants nothing to interfere with our marriage." And its consummation, Delphine thought but chose not to say.

Maddy was shaking his head. "I am amazed. That is going beyond being good hosts."

"Well, now that you can put your mind at rest on that score, would you like me to tell you about some of the other arrangements Phillida and I have been discussing."

He chuckled. "If you could spare me that, I would be grateful."

Starting to walk again, Delphine said, "Suffice to know the wedding will take place here at the keep. Berold spoke with the Justice of the Peace, and he is more than willing to perform the ceremony here. I would guess he is expecting to be asked to stay to the celebration."

They had reached a pebbled path leading into Phillida's private garden. It was a lovely garden with shade trees and benches in one corner, and pretty paths through various beds of flowers and bushes where the sun could bathe them. "Let us take a bench in the shade," Delphine said, pleased the garden had no other occupants.

Maddy chose a bench under low hanging branches. The selection afforded them a measure of seclusion. Once they were seated, she noted he was again looking at her in that new way. He seemed to be studying her. "Yes," he finally said, "Preston is right. You really are quite lovely, Delphine. Venetia is a beauty unlike any others, but I find I have done you a disservice. I have been enjoying your company, your companionship, but I failed to pay heed to your beauty."

Delphine knew not whether to blush or be angry that he had needed Preston to point out her attributes. Having no response, she but looked at him. He took her hand and said, "I have seen your inside beauty. Your kindness and concern for others. I could not help but see that, but I now realize you are as lovely on the outside as you are on the inside. I find I am a dunce for not noticing sooner."

She had never thought herself a beauty, but then, she, too, had compared herself to Venetia. She liked that he thought her kind and caring.

But what might he be seeing in her eyes. Ebony eyes she inherited from her mother. Her best features were her eyes encased in thick dark lashes and set under perfectly arched brows. Her high cheek bones and dark wavy hair were also pleasing, but she could not think her jutting chin and firm-lipped mouth added to her appearance.

Still unable to think how to answer Maddy's sudden revelation, she but smiled, and to her surprise he put a finger to her lips. "I have kissed you but once, Delphine. I think as we are soon to be wed, 'twould not hurt did we kiss again."

"N...no, Maddy," she stuttered and swallowed. "I cannot think 'twould be improper."

Tilting her head back with his fingertip under her chin, he leaned forward. Their eyes met, then his lips were on hers. She closed her eyes and let the sensations coursing through her claim her complete attention. The kiss was sweet and gentle but after a moment, his lips parted hers, and she felt his tongue caress her lips before dipping inside her mouth. Without thinking, her tongue met his, and at that instant, she felt an intense need stir between her legs. That need only increased when his arms went around her, and he drew her tight against his chest.

Pressed against his chest, her breasts throbbed. Somehow, she managed to get her arms up and around his neck. Then one of his hands went behind her head that he could tilt her back more, and his other hand found her breasts and gently caressed first one then the other. His fingertips slipped into the cleavage exposed by her gown, and before she knew what was happening, he stopped kissing her lips to run his tongue along the top of her breasts. Her passion rising, she was near to screaming. Instead, she moaned. The sound seemed to increase his fervor, for he again drew her tight against him, and he brought her hand down to touch him. At her caress, he groaned, and his kiss became more intense, more demanding.

He was introducing her to magical new sensations. She knew what to expect when a man and woman bedded. She knew that a man's organ grew and hardened when aroused. Was she judging Maddy correctly, she would definitely say he was aroused. Aroused by her. The thought made her giddy. Mayhap this could be the first step in winning his love. She was also very aroused. The moistness between her legs was

212

increasing, and she knew the clean shift she had donned that morning would need to be changed before she sat down to dinner.

Waiting for their wedding night was going to be difficult. She would have no problem bedding Maddy right now did they have a place to call their own. But they had no place private. Even now, they could be interrupted by others wishing to enjoy the garden. She felt bereft when Maddy pulled away from her. His breathing was hard. He took her hand, raised it to his lips, and kissed it.

"Oh, Delphine," he said, "how I wish tonight was our wedding night."

"I was just wishing the same thing, Maddy."

"Were you?" he sounded surprised, then he smiled. "That thought makes me wish even more that we had not three weeks before I may make you my wife in every way."

"Had the Puritans not done away with bishops. Could weddings be performed by parish priests rather than by the Justice of the Peace, we could now have a special license and already be married."

"Damn the Puritans," he said. "Another reason to hate them. But come, tell me more of our celebration that I can get my mind off my desire for you."

Smiling, she began telling him how Phillida and Sidonie were planning decorations for the hall. It would have to be a holiday for the tenants. They would have to be invited, so an oxen or two would have to be butchered." She rambled on, but her thoughts were on Maddy. She was beginning to think that indeed, she would be able to make him love her. She would.

❧   ❧   ❧   ❧

Madigan listened to Delphine ramble on about the plans for their wedding celebration, but his thoughts were more on her passionate response to his kiss than on anything she was saying. She stirred him in ways he had never before experienced. He had felt her heart pounding against his chest. Unlike Venetia who had claimed his kiss started no flurry in her heart, his kiss had definitely started a flurry in Delphine's heart. And in his own. He had thought he would remember Venetia's kiss forever. It should have singed itself into his brain, yet at the moment, the only kiss setting him on fire was the kiss he had just shared with Delphine.

What that revelation could mean, he was not certain. It would take some study, but in the meantime, he meant to discover some place he could be more intimate with Delphine. He might have to wait until they were married to bed her, but he was already longing to again have her in his arms. He wanted to taste her, touch her, and revel in the sensations he stirred in her. Her fervor increased his own, and he could hardly wait until he could again be alone with her. He hoped it would be soon.

Chapter 29

Venetia loved the pavilion Berold had built for Phillida. Situated at the southwest corner of the wall enclosing the keep, and shaded by a tall and ancient oak, its first story windows offered a grand view of Lake Grasmere. The ground floor was furnished with a trestle table and benches. Perfect for picnicking or serving desserts on warm summer afternoons or evenings. A narrow winding staircase led up to the first floor that was furnished with a plush day bed, two comfortable, tufted chairs with side tables and decorative lanterns, and a candelabra hanging from the center of the peaked ceiling.

In leading Henry up the winding stairs, Venetia had more in mind than the view or of discussing their eventual wedding date. She wanted Henry to kiss her, but this time, without an audience and with no interruptions. She wondered if she would have to finagle a kiss. Would Henry again be shy about kissing her. She need not have worried, the moment they were upstairs, and she turned to him, he took her into his arms.

"My love, my love," he said before lightly kissing her lips. Pulling her closer, he deepened the kiss, his tongue searching, probing, demanding.

She thrilled to his kiss, his tight embrace, and slipping her arms inside his coat and around his back, she clutched him to her. The feel of his muscles under his shirt excited her, and had her wishing she could be caressing his bare skin. Her breasts, pushed firm against his chest, ached to be free of the bodice securing them in place. Her wish came true when he loosened his hold and pulled away from her enough to tug at the laces holding her stomacher in place. She helped him, and in a matter of moments, the stomacher dropped to the floor and naught but her frilly shift covered her breasts. The ties to the shift Henry quickly loosened and exposed her breasts to his sight and touch.

His gaze and hands caressing her breasts had her breathless, but when he licked first one nipple and then the other, she near went into a spasm. Grasping his head and entwining her fingers in his hair as he suckled her breasts, she believed she was having a glimpse of heaven. Nothing had ever stimulated her in such a fashion.

"I must have you now," she whispered into his ear. "I must!"

Scooping her up, he carried her to the day bed and laid her on it. He then knelt down beside her. "Nay, my love. I cannot take you in this manner, but I can give you some relief." Reaching under her skirts, he began touching her in a manner that had her writhing in longing. His mouth returned to her breast, and with a yelp of surprise, she exploded in a delirious frenzy of shudders and shakes. As her passion engulfed her, Henry wrapped his arms around her and held her until she floated down from the heavens and regained some control of her senses.

"Oh, my," she at last said. "What was that?"

He smiled. "That, my love, is what I promise to tender you each and every time we go to bed. I hope that meets with your approval."

Slowly she nodded her head. "I should say it does."

"Good." He looked down at himself. "Now, we must do something to relieve me, or I will be unable to return for dinner."

She looked at his groin and saw a bulge that appeared to be throbbing. Looking back up at him, she asked, "What are we to do?"

Untying the cord of his breeches, he reached inside to draw out his member. She could do little but stare. Phillida had discussed with her and Delphine what to expect when they bedded their husbands, but seeing Henry's erect privates was stimulating. Then when he took her hand and showed her how to stroke him, she was completely intrigued. Her touch on him seemed to be as exhilarating to him as his on her. In a matter of moments he was groaning jubilantly, and he erupted in a shuddering ecstasy and a shout that she guessed could be heard from anyone who might happen to be close to hand. She hoped no one would come rushing into the pavilion thinking someone was being killed.

He pulled a kerchief from his coat pocket, and after cleaning himself and tucking away the soiled kerchief, he looked at her rather sheepishly. "I do believe I will need to learn to be more circumspect or everyone will know what we are about."

"That might be a good idea," she said, but she smiled and reached up to touch his face with the palm of her hand. "Oh, Henry, I do love you so. Thank you for this interlude. I think this may well be the most thrilling moment of my life."

"Hmmm, I hope you will have even more thrilling moments when we can enjoy ourselves in our own bed. God, Venetia, I am not sure how I am to wait until we return to Harps' Ridge. I could well go mad with desire."

"Then I think we should not wait."

Grabbing her hands, he placed them on his chest. "Do you mean we may post our banns and be married here?"

She nodded. "Yes. I cannot think that I like the idea of waiting any longer than we must. I see no reason we cannot be married by the Justice of the Peace here, then be married in the church when we return to Harp's Ridge. That way, Grandmother can enjoy what she and I will consider the true marriage before God."

Grasping her and pressing her against his chest, he said, "Venetia, I do think I must be the most fortunate man in all of England. Mayhap in all the world."

She laughed and said, "Well, 'tis pleasant you do think so. But now, do hand me my stomacher. I must put myself back together, and you must help me. 'Tis near time to ready for dinner. Goodness, what will Bethel say when she sees me."

※　※　※　※

Phillida looked down the table at Delphine and Venetia. Both were sitting erect and behaving properly, but by the blushes they each experienced when they looked at the men beside them, she would guess they had been more than a little intimate with their lovers.

Sitting next to Phillida, Sidonie leaned over and whispered, "Delphine and Lady Venetia look very happy, do they not? They both seem to glow."

Chuckling, Phillida agreed. "Yes, and it would seem, Venetia is now as eager to marry Lord Tuftwick as he is to marry her. Leads me to believe he did a good job of convincing her."

"Hmmm," Sidonie said. "I think both sets of lovers are good matches. I predict they will enjoy very happy marriages."

"Yes, I have no doubt you are right." Phillida glanced at Preston and Yardley who were to her left. Involved in their own conversation, they were paying no heed to her and Sidonie. Turning back to Sidonie and keeping her voice low, she said, "At first I thought Mister Madigan might not be suitable for Delphine. I thought mayhap he was in love with Venetia, but I can see I am wrong. I now think he is marrying Delphine because he loves her and not because she is a wealthy heiress."

Sidonie nodded her head. "Indeed. I have felt the same for some time now. They seem to truly enjoy conversing with one another. And the way they look at each other." She giggled. "'Tis like they could gobble each other up. I do love it when Caleb looks at me that way."

"Indeed, I know what you mean. When Berold gets that look in his eyes," Phillida smiled, "then I know we are in for an exciting evening. And since Delphine became betrothed, and her marriage is imminent, he has been much more relaxed and more in the mood."

Phillida noted that her husband and Caleb Hayward, seated at the opposite end of the table, had stopped their conversation and were looking at her and Sidonie. "I think our husbands have noticed all our whispering," she said.

Sidonie grinned. "You are right. We shall change the subject. So, when are you expecting your brother to return?" she asked, no longer whispering.

"I could not say. But I hope he will have a letter for me from Ranulf. 'Tis hard to think Ranulf will be so near and yet, I may not see him."

Sidonie looked sad for a moment. "Yes, I have dreams about my brother, William. In my dreams he is alive and well. Caleb says he has dreams of his brother, Adler. And even though Adler is alive, Caleb knows he will never see him again."

"His brother is happy in that Dutch colony?"

"Yes, he writes that he has learned to understand, if not speak well, both French and the Dutch tongue. And he is very happily married. His parents miss him terribly, but at least they have Caleb, and now our baby, William."

"How different our lives and our situations would be had King

Charles II not decided to try to regain his crown. My brothers would not be fugitives, your brother would still be alive." She sighed. "I support the King, but I do wish circumstances had been different."

"Yes, yes," Sidonie said, nodding slowly. "'Twas bad enough this dreadful revolution took place. So much grief and heartache it has caused. Homes destroyed, families separated. But how fruitless was Charles II's attempt to defeat Cromwell with the Scottish army and the few Englishmen who were willing to again risk not just their lives but their fortunes."

"Well, 'tis done, and we now live with the consequences." Phillida shook her head. "Let us speak of happier things."

"Yes, let us. Have you told your cook he will be having to prepare a feast for Delphine and then the next week for Lady Venetia?"

Phillida grimaced. "That is not a happier subject. No, I have yet to tell him as we have only just learned of Venetia's change of plans. I cannot think he will be happy. Even though neither celebration will be large, preparations for the tenants' meals will be what causes him grief. I may suggest Berold have help come from the village. Not just to help with the serving, but to do the oxen roasting. That way, Cook will only have to be responsible for our personal guests. What say you?"

Sidonie nodded. "I would think that a good idea. Mother had extra help from the village when Caleb and I were married, and Father has not near as many tenants as you have here at Knightswood. You may need to get in your ale order soon, though, as you will be having the two celebrations."

Phillida enjoyed having Sidonie's input, enjoyed sharing her thoughts with her. She was going to miss Sidonie when she had to return to her home. She could not help but wonder how different things would now be had her brother, Nate, not decided to be a highwayman and rob Puritans to send the proceeds to King Charles. Caleb would never have been shot. Had Caleb not been shot, Sidonie would not have needed to insist she would travel with him to Harp's Ridge. Had the Haywards not showed up on her doorstep that rainy night, Madigan and Tuftwick would not have shown up there either. And without Madigan and Tuftwick to help rescue Delphine, she might now be married to Flynn and carted off to France.

So many events and circumstances had to happen to bring about what appeared to be such happy results. Delphine and Venetia were both now betrothed. Caleb was fully recovered. Sidonie was fully recovered, and her baby was strong and healthy, and Sidonie was enjoying a change of scene she most likely would never have had the opportunity to see. Indeed, might never see again. And best of all, Berold no longer had to spend his nights worrying about Delphine. Phillida sighed. Berold could instead spend his nights making love to her.

Fate certainly had its own way of changing lives.

Chapter 30

"Utterly ridiculous," yelled Berold, and while Maddy echoed him, Delphine could do little but sigh wearily. Flynn had sent an attorney to protest her right to marry Maddy. Flynn was asserting she had agreed to marry him.

"Flynn abducted Mistress Lotterby and my sister," Berold boomed.

The registrar was looking confused, glancing first at the attorney and then at Berold, then at her and Maddy. "You say he abducted Mistress Lotterby?"

"Sir Milton has witnesses who will swear Mistress Lotterby went with him of her own free will," the attorney said. "And the banns were duly posted in Glasson for three weeks and no one opposed them. Then in front of witnesses at Mister Crutcher's house, she did agree to marry Sir Milton."

Berold was again sputtering until Delphine interrupted him. "Berold, let us see the Justice of the Peace now that we may end this charade. I grow weary of it."

"Fine idea," the registrar said. The banns had been posted and read in the village center. Berold, Delphine, Maddy, Venetia, and Tuftwick had been present for the reading. After the banns were read, and they started to leave, Flynn's attorney had made his protest. With a number of the villagers watching, the registrar lead the way to the home of the Justice of the Peace.

A portly man with the Puritan short hair, but without their plain dress, welcomed them into his hall. His home was not large, and he was not particularly wealthy, but he was well respected, and he took his position seriously.

He listened first to the attorney and then turned to Delphine. "How do you answer him, Mistress Lotterby. Did you go with Sir Milton of your own free will?"

"If you would say I went with him freely because he had no gun to my throat, then I would say yes. But he held a gun to Lady Venetia's throat, and his threat to her, my beloved cousin, was a threat to me."

The Justice looked back at the attorney. "Your client held a gun to Lady Venetia's throat?"

"'Twas harmless. But a jest. And she is over twenty-one," the attorney said. Had she been under twenty-one, with the new Puritan laws against the abduction of minors, Flynn would have been in considerable trouble.

Berold began blustering again, but Delphine repeated, "I followed after Sir Milton only because he was abducting Lady Venetia. As to the banns he posted in Glasson, I never gave my consent to them. The Glasson registrar would have to swear to that. Besides, when those banns were posted, I had not yet even met Sir Milton. The Phelpses, whom we stayed with, as well as Lord Rigdale who was Sir Milton's host, will testify that we met Sir Milton for the first time at the Phelps' home. As the banns were posted three weeks before I had ever even met Sir Milton, I doubt I could have agreed to them.

"And as to my agreeing to marry Sir Milton when at Mister Crutcher's home – I said naught but that 'I had to marry someone.' I never said he would be the someone. Lady Venetia and Mister Crutcher, Crutcher's steward, Simpson, will testify to that."

The Justice looked at the attorney. "What have you to say to that?"

"I say Sir Milton will wish to challenge her statements."

"Nonsense," shouted Berold. "He but wishes to hold up Delphine's marriage to Madigan so he can have another chance to abduct her."

"I should have killed him when I had the chance," Maddy said in a whisper to Delphine.

She smiled up at him, then again addressed the Justice. "I see no reason sir, you cannot make a ruling at this time. We can produce everyone who was in our company if need be, and they will all swear Lady Venetia was abducted at gun point. They will also testify Sir Milton stole a number of our horses. He and his ruffians threatened the lives of Lord Grasmere, Lord Tuftwick, and Mister Madigan, and they terrified Lady Grasmere and her companion, Mistress Hayward, not to mention our servants."

The Justice was now angrily shaking his head. "Indeed, I have heard enough. Lord Grasmere and his wife are highly respected. Does Lord Grasmere swear to all Mistress Lotterby has just proclaimed, then I rule the banns may proceed, and Mistress Lotterby and Mister Madigan's wedding may be held as planned."

Berold, clapping the Justice on the back, was saying, "I do so swear to all she has said. You have made a wise ruling, sir." The attorney complained ardently. The Justice, however, brushed off the attorney's complaints, and told him to return to Sir Milton and tell him his suit to stop the marriage would not be upheld.

Delphine thanked the Justice of the Peace, and after affirming the wedding dates for her and Maddy as well as for Tuftwick and Venetia, she allowed Maddy to give her a hand up on her horse. Soon they were all mounted and headed back to Knightswood.

"I cannot believe the effrontery of the man," Berold said, his face red, his eyes angry.

"Aye," Maddy said. "The man is vile."

"When I think what he did to Venetia," Tuftwick said, "I wish I had throttled him instead of letting him live."

"That will be enough," Delphine said. "Venetia and I try to keep that memory buried. We wish to speak of it no more. However, Berold, I would appreciate it if you would write to Mister Blomster and ask him to make certain Mister Crutcher and his steward have not been harmed. With Flynn refusing to give up, I worry about Mister Crutcher's safety."

"I will see to it," Berold said. "And as you wish, when in your presence, we will refrain from discussing Flynn or our ideas on how he should be dispatched."

"Thank you, Berold," Venetia said, her silken voice vibrant with feeling. "I hope I may never hear the man's name again."

"So be it," Maddy said. "Let us instead admire the beauty of the lake today. 'Tis like a looking glass, the clouds and hillsides reflected in it."

"I have never seen it look more lovely," Delphine said. "How splendid Phillida decided to have a picnic in the pavilion today. 'Tis perfect." She was glad they would have the diversion to take her mind off Flynn's continued attempts to force her to marry him. She would not feel safe and free of him until she and Maddy were truly wed.

The thought of the wedding bed brought a slight smile to her lips. Whenever she and Maddy found time to be alone together, they found themselves wrapped in an embrace. She loved his kisses and his caresses. They left her breathless and lightheaded. She believed he was giving her a glimpse of a future paradise. What thrilled her the most, though, was his reaction to her caresses. She had no doubt he wanted her as much as she wanted him. He might not love her yet, but she was becoming more and more certain she could make him love her. Maybe not the way he loved Venetia, but he would grow to love her.

❈ ❈ ❈ ❈

Madigan enjoyed the picnic in the pavilion because he saw how much Delphine enjoyed it. The morning's episode with Flynn's attorney had been hard on her. When Flynn abducted her, she had come near to being forced into a marriage with a man she loathed, and the memory preyed on her. Gads, but he wished he had killed Flynn when he had the chance. Yes, it would have delayed their trip, but it would have been worth it.

Despite the disagreeable morning, Delphine, with her usual good humor, enlivened the picnic, and amused the Haywards with accounts of various intrigues she and Venetia and their friend Clarinda had been involved in when fostered at Wollowchet. The Haywards reciprocated, recounting a couple of adventures from their younger days, but their most diverting tale involved Sidonie's younger sister, Arcadia. The girl was unquestionably a minx. Having met her on several occasions, and seen the mischief ever present in her dark eyes, Madigan knew the Haywards' tale was not exaggerated – but it was entertaining, even though at the time, Sidonie's brother came close to losing his freedom. The tale revolved around Cyril Yardley's marriage to Tamar Jagger.

The Knightswood servants had been dismissed to partake of their own dinner, so the Haywards had no need to mind their tongues. "Poor Mister Moreland, the captain of the local militia," Sidonie said with a chuckle. "He thought he had caught Cyril."

"Most likely would have if not for Arcadia's antics," Caleb added.

Sidonie frowned. "We know not who tipped off the militia about Cyril's and Tamar's wedding, but when three households are involved, 'tis hard to be certain all servants and tenants are loyal. Sadly, rewards can be tempting." Shrugging her shoulders, she added, "Tamar and Cyril, poor dears, were supposed to marry in October of fifty-one, after the fall harvest. The banns had been posted, they had their license, and then Cyril and William decided they must fight for King Charles, so off they rode. They insisted Caleb," she looked at her husband, "and his brother, Adler, go with them. We lost my brother, William." Her dark eyes saddened, before a light smile touched her lips. "My son, of course, is named for my brother."

"Oh," Delphine said, her voice soft. "I am sorry about your brother."

Sidonie acknowledged Delphine's sympathy before continuing, "Anyway, Cyril and Tamar were finally able to arrange a quiet wedding ceremony at the Jaggers' home in April. Their license was still valid, and the parish vicar, being a Royalist, agreed to do the ceremony at the Jagger's house. This was before these new Puritan laws that now make marriages be performed by the Justice of the Peace. I stood as Tamar's witness and Caleb stood with Cyril."

"The Jaggers," Caleb said, "have a good size manor bordering on the north and west of Woodspring Hall, the Yardley estate. My family farm, though it dates back to the time of the Conqueror, at least so I have always been told, 'tis not near as large. It is directly to the south of Woodspring Hall. We," he nodded at Madigan before his gaze rested briefly on Tuftwick at the end of the table, "and D'Arcy, Chapman, and Preston spent the night after the wedding at the farm. Cyril and Tamar spent their wedding night at Woodspring Hall."

Picking up the tale from her husband, Sidonie said, "The Hayward household was up early. Mister D'Arcy believed he and his, ah," she cleared her throat, "his, ah, friends should not delay their departure, so I hurried over to my parents' home to tell Cyril they were awaiting him. I had just arrived on the grounds when Arcadia came running from the house. I barely recognized her, dressed as she was in a man's apparel. Before I could say anything, she jumped astride a horse the groom held for her, and took off at a mad gallop right as six militiamen came racing up the front lane to the house. Seeing her, they spurred their horses and went racing after her. While I stood there with my mouth open, Cyril burst out the door with Tamar at his heels. He swept her into his arms, kissed her, then pulling away from her, he sprang down the steps, grabbed me and kissed my cheek, and sprinted off to the edge of the woods where his horse had been left. He disappeared into the woods as Arcadia came racing back around to the front of the house with the militia following her."

Her eyes wide, Sidonie looked at Madigan and then Delphine, and shook her head. "I had no idea what was happening. My parents joined Tamar on the front steps, but I still stood in the courtyard in front of the house, dumbfounded. Arcadia sprang from the saddle tossed the horse's reins to the groom, and as the militiamen drew up in front of the house, their horses kicking up dust in the air, Arcadia swept off the hat and shook out her hair.

"My heart was in my throat, for the militiamen had guns out and rapiers raised. Their horses were stamping about as they tried to get them under control. And their eyes. If you could but have seen their eyes. Bulging out. Their mouths contorted, drooping open. And Arcadia stood there laughing.

"'My, my, Mister Moreland,' she said, 'whatever brings you to Woodspring? And why would you be chasing me in such a manner?' Of course, she knew full well why they had chased after her. That had been her plan."

When Sidonie described the befuddled look on a militiaman's face at being confronted by Arcadia dressed in the man's hat and clothing, Delphine laughed until tears sprang to her eyes and ran down her cheeks. "But how did Arcadia know the militiamen were coming?" she asked, wiping the tears of laughter from her cheeks.

"The vicar who married Cyril and Tamar warned them. Mister Moreland, having learned of the wedding, came by the vicar's house to check his register, to see if indeed he had performed the ceremony. Mister Moreland then went off to round up his men, and the vicar hopped on his horse and came to warn Cyril.

"His horse being old, the vicar knew the militia could not be far behind him. Father sent his valet to the stables to have his horse saddled and brought out front and to have Cyril's horse left in the woods near the path to the Haywards' farm. Father meant to lead the militia off on a merry chase, but Arcadia beat him to it. And indeed, 'twas good she did. Father could have been shot or mayhap arrested. 'Twas naught they could do to Arcadia."

"Could they not have arrested Arcadia?" Madigan asked. He remembered well when Cyril came racing from the woods and across the fields to the Haywards', but he knew nothing of Arcadia's role in Cyril's escape. D'Arcy had ordered his gang to mount up, and when Cyril reached them, with naught but a wave to the Haywards, they had all departed. All but Caleb, who was not suspected of having fought for the King, so unless they had plans for a robbery, he remained in his home. Not until they were a ways down the road, did they pause long enough to learn what had happened. And all they learned was that Cyril had escaped just as the militia arrived. Fact was, Madigan had given the episode no more thought until Sidonie's recitation.

"Arcadia told them she was an early riser, which is true," Sidonie continued, "and she often goes riding in the morning is the weather not blustery. The groomsman confirmed the truth of her statement. Mister Moreland also questioned the groomsman if 'twas normal for Arcadia to ride astride, and the groomsman admitted she was known to do so upon occasion – though he failed to mention 'twas never in a man's clothing.

"Mister Moreland knew he had been fooled. He knew Cyril had escaped, but still he had the house searched. He knew, too, 'twould do no good to arrest Arcadia. He has known her all her life, and he, like everyone else in the parish, knows she is eccentric. Not a person in the parish would have any trouble believing she would dress as a man and ride astride. That he and his militia had chased after her was Moreland's doing, not hers."

"That would be my sister," Yardley said. "Never a fear, never a thought for future consequences."

"She was very brave," Delphine said and turned to Sidonie. "It must run in your family. Look what you have done for your husband at great risk to yourself."

Madigan could hear the admiration in Delphine's voice, see it in her face. Another quality to like about her.

Sidonie blushed but took Caleb's hand. "I could not live did anything happen to him."

Caleb raised her hand to his lips. "No man could be as fortunate as I am."

After the meal ended, everyone was lazing about in the glow of the beautiful day. Phillida declared she intended to relax on the daybed upstairs. Sidonie said she would go back to feed her baby, then take a nap, and Berold enlisted Hayward, Preston, and Yardley to go with him to select the two oxen he would need to have butchered for the two upcoming wedding feasts. Berold seemed to understand that Tuftwick would want to be with Venetia, and that Madigan would want to be with Delphine.

And Madigan did indeed want to be with Delphine. He had discovered a pretty glade amongst the trees at the top of the hill. It would give them the privacy he had been longing for ever since he first kissed Delphine. His need for her had enveloped him, kept him awake at night, and in sharing a room with Tuftwick, he had not been able to relieve his ache with his own hand. How he longed to have Delphine stroke him. He was in such need, he feared he would explode the moment she touched him. No woman had ever so stimulated him. Not that he had known many women. All the same, Delphine brought out a passion in him he had not suspected he possessed. Now, all he had to do was find a way to get her away from prying eyes so they could discreetly make their way up the hillside.

And then – and then he could revel in his need for her and hers for him.

※　※　※　※

Venetia felt incredibly frustrated that Phillida had decided to nap in the pavilion daybed. She had come to consider the pavilion hers and Henry's personal hideaway. The weeks on end when she could not get Henry to even kiss her had been irritating, but since he had claimed her as his own and kissed her at Crutcher's, he had not again been shy. He was as eager to find time alone with her as she was with him. And, oh, how their passions soared when their lips met. And what incredible sensations he stirred in her. He seemed to find new ways to bring her to ecstasy. Each way thrilling and wondrous.

But what were they to do now? Where could they be alone? She needed to feel his body pressed against hers. Needed to taste his lips. Needed him to caress her in ways that drove her mad, but a madness she craved. She looked at him and saw him looking at her with the same longing. Mayhap they could sneak into his room. Madigan looked as though he was planning to take Delphine for a walk. The room Madigan and Henry shared would be empty. Why not? It was perfect. She smiled knowingly at Henry. He straightened and looked questioningly at her. She raised her eyebrows, glanced at the pavilion door and said, "Henry, let us go back to the garden. It is so lovely there. We will sit under a shade tree."

"As you wish, my dear lady." Joining her, he took her arm and directed her out the door.

Glancing back over her shoulder, Venetia saw Madigan taking Delphine by the arm and leading her up the grassy hill toward the new sheep pasture. She had no idea where they might be going, nor did she care. She would learn more that evening when she and Delphine snuggled into bed together. They had been sharing secrets for so many years. Now they both had exciting, stimulating revelations to share. She could not be more pleased that Delphine had fallen in love with Madigan, and he with her. What she found most amazing was that Delphine had loved Madigan for so many years, but it was one secret she had not shared. Venetia knew she would never have been able to keep such a secret, but then Delphine had feared Madigan would never return her love. Fact was, Delphine still feared Madigan might not return her love, but Venetia knew better. Madigan was as much in love with Delphine as Henry was with her. Eventually, Delphine would realize how much Madigan loved her. She hoped it would be soon. She wanted Delphine to be as happy in her love as she was in hers.

And, oh, she was happy. Very happy.

※ ※ ※ ※

Anker watched Madigan lead Mistress Lotterby up the hillside toward a remaining stand of woods near the top of the hill. Not good, he thought. Not good. Before leaving to search for an estate near Tuftwick Hall that Mistress Lotterby could purchase, Purdy had given Anker strict orders to continue a watchful diligence of Mistress Lotterby – and of Madigan. Knowing Anker could not watch both Mistress Lotterby and Madigan, did they separate, Purdy advised him to look among Lord Grasmere's tenants and try to find someone he could trust to help him.

Having explained his need to Lord Grasmere, his lordship had given him permission to make inquiries amongst the tenants. Lord Grasmere agreed that until Mistress Lotterby was married, someone might yet attempt to abduct her. The person Anker chose to help him was a youth, Wiggin. A bright boy of fifteen, he was tall for his age, slim of build, and he had a winsome disposition. He thought the boy showed potential. He might well learn to be a footman. And Mistress Lotterby would be needing a new footman once Purdy became her steward.

With Wiggin trailing him, Anker adopted an easy jog. He intended to reach the hilltop ahead of his mistress and Madigan. Having followed Madigan the day before, he had a good idea where Madigan would be taking Mistress Lotterby. A shady glen hidden amongst the trees. It would be a secluded place for lovers. Anker could not blame Madigan for wanting to take Mistress Lotterby to the glen. Lovers needed time to love. After Mistress Lotterby was safely tucked away for the night, he had been pleased to enjoy time alone with the Lotterby maid, Lucy, a spritely wench with a lively laugh and a shapely figure. He and Lucy had been growing more and more intimate, and he was hopeful they would become even more intimate.

He liked Lucy. Once Purdy became Mistress Lotterby's steward, Anker expected he would be second in command. That could mean a more settled existence. It could mean he could take a wife. A man could look far and not find a more suitable woman to take to wife than Lucy. She was smart and hardworking. Might be, she could become the housekeeper for Mistress Lotterby. Between the two of them, he and Lucy could make a goodly income.

Keeping low and making a wide circle around Mistress Lotterby and Madigan, he believed the couple, lost in each other, had not observed him and Wiggin. 'Twould not do for his mistress to think he was spying on her. At the same time, he had to ascertain no one else was. He and Wiggin reached the trees long before his quarry. After a quick glance to ascertain the couple were indeed headed where he expected them to be going, he hit a narrow path through the woods and before long, he broke out of the woods and trotted up to the top of the grassy hill.

"All right, boy," he said, "now we search the area. From here we can see a goodly distance. We want to determine if anyone else might be observing Mistress Lotterby."

"Yes, sir," Wiggin said. "Do you wish, I could shinny up that lone oak there. 'Twould give me an even better view."

"Good idea, but first, we must give careful scrutiny to this hill. When I was here yesterday, I saw some horse dung. Would it be normal for horses to be up here?"

Wiggin frowned and shook his head. "Nay, sir. Sheep or cow dung, but I cannot think any o' the tenants would be having a horse up here."

"That is what I thought. Now, we will each take a section, and see do we find any other signs that a horse and rider might have come through here."

"Why would it be important, sir? I mean, why important did a rider come by here?"

"As I told you, the view from up here of all the surrounding area is very good. A man wanting to watch the castle would have a clear view of the comings and goings of everyone."

The boy nodded and set about examining the hill. Anker was not pleased a horse had been on the hill, but he needed more evidence. And he found it. A tuft of grass had been scuffed, and in the dirt was a portion of a man's boot print. "See here, Wiggin, he called. A man's boot heel. See do we find any more."

Wiggin looked at the mark, bent low, and began examining the ground, pushing back taller grasses and brushing aside small heather bushes that here and there dotted the hilltop. Anker searched for the trail of horse hooves. Where might the rider have gone when he left the hill? The grass on the top of the hill was thick. The sheep herders had not yet brought their sheep up from the lower pastures. He saw smashed grass here and there, but whether smashed by man or beast, he could not determine.

"Anker, Anker, sir," Wiggin called. "I have found prints. They go into the woods."

Hurrying over to where Wiggin awaited him, Anker said, "Good lad. Later we will see can we find more and follow them." He imagined by this time Madigan and Mistress Lotterby had arrived in the glen. It would not do for him and Wiggin to barge in on them. No, that would definitely not do. "What I want now is for you to help me discover where that rider rode off to."

Together, he and Wiggin searched the grasses. Having no luck, Wiggin said, "I know where a path is, Anker. It bypasses the more craggy fells and leads to Chapel Stile or to Ambleside. 'Tis not used much."

"Show it to me."

Wiggin led Anker along the top of the hill until it swept down away from the lake. They trudged down through a wooded area and broke out onto a path. Sure enough, recent horse hoof prints were in evidence. In examining the prints, Anker thought it looked to be but a lone rider. But what had that rider been doing up on the hill looking down at Knightswood?

"You have done good, Wiggin. Now let us go back up and have you climb that tree and see what all you might be able to see."

What he saw was Mistress Lotterby and Madigan headed back to Knightswood. That was good. Now it was safe for him to see if the foot prints Wiggin had found led to the woodland glen that Madigan and Mistress Lotterby had so recently vacated.

Chapter 31

Clinging to Maddy's arm, Delphine let him lead her back down the hillside. Without his strong arm for support, she had no idea how she would manage. She was still delirious, still dizzy. She had never imagined lovemaking could be so glorious. Oh, she had known it could be pleasurable. She had certainly been enjoying her brief interludes with Maddy, but kisses and fondling could not compare to bare skin pressed to bare skin. It could not compare to his mouth suckling her breasts or to the touch of his hand between her legs.

She loved the feel of his bare chest beneath her fingertips, the feel of his arm and thigh muscles. She loved touching every inch of him. And knowing that she aroused a passion in him that was equal to her own, made her feel she could make him happy, and that was what mattered most to her. If she could make him happy, surely she could make him love her. He might not ever love her to the extent she loved him. But if he loved her at all, that would be enough.

When he had led her up the hill and into the woods, he told her he had a surprise for her. And indeed it was a surprise. The most beautiful little glen, surrounded by ferns and with a babbling little brook running through it. She had laughed when he pulled a blanket and a jug of wine from under a bush. "Are we to have another picnic?" she asked. The look he gave her had set her head to spinning and her heart to drumming.

"A picnic of a sort," he said, spreading out the blanket. "Come, sit and have a sip of this wine. 'Tis good, sweet."

She sank down on the blanket, and he joined her, then handed her the jug. She took a sip. It was lovely. He took a sip, recorked it, and said, "Do you get thirsty, know it is handy."

She nodded, not knowing what to expect next. He leaned over and kissed her softly. She responded, her lips hungry for his, but he drew

233

back. "Delphine, I know we are soon to be wed, but I think I could well go mad do I not get some release."

"Some release?" She looked at him questioningly.

"I want to make love to you, Delphine. I want to touch you, caress you, I want to send you up into the clouds, and I want to go there with you. What I am saying is, I need you."

You need me, she thought. You need me, and oh, how I need you. "I know nothing of making love, Maddy. You will have to teach me."

"That, Delphine, will indeed be my pleasure."

Oh, the way he looked at her, hungrily, but he was ever so gentle. Together they removed the various pieces of her gown until she lay naked before him. His eyes ravished her before he hastily shed his own clothing, and she got to feast on his naked body. She had never dreamed a man could be so beautiful. He stretched out beside her and slowly kissed her. The kiss deepened and his hands began roaming her body, sending shivers wherever he touched her. She reached up to touch him. His skin was so smooth, and the dark hairs on his chest felt satiny.

As much as she enjoyed touching him, when his hand went between her legs, she lost all interest in everything but the sensations he was stirring in her. In a matter of moments, she was climbing skyward then her body was racked with shudder after shudder that she prayed would never end. However they did, and she came back down to earth to find Maddy grinning at her.

"Now, 'tis my turn," he said, and spreading her legs, he positioned himself over her. "This may hurt some, Delphine, but it will hurt but this one time. Afterwards, our love making will never hurt you again."

Before she could answer, he began kissing her, and again fondling her breasts, then she realized he had slipped inside her. She felt no pain, just a fulfillment. At last Maddy was hers. Hers and hers alone. After Maddy's first couple of strokes, she reached up and grasped his buttocks to pull him deeper inside her. At her touch, he gasped, and drove into her. She felt a little pull, but nothing to cause her to cry out. Then he was moving in and out of her more and more rapidly until with a wild yelp, he found his release. He clung to her as his body shook and shuddered. When he stopped shaking his lips again met hers.

Finally, he raised his head to look down into her eyes. "Oh, Delphine,

234

you could not possibly have given me any greater pleasure. I hope you were not pained too much."

She wobbled her head from side to side. "Nay, Maddy. I felt next to no pain. But I like that we are now one. I like that we may already have created our first child."

He smiled. "Our first child. To have a family, Delphine, I cannot tell you how much that will mean to me. Tuffy has been my only family for so many years now." His eyes shifted from hers, and a sad look descended on him. "At times, I cannot even remember my mother's face."

Reaching up, she touched his face, and his eyes returned to hers. "I know how you feel, Maddy. I was but six when my mother died. My memories of her are so limited. But I had Father and Grandfather, and of course, Venetia and Berold and Grandmother Marietta. I am very glad you had Lord Tuftwick."

Brightening, he said, "Aye, but enough of the past. Now we must get dressed and get back to Knightswood ere we are missed. Would not do to have a search party looking for us."

She chuckled. "That it would not."

Before he rolled off her, he kissed her lightly. "Thank you, Delphine."

"'Twas delicious, Maddy. A marvelous picnic."

"We will have to have another ere long, hmmm?"

"We will," she agreed, rising and starting to put her shift on.

"God, but your body is beautiful," Maddy said, watching her raise her arms to slip the shift over her head. "I am a lucky man."

Letting the shift drop down over her, Delphine said, "I am glad you think so, Maddy." Did he really consider himself lucky? She prayed he did.

When he finished dressing, he helped her with her gown. There was little they could do about her hair. "I will but say a branch caught it, but do we have another picnic here, they may become suspicious if my hair keeps getting caught in tree branches."

He laughed a hardy laugh. A laugh that made his eyes glow warmly, and he swept her into his arms and gave her a kiss on her nose. "That is one of the things I love about you, Delphine, your humor. 'Tis good to laugh."

One of the things he loved about her. Had he really said that? Could

that mean he had other things he loved about her? She would take anything, any morsel. With her heart beating a tattoo in her chest, she
hoped she would learn more of the things he loved about her. She
watched him hide the blanket and wine jug before he turned to her and
took her arm.

"Come let us hurry."

And so they were hurrying back to Knightswood, she clinging to his
arm, but cherishing the thought that even now she might have the start
of a baby in her. Maddy's baby.

❦ ❦ ❦ ❦

Sitting at the supper table next to Delphine, occasionally touching
her hand or brushing his knee against hers was forcing Madigan to use
all his self-control to keep from grabbing her and carting her off to one
of the bedchambers so he could again make love to her. He had never
experienced anything so marvelous, so all-enveloping as his lovemaking with her. That he had been able to bring her to a euphoria was as
satisfying to him as finding his own fulfilment. And how heavenly
that had been, having her luscious, naked body beneath his and then
entering her and claiming her as his own. He could hardly wait until
he could have her in his bed every night. 'Twould be paradise. Indeed
it would be. He knew he would have to get her back to the woods ere
too many days. Even now, her nearness was driving him mad. He had
never thought he could so desperately need any woman. Oh, but he
needed Delphine.

That thought grabbed him. He stopped with a chunk of bread ready
to be popped into his mouth. He needed Delphine. Needed her. Did that
mean he loved her? He glanced at her. She was smiling at something
Venetia had said. He looked at Venetia. Venetia was beautiful beyond
description, and she was sweet, and he had thought himself in love with
her. Any man looking at Venetia could imagine himself in love with
her. She was a goddess, an angel – but she was not Delphine.

Delphine was lightness and laughter. She was strength and courage.
She was kindness and generosity. And she stirred in him more sensuous and sensual emotions than he had known he possessed. He hun-

gered for her. Yet he wanted her to need him as he needed her. Certainly she responded to his lovemaking with an eagerness that mirrored his own desires. He knew she liked him. That was obvious. Otherwise, she would not have asked him to marry her. Yes, she needed a husband, and because she found him companionable, she had chosen him. But was there any chance she might grow to love him. What he would not give to be able to experience the kind of love that Tuftwick and Venetia shared. That Caleb and Sidonie shared. He craved that kind of devoted love. Might he and Delphine someday know that radiant love?

He wondered that he had not recognized sooner that he was in love with Delphine. He should have realized it when Flynn abducted her. His entire being had been intent on finding her and freeing her. He had given little thought to Venetia. But then Venetia was not the one at risk of being forced into an unwanted marriage. His rage had been so intense, he had wanted to kill Flynn for having the nerve to so much as touch Delphine. Only Delphine's plea to spare Flynn had saved the man's life.

Once he knew Delphine had not been harmed, had not been forced into marriage to Flynn, he had felt lightheaded. Then that first kiss they had shared – so different from the kiss he had pressed on Venetia. Kissing Delphine had aroused his senses, stirred longings in him that had grown daily. Why had he not known what he was feeling was love? Now with the consummation of his need for her, he found he could scarcely wait until he could again possess her and be possessed by her.

A bark of laughter from the other end of the table made him look with irritation at its perpetrator. D'Arcy and Chapman had returned. D'Arcy, seated next to Phillida, was entertaining her with news of their brother, Ranulf, who had risked his life to return to England to collect the funds D'Arcy and his highwaymen had gathered for the King. Well, if D'Arcy thought he would be leaving Delphine any time soon, he would have to think again. Fact was, he might never rejoin D'Arcy. Why should he?

"Where are your thoughts, Maddy? You look almost angry," Delphine said with a touch to his hand. The touch sent shivers racing up his spine.

Bringing his eyes back to her, he said, "To be honest, I was thinking

I care not much for the idea of again riding out with D'Arcy."

She smiled. "I would be pleased did you not wish to put your life at risk. All the same, as I promised, I will not stand in your way."

"I am torn. D'Arcy has been good to me. I have learned much from him, but I cannot think, as we start our new family, that I have any wish to take up that life again."

"Well, 'tis not something you must decide right now." She leaned closer and whispered. "Think instead on when we may have another picnic."

His breath caught in his lungs as he looked at her. Her eyes were telling him she was again as hungry for him as he was for her. God, how had he been so blind not to have seen Delphine was all he could ever want in a woman. He would make her love him. If she liked him enough to ask him to marry her, she could come to love him. He would know the same kind of love and devotion that he had so longed for. Yes, Delphine would grow to love him.

❈   ❈   ❈   ❈

Phillida loved having her brother back with her. And the fact that he planned to stay at Knightswood until Madigan and Delphine and Tuftwick and Venetia were wed surprised her. He was ever wary of staying in any one place too long. At least Knightswood was a goodly distance from any large towns or cities. And it was in royalist territory. She knew, too, her brother was ever alert. He would be watchful of anything out of the ordinary. Any servants that seemed nervous, tenants that were too curious. She should relax and enjoy his company.

She was pleased Venetia had decided to marry Tuftwick a week after Delphine and Madigan were wed. To have Berold's sister and cousin safely ensconced in their own homes would make Berold rest more easy at night. She liked, too, that Venetia had come up with the idea of having a church wedding when they returned to Harp's Ridge so their grandmother could attend. Grandmother Marietta was a lovely woman. Phillida loved her dearly. She felt she was as much her grandmother as she was Berold's. When Phillida had first come to live at Harp's Ridge, Grandmother Marietta had done all in her power to make her feel welcome. She deserved to get to see her granddaughters' weddings. And, somehow, a wedding performed by a Justice of the Peace, as the Puritans decreed it must be to be legal, seemed unholy. A marriage in the church would make the marriages legal in God's eyes.

What saddened her was that Sidonie would be leaving for her home after the weddings. She had grown very fond of Sidonie and of her baby. Even though baby William did little more than eat, sleep, and soil his napkins, when he did wake, he was adorable, blinking his eyes and gurgling. He had red hair, like his father. Funny, she thought, how Caleb Hayward's coloring was so like her brother, Ranulf's. Caleb and Ranulf looked more like brothers than did Nate and Ranulf. She supposed it was because both the D'Arcy and the Hayward families had Welsh, or Celtic ancestry. Everyone knew the Welsh and the Irish were more likely than most to have one of the varying shades of red hair. She found the trait interesting and wondered if she might someday have a baby with red hair. Ranulf was proof that red hair ran in the D'Arcy family, though according to her father, who had had dark hair like her own, none of his siblings had sported a flaming bush atop their heads as did Ranulf. However, her father declared his father's hair and beard had been a vibrant red.

She wished they had portraits of the D'Arcy ancestors. Now, so many people were having their portraits painted. She and Berold had decided to have a portrait made with Timandra when she was but a new born. The first Lotterby portrait was of Grandmother Marietta. She had been a beautiful woman. Venetia looked so much like her. The portrait of Berold's grandfather was a poor likeness according to Grandmother Marietta. Berold said 'twas most likely because he had no wish to sit for one. Berold's father had been the same. They had but a drawing of him, but they had a portrait of Berold's mother and of Venetia. The gallery at Harp's Ridge housed all the family portraits as well as a landscape Berold had recently purchased for her.

Sidonie had greatly admired the landscape, a scene of a brook running through a green meadow surrounded by oak and elm trees, and a path meandered off through the trees. "Do you not wonder where that path may lead?" Sidonie asked. "I picture it leading to a small vine covered stone house with roses by the front door and bright green shutters on the windows."

Phillida laughed. "Sounds lovely, but why do you see such a cottage?"

"Sometimes in my dreams, I am there with Caleb, and he never leaves me to go off with your brother." Her eyes misted. "Always, I have the fear I will lose Caleb, and how I could live without him, I cannot imagine."

Phillida had hugged Sidonie. "I can only imagine how you feel. I thank the lord that Berold is confined to his two parishes, otherwise, I fear he would want to join my brother in his nefarious activities."

She could not help but wonder if Tuftwick and Madigan would leave Venetia and Delphine when Nate called. How much must Venetia, Delphine, and Sidonie give up to keep King Charles in his finery? She, herself, could do little but keep them all in her prayers.

Chapter 32

Delphine knew she should not be sneaking off with Maddy. Her wedding was in two days, and Phillida and Sidonie had been working tirelessly to have everything just right for her. She should be there helping. But when Maddy looked at her with that hungry look, she had not been able to resist him. Over the past week, they had been able to sneak away to their woodland haven twice, and each time Maddy had introduced her to new delights. That he took pleasure in pleasuring her increased her love for him. Indeed, she had not been wrong those many years ago when she had given her heart to Maddy. Even then, she had seen into his inner soul and had known his soul was filled with honor, kindness, courage, and generosity.

At night, she and Venetia confided some of the delights their men had introduced them to, but she had not told Venetia she and Maddy had consummated their love. That Venetia was enjoying a sexual feast with Tuftwick was reassuring. She liked knowing Venetia was happy in her choice for her husband. She was amused to learn they considered the pavilion their private hideaway, but upon one occasion, they had used the room Maddy and Tuftwick shared. She wondered if Phillida and Berold knew she and Maddy and Venetia and Tuftwick were having these sexual interludes. If they knew, they had not tried to stop them.

Delphine was certain Tatty knew what was going on, but she said nothing. She simply listened to Delphine's excuses about her mussed hair and clothing and helped her right herself before she had to join the others for supper. Venetia said Bethel was just as discreet. Neither maid sought to chastise their mistresses.

Besides her need to be with Maddy and make love with him, Delphine was eager to tell him about the letter she had received from Purdy. Purdy had found a location he believed they would like. It lay between Tuftwick Hall and Wollowchet. Purdy's brother, Benjamin, had arrived and was discussing the price of the property with the owner. A royalist in need of money to pay off his fine, he was willing to sell a portion of his estate. The portion would include pasture land and cropland in the demesne, and several tenants' and cottagers' acreage. The section the royalist was willing to sell had no housing other than the tenant homes. Delphine rather liked that she and Maddy would be able to design and build their own home. She knew they could stay at Tuftwick Hall while their house and outbuildings were being built. At least, they could stay there would Maddy not be too distressed being in Venetia's company, but knowing she was Tuftwick's wife.

In the letter, Purdy also promised he and Benjamin would be arriving on the following day. They had no intention of missing her wedding. Besides the message from Purdy, Delphine had received a letter from her trustees concerning Maddy. Near skipping along beside Maddy as they made their way to their woodland hideaway, she debated whether to tell him about the second letter or whether to wait until after they were married. The letter could make him decide he had no need to marry her. But Maddy was honorable. He would not attempt to back out of their wedding. At least, she prayed he would not. Just to be safe, mayhap, she should wait until after they were married to give him the letter.

No sooner did they emerge from the woodland path into their grassy retreat than Maddy had her in his arms, and his lips devoured hers. Melting against him, she wrapped her arms around him, reveling in the feel of his muscled back. When he released her enough to let her grab a gasp of air, she said, "We have not much time. I had to sneak away."

"Aye, between Preston, Yardley, and Hayward, and all the pieces of advice they felt they needed to give me, I, too, had to be a little wily," he said, his fingers fumbling with the buttons running down the front of her gown bodice.

"Well, now, I am glad you both managed to slip away."

Delphine and Maddy jerked around at the sound of the too familiar voice. To Delphine's horror, Flynn and three men stepped out of the woods. They had guns pointed at her and Maddy.

"No," she breathed. "This cannot be."

"Not you again, Flynn," Maddy said, his voice a growl. "Have you not learned Mistress Lotterby will not be marrying you. She is betrothed to me. We are to marry in two days."

Shaking his head, Flynn was smiling that smile Delphine hated. "Nay. Mistress Lotterby will be marrying me. And much as I would have enjoyed seeing her with her clothes stripped away, I will have to await that pleasure. We have a long way to ride. So, the two of you. Get moving." He pointed his gun toward a path revealed when one of his men pulled a bush aside.

"You will not get away with this, Flynn. You have to know that," Maddy said, but he took Delphine's arm and directed her toward the path.

Stumbling along in front of Maddy on the narrow path, Delphine wondered if they could not dart into the woods. Make their escape, but Flynn was too close to Maddy, too close not to miss should he shoot. They were climbing up the hill, and a couple of times she stumbled over roots and bushes in the seldom used path. She had no idea what Maddy was thinking, but her thoughts were only on keeping him alive. Nothing else mattered. Nothing.

❦ ❦ ❦ ❦

Anker's fears had been realized. When he and Wiggin arrived at the top of the hill, he saw six horses and two men. Stopping before he could be seen, he grabbed Wiggin's arm and hissed, "Go as fast as you can and bring Lord Grasmere or Lord Tuftwick or anyone. Just get as many men here as you can. I fear this is another attempt to abduct Mistress Lotterby. Run, boy."

Wiggin took off on the instant, and Anker looked again at the two men. He recognized one of the men as one of Flynn's retainers that he had apprehended at Crutcher's. The second man had his back to him. Slumped over, the man looked weary and dejected. Six horses meant four men were somewhere in the woods. One horse had a pillion behind the saddle. The pillion could only be meant for Mistress Lotterby.

His heart hammering in his chest, he tried to decide what he should do. Should he shoot the man he recognized and shoo away the horses. And what of the other man? Should he shoot him also? What if he was but a villager caught in the wrong place? To shoot accurately, he would have to leave his hiding place. The men were too far away for him to hit them. And the shot would give warning to the men who by now could have captured Mistress Lotterby.

What a fool he had been not to warn Mister Madigan that he had seen signs indicating someone might be watching him and Mistress Lotterby. He should have said something to Lord Grasmere. In both cases, he had thought he had no real proof anyone had been spying on his mistress. Only he and Wiggin had been spying on them, and how did that make him appear?

As he tried to determine what would be his best move, two men emerged from the woods. They were followed by his mistress and Madigan. After them came Flynn and the man, Treadwell, who had helped abduct Mistress Lotterby and Lady Venetia on the road to Lancaster.

"Spice!" Flynn called, and the weary looking man turned around. Anker recognized him. The Justice of the Peace from Glasson. "Come here and you may perform the long awaited wedding ceremony." He looked at Mistress Lotterby. "You see, we have plenty of witnesses."

"I will not marry you, Sir Milton." Mistress Lotterby looked at Spice. "If you marry me to him, it will not be legal because I have no wish to marry him."

"That is right, Spice," Madigan said, and Treadwell whopped him on the back of his head with his pistol causing blood to spurt from his head and trickle down his hair. Madigan bent forward with the blow, but regained his posture.

"Bind and gag him as he did me," Flynn said, and Treadwell and another man soon had Madigan's hands tied and a kerchief stuck in his mouth.

Mistress Lotterby protested and glared at Flynn, but Flynn but chuckled. "Had I taken Madigan as hostage instead of Lady Venetia, we would already be married and in France," he said. "I realized by the way you were always watching him, by the way you looked at him, that you were in love with Madigan, but I foolishly abducted Lady Venetia instead of him. You knew I would never harm Lady Venetia, but you must know I will happily dismember your lover."

244

At her gasp, Flynn chuckled again. "My first thought is to cut off his right hand, and does that not convince you to marry me, next will be his right foot."

Her chin raised, Mistress Lotterby said, "You are right, Sir Milton. You need not harm Mister Madigan. I will marry you." She looked at Madigan. "No, Maddy, 'twill do you no good to protest. I will not see you harmed." She looked again at Flynn. "What guarantee do I have that after I have married you, no harm will come to Mister Madigan?"

He smiled. "Glad you are being sensible. I have no reason to kill your Mister Madigan. He has served his purpose. I will simply leave him here, bound and gagged as he left me at my cousin's. Someone will eventually find him. Now, let us get on with the ceremony. We have a long ride ahead of us. And once we reach the sea, we have a boat to catch."

"Know this one thing, Sir Milton. Do you harm Mister Madigan after we are wed. I will see you dead the first chance I get."

Flynn but laughed and called to Spice.

Anker feared he had no choice but to take his best shot at Flynn, and hope he would not miss, or worse, hit Mistress Lotterby who was entirely too close to Flynn, but before he could step from hiding and aim his pistol, a voice said, "Now, Flynn, I fear you will not be marrying Mistress Lotterby." To Anker's amazement, D'Arcy, pistol in hand, stepped from the woods. With him were Preston, Yardley, Chapman, and Hayward, their pistols leveled at Flynn's men. Ignoring the grunts and gasps that emerged from the various throats, including Anker's, D'Arcy said, "My sister, Lady Grasmere, has done so much work preparing for the wedding between Mistress Lotterby and Madigan, that I could not possibly allow you to disappoint her."

His head titled questioningly to one side, Flynn said, "Nathaniel D'Arcy. I recognize you. I thought you on the continent with the King. But no matter, this is no concern of yours."

Hayward shook his head and waved his pistol from side to side. "It is our concern. My wife has been helping Lady Grasmere. She, too, would be disappointed did anything interfere with the wedding celebration, and I do my best never to let anything disappoint my wife."

Near sinking to his knees in relief, Anker gave thanks to God. Mistress Lotterby was safe. And Purdy would not have his head after all.

※　※　※　※

Delphine had never been so glad to see anyone in her life. How D'Arcy and his cohorts came to be there, she had no idea, but hastily drawing her knife from the decorative scabbard at her waist and slashing at Flynn when he reached for her, she stepped away from him. D'Arcy's men circled Flynn's men, and D'Arcy gave Flynn's men orders to drop their arms. At that time, Delphine was not surprised to see Anker emerge from another section of the woods, the relief on his face was telling. He must have been watching the whole proceeding and been attempting to determine how best to save her. She should have known her footman would not be far away.

Wringing his hands and stepping between Treadwell and D'Arcy, Spice said, "Mistress Lotterby, you have to know I had no choice. Sir Milton forced me to come with him."

Spice's movement gave Treadwell the opportunity he needed. Pulling a knife from his waistband, he grabbed Maddy and held the knife to his throat. Delphine gasped and no one else moved. All eyes were on Treadwell and Maddy.

"Now I got no intention o' bein' turned over to no magistrate or bailiff," he said. "All I did was keep an eye on Madigan here like Flynn paid me to do. When I discovered he and his lady was a-dallying in the woods, I reported back to Flynn. 'Twas Flynn's idea to come here and wait to see did the lady and Madigan set about doin' some more dallying. Sure 'nough, after but two days o' watchin', here they came."

He looked at D'Arcy. "Had we not caught them before they was married, Flynn would have killed Madigan after they was married. He is that set on marrying Mistress Lotterby."

Flynn protested, but Treadwell went on. "Ask any of his men." He nodded his head at the other men who stood nervously waiting to see what was to happen to them. "I am tellin' ye the truth. Now, that should be worth something."

"It is," D'Arcy said. "It tells me you are a man of poor morals who most likely would have helped Flynn kill Madigan. Just as you would

246

have stood by and watched Flynn cut off his hand. As to these other men, I doubt they are any better than you. However, I will leave it up to Mistress Lotterby as to what to do with you and them." He looked at Delphine. "What say you?"

"He needs to take that knife away from Maddy's throat and free him ere I make any decision," she said, her heart in her own throat. What would Treadwell do?

He must have realized he had no options, for he lowered the knife and slipping it behind Maddy, slit the rope tying him. Maddy immediately ripped the gag from his mouth and grabbed Delphine into his arms. But he looked over her head at D'Arcy.

"I have unfinished business," he said.

"I would guess you do," D'Arcy agreed, but at that moment Berold, Tuftwick, and several of Berold's men, all armed, came bursting out of the woods.

"What is this!" bellowed Berold, waving his pistol. Spotting Flynn, he yowled, "Not you again. By God, I will have your hide this time."

"Nay, Grasmere," D'Arcy said. "That pleasure belongs to Maddy."

"What of these other men?" Berold asked. "Do we take them into Grasmere village?"

"That is up to Mistress Lotterby," D'Arcy said.

Delphine looked up at the man holding her in his arms. "What say you, Maddy? What are we to do with them? I want nothing to delay our wedding."

"Send them on their way. All but Flynn." Releasing her, he turned to Flynn. "Without Flynn as their leader, I think we will ne'er see any of them again."

"That is right, that is right," the men loudly proclaimed, vigorously nodding their heads.

"Someone will need to see Mister Spice gets safely home," Delphine said. "This was not of his doing, though had he not obliged Sir Milton in the first place, he would not now be here."

"Mayhap you have learned a lesson," D'Arcy said, eyeing the man clawing at his goatee while his Adam's apple bobbed about with each nervous breath he took. "Mayhap you will not again take money for acknowledging banns that are fraudulent."

Shaking his head, Spice proclaimed, "No, no, I will hereafter make certain the bride is willing, and the banns are legitimate. That I do swear."

"We will see Spice back to his home," said a man Delphine recognized as being one of Flynn's retainers.

"Very well, the lot of you, be gone," D'Arcy said.

"Thank you, thank you," Spice said before hurrying to his horse.

"Our arms?" questioned Treadwell.

"They will remain with us," D'Arcy said.

Treadwell looked as though he might protest, but shaking his head, he joined the other men. Soon they were mounted and were making their way back down the hill toward the seldom used trail that would lead them back to wherever their homes might be.

His eyes angry slits, Flynn said, "And what of me? You think to take me to the bailiff, the magistrate? What can you charge me with?"

D'Arcy shook his head. "No. I believe we will have to deliver you to the coroner."

Flynn stiffened and his eyes widened. "You mean to shoot me?"

"That would be too easy," D'Arcy said, and turning to Maddy, he handed him his sword. "'Tis all yours, Maddy. Rid us of this cursed fiend."

Brightening, Flynn drew his own sword. He must think does he kill Maddy I would let him live, Delphine thought. Even now, all she had to do was pick up one of the pistols off the ground. She knew how to use a pistol. Had used one before. Why let Maddy risk his life? She felt a hand on her shoulder. Turning, she looked into D'Arcy's twinkling blue-green eyes.

"You could not think I have ridden with Maddy for these three years and not know the swordsman he is," D'Arcy said. "Flynn has not a prayer. And after all the pain Flynn caused you, dispatching him will let Maddy sleep easy at night. Trust me. Trust your future husband."

Delphine prayed D'Arcy was right. Maddy had fought Flynn once before. It had been a hard fought fight, but Maddy had prevailed. Tuftwick came to stand beside her. His presence helped keep her from screaming each time Flynn lunged at Maddy. After what seemed an eternity to her, she noticed Flynn was tiring. His thrusts and parries were more

248

jerky. His breathing came almost in gasps, but Maddy seemed as fresh as when the battle started. He was not winded at all. He even seemed to be toying with Flynn, like a cat toyed with a mouse.

Then suddenly, it was over. Maddy's sword went directly into Flynn's heart. A look of shock spread across Flynn's face. His sword dropped from his hand. For a moment, he swayed on his feet, and when Maddy pulled his sword free, he had to step aside as Flynn fell forward.

Delphine gasped. It was over. Maddy was safe, and she need never fear Flynn again. She looked from Flynn, lying on the ground to Maddy, standing over him. Taking his kerchief from his pocket, Maddy wiped the sword, and returned it to D'Arcy. Then he had her in his arms, and she buried her head in his shoulder. He had not even a nick on him. Flynn had never so much as touched him. She offered up a silent thanks to her Uncle Gyes who had taught Maddy so well.

"Let us go back to Knightswood," Berold said. "My wife and sister will by now be in hysterics, wondering what has happened."

"No we will not," Venetia said from the edge of the woods.

How long Venetia had been standing there, Delphine had no idea, her eyes had been only for Maddy, but that her cousin would come to do what she might to help, was no surprise. She carried Delphine's pistol. Phillida, Sidonie, and Tatty, armed with a fire poker, were with her. Their skirts torn from their hurried scramble up the hillside, they looked tired, but determined.

Berold ordered two of his men to take Flynn's body down to Knightswood, and another to see to Flynn's horse and the confiscated weapons on the grass. "Place the body in the stables. We will send for the coroner, but hopefully, the inquiry will not interfere with the wedding."

"It had best not," Phillida said, eyes narrowed and chin raised. "I will have strong words with the coroner and the Justice of the Peace do either one think to spoil all my preparations."

"That would be my sister," D'Arcy said. "I told Flynn would not do to interfere with her plans."

After receiving hugs from Venetia and Tatty, Delphine asked D'Arcy, "How came you be here?" She swept her arm around. "All of you, how came you to be here?"

"'Tis my business to be ever wary. Before Chapman and I returned at

Knightswood, we did some reconnaissance. We determined someone had been spying on Knightswood. 'Twas not until we saw you and Maddy making your way to the woods that we realized you were the ones being spied upon. We saw Anker keeping a respectful distance, but still monitoring your movements. Anyway, we kept watch, and yesterday, Chapman discovered Flynn and his men at the top of the hill. From a nearby tree, they had a lookout who could see all that was occurring below. We knew Flynn had to be after you, Mistress Lotterby, not us, so we decided, 'twas best to wait to see what was his scheme. Today, when we saw you and Maddy planning to make for the woods, we simply made our way there ahead of you."

"How did you keep Flynn's lookout from seeing you?" Berold asked.

"You should know your property better, Grasmere," Chapman said with a chuckle. "The way the hillside slopes off on the left, it forms a gully. Nothing in that gully can be seen from the ridgetop. We headed down the path to the lake. But when we reached the gully, we cut into it and entered the woods where it meets up with the gully. I could not say whether Flynn or any of his men saw Anker and the boy, Wiggin, flanking Mistress Lotterby and Maddy. Most likely if they did see them, they thought them shepherds searching for lost sheep. That would be why they would not have been more concerned about Anker, mayhap set a trap for him."

Maddy slipped an arm around Delphine, and she looked up at him. "I cannot be more grateful to all of you," he said, "but I would like to get Delphine back down to Knightswood."

"Aye," Phillida said. "We need all make our way back down. Sidonie and I have more preparations to finish, but I believe they may wait until the morrow. Now, I want nothing more than to relax with a glass of claret. Mayhap two glasses. Berold, do give me your arm."

Her husband obliged. Tuftwick took Venetia's arm, and Hayward, Sidonie's. Anker, gallantly offering his arm to Tatty, suggested they skirt the woods and go back down the grassy slopes of the sheep pasturage. Delphine thought they made quite the parade all traipsing down the hillside. Though relieved to know Flynn would never trouble them again, she had a feeling when the shock of the afternoon events wore off, she would be highly embarrassed.

So many people had known she and Maddy were slipping off together. Anker, and the boy, Wiggin, D'Arcy and his cohorts. And now, everyone else at Knightswood would know. Everyone down to the cook, the maids, and the scullery lad. Yes, she could well feel embarrassed when the shock wore off, but for the moment, nothing mattered but Maddy was safe and in two days, she and he would be married.

Chapter 33

Madigan tried to get sleep to take him, but his thoughts kept revolving around Flynn. More specifically, what Flynn had said to Delphine. "I could tell you were in love with Madigan," he had said. Could it be true? Could Delphine be in love with him? He had no doubt she liked him, enjoyed his company, and reveled in their lovemaking. But might her feelings for him be as deep as his for her? Might he and she come to know the all-encompassing love he so envied his friends?

Having escorted Delphine back to Knightswood, he released her to Tatty who shepherded her, with Venetia at their heels, up to her room. Sidonie and Lady Grasmere, after seeing his head bandaged, retired to Lady Grasmere's chamber, and he joined the men in the hall where Berold had ordered mugs of ale served. They had to await the coroner. What to do with Flynn's body once the coroner finished his examination had been discussed. Berold thought an unmarked grave outside the church cemetery would serve best, did the Justice of the Peace not object.

Tuftwick had said he would write to Crutcher, Flynn's cousin, and inform him of Flynn's demise. They knew of no other relatives. Did Crutcher want Flynn's body returned, he could make the arrangements, but Tuftwick doubted Crutcher would want the expense of having the body carted from Grasmere to Glasson, though he might pay for a marker.

They had not long to wait for the coroner. The Justice of the Peace came with him. After listening to the account of the attempted abduction, the death of Flynn, and escape of his men, they went out to the stable to view the body. Dueling in itself was not legal, but as Berold explained, Madigan had been fighting to protect Delphine from Flynn, so it should not be considered a duel. After hearing the testimony of several other witnesses to the attempted abduction, the coroner and

Justice of the Peace agreed with Berold. A man was allowed to defend his home and family by whatever means at his disposal. Everyone then went back to the hall where they were treated to more ale, and Berold assured the coroner, he would see the body carted into Grasmere. And, as they found a plump coin purse on Flynn, Flynn would pay for his own burial, and the remainder of the money would go into the town's poor fund.

Relieved all was settled amicably, and there would be no cause to delay the wedding, Berold said, "'Cannot tell you how much effort my wife has put into the plans for first Madigan's and my cousin's wedding, and a week later, Tuftwick's and my sister's wedding."

"I am pleased to officiate at both," the Justice said. "And 'twas kind of Lady Grasmere to invite my wife to the celebration after the ceremony. She is looking forward to it."

"Wonderful, wonderful," Berold said, escorting the coroner and Justice out the door.

Not long after they left, supper was ready, and the ladies joined the men. Delphine looked flushed, but in control of her emotions. That was good, Madigan thought. He had feared the day's trauma might have affected her poorly. He had chastised himself for allowing his lust for her to put her in danger. Yet, even as she sat beside him, he could feel his need for her grow. Supper might have been somber after the events of the day, but D'Arcy would not have it. He started a banter with Venetia about the merits of hunting small game with a falcon or larger game with a gun. Since both Venetia and Delphine could ride with the best of men, they had often joined various hunts, and soon the whole table was involved in the debate.

Delphine became animated and expressed her sympathy for the poor fox. Venetia agreed with her, saying she tried never to be to hand when the fox was killed. "I like best, if we kill nature's creatures, that we kill ones we can eat."

"Yes," Delphine said. "Though I can see at times the fox can be a nuisance when he gets into a chicken coop."

"I never went on a hunt," Sidonie said. "Unlike my sister, Arcadia, I am not a good rider. I prefer to travel on the pillion as I did all the way to Harp's Ridge." She looked at Madigan. "And I had a good strong back to lean against."

"Well," Delphine said, "you will be returning home in my coach. I will have no immediate need of it."

"You are most kind," Hayward said. "I will feel much better knowing the baby will be in the coach and protected from the weather."

And so the conversation had circled around the table, but while awaiting the dessert to be served, Delphine told Madigan about her letter from Purdy. The possibility of having a home near Tuftwick's was Madigan's greatest desire, and so he assured Delphine. She seemed pleased. He wanted to please her, please her in every way he could.

When supper ended, Phillida spirted Delphine and Venetia away, saying they had things to discuss. Madigan had not seen Delphine again that evening. How strange it felt not to sit down to a game of cards or chess or backgammon with her. Just being in her presence brightened his mood. But this night, despite the fact he had had his revenge on Flynn, he was in a dark mood. What he would have done had D'Arcy not been far more astute than he, he could not say, but he knew he should have been more alert. 'Twas his job to keep Delphine safe, and he had botched it. Even Anker had been a more reliable protector.

Having no wish to join in a game of dice or cards, he had retired early to bed. And there he lay, wide awake, willing sleep to take him, but unable to think of anything but the possibility that Delphine might be in love with him.

※　※　※　※

Delphine and Venetia both listened to Phillida and Sidonie, even asked questions. Phillida and Sidonie both assured them, as they loved the men they were marrying, they would find the act thrilling, though they explained their first experience could be somewhat painful. "'Tis but the first time when you become one with your love that it may hurt. After that, it will be heavenly," Phillida said, and Sidonie agreed.

Before heading off to bed, Delphine and Venetia thanked Phillida and Sidonie for enlightening them, but later when they snuggled into bed together, they burst into laughter. "They have to know we have already been enjoying relations to a certain degree," Venetia said.

"Indeed, they must," Delphine said. "Fact is, everyone has to know as Maddy and I were sneaking off to the woods, that we were not going to the woods to pick flowers."

Venetia laughed and hugged Delphine. "You are not to let such thoughts bother you. Day after tomorrow, you will be married. The fact that you were enough in love to want to sneak away simply tells everyone you are marrying for love."

Delphine knew she was marrying for love. She also knew she had come close to killing a man this day. To save Maddy from harm, she would have married Flynn, or at least let Spice perform the ceremony, but once they were far enough away from Maddy that Flynn's men could not do him harm, she would have driven her knife into Flynn's back. Strangely, she could feel no remorse at the thought of such an action. What Treadwell and Flynn's men would have done, she had no real idea, but she guessed, she could have bribed them to release her. With Flynn dead, they would have no reason to keep her a captive, especially as she would have been more than ready to pay each of them a huge sum.

She was glad she had not had to marry Flynn to save Maddy. Glad D'Arcy had come to their rescue. And had D'Arcy not been there, Anker would have done something. Perhaps shoot Flynn. She would have to see Anker, and the boy, Wiggin, were well rewarded for looking out for her. Anker thought the boy had a lot of potential. That was good as she would be calling on both Anker and Purdy to perform other duties once she was married and had a new home.

"Delphine?" Venetia's soft voice interrupted Delphine's thoughts.

"Yes, dear," she answered.

"Are you planning to let Mister Madigan go off with Mister D'Arcy?"

"I promised Maddy I would not interfere did he wish to continue to ride with Mister D'Arcy, though I cannot say I like it."

Venetia sighed. "I know, do I ask Henry not to go, he will not go, but does he see Mister Madigan ride off, and he cannot go, I wonder how he will feel."

"With men, 'tis hard to say. They are such sticklers for honor. And our two men are like brothers. I could guess, Lord Tuftwick will feel shamed that he cannot ride with his friend."

"I was afraid you would say something like that. I suppose, I will have to let him go."

"At least we will still have each other, and hopefully, we will soon have babes on the way. I hope to have many children."

"I hope to have at least one boy," Venetia said. "Then I hope all the others are girls."

Delphine chuckled. "Why all girls?"

"They are easier. Boys must always be fighting and pushing and calling each other names. Girls are more settled."

"Hmmm, I cannot remember that we were all that settled."

"Well, that may be true, but at least we were not required to go riding off to war."

"Yes, now that is a very good reason to have girls instead of boys. However, we will have what we will have, and we will love them as Sidonie loves little William."

"You are good to offer your coach to take the Haywards home."

"'Tis of no note. I love to ride, and I can use one of Berold's coaches to cart Tatty and my trunks to wherever Maddy and I may go once we are married. Besides, the coach will be back ere 'tis time for us to return to Harp's Ridge so we may have our church wedding that Grandmother may attend. Are we both married on the same day, 'twould cut down on the work Phillida must do to put together yet another celebration."

"Hmmm, that sounds a good idea. Phillida and Sidonie have done so much to make our celebrations special. I believe Phillida will miss Sidonie. They have become close friends."

"Yes, I believe with all that has happened, it has been a blessing for Phillida to have Sidonie with her. It has been good for Timandra, too. She has grown attached to William and no doubt will cry when the Haywards leave, but for the present, he has helped keep her entertained."

"So, you say Mister Madigan is pleased Purdy found a place near Henry's that you will consider? You must know, Henry and I hope you will stay with us while your home is being built. Fact is, Henry will be hurt do you not stay with us."

"We shall see, but for now, I think we had best get some sleep. Tomorrow promises to be a busy day. I have my final fitting, and Purdy and his brother should be arriving with news of the estate. So, I bid you good-night, dear one."

"Good night," Venetia answered, and they both settled comfortably on the bed.

Chapter 34

Delphine's wedding and the celebration following it were all she could have wished for. She thought the local seamstress had done a wonderful job with her new gown. Maddy had said the bright green color looked beautiful on her. The feast following the ceremony had shown off Phillida's cook to the utmost. From his fish in a saffron sauce to his dove in plum stew to his beef roll in a puff pastry, everything was superb, and Berold chose his best wines from his cellar. The hall was splendidly decorated with bunting and greenery. The long trestle table was laid with white cloth and pewter dishes, and flowers were everywhere.

At trestle tables set up in the front courtyard, Berold's tenants and servants were served a roasted oxen and mutton stew along with the various side dishes the tenants provided. And there was plenty of ale for all. Musicians from Grasmere kept up lively tunes as well as romantic ballads, and after the meal, the tenants enjoyed much dancing and frolicking. The entertainment carried on until late into the afternoon, but finally the tenants began drifting home. They would have their animals to tend and most likely, after feasting and drinking heavily, they would be ready for an early bed.

Delphine was also ready for an early bed. But not to go to sleep. She appreciated all Berold and Phillida had done to give her the beautiful wedding day, but what mattered most to her was the ceremony binding her and Maddy for the rest of their lives. For so many years, she had doubted she would be able to marry Maddy. She had feared he would marry someone he came to love, and she would end her life alone and barren, for she could never have married anyone else. But now Maddy was hers, and at long last, Phillida said 'twas time she and Sidonie and Venetia and Tatty should escort her up to the solar chamber and prepare her for her groom.

258

Ensconced in the bed, her dark hair floating about her shoulders, her new chemise of creamy silk revealing much of her figure, Delphine laughed when Venetia and Phillida backed up to look at her.

"So lovely," Phillida said.

"Indeed, you look like a fairy princess," Venetia said. "What say you, Tatty? Did you think this day would never come?"

Her nose quivering, Tatty said, "I have never known a happier day in my life. Delphine has been in my charge since she was Lady Timandra's age. I could not have loved her more was she my own child. The years in her grandfather's house, then in Lord and Lady Grasmere's, and when you, Lady Venetia, and she were fostered at Lord and Lady Wollochet's, I was always there to see to her needs. God willing, I will see to her needs for a few more years to come, but now at least when the Lord calls me, I can go to him knowing Delphine is well cared for."

Tears filled Delphine's eyes. "Oh, my dear Tatty. What would I have done all these years without you. And, yes, I hope you will be with me many years to come, and that the good Lord will not be calling for you anytime soon."

Venetia laughed. "Amen. But now I think 'tis time we invite the groom to join us. Get him up here before he has one too many drinks."

"Venetia is right," Phillida said with a sly look at Delphine. "Mister Madigan looked as though he would have preferred to kick us out and come up here with you himself. Tattersall, do go tell Mister Madigan he may come see his bride"

❋ ❋ ❋ ❋

Madigan could do little but stand in the doorway and stare at Delphine. Her dark eyes glowed, and she smiled brightly at him. "Why do you but stand there, Mister Madigan?" Venetia asked. "Are you not eager to come in?"

"He is eager and then some," Tuftwick said, giving him a push into the room.

Hearing the laughter of the other well-wishers behind him, Madigan turned to them and snapped, "Off with you, the lot of you. My wife is not on display."

They all laughed some more, but did as he bid and headed back to the hall. Madigan had no doubt they would be doing a lot more drinking. The women, too, were laughing at him, but Lady Grasmere was shepherding them to the door. Before exiting, she said, "There is wine and cheese and bread on the table do you thirst or get hungry." With that, she closed the door, and Madigan was left alone with his new wife.

"You look so beautiful," he said, "I am speechless."

"Then you have no need to speak. Instead, join me here in bed."

"Splendid idea," he answered with a grin and hurriedly undressed.

She watched him disrobe, and when he stood before her in the buff, she held up her arms and said, "Help me slip this chemise off. Its silkiness feels lovely, but not near as heavenly as the feel of your skin next to mine."

He happily obliged her, and as he had done since the first time they made love, he marveled at the beauty of her body. Breasts, hips, legs, every inch of her stirred him to a frenzy, but he would not let this, there wedding night, be rushed. He wanted to pleasure her to the utmost before he found his own release. When under his touch, she reached her rapture, he muted her fervent cry with his lips on hers, and reveled as her body shook and shook before finally subsiding and resting exhausted beside him.

When she looked up at him from under lazy eyelids, and a soft smile touched her lips, he was undone. Spreading her legs, he entered heaven, but he was too aroused and desperate to last more than a few strokes before exploding in delirium. How anything could be any better, he could not imagine. With Delphine, he was visiting paradise.

His passion eased, he rolled off her, but pulled her into an embrace. "I have never known such happiness," he told her. "You have made my life complete."

She pulled back enough to look into his eyes. "Have I, Maddy? You are truly happy?"

He snuffed. "How could I not be?"

"I am so glad to hear that. And now, I have a surprise for you."

Rising on his elbow and cocking his head, he smiled. "A surprise?"

She sat up and reached for a folded paper on the stand beside the bed. His eyes devoured her as each movement revealed enticing portions of her body. He had little doubt but that he would be in need of her again soon, very soon.

"This letter is from one of my trustees, Mister Norwell. I asked him to try to find any information about your sister."

"You found my sister!" Madigan sat up and clenched his hands together. Could it be true? But Delphine was shaking her head.

"Nay, I am sorry, Maddy. All they discovered was that your step-father left with her a couple of months after your mother died."

He shrugged, exhilaration seeping out of him. "I could have told you they would find nothing. Did you have to pay for the search, was a waste of your money." He smiled. "Though sweet of you to try."

Returning his smile, she said, "They could not find your sister, but they did find your grandmother. Or at least, her executor."

"What!" At first excited, he quickly sobered. "Oh, you mean my mother's mother. She disowned my mother when Mother married my step-father. I never saw my grandmother after that. I think I already told you I never knew my father's parents. They both died years before I was born, and neither father nor mother had any siblings."

"Yes, you told me of your father's parents. 'Tis sad, but that aside, your mother's mother may have disowned your mother, but you were not disowned. You do know, do you not, you were given your mother's family name as your first name."

He snorted. "I may have a vague memory of that."

"Well, Torrance Madigan, seems your grandmother loved you dearly. And she left you a rather substantial inheritance."

"What! What do you mean?" He could do little more than stare at Delphine. An inheritance? He was not penniless?

"When Mister Norwell's man could learn nothing from your mother's neighbors or her former trustees, he decided to try to find anything he could of your grandparents or other possible kin. What he found was Nolan Bristow, a now established attorney, but a mere youth when your mother's mother died. She died but a few weeks after your mother. Bristow's grandmother was your grandmother's dearest friend, that is why your grandmother entrusted management of her estate to Bristow even though he had not yet completed his schooling."

Madigan frowned. "I am getting confused."

261

Delphine smiled. "What it comes down to is, you are a man of considerable wealth."

Shaking his head, he asked, "How can that be?"

"Your grandmother had property, prominent property in Dublin. Her husband, your grandfather was a woolen merchant. Very prosperous. But he died shortly after your mother married your father. Your grandmother and grandfather Torrance highly approved of your father, by the way. When your grandfather died, your mother became a wealthy heiress. But then your father died, and the trustees of her wealth had no real control over her fortune should she remarry. And she did remarry. As you know, your step-father went through her fortune, and when she died, he sold off her home, and where he went with your sister, no one knows."

"But you say my Grandmother Torrance had property?"

"Yes. Property in Dublin plus a house in a small village outside Dublin. They are now yours. Mister Bristow has kept both properties rented and has kept your money safely invested for you. It but awaits you claiming it."

Delphine was smiling at him, but his head was spinning. All these years of living off Tuftwick's generosity. All these years thinking he was a penniless nobody. "How long have you known this?" he demanded, his voice sharper than he meant it to be.

She looked at him a little questioningly, then said, "Since two days ago. The letter arrived the same day Purdy's letter arrived."

"And you are only just now telling me of it!" He knew his voice sounded harsh, but why had she not told him something of this magnitude sooner?

She frowned. "When was I to tell you, Maddy? While Flynn was dragging me off to force me to marry him. Or mayhap after we were rescued, and we marched down the hill with everyone around us, and I was attempting to keep my footing."

He started to protest, but she held up her hand. "No. You must think I should have told you this exciting news in front of everyone at the supper table. Yesterday, I was given no time alone with you, and this morning we were busy getting married. So pray, Maddy, do tell me when I should have shared this information with you."

262

He shook his head. "God, Delphine. I am sorry. How foolish of me. I suppose you planned to tell me in our woodland haven, but circumstances made that impossible. Say you forgive me for being so harsh with you."

Tilting her head, she pouted a moment then sighed. "Oh, Maddy, I am sorry to say, but you may have a right to me angry with me."

"Nay!" he said, reaching for her, but she pulled back.

"Please, I must tell you, I had not made up my mind whether I should tell you before we were wed. I was debating it even as we made our way to our haven."

"Why? Why would you not wish to tell me?" He stared at her trying to read her face. What would make her want to wait to tell him this astounding news?

"Maddy, though you still bear the scars on your legs," she pointed to dim scars he had long forgotten and ignored, "you may not remember that you have those scars because you jumped between me and a dog. The dog that might have killed me, he badly mauled you."

"Now you mention the incident, I remember it well. Those bites hurt like the devil, but your Uncle Gyes told me it would help condition me to pain. I guess it did." He shrugged. "But what has that to do with your indecision about telling me of my inheritance."

She looked down and would not meet his eyes. "I was afraid," she said in a low voice.

"Afraid! Afraid of what? Look at me Delphine."

She raised her eyes to his. "I was afraid that if you knew you had a large inheritance, you might decide you had no need to marry me." Before he could say anything, she raced on. "You see, I have loved you forever. I never loved anyone else. Never will love anyone else. Never could love anyone else. Had you not agreed to marry me, I would have given my fortune away so I would not be constantly pursued, and would have lived out the rest of my life alone."

He caught her hands. "You say you love me?"

"Remember when I saw you kiss Venetia?"

"Oh, that." He shook his head trying to indicate it was long past.

"Remember I said you were a fool not to fight for her love. And I told you I would lie or cheat or do anything else to win the man I loved.

That man is you, Maddy, and I have done all I could to get you to the altar. I feared did you know you are not penniless, you might want to back out of marrying me that you might marry someone you loved."

She bowed her head again, but he placed his fingers under her chin and raised her head that he might look at her. Her eyes were still downcast, but he said, "Delphine. I have been the fool. I should have recognized much sooner than I did that 'twas you I love, not Venetia."

With his words, her gaze flew up to meet his. "You love me?"

He smiled. "Yes, and for any number of days now, I have been wondering how I might go about winning your love."

Her eyes widened. "Have you really?"

He chuckled. "My guess is you and I are the only ones who have not known how much we are in love."

She reached for his face, and taking it between her hands, purred, "Oh, you dear, dear man. That you really love me makes my every wish come true."

He pulled her closer. "Right now, I would like to make a lot more of those wishes come true, along with a number of mine."

Reaching down, she touched him. "Oh, yes, I do believe we shall share a wish or two."

Her touch was his undoing, and he dragged her down beside him on the bed. "My love, my love," he whispered before setting about proving his love for her and taking them both off to a world where wishes do come true.

Chapter 35

Delphine, seeing the tears welling in Phillida's eyes as she hugged Sidonie good-bye, could tell their parting was difficult for the two women. They had become very attached, and poor little Timandra was sobbing piteously as she watched William, tucked securely in his basket, being set into Delphine's coach. Timandra's nurse had to take her aside and threaten her with a return to the house could she not control herself. The little girl hiccupped, and knuckled her eyes, and did manage to cry more quietly.

Sidonie's husband, turning from Lord Grasmere to Delphine, said, "We cannot thank you enough for the loan of your coach. Not to mention the loan of your footman, Anker."

"You are more than welcome, Mister Hayward. Besides, Anker can use this journey to train young Wiggin. I have swiped Wiggin away from my cousin and intend he be trained as a footman as someday he will replace either Anker or Purdy as they will have other duties."

When Phillida finally released Sidonie, Hayward turned to her and took her hands. "Lady Grasmere, you and Lord Grasmere have given us a treat we will always treasure. Was I not needed at home, and were both sets of grandparents not eager to see their grandson, we would continue to partake of your generous hospitality. 'Tis hard to leave this lovely, peaceful area. We thank you, too, for the loan of your maid, Lucy, for our journey home. To have her to help Sidonie with the baby is a true blessing."

"Lucy is a good girl. I know she will help in any manner she can," Phillida said, her eyes welling up again. "Dear me, how I am going to miss your wife, Mister Hayward."

Delphine cast a glance at Anker as he helped Lucy up into the coach. She believed a romance could be blossoming between those two. If it developed into marriage, she would find a position for Lucy in hers and

Maddy's home.

That consideration brought her thoughts back to her husband. Maddy, dear, Maddy. They had been married a week and two days, yet she was still floating on air. How she could be any happier, she could not fathom. The week they had spent in the solar chamber had been glorious. They had forced themselves to go down for meals, and had spent time playing chess or cards or taking walks with Phillida and Berold and their numerous guests. She had helped Phillida with plans for Venetia's wedding, but as often as they could, she and Maddy had kept to their room, reveling in their love.

Venetia's wedding had been as lovely as her own, the celebration identical. But as Venetia and Tuftwick were to be given their turn in the solar, Maddy, with a look that sent delightful tingles down Delphine's back, had insisted, "The inn in Grasmere will serve us for a couple of nights. At least until the other guests leave for their homes, or in D'Arcy and Chapman's case, wherever it is they may be going." In five days, when Venetia and Tuftwick's honeymoon in the bridal bower ended, they would join Delphine and Maddy and the four of them would set out for Tuftwick Hall.

Delphine was pleased she and Maddy would be staying at Tuftwick Hall while they viewed the property they might well purchase. Once they made their decision, they would head to Ireland to see the properties Maddy inherited and to learn just how wealthy he might be. His rent money had been accumulating for a lot of years.

At the dinner table the day after their wedding, when she and Maddy announced the news of his unexpected inheritance, his friends were delighted for him. Tuftwick sprang from his chair to pound Maddy on the back. "By George," he proclaimed, "now I will see no more long faces when I offer to purchase you a new horse or new clothes. Now you can very well buy your own."

"Having married Delphine," Maddy said with a chuckle, "I believe that would be true anyway, but yes, I am more than a little pleased I will not have to ask my wife every time I want to purchase something."

"Oh, Maddy, you will have your own account," Delphine said. "You will never have to ask me for money. You must know that. Fact is, my wealth is now yours."

266

He leaned over and kissed her. "I know that well, but 'tis even better that I will have my own finances. No one need think I married you for any reason but the overwhelming love that consumes my every waking moment."

"Oh, Maddy," she whispered.

"Beautifully stated," D'Arcy said with a laugh. "Such love is grand to behold. I offer another toast to the lovers. May they always be as much in love as they are now."

Everyone raised their glasses, and the look in Maddy's eyes told Delphine they would soon be making their way back to the solar.

At present, Maddy was chatting with Yardley and Preston. The two would be escorting the Haywards back to their home before enjoying brief, but clandestine, visits with their own families. They would then meet up with D'Arcy and Chapman for a few more summertime highway robberies of various Cromwellians. Delphine and Venetia were relieved Maddy and Tuftwick would not be joining in the robberies. At least not for the time being. Too many matters needed attending, including just settling into married life. Eventually, though, they would again join D'Arcy, and the two women would be left to console each other.

Venetia joined Delphine as Hayward handed Sidonie into the coach. "Think you they will be safe," Venetia asked. "'Tis a long journey and your coach is so rich, it could make bandits think it carries rich passengers."

Delphine chuckled. "You think bandits would attack a coach with three armed men escorting it." She waved her arm at Yardley, Preston, and Hayward. The three were mounting their horses. "Plus the coach has two armed footmen, albeit one is yet a youth, but the coachman and the postilion are both armed as well. No, I think they are easily as safe as we were when we returned from visiting Clarinda."

"Yes, I suppose you are right, though we did have four outriders and Purdy as well as Anker. I must say, I am pleased Purdy will be accompanying us to Tuftwick Hall."

"I, too. He says 'tis still his duty to see I am kept safe. His brother, Benjamin, will join us at the proffered estate to negotiate the purchase, do we decide we like what Purdy found."

Venetia put her arm around Delphine's waist. "Oh, you must like it. I must have you near to hand. We have been together too many years to ever be far from one another."

Leaning her head against Venetia's, Delphine said, "I agree, dear cousin."

They both straightened to wave good-bye to the departing party when the coachman slapped his reins and yelled, "Haw!" and the coach jerked and started forward. Delphine wondered if she would ever see Sidonie again. She hoped Phillida would be able to continue her friendship with Sidonie. Frodsham was little more than twenty-five miles from Malpas. Not a far distance, especially if traveled by horse and not coach.

Maddy and Tuftwick joined their brides to shout and wave until the coach and riders were too far distant to return their waves. In less than a week, the four of them would be waving good-bye to Berold and Phillida. They would ride by horseback, but their luggage and Tatty and Bethel would travel in one of Berold's coaches. The coach would then be returned to Berold for his and Phillida's trip home.

"Well, my sweet," Tuftwick said to Venetia, "they got an earlier start than I might have expected. Rising early as we did to bid them farewell, I wonder if we might go up for a bit of a nap before dinner."

Venetia laughed her enchanting throaty laugh and said, "Oh, indeed, my husband, I do believe a nap would be most advisable."

Delphine doubted any napping would be taking place in the solar, but she and Maddy had used the same nap excuse any number of times when they had been blessed with the solar. Now, with all the other guests departed, she and Maddy were returning from the inn to take the room the Haywards had shared. Berold and Phillida would take one of the other vacated rooms. The housekeeper, Claudia Burch, had the staff busy airing out the rooms and changing sheets and toweling.

"I suppose we may not go to our room for a nap," Delphine said. "The maids have not finished readying it. I wonder might we take a walk in the garden."

Slipping her arm into the crook of his arm, Maddy said, "I know a nice secluded bench under some trees that we might sit on."

She smiled and glanced sideways at him. "Do you now?"

She noted Berold and Phillida and Timandra and her nurse were headed back into the house. Tatty would be busy seeing to her chamber once the maids were finished. She and Maddy could expect not to be disturbed. She liked that Maddy would remember the bench where their first real kiss had taken place. He had stirred longings in her that she had not then understood, but she certainly understood them now. Too bad they could not use the nap excuse. She would not be surprised did Phillida and Berold decide they, too, needed a nap. They had been sleeping in separate chambers for over a week, and by the way Berold slipped his arm around Phillida's waist and looked down at her when they headed back into the house, Delphine had little doubt he had designs on his wife. And his wife on him, if the way she looked up at him was any indication.

Timandra would miss baby William, but Phillida had arranged for the daughter of one of the tenants to come and play with Timandra for the summer. The little girl was but a year older than Timandra, so the two should have fun together. Timandra needed more playmates, that was for certain.

"Where are your thoughts, my dear?" Maddy asked as they strolled arm in arm down a pebbled path in the garden.

"I was thinking of Timandra. She needs playmates."

"Aye, all children do. When I see Timandra, she makes me wonder what my sister would now look like. Assuming she is still alive. 'Tis like she vanished into thin air. Where could Lawford be? Where did he take her? Since I have never seen her, she could walk down the street, right past me, and I would never know her."

Delphine patted his hand. "We will not give up on our search for her. Someday, we may find her. And what a glorious day that will be."

Nodding, he pulled her down on the bench beside him. "Delphine, you are the most wonderful thing that has ever happened to me. I thank God you love me. That for all those years, you never gave up on me. You truly astound me. And you were right all along about Venetia. Had I truly loved her, I would have fought for her. When it was that I realized I had fallen in love with you, I cannot say for sure, but I think mayhap it first dawned on me here on this bench when I took you in my arms, like this."

269

He proceeded to pull her into his arms, his eyes glued to hers. "And when I kissed you, I knew how desperately I needed you. How I will need you for all the rest of my life."

His lips met hers, and she melted into him. Oh, my Maddy, she thought. How I need you. Have always needed you. Always will need you. That she had won his love would forever leave her amazed, but that he loved her with a passion that matched her own, she had no doubt. And was fate still on her side, they would soon be having a family. Then all the wishes she had made over so many years would at last come true. With those happy thoughts, she lost herself in her husband's embrace.

The End

Look for my Next Novel!

Excerpt from
Precarious Game of Hide and Seek

Chapter One

Derbyshire England 1656

Rowena Plaisance Crossly, Lady Crossly, paced back and forth across her bedchamber wringing her hands and cursing in a most unlady-like fashion. That her husband, Sir Lindell Crossly, Baronet of Crossly Oaks, had forcibly locked her in and placed a guard at the door had her rabid. Her fists ached from pounding on the door, and her throat was raw from yelling. Below her in the Crossly Oaks hall, her fourteen year old daughter, Cecily, was being compelled by her father to marry Orrin Haspel, a Puritan tax commissioner appointed by Cromwell's Major General in charge of Derbyshire.

A decimation tax being imposed on Royalists or even just suspected Royalists was meant to finance the county militia. The zealous Haspel had been intent on assessing a massive tax on the Crossly Oaks manor whether the property merited such a great increase or not. Sir Lindell would have needed to sell off much of his land to pay the taxes. Then Haspel had spotted Cecily. Just beginning to blossom, her figure still svelte and youthful, Cecily was small for her age, but her beauty was undeniable. She favored her father in her coloring, light blond hair and vivid blue eyes, but she had her mother's straight, slim nose, sculpted jawline, and full, finely-molded lips. Being sweet-tempered, she perennially wore a smile and had a ready laugh.

Unbeknownst to Rowena, her husband made a bargain with Haspel – the tax assessment would be minimal in exchange for Cecily's hand in marriage. When told of the arrangement, Rowena had raged, "In no way will I allow Cecily to be married off to that Puritan ogre. First off, she is barely turned fourteen, but was she twenty, I would not consent to such a marriage."

Sir Lindell, his blue eyes sad, but his mouth set, responded, "She must marry him. Does she not, we stand to lose half the manor. Besides, she is but a year younger than you were when you married me."

"I might have been but fifteen, Lindell, but you were our neighbor. I had known you all my life. With my grandmother's illness, and my mother's continual absences to care for her mother, I had been helping to care for my family from the time I was ten. My childhood was limited. By the time I was fifteen, I was already a woman. But Cecily is yet a child. And I intend she shall continue to enjoy her childhood for several years to come."

Shaking his head, Sir Lindell said, "That cannot be Rowena. I have already betrothed her to Haspel. The banns are being posted and read on the next three Sundays. A month from next Sunday, the local magistrate will perform the wedding ceremony here in our hall. I thought having the ceremony in our own home would make it easier for Cecily. You have a month to prepare her for her new duties as a wife."

As her husband spoke, Rowena stared at him in wide-eyed disbelief. "Never! Never!" she stormed. "Never will I let you marry Cecily off to that man. We have my dowry. We can use it to pay the higher tax assessment. We need not sell any of Crossly Oaks."

Sir Lindell reached out to take her hands, but she snatched her hands away and glared at him. Frowning, he said, "Would that we could use your dowry, but your grandfather tied it up in such a way we cannot touch it. It is in trust, and the monthly stipend is all we can ever have of it. I know you had planned to have a portion of that stipend transferred to Cecily as her dowry, but Haspel has asked for no dowry, so you will retain your full portion."

"My uncle controls the trust. Could he not release it to us?"

Twisting his mouth over to one side, Sir Lindell shook his head. "Nay. I have already spoken with him. Before I consented to Haspel's request for Cecily's hand, I went to see Gaylord. He could find no way to break the trust. Nor could he offer us a loan. He, too, is being pressed financially. Due to a storm at sea, he lost a large cargo of woolen goods being shipped to Sweden. Right now he is barely able to make good on his debts besides keeping up with yours and your brother's stipends."

Rowena brightened. "What of Artus. Could he not loan us what we need?"

"Your brother will be lucky does he not lose more of Elkton Hall. He, too, has been assessed massive taxes, but he still has a good stand of woods he can sell off. That may save him. We had to sell off our timber to pay the fines and buy back Crossly Oaks after it was confiscated, so we have nothing more to sell.

"Had your mother willed Glenwood House to you instead of to Godwin, we could sell that land, but it is in trust to Godwin and cannot be sold until he turns twenty-one, does he then choose to sell it, which I would advise against."

"'Twas right Mother should will Glenwood House to Godwin. Milo will inherit Crossly Oaks, and Cecily will have a portion of my stipend for her dowry, plus the two-hundred pounds you have designated for her dowry. Besides, Godwin was named for Mother's father."

Rowena's two sons, Milo age ten and Godwin age seven, could not be more different. Milo looked like his mother, tall and slim with dark hair and brown eyes. Godwin looked like his father short and stocky with blond hair and blue eyes. Their personalities were also different. Both were cheerful boys, but Godwin was more serious and studious where Milo cared more for the outdoors and for horseback riding and hunting.

"Well then, Lindell, there is naught for it but to sell off some of Crossly Oaks to pay the tax assessment, for I will not have Cecily married to Orrin Haspel or anyone else at her young age. That you could even consider such a thing is a sad disappointment to me. And until you have informed Haspel that he will not be marrying Cecily, you will not be sharing my bed."

274

But her threats and her haranguing had not moved her husband, and Rowena had found herself sharing her daughter's bed instead of her husband's. She had given Cecily her word she would never let her be forced into marriage with Haspel, but here she was, locked in her bedchamber, unable to save Cecily from her fate.

Hearing a coach being brought around to the front of the house, Rowena hurried to her chamber window. Pushing open the casement frame with its diamond-paned glass, she leaned as far out as she could that she might see what was happening. She had been praying the magistrate would not sanction the marriage, Cecily being so young and Haspel being well into his middle years, but her prayers had not been answered. With a mournful gasp she watched Haspel lead Cecily to his coach. Lindell, following in their wake, was saying something to Cecily, but Rowena could not hear what he said. She but saw the hopeless look on her daughter's face. Then Cecily looked up, and her eyes met her mother's.

"Oh!" sobbed Rowena, stretching out an arm and leaning further out over the edge.

"My lady! Do have a care," cried her maid Liverna, tugging at Rowena's arm in an attempt to pull her back into the room.

Her heart in her throat, Rowena watched the hated Haspel hand her daughter up into his coach. He clambered in after her, and Lindell shut the door. A footman swung up on the stand at the rear of the coach, the coachman flapped the reins, and the coach jolted forward, disappearing around the house and up the road. Eager to escape with his young bride, Haspel was not even staying for the wedding breakfast Lindell had ordered prepared. Rowena guessed Lindell would be sitting down to the elaborate breakfast with no one but the magistrate.

Frustrated and sickened that she had not been able to save her daughter, Rowena angrily plucked at the ivy climbing up the outside wall. Rage pummeling her soul, the small destructive action was not enough. Desperately needing to assuage her wrath, she tugged on a thick vine. She could not budge it. It clung to the weathered stone that had been its home for so many years. Straightening, she studied the vines – then whipping about, she demanded, "Liverna! Get me a pair of Lindell's breeches and be quick!"

Liverna eyed her mistress warily. "Rowena, what do you mean to do?" She had been Rowena's nurse when Rowena was young, and had come to Crossly Oaks as Rowena's maid when Rowena married the baronet. She knew her charge well, and Rowena knew better than to try to fool her maid.

"I mean to go after my daughter. I care not do I have to shoot Haspel, he will not take Cecily to his bed. Now get me those breeches."

Casting a doubtful look at Rowena, Liverna nevertheless obeyed. Though muttering loud enough for Rowena to hear that she wondered how Rowena thought she would get a chance to shoot Haspel, she began digging into the large chest at the foot of the four-poster bed. Her brow creased in a frown, Liverna pulled out a pair of the baronet's breeches while Rowena, ignoring her maid's mutterings, yanked off her lappet cap, grabbed a garter from the chest, and tied her hair behind her at the nape of her neck. Snatching the breeches from Liverna's hands, she kicked off her shoes, jerked up her skirt and petticoat, and hastily donned the breeches.

"Get me my riding boots," she said, taking a sash from her gown and tying it about the waist of the breeches to hold them up.

Liverna found the boots in a corner, and handed them to Rowena. "Now how is it you plan to go after Cecily?" she asked, brushing a lock of her graying hair off her forehead.

"I intend to take Sir Lindell's gelding. He is the fastest horse in the stable."

"And how do plan to get out that door?" Liverna pointed to the locked door.

"I have no mind to go out the door," Rowena said, returning to the window. "I intend to go down this ivy."

Shaking her head, Liverna said, "I feared that was what you had in your head. Well, I cannot let you do that. You could fall. The vines could pull lose."

"I trust the vines will hold. And you cannot stop me." She caught her maid's hands in her own. "I must do this. You must see that, Liverna. Cecily is an innocent. Would you have me leave her in Haspel's evil hands?"

"No, my lady, but I fear for you."

"Have no fear for me, faithful friend. But know that I might be unable to return immediately. I might need hide out somewhere with Cecily." She thumped her forehead with her palm. "In my haste, I am near forgetting my pistol. And I will need something to fund us." Hurrying to her jewelry case, she pulled out everything in it, including her small six-inch flintlock, and stuffed first the jewelry then the pistol into her pockets.

"My lady!" Liverna cried. "You would not part with your dear mother's emeralds?"

"Mother would forgive me does it mean I use them to save Cecily." Returning to the window, she looked out. Seeing no one around, she dropped her boots out the window. Turning back to Liverna, she swallowed and said, "I will trust you to care for Milo and Godwin and make certain they understand why I must leave them for I know not how long."

"I will see to them, my lady. Like they were my own blood." She clutched Rowena's shoulders. "Oh, do have a care. Come home to us safe and well."

Wrapping her arms around the aging body of her beloved maid, Rowena gave her a quick hug and said, "I will. And with my daughter. I promise."

With that, she climbed onto the windowsill, and taking a deep breath, she placed first one stockinged foot and then the other onto thick vines in the ivy. Her footing secured, for a moment she clung to the windowsill. She looked up into Liverna's worried eyes then released one hand to grasp a vine. Not daring to look down, she moved one foot to a lower vine and released her hold on the windowsill. Totally supported by the vines, she slowly made her way down the wall.

When she touched the ground, she offered up a prayer then sat down to tug on her boots. Rising, she looked up at her maid. She offered Liverna a smile and a wave then turned and raced off to the stables. Upon entering the stable, the musty smell of hay and muck assaulted her nostrils, and the dim light made her halt until her eyes could adjust to the dark interior.

"Milady," a stable boy addressed her, obvious surprise in his voice. Standing with pitchfork in hand, he had been mucking out a stall.

"Where is the stableman?" she questioned.

"Why, milady, he be with the other members of the household having a bit of the cake and ale that Sir Lindell set out to celebrate Mistress Cecily's marriage. I was told to finish my work here afore I got any of the treat." He ducked his head then sheepishly looked back up. "I fear I was late rising this morning, so I be behind in me duties."

"Well, I am glad you are here. I need you to saddle Sir Lindell's horse."

"Saddle Sir Lindell's horse, milady?"

"That is what I said, and be quick about it."

Dropping the pitchfork, the boy said, "Aye, milady, and hurried to do her bidding."

Nervously grinding her teeth and knotting and unknotting her fists, Rowena willed the boy to hurry. The magistrate could choose to leave at any time and send the stableman to fetch his horse. How would she then explain her presence? At last the horse was saddled, and the boy asked if he should lead the horse out front.

"No," she snapped. "Go saddle my horse. I will lead Dalton out."

"Aye, milady." The boy looked at her a little warily. She had never been known to be cross with the servants. Feeling guilty, she gave the boy a smile, but fluttered her hand at him. "Go ahead. Get my saddle onto Flyaway."

Nodding, the boy hurried to saddle the mare, and Rowena, after peeking outside and seeing no one around, led her husband's horse out the stable door. Having Flyaway saddled was but a diversion, though she wished she could take her mare with her for Cecily to ride after she rescued her. The mare, however, would never be able to keep up with Dalton, and Rowena meant to ride hard and fast. Leading the horse over to the stump her husband used when mounting his horse, she tossed the reins over the horse's head. She had never straddled a horse before, but she thought it looked like a far easier way to ride than on a sidesaddle as she had always ridden.

Before mounting, she reached into her pocket and fingered the small flintlock she had taken from her jewelry box. It was not a powerful pistol, but at close range, it would do the job. She hoped she would not have to shoot Haspel. She meant but to threaten him, but shoot him she

278

would if she had no other way to save her daughter.

Fear returned as she heard voices coming from the back of the house. In an instant, she placed her foot in the stirrup and swung herself up onto the saddle. With no set plan in mind, but without a second thought, she shook the reins, dug her heels into the side of the horse, and Dalton took off. As she raced past the side of the house, she saw Liverna in the window, but she dared not wave. She needed both hands on the reins to stay seated on the fast moving horse.

She might have heard shouts as the horse thundered up the drive, but she paid them no heed. She had to catch Haspel's coach before it reached Derby.

Biography

Celia Martin is a former Social Studies/English teacher. Her love of history dates back to her earliest memories when she sat enthralled as her grandparents recounted tales of their past. As a child, she delighted in the make-believe games that she played with her siblings and friends, but as she grew up and had to put aside the games, she found she could not set aside her imagination. So, Celia took up writing stories for her own entertainment.

She is an avid reader. She loves getting lost in a romance, but also enjoys good mysteries, exciting adventure stories, and fact-loaded historical documentaries. When her husband retired and they moved from California to the glorious Kitsap Peninsula in the state of Washington, she was able to begin a full-fledged writing career. And has never been happier.

When not engaged in writing, Celia enjoys travel, keeping fit, and listening to a variety of different music styles.

Visit my web site at:
cmartinbooks.kitsappublishing.com

CPSIA information can be obtained
at www.ICGtesting.com
Printed in the USA
FSHW021643090120
65915FS